THE HOLY TAKE

M.S. Canton

Dedication

To my wife, Jodi, whose unconditional love, and support, has made all of this possible, and my sister, Carolyn, who spent countless hours reviewing this novel, and making key suggestions to provide a more enjoyable read.

ISBN: 979-8-9948029-1-5

Cover design by Glenn Weintraub

Table of Contents

Prologue - The First Ledger

April 10, 1865i

Fog sat low over the road as if the night had decided to stay. Trees crowded the ruts. Horses blew white from their nostrils and stamped, iron ringing against mud and bone. Far off, artillery muttered like thunder that had forgotten how to end.

Down in a cut near a creek, gray trousers already stained to the same dark as the road, moved among wagons that had been brought up short and opened with care. No flags. No field music. Just men and a lieutenant with a tight beard seemingly cut down to the bone, a clipboard in his hand, and a pencil he had chewed until it looked like a stick. He walked the line of crates that had not been burned and ticked off numbers that would never agree with any list in any office.

"Church silver," he said without ceremony. "Two crates. Mark them separate."

The boy's eyes lingered on the crosses stacked in straw, the faces rubbed thin by a century of prayers. The lieutenant followed the look, tapped the clipboard once, and said again, "Two crates. Mark them separate."

They had a wagon pulled from a hedgerow and two mules lifted from the kind of farm that could not argue. The boxes went up like this had been done before. Brands were on every plank: F & F.

The lieutenant paused as another small party rode in from deeper in the trees. He handed the clipboard to his sergeant without comment and stepped away from the wagons.

These men did not wear gray. Their coats were plain, dark wool, their hats without insignia. They moved with the easy self-possession of men who answered to no regiment. One of them broke from the group and followed the lieutenant toward the canvas tent set back from the road.

The lieutenant lifted the flap and went inside first. Lamplight cut a narrow lane through shadows. A moment after entry, the canvas fell closed behind them.

Outside, the wagons creaked forward. Brands on the planks caught the gray light once and then turned away.

By dawn, there would be no record of who had ordered it.

Only that it had been done.

The second figure paced behind the cloth—his shadow long and restless. Every few steps, the pacing figure lifted a hand in a gesture too wide for ten feet of canvas, shaping invisible words in the air like a preacher or an orator or an actor hitting marks no one else could see.

The lieutenant did not speak at first. He reached into his coat and produced a small ledger bound in calfskin gone nearly black with handling. He opened it only far enough to expose the middle, where a single page had already been folded once along a careful crease.

With a practiced motion, he slid a knife from his sleeve, slipped it under the fold, and lifted the page free without tearing the margin. The rest of the ledger remained closed in his hands.

“You’ll have a courier for that page?” one of the plain-clothes men asked.

The stranger nodded. "The gentleman from the theatre will see it north. They have plans for him. He is very keen on moments." His mouth twisted. "Men like that usually get them."

The lieutenant closed the ledger and nodded once, which signaled the visitor, who took his leave from the tent.

He disappeared from the tent and handed the folded page to one of the others who had ridden up to the camp with him, minutes earlier. His coat sat on him like a borrowed character; his boots shone too much for war. Dark hair, carefully parted. A face made more for balconies than for trenches.

He read the message once and smiled. The role of his life had finally been cast. History would record the performance exactly as intended—his contribution to the war effort.

The lieutenant did not know his name. He did not need to. He knew the type.

"Where are you headed?" he asked.

The rider smiled, a thin, bright slice. "I go wherever the stage is widest, sir."

He took the small, folded slip and tucked it into his inner pocket with a care he had not shown the reins. His fingers brushed his pocket for half a second, as if he wanted to touch it longer but didn't. Then he mounted, turned his horse toward the river road, and rode off at a pace almost too jaunty for the errand.

The lieutenant watched him go. "Damn actors," he muttered. "Always think they're in charge of the ending."

Prologue - The First Ledger

The ledger was not the sort of book issued by any quartermaster. Its pages held no printed columns, no headings meant to guide a clerk's eye. What writing there was had been set down by hand, careful and restrained, as if space itself were valuable. Whatever the ledger measured, it did so quietly.

COINS – NASHVILLE

CHALICE – SAVANNAH

ALTAR PLATE – CHARLESTON

There were also symbols. Small. Deliberate. Triangles. Circles. Lines crossing at wrong angles. A grammar that did not belong to soldiers.

The ledger was not a battlefield document. It did not care who won. It recorded movement, custody, obligation — the quiet mechanics beneath belief.

A scout came hard down the slope from the east, breath torn and eyes bright. He bent close and spoke low.

The lieutenant did not ask how many or how near. He had already heard it in the way the fog thinned and sound carried farther than it should have.

"Fire," he said. "Burn what wasn't marked. Burn the book. Leave nothing that teaches a man how to count twice."

Only after the gray coats were already breaking away did the sound of hooves rise again — heavier, less certain.

A Union courier detachment came on slow through the pines, six men and a sergeant who had learned to keep his voice for things that mattered.

They were not looking for a fight. Their orders were ink and math: intercept a specie train—wagons carrying hard coin, not rations—log the crates, deliver them to the quartermaster who kept his own kind of scripture. On the sergeant's breast, the leather case with his blotter and lead pencil lay flatter than his heart.

The first wagon they found had already bled out.

The tongue lay snapped in the ruts; one rear wheel leaned like a drunk against the ditch. The tarpaulin had been slit and folded back as neatly as a surgeon lifts skin. Inside, straw was salted with gold dust and torn paper. The sergeant put his hand in and came up with ash and a solitary button.

"Skirmish?" one man asked.

"No smoke," another said. And he was right. The air smelled of wet iron and mule, not gunpowder. The damage had been patient, not loud.

They followed the gouged track down to the creek and up again. Two more wagons, then three. Each had been opened and closed by hands that knew latches in the dark. Rope ends lay cut on diagonals, not chewed. A ledger board had been pried from a side rail and set back with care—the long interior plank that stiffened the wagon wall, removed to reach what had been hidden behind it and then returned so cleanly it nearly vanished into the grain.

Whoever worked here believed in putting tools away.

The sergeant lifted a splintered lid and read the brand burned into the plank: F & F, the ampersand shoved too close to the F as if the iron had been hotter than the man could bear. He traced it with his thumb.

It wasn't a regimental mark or an arsenal stamp. It was a commercial brand — the kind burned into crates meant to travel.

"Faith and Freedom," someone said behind him, half-catechism, half-curse.

Across the creek, faint as smoke, a hymn rose and fell and went out again.

"Company," the sergeant said. He flattened his palm, and the men sank into the ditch and waited.

No one came.

Past noon the sky dragged more fog down over itself. A jay scolded from a treetop like a clerk who had found an error. When the sergeant crossed the creek for the fourth wagon, the gray lieutenant's men were already gone—no wheel tracks where there should have been, no ash where there should have been fire, only straw lying in the mud and a spoon sunk bowl-deep as if someone had given up mid-meal.

The sergeant stood in the road between two emptied wagons and pressed his pencil flat along the spine of his blotter—his recording book of crates that no longer balanced—until it snapped.

The youngest man lingered near the ditch, staring at the open beds and the straw pressed deep into the mud, as if the ground itself had swallowed something it shouldn't have.

The sergeant followed his gaze without answering.

"Look at the latches," the sergeant said at last. "Cut clean. Re-tied. Same with the ropes. No breakage."

He stepped to the nearest wagon and ran two fingers along the edge where the lid had been lifted and set back down.

"That's not theft," he said. "That's transfer."

The youngest man nodded once, relief and unease mixing on his face at having an answer that did not require him to guess further.

"Write what you see," the sergeant added. "Nothing else."

He lifted the lid of the next smoldering crate and found straw, two coins that had fallen out of their paper like teeth, and a little book charred down the spine. He eased it free. It had been bound in calf skin, handsome once, now bubbled along the edge where the fire had licked it like an animal. The first pages were a neat hand and numbers—weights, dates, places. In the margin, under an entry that read CHALICE – SAVANNAH, a column of smaller marks—crosses, triangles, a circle with a notch—ran like private punctuation.

"Who writes like that?" the young man asked.

"Someone trained to know things without saying," the sergeant said.

He closed the book and held it for a second, then put it under his coat because he had learned that the Army could lose a crate but a man with a conscience could keep a book.

He was turning to call for the second squad when a cough of flame lifted from the close thicket down the cut. Not gunfire. Kerosene. A small, patient fire—enough to blacken wood and not enough to call a brigade.

The Union sergeant slid the blotter deeper under his coat and climbed into the last sound wagon. It held nothing but old straw and a single board across the bed, a plank pulled from something that had known prayer. He knocked, and the sound came back hollow.

He pried the plank up with his knife and saw the hollow cavity beneath, clean, dry, lined with paper that had not seen light since it had been put there.

In the box, a ledger the size of a hand, the edges singed where the fire had found it and then changed its mind.

He opened it because he could not not open it.

The page held no letters. Only marks—a little parish of symbols lined in soldier's ranks: squares with notches, circles with tails, stars with one point longer than the others. They ran in rows, twenty across, then turned and ran again. A cipher, or a prayer written by a man who did not trust words anymore.

Some lines were darker than others, as if the hand had trembled or pressed harder to make the mark stay.

The marks had been laid down by hand, not carved or stamped.

Ink pooled unevenly where the nib had paused. The rows weren't straight so much as forced—kept in line by patience rather than skill.

The sergeant did not know what the marks meant. He knew only that they were not idle. Not decorative. Not the sort of thing a man scratched while waiting for orders or killing time between meals. Soldiers doodled. Clerks scribbled. This was neither.

He turned a page once, then again, checking for words. There were none. Only symbols.

01 ●◆✚■ ★◇☑✦ ■●□▲ ◆◇✖◆ ◇✚☒★

02 ▲◇■□ ■●◆◇ ✶☑◆◇ ●◆◇▼ ■◆◇★

03 ★✚◇■ ●☒✦◆ ■◇□★ ◆◇■◆ ●✶☑◇

04 ◇■●◆ ■□✚■ ◆★●◇ ◆◇■☒ ●◇✖■

05 ◆◇☒★ ✦◆◇● ◆□■◇ ●◆◇▲ ★◇◆✶

06 ■●☑◆ ◆◇▲□ ●◆✚■ ☒■◆◇ ✶◇■★

07 ◆◇■● ★●☒◇ ■◆✦□ ●◆◇■ ▲◇☑◆

08 ◆◇✶★ ◇☑■◆ ●✖□■ ◆◇■★ ☒■●◆

09 ★◆◇☒ ■◇◆● ●☒◆✚ ▲◇■◆ ■●◆□

10 ◆☒■● ◆◇■□ ●☑■◆ ◆◇☒◇ ✶■●□

11 ●◆◇■ ◆◇☑◆ ■☒◇✖ ●◆□■ ◇◆■★

12 ◆◇☒■ ■◇◆□ ●◆◇■ ★◇☑◆ ■◆◇●

13 ●☑◆◇ ◆◇■□ ◆◇☒■ ★■●□ ◆◇☒▲

14 ■□◆◇ ●◆☑■ ◆◇✖□ ★◆◇■ ◇☒◆■

15 ★◆◇☒ ■●□◆ ◆◇■★ ●☑✶◇ ◆■□★

16 ◆◇■☒ ◇☑■◆ ●◆☒◇ ■□◆◇ ◆◇✖●

17 ◆☑■◆ ■◇✦● ●□◆◇ ★◆◇■ ◆◇■☒

18 ■☑●◆ ◆◇☒■ ●◆◇□ ◆◇■★ ◇☑■✶

19 ★◆◇■ ●☑◆◇ ◆◇☒■ ■□●◆ ◆◇☒★

20 ■☑◆◇ ●◆◇■ ★◇□◆ ◆■☒◇ ●□◆■

The sergeant did what he always did when faced with confusion. He looked for numbers. In the corner of the page, someone had written them in a hand too small for war.

01, 02, 03… to 20, then again.

That much, at least, he understood. The rest was not his to interpret.

“Sir?” the young private called from the road. “Orders?”

He did not try to read them. He folded a sheet once, then again, testing the crease, and closed it back into the ledger. The book went under his coat, settled flat against his ribs—the way he had been taught to carry anything that did not belong to him but did belong to the Army.

“Orders are the same,” he said. “We write what we find.”

By first light, the detachment was moving again, wagons reshaped by fog, tracks already softening in the road. The ledger rode beneath his coat, unopened, its contents intact and unexamined.

The fog took the wagons’ shape and made them nothing.

What it did not take was the book itself—carried forward not because it was understood, but because it had been found.

Chapter One – Practice Makes Perfect

February 27, 2020

+30 Days

The warehouse echoed with failure.

Yellow tape marked crooked aisles across the concrete, an improvised grid laid out to match a vendor map none of these men had seen in person but all of them had memorized. Folding tables wobbled on uneven legs, pretending to be display cases and coin show booths. Two scissor lifts dozed near the back wall, their yellow arms folded like sleeping animals, proximity alarms chirping whenever someone swung too near a beam.

The air inside was colder than outside. Concrete held the night. Every misstep bounced back off cinderblock and metal, magnified, judged.

Ten men in gray coveralls moved through the taped floor, clumsy in places, too cautious in others. Outside, under a sodium lamp buzzing with insects, the Driver walked a tight path between a white panel truck and a compact sedan, stopwatch in hand, pacing out seconds until numbers felt like weight.

Farther out, in the dimmer reaches beyond the warehouse, engines rolled and coughed. A motorcycle revved, then died. Another spun gravel in a practiced half-circle. The sound echoed, but the men on the taped floor had been told not to look that way. Their world, for now, was the grid inside.

“Reset,” the team Leader called from the floor. “Again.”

His voice wasn’t loud. It didn’t need to be. It carried the way a closing lock carries.

They shuffled back to the starting points. The coveralls were already dark at the collar and under the arms. The warehouse lights came up in staggered rows, humming and flickering before settling into the sickly, honest brightness of cheap fluorescents.

They moved.

A bin tipped, spilling masks, nitrile gloves, and adhesive tubes that scattered like startled insects. A mop handle slipped, clanged off a ladder, and the metallic ring ran the length of the rafters like a bullet in a barrel. One of the cutters misjudged a turn, clipped his boot on the edge of a taped aisle, and dropped to both knees as his pliers shot under a fake table.

In the mock equipment room—built to mimic a building's phone and data hub—a man cut the wrong cable and killed a strip of work lights. Another slammed the flimsy door hard enough to crack the frame, undoing an hour's work with a single careless motion.

Overwatch fared worse. One operator's boot slid out of his loop harness, sending him backward into a stack of plastic bins. Another goosed the lift control too sharply and swung into a steel beam, the small motor screaming in complaint while he scrabbled to stabilize.

From outside, a diversion caller stumbled through a panicked 911 script, his voice climbing and falling in all the wrong places. His partner delivered his lines in the flat monotone of a man reading a grocery list. Somewhere beyond them, a motorcycle skidded, tires squealing just a little too long.

The Leader lined the interior crew shoulder to shoulder. He didn't frown. Didn't scowl. He just stared at them until everyone remembered to stand still.

"You'd be dead," he said, quiet and level.

It landed harder than a shout.

He tapped his watch with a knuckle. The sound was crisp enough to sting.

"Reset."

They started again.

And again.

Every small failure earned a repetition. The lift alarms shrieked whenever a basket drifted too close to a beam. Adhesive went on too thick and sealed doors that were meant to be reused. Hand signals—two fingers for hold, flat palm for stop, wrist flick for drift—went soft at the edges. The Leader rapped each slack gesture with his knuckles, not hard enough to bruise, just hard enough to remind them that bones were finite.

By night's end, they weren't perfect. But they were tired enough not to repeat the same mistakes.

In this place, that counted as progress.

March 19, 2020

+21 Days

The tape no longer looked like tape. It looked like fate.

A two-man cut team drilled their five-minute disappearance until it no longer felt like a trick; it felt like something they had always done. Their boots found the same path every time, the same corners, the same false distractions. First run: one of them forgot the laminated MAX OCCUPANCY REACHED placard and had to jog back for it, ears burning. Second: they walked too quickly, shoulders hunched, eyes down—too much guilt, not enough boredom.

By the fifth run, they had the rhythm right.

Leave the floor like men fetching supplies.

Badge the PBX door.

Green light.

Snip the trunk lines in order: PBX voice, data, backup.

Run glue along the frame in two clean beads.

Soft-close the door—no shudder, no bounce.

Re-enter using the same route used to exit the mock facility.

Slap the placard into the frame.

Seal the seams from inside.

Melt back behind the guards, close enough to smell their breath and not be noticed.

On the far side of the warehouse, through an open side door, outside, another crew could be seen between sawhorses and chalked-out rectangles. Wooden barricades went up and came down. Cones marked lanes as if asphalt ran through the dirt. A motorcycle traced a narrow figure-eight between them, wheels whispering instead of screaming. A second bike followed at exactly the same distance, the two of them learning how to move like a pair of scissors closing.

From the heist floor, the sounds of their work—engines, muted shouts, the pop of training blanks—bled in as texture. The heist crew didn't turn their heads. That was rule one: you knew your piece, not the whole.

Overwatch learned their loop rigs by pain and repetition.

Foot in. Thumb on. Rise smooth.

Knees drawn in tight. Ribs grazing steel.

Prone across the beam, rifles laid flat where no one but the dust could see them.

One of them shaved a knuckle on a bolt and watched the brown half-moon soak into his glove. He flexed his fingers and decided to keep the glove; pain taught faster than speeches.

The diversion callers improved, too. Scripts shortened as they learned what mattered.

"Shots fired… west lot… two down…"

Then nothing.

Dispatchers feared silence more than details.

The earbuds almost undid them.

One click meant hold.

Two clicks: ready.

Three: go.

Twice, someone misread the rhythm and rolled into an aisle just as someone else cut across. Plastic bins collided. A mop bucket tipped, water sliding in a thin wave across the taped floor.

The Leader didn't rant. He walked over, pressed the buds back into the man's ears, and tapped the casing once.

"Your life lives in there," he said. "Learn the language."

By the time the lights went out that night, there had been several rehearsals instead of one—one for what would happen inside a hotel, others for what would happen outside it.

None of the crews knew the other team's script.

Chapter One - Practice Makes Perfect

March 12, 2020

+10 Days

Mistakes thinned into ghosts.

Radios vanished into hidden compartments without so much as a bump. Adhesive laid down like invisible caulk, sealing mock doors that didn't exist anywhere but here. Overwatch rose and dropped with the silent precision of ghosts. Diversion calls hit their cues with unnerving accuracy, panic honed into something almost musical.

The Driver outside wore the stopwatch like a sacrament. By now, the route wasn't movement—it was choreography, and choreography meant the same order every time.

The panel truck stayed parked once it was in its service mark—backed in, aligned, and left alone. It didn't prowl. The whole point was that it looked like a delivery that had already happened.

He stepped down, cracked the rear doors, and made the first part look boring: one trip to the sedan trunk, one trip back—weighted dummy boxes lifted out in plain cardboard, crossed over, and set just inside the truck bay like supplies being staged.

He paused between trips—not because he was tired, but because the stopwatch said the interior crew would need those seconds to take the load, step clear, and move inside without noise or overlap.

When the count hit its mark, he shut the rear doors and latched them by feel.

He waited through the interior count—long enough for the cut team to vanish inside, long enough for the floor crew to be fully committed. He listened to the band, not for drama but for density—the way units stacked and reassigned, the way response stretched thin when too many things asked for the same cars at the same time.

Before leaving the truck for his next tasks, he reopened the rear bay and left it wide—ready for returning hands, no latch to fumble, no bottleneck waiting to happen.

Only then did he move to the staff entrance—the door the janitors had already used to reach the trash corridor. He ran one clean bead of adhesive along the frame, pressed once with his palm, checked the seam, and stepped back.

That entrance was sealed behind them, not ahead of them.

Now the compact sedan moved.

He slid into the driver's seat, eased it forward, and nosed it to an emergency exit—but stopped short, leaving the door usable until the stopwatch told him the crew's exit window was open. He sat there, hands light on the wheel, letting that dead time sell normal.

When the mark hit, he pulled the sedan within the last foot—prepared to pull the vehicle flush, hard on the door, blocking it completely—then he would kill the engine, and pocketed the keys. He waited exactly long enough for "exit traffic" to clear, then pulled up to the door, sealed the seams with adhesive and a shoulder press.

He returned to the panel truck, confirmed the bay was open, then latched it closed once the simulated load was complete. He climbed into the cab and checked the stopwatch.

When the day arrives, this would be the moment the truck rolled. In rehearsal, it was enough that the order never changed.

On the outer side of the compound's gravel lot, another team practiced what their Leader called corridor drills.

Old fence posts marked imaginary roads. Fluorescent paint labeled them simply: NORTH, SOUTH, CUT, CHOKE. The men drove sedans and pickups through the lanes, then stopped on commands that came over earpieces:

"Lock North."

"Release East."

"Choke South at thirty."

They left tire scars in the dirt, adjusted, then ran it again. They repeated the same half-mile in place.

Inside the mock industrial layout, the heist team practiced boredom like it was an art form.

This was rehearsal, not execution. They ran it slow first, then at speed, then blind—no improvisation, no shortcuts—until every man understood not just what he did, but when he was allowed to do it.

The communication system was the spine of the plan. Outside the building, the driver would listen to a live police scanner and internal communications. He would be the only one tracking when law enforcement had been pulled apart far enough—North, South, East, and West—when no local unit would be free to answer a call tied to their assignment, barely a mile from the station. Until he confirmed that condition, the operation did not exist.

When the driver sends that confirmation, control passes inward, but nothing moves. Inside the pavilion, authority belongs solely to the Leader. Like everyone else, he takes his assigned position and waits.

The Leader's first signal marks the beginning of the count. It releases the team from stillness and authorizes Phase One only—PBX disruption, sealing doors and windows, overwatch movement into position, lifts raised, secondary systems staged. No weapons are exposed. When each task is complete, every man returns to his position and signals ready.

The Leader's second signal authorizes preparation without execution. Weapons are retrieved, safeties checked, lasers aligned, hands set—but no one advances. Each man signals ready again.

The third signal is execution. It goes to everyone at once—the interior team, the driver, and the secondary elements already in place outside.

Too early, and response arrives before the pavilion is sealed. Too late, and secondary pressure chokes the escape routes they depend on.

They practice until no one confuses permission with motion.

Four hours of fake cleaning.

Mop strokes on clean floors that don't need them.

Metal polished to a mirror shine.

Bins rolled endlessly up and down aisles.

One wheel squeaked, high and thin. They left it that way on purpose. Every man learned its sound. If they heard that note during the operation, they would know exactly where that bin—and whoever was behind it—stood.

By the end of that day's session, no one moved their eyes off the tape grid.

You didn't need to see what wasn't yours to execute.

You just needed your marks. And the clock.

March 21, 2020

+7 Days

A week out, the work went quiet in a different direction.

A four-man advance went to the pavilion under the cover of licensed trades. They had paperwork. They wore shirts with a company name that existed long enough to be looked up and then disappear again. The building swallowed workers without learning their faces.

They didn't rush. Rush is memorable.

They rolled in equipment that would look ordinary to anyone who signed a clipboard—compact lifts approved by a bored glance, staged in corners where sightlines would be clean later. They walked the floor like men taking measurements for someone else's job. They learned the small geography: freight doors, shadowed corners, the aisles that woke first.

They watched security without making it look like watching. One guard always finished coffee near the freight doors at the same minute. Another ran his key ring like worry beads at the end of every lap. Notes went onto a page that, to anyone else, read like nothing—and to them read like a score.

Back at the warehouse, the Leader had them draw the floor from memory—columns, doors, hidden turns. Where would you stand to see more than see? Where would you park a bin to look like someone forgot it there?

No one asked how they knew. That wasn't a question that helped.

March 27, 2020

Night Before — Staging

Evening settled on the storage-unit complex like a lid. Rows of corrugated doors. Sodium lights. Moths circling themselves out.

The white panel truck waited in its stall, plain as a pantry item. Its sides had been wiped with a dirty rag. It looked clean in the way something looks when the person cleaning it is rushing to leave.

The men opened the door enough to slip inside and eased it back down behind them. They moved without the warehouse echo. There was satisfaction in that—the quiet of progress.

On the truck's side racks, cleaning equipment rode in a neat comb. Flattened cardboard leaned like tired shingles. Boxes of supplies visible in the faint light, items a normal delivery truck might carry.

Everything you would expect to find and nothing you would think to look inside.

They brought in the last cases. Straight lines and folded cloth. If anyone hurried, the Leader slowed him with a hand on the shoulder. Panic thrives in rooms that try to sound like a movie. This room sounded like work.

Two men went to the pavilion after midnight and moved like they belonged there. They rolled in a set of lined trash cans that would be waiting by dawn. They put a handful of the right kind of litter in each so no one would think to ask why a bin was too clean. They wheeled them to a service alcove and set the lids down and left without looking back.

A blocker car slid into a space where it would later look like an accident of convenience—nobody's car and everybody's car, dented just enough to be forgettable.

They tested the comms—the cheap earbuds, the clicks with their plain meaning—and then they didn't touch them again.

Some slept where they could. Concrete doesn't offer. It accepts. A few found cots tucked behind a stack of boxes. A few slept sitting up with backs against the truck's tires.

The Driver did not sleep.

He sat in the cab with the key in his hand and rolled it end over end. The weight steadied him in a way sleep could not.

March 28, 2020

Day 0 — Zero Hour

Second earbuds slid into place. First buds—the ones that had carried pre-chatter, corrections, complaints—came out and went into pockets.

From now on, there would be no more talking in the open.

To anyone watching, they would look like men killing time at the edge of their shift, listening to music to get through a morning of cleaning. No one looks twice at a janitor with earbuds in his ears.

Inside the system, the tones were the leash.

Out in the gravel lot, the white panel truck gleamed under a washed-out sky. Dew beaded on its sides. The Driver walked the length of it, fingertips brushing the metal, checking for things he couldn't have seen anyway—anything out of place, any sound that didn't belong.

He cracked the rear bay just enough to look inside, confirming by sight and touch that everything sat exactly where it should—nothing loose, nothing arranged, nothing that would rattle or shift once the engine stayed running.

Everything sat exactly where it should.

Nothing looked disorganized. That was the idea.

He watched the second hand of his wristwatch sweep toward the mark he had picked weeks ago, when this was still theory and tape and error.

In the distance, beyond the compound's fence, a dog barked twice and then stopped. A truck down on the county road rattled over a seam and kept going. Somewhere deeper in the trees, a motorcycle ticked as its engine cooled.

He checked the time again.

06:00.

Eleven men would make this work. With the Driver, twelve.

He counted them every time.

Anything less than eleven was failure.

They moved out from the shadows in ones and twos, each with a soft-sided bag slung close—backpacks and duffels that read as janitorial supplies if anyone bothered to look. Their coveralls showed creases from weeks of sweat. Their ball caps sat low on their brows. From a distance, they were just men hauling what men always haul when someone pays them to clean up after other people.

Inside, the backpacks would be set aside quickly and without ceremony.

By the time the first vendors began setting up tables, nothing dangerous would be carried in the open—only tools waiting to be used.

The bags went up the ramp with the same rhythm they'd practiced a hundred times in the dry run—open, lift, pass, slide, settle—because even "supplies" have to look boring when a hotel window might be watching.

Open. Lift. Pass. Slide. Settle.

The real transfer—the part that couldn't be seen from the lot—would happen inside, where their staged bins waited in maintenance shadows like they'd belonged there for years.

The panel truck eased into the Hilton/Marietta pavilion lot like it belonged there. Early deliveries always did. Sprinklers had left beads of water shining along the painted lines. The compact sedan was already parked where it needed to be, just as it had been in every rehearsal: screening the best exit lane, making their path out look like an accident of convenience instead of design.

The truck backed into place. Mirrors aligned, angles checked, corners matched.

The engine stayed running. The Driver popped the latch and cracked the rear bay just enough for some of the men to step down one by one, waiting to help transfer the contents staged in the sedan beside them.

Boxes moved hand to hand. From the hotel windows, it read as supplies—cleaning stock, paper goods, nothing worth remembering. Waiting hands slid them forward toward the cab without a word.

Only when the last box was staged, and the count hit its mark, did the rest of the men drop to the ground and head for the service entrance with those already on solid ground.

At the locked door of the service entrance, the Leader swiped a badge.

Green light.

Muted click.

Hinges moved almost without sound.

The corridor smelled of mop sink water, hot dust, and a faint hint of last night's coffee. It looked exactly as it had in the warehouse—because they had spent a month forcing it to.

They moved to their assigned bins.

From their duffles, masks and rifles vanished under trash bags and rags.

Cutters hid beside spray bottles.

Compact projectors slid into false bottoms.

Their hands checked everything by touch.

No one needed to look down.

They had done this too many times.

They broke cleanly and immediately.

No clustering. No hesitation. Each man took the route he'd been assigned weeks ago—one toward restrooms, another down the vendor hall's outer edge, two splitting toward service alcoves where trash always accumulated and no one ever lingered. Mops dipped. Carts rolled. Gloves snapped on with the casual impatience of men already behind schedule.

To anyone passing, it would have looked like a crew starting early, not a crew starting something else.

Inside the pavilion, the heist crew wheeled their bins through the vendor hall, mopping at nothing, wiping at already-clean chrome, leaning into their roles like men who depended on not being seen.

On the far edge of the lot, secondary elements waited where waiting looks like nothing.

Behind some drapes on each side of the pavilion, two scissor lifts waited, arms folded, already locked into their marks.

Feet to go into loops.

Thumbs on controls.

Motors would hum.

Then rise.

They would settle along the beams like shadows learning where to lie.

Inside, the props and masks and rifles waited under trash bags in the bins. Outside, vehicles waited at the edges of lanes no one had closed yet.

For a moment, nothing moved.

Chapter Two – Time to Go

Engines idled low in three corners of Cobb County, each one tucked into the kind of ordinary lots no one bothered to remember. A rusting SUV waited behind a laundromat; a pair of sedans sat nose-out in strip malls where neon signs still slept. To anyone passing, they were just cars burning gas, another irritation in a county already thick with traffic and noise.

Inside, the drivers held themselves still. No one spoke. No one checked phones. Stillness had been drilled into them until it felt like posture instead of absence, as deliberate as any movement they had practiced. One driver tapped a thumb once against a thigh—caught himself—and pressed his palm flat to his knee. Another leaned her head back against the seat and counted breaths slow enough not to show.

Identical plastic watches glowed faintly on their wrists, seconds sliding past without ceremony.

The cabins smelled of old vinyl, cold coffee, and the faint metallic tang that clung to gear no matter how often it was wiped down. They weren't rehearsing lines anymore. That part had been burned into them weeks ago. What mattered now was listening—waiting for the shape of activity to change.

Outside, a fast-food wrapper skittered across asphalt, lifted briefly by a swirl of air before slapping flat against a curb. It was the only thing moving.

Inside the vehicles, the world felt balanced on a moment that hadn't decided what it would become.

The Driver listened. He wasn't counting calls. He was counting patterns—listening for units being stacked, how often they were reassigned before they arrived, how many times supervisors stepped in where they usually didn't. The police band was still orderly enough to pretend it was a normal morning. The Driver did not let it fool him.

He watched for the sound that mattered: constraint.

At 10:40, the first diversion call to 911 hit.

“I—please—there’s a man with a gun, I think he just—oh my God, he just fired—people are running, I can’t—”

The line went dead before the operator could anchor it to an address. The Driver didn’t move.

A second call followed, thirty seconds later, from another part of the county.

“Listen, I’m in the parking lot on Roswell Road—there’s someone shooting, I saw glass blow out of a car, there’s blood on the pavement—please, you have to send someone—”

The dispatcher cut in with questions. Units were logged. A supervisor’s voice sharpened in the background. Still not enough. The third call came from the SUV further west.

“He’s screaming—he’s got a rifle—people are down, I don’t know if they’re dead, I don’t—”

A scream tore through the background, sharp enough to distort the line. The call ended mid-syllable.

Screens bloomed red across the GIS, a computer-based system for capturing, storing, analyzing, and displaying geographically referenced data, linking location information with descriptive details to reveal patterns, relationships, and trends on maps, tiles.

The call-takers started chasing fragments. None of the calls referenced one another. Different voices, different locations, the same kind of fear arriving within minutes of itself.

A veteran dispatcher raised her hand for silence and got none.

“We’re chasing echoes,” someone said, and nobody contradicted them.

Chapter Two - Time to Go

A rookie wiped her hands on her jeans twice before typing. A gray-haired operator pinched the bridge of her nose and murmured, "Not like last time," before remembering the line was live. In the glassed-in office, a supervisor snapped the OVERFLOW binder shut and reached for a phone.

"Get Cobb Police command," she said. "Now."

After a beat, she added—almost to herself—

"Didn't the Vice President land this morning?"

Out in the lots, the drivers pressed END and went still again. Pressing END felt the same as pulling a trigger. The difference was that nobody died when you hung up. The point wasn't death. The point was bandwidth—making the county's attention so wide it couldn't focus.

Then Kennesaw State began.

It didn't begin on the dispatch board. It began in motion.

Two sedans slid into opposite ends of Kennesaw State University's sprawling parking lots. To anyone watching, they looked harmless—one idling beneath a row of trees, the other coasting in with its blinker still ticking, as if a student had paused to check directions. They held that posture long enough to look forgettable. Then doors cracked open at the same second.

Boots hit asphalt in rhythm. Rifles cleared door frames in a single practiced motion.

The first bursts rattled into parked cars, windows bursting into glittering spray. Alarms shrieked, horns bellowed, and the panicked chorus carried across the lot like a siren no dispatcher could mute. Students scattered before they even saw who fired, flight primal and uncoordinated—backpacks dropped, phones clattering, voices breaking into screams. A girl tripped on a curb and was dragged to her feet by a friend; another clutched her inhaler and forgot to breathe.

The shooters didn't linger. Their rifles swung across hoods, chewing metal, shredding tires until the smell of burnt rubber rose sharp into the morning.

Only after the first wave of screaming bodies hit cover did the campus calls start to pour in—fast, messy, climbing over one another.

"Shots fired—Kennesaw State—west lot!"

"Active fire—lockdown procedures!"

"Multiple calls—multiple shots—"

Campus radios lit up instantly, officers shouting over each other.

"Shots fired, west lot!"

"Lockdown procedures!"

"Multiple calls, multiple shots—"

On the second floor of a dorm, a freshman crawled under a desk and texted his mother," I love you," then followed with "password is the pet's name 2x," staring at the bubble that never turned blue. Across campus, a sophomore pressed Go Live with shaking hands and streamed a sliver of the parking lot—a siren, a scream, the stuttering flash of hazard lights—two hundred watchers in seconds, then guilt slamming the phone facedown. Group chats bloomed with rumors: five shooters, library bomb, SWAT on roof. Someone typed," it's a drill," and fifty replies screamed back, "no".

In less than two minutes, the sedans were gone—doors slamming, engines howling. They melted back into traffic like ordinary cars, taillights vanishing into the sprawl. Behind them, the lot echoed with alarms, sobs, and the high ragged voices of people trying to make sense of what had just happened.

The point had never been casualties.

The point was fear and distraction, and fear was already spreading like flame across dry grass.

On the police band, the Driver heard what he needed: units pulled toward KSU, units pulled toward earlier calls, supervisors stepping into channels, county lines blurring. It wasn't chaos yet. It was load.

He waited for constraint to become the only story.

Because until it did, the operation did not exist.

The first motorcycle rolled onto the shoulder of the I-75 overpass and idled, its engine dropping to a steady thrum that blended with traffic noise below. The rider kept his visor down, reflecting nothing but pale sky, body angled like a man resting before the next mile. From a distance, he looked like another commuter pulling over to check directions.

At the appointed second, he leaned forward, bracing the rifle against the tank.

The first burst cracked into the southbound lanes, bullets shattering the windshield of a silver sedan and sending it fishtailing hard into a center divider. A blue pickup tried to dodge, clipped steel, and spun broadside across two lanes, its bed slinging tools like shrapnel. Brake lights flared in a red wave. Behind them, three cars folded together in the screech of rubber and the soft, sick thump of metal kissing metal too fast.

A tractor-trailer locked its brakes; the cab dove and the trailer yawed until the rig jackknifed across three lanes, its side a sudden wall. A compact car knifed under the trailer by a hand's width, scraping paint and prayers. Horns screamed. Someone's airbag blew and powdered cornstarch burst in a white cloud. Plastic and glass lifted like a flock and fell as a rain of glittering knives.

Inside a minivan, a mother clawed at her seat belt with one hand while reaching back for her toddler with the other. The little girl wailed, high and shrill, the sound lost in the chorus of horns. In the next lane, a man fumbled for his phone only to find SOS calls choking—towers already strangled by hundreds of frantic dials.

A patrol cruiser, lights hot, came blind into the bottleneck and fishtailed sideways, tires shrieking, bumper kissing a barrier. The officer slammed his fists into the wheel and shouted into a radio that returned only carrier hiss. Thirty yards ahead, everything was noise and steel. Thirty yards behind, more was coming.

The rider didn't wait. He slid the rifle back into its scabbard, twisted the throttle, and the bike leapt forward. The sound rose sharp and angry, then bled back into traffic. To the drivers clawing at their phones or staring into bent steel, he was gone—just another taillight dissolving into confusion.

Southbound was dead. The county's artery was clotted, and every unit that might have rushed toward the pavilion was now stranded in a snarl of wreckage.

Across the median, at the same time, a second motorcycle eased onto the northbound shoulder, engine rumbling low. The rider shifted his weight, visor hiding his eyes, one boot steady against the guardrail. Southbound was already a wall of twisted metal and smoke. Now northbound was about to be carved into silence.

He raised the rifle and squeezed.

The first burst punched through the windshield of a delivery van; glass exploded outward and the van slewed across two lanes. An SUV behind it fishtailed, kissed the rail, threw sparks, and scraped sideways through a lane of braking cars. Then a tractor-trailer in the fast lane stamped brakes and folded, its trailer swinging like a blade across the blacktop until it blocked every lane corner to corner.

Drivers panicked. Some stood on brakes and stacked into each other like a line of falling dominos—steel, plastic, skin. Others jerked wheels across medians and bounced through ditch grass that sucked them down with mud. One compact spun and ended up sideways in the center lane, doors flung open, its driver sprinting away with arms pumping like wings. Someone tripped on a bumper and vanished under smoke.

Within a minute, northbound froze into a solid mass. Engines hissed. Radiators steamed. Horns bellowed. People spilled from cars and ran along shoulders, one woman in heels carrying her dog to nowhere at all.

The shooter lowered the rifle, slid it away, and twisted the throttle. The motorcycle leapt forward, taillight flaring once as it threaded the gap between wreck and rail. He vanished into brake-light glow and dust.

On both sides of the interstate, red and blue lights lit on vehicles that could no longer move. EMT crews tried to snake ambulances along the shoulders and found their way choked by abandoned cars and the geometry of panic. A paramedic jumped out with a bag and ran, because a bag can run farther than a box can roll.

In the 911 center, calls from the interstate started to eat the calls from everywhere else.

"Multi-vehicle collision—southbound I-75—"

"Northbound too—tractor-trailer jackknifed!"

"We've got entrapments—multiple vehicles—"

"Nothing's moving—units can't get through—"

The wall of monitors became a wall of fire ants. An analyst drew a red bar through the interstate on the map and wrote NO FLOW in a corner box no one had time to read.

That was the change the Driver listened for.

Not noise. Chaos.

On the police band, he heard the gap where responses should have been. A unit reassigned before it ever spoke. A supervisor breaking in where she normally stayed out. A medic abandoning his rig and running. Delay stacking on delay until response became guesswork.

He listened until the pattern stabilized into something he recognized as irreversible.

Then he thumbed the shortwave and pressed the button once.

No voice followed.

A tone slid into earpieces inside the pavilion and out across the lot. No one outside the operation heard it, but its effect was immediate—not movement, but awareness. Conditions met. Safe to proceed. Control passed inward.

Inside the Hilton/Marietta pavilion, nothing moved. Not yet. Men in gray coveralls continued to mop floors that didn't need mopping. Bins rolled their endless circuits. Gloves snapped on and off with casual impatience. To anyone watching, it was still a morning trying to get organized.

Near a vendor hall column, the Team Leader felt the tone settle. He didn't look at a watch. He didn't need to. Thirty days of rehearsal had pressed the timing into his ribs.

He waited exactly two seconds longer than instinct wanted—just long enough that every internal clock could be trusted.

Then he sent the signal.

Phase One.

Not words. A distinct, practiced signal.

Chapter Two - Time to Go

Every member of the inside crew heard it.

So did the outside team.

Watches synchronized without being touched.

Two men peeled away from the floor at the same instant—not rushing, not breaking character—one angling toward the main public entrance, the other angling toward the designated exit. Their bins rolled ahead of them with the same unremarkable squeak. To anyone watching, they were heading to do what janitors always do: check doors, check hallways, respond to "something" that looked like "nothing" on a schedule.

Hidden from the pavilion floor, the scissor lifts began to rise.

Not after the first shots.

Not later.

Now—during Phase One, while the room still believed the day was normal.

The lifts moved with the patient pace of approved work. At the top, harnesses settled. Boots found beams. Rifles were brought into position but kept low, angled along steel rather than down toward the room. Automatic laser units—mounted earlier and wired to remote activation—were armed, not live. Overwatch did not scan yet. They waited.

On the far edge of the lot, the outside team stopped waiting.

They didn't move like men planting anything. They moved like men killing time around vehicles—checking a tire, stooping to pick up a scrap of paper, leaning down as if to retie a boot. Under those ordinary motions, magnets kissed metal. Compact charges disappeared against underbellies of vehicles in the parking lots—placed where a restless visitor could leave early and still carry the problem with them, placed where a tire couldn't expose it and a bumper couldn't scrape it loose.

When the last vehicle was seeded, they drifted toward the perimeter trees. The trees had been prepared days earlier—small brackets nested into branches, hardware darkened, silhouette broken by bark and leaf.

What remained was assembly, not installation. Cases opened briefly and closed again. Barrels slid into waiting mounts. Optics clipped home. Safeties stayed on.

No one fired.

No one rushed.

Phase One was not violence.

Phase One was alignment.

The two men who had peeled out of the pavilion moved through the lobby on opposite sides—one coming out the public entrance, the other out the designated exit—never together, never looking like a pair. They crossed the open lobby like staff running errands: shoulders relaxed, eyes on nothing that mattered, bins rolling as if they were headed to a supply closet.

From the outside glass, the lobby looked like a convention morning—vendors and volunteers, signs and tape, the usual boring confusion. That was the cover: that nothing looked like a countdown.

The equipment room sat off the lobby corridor behind a keypad door that most attendees never knew existed. The two men converged there without converging—arriving within the same minute from different directions. One paused as if reading a notice on the wall. The other stopped as if shifting his bin's weight. Then the first hand went to the keypad.

Chirp. Green.

Muted click.

The door opened into the smell of hot electronics.

PBX first. Then data. Then backup.

Wire cutters flashed. Bundled lines fell away in quick, hungry snaps. Copper twisted and sprang. They didn't test. They trusted the order.

They stepped back into the main hall together and pulled the door shut. A thin bead of adhesive traced the frame as one of them wiped, slow and methodical, like finishing a job that didn't need checking. The other smoothed the line until it looked like an old seam that had always been there.

The keypad blinked uselessly behind the filmy skin of glue.

That door would not open again today.

They split immediately—one returning toward the entrance, the other toward the exit—retracing the exact paths they had used to leave the pavilion.

At the outside of each door, each reached into his bin and drew out a laminated MAXIMUM OCCUPANCY placard. They fixed them where management would have posted them—clean, centered, official. The numbers were deliberate lies.

Then they reentered—one through the entrance, one through the exit—so that from the inside they could do the part that mattered most.

From inside the pavilion, adhesive guns whispered.

A stitch along the jamb. A seam at the threshold.

Handles were tested once, then left alone.

The doors did not argue. Glue made them walls.

Both men drifted back into the hall and took up position directly behind the guards assigned to those doors—bins parked where bins always parked, mops leaned where mops always leaned. They became background again, because that was the job.

At the same time, outside, the Driver exited the panel truck. The engine stayed running. He closed the cab door carefully—because doors make different sounds when they're slammed, and sound carried farther than people thought. He crossed the short distance to the service entrance the team entered, with his head down, like a man sent to check a door he expected to be used all day.

He ran one clean bead of adhesive along the exterior frame.

Pressed once with his palm.

Checked the seam.

Stepped back.

The service entrance was now sealed behind the crew, closing the next to last portal to the pavilion.

That was critical.

He returned to the cab and climbed back in, eyes lifting to the rearview mirrors. From here on, he would not leave the vehicle again until instructed by the sequence.

Inside the pavilion, readiness signals began to return.

One click.

Ready.

Another.

Ready.

They came from the two men on the doors.

From overwatch in the rafters.

From floor positions.

From the outside perimeter team—charges placed, mounts set, lanes covered.

Each tone meant one thing only: Phase One tasks complete.

The Driver counted them. He did not respond early. The operation did not reward optimism.

When the last ready signal arrived and nothing remained outstanding, the Driver pressed the shortwave again—one tone only, the agreed confirmation: all positions checked in, board clear.

The Team Leader received it without looking.

Phase One complete.

He sent Phase Two authorization—the next sound, practiced until it lived in muscle: preparation without exposure, retrieval without movement. Inside, hands reached into bins, safeties checked, lasers aligned—but no one advanced.

Then, when every man had signaled ready again, the Driver sent the final confirmation tone—everything aligned, timing window open.

The Team Leader waited half a beat.

Then he sent the last sound.

Execute.

Inside the pavilion, it began at the doors.

Hands came up from behind the guards. Radios were crushed into silence. Arms were trapped before they could rise. Weapons were fouled before they could clear leather. One guard staggered, surprised more than hurt; the other never got that far. Plastic ties snapped closed. The men did not linger.

The first shots cracked upward—deliberate and angled—into ceiling tile and steel beam. Plaster burst. Dust rained down in a white sheet that covered banners, cases, and shoulders alike. The sound flattened thought and erased choice.

Above, overwatch activated. Rifles stayed disciplined; lasers did the talking. Red dots swept backs and shoulders, paused at necks, drifted again, patient and merciless.

Outside the building, the perimeter denial began: jammers activated, short bursts into glass and steel at secondary points of the conference center—lobby line-of-sight, outer doors, anything that would tempt a panicked rush. Not a firefight. A message: stay inside.

Then the parking lots spoke.

A detonation rolled through the nearest row of vehicles. Then another. Suspensions jumped and slammed down. Alarms shrieked into the morning. Windshields spidered. People who still believed they could sprint to their cars learned, in a single second, that cars were no longer refuge.

The building was not just sealed.

It was isolated.

Inside, the Team Leader stepped into the center aisle. He did not raise his voice.

"Face down," he said calmly. "Phones. Wallets. Jewelry. Firearms. On the floor. Now."

The pavilion obeyed before it understood why.

And the morning that had looked like setup stopped being morning at all.

Chapter Three – In Charge

Screams flared, then choked into silence. Instinct took over—vendors, collectors, staff pressed their bodies low, arms over heads, trying to vanish into carpet. Coins spilled from trays, glittering in dust like discarded teeth.

The crew didn't fire again right away. They didn't need to. The first volley had already rewritten the room's rules.

From that first burst, obedience was the only currency left.

The Team Leader's voice again cut through the dust, calm and level, the opposite of the storm he had just created.

"Face down. Phones. Wallets. Jewelry. Firearms—on the floor. Now."

No shouting. No bark. Certainty did the work.

A man hesitated, clutching his phone like it could anchor him to the world he had been in five minutes ago.

A rifle cracked once—upward—chewing plaster from the ceiling inches above him. Dust peppered his hair. He flung the phone forward and dropped flat.

The sound of surrender filled the space—phones skittering across carpet, wallets slapped down, watches and rings stripped from fingers. A pile began to form, obscene in its ordinariness. Sweat sharpened. Gunpowder lingered.

Somewhere beyond the walls, sirens rose—distant, multiplying, useless.

Somewhere above them, red dots moved across the pavilion floor.

Chapter Three - In Charge

They came from the rafters—rifle lasers and scopes steadied on beams—sliding across backs, pausing at the base of a neck, drifting on. Nobody needed to understand optics to understand the message. The ceiling owned the room.

The room had been trained by every movie it had ever seen to recognize what red light meant.

A woman whispered, "It's okay," to someone who wasn't her child—just a stranger pressed so close their shoulders touched. A boy slid his hands forward with palms up and felt carpet burn. A dealer pried his wedding band loose, skin pale where metal had lived for decades, and set it down like an offering he hated giving.

The Team Leader moved the room from control to work.

At a gold booth near the north aisle, an older man in a vest lay with his cheek against the carpet and watched gloved hands empty his case. Krugerrands winked and vanished. American Eagles slid against each other with a sound that was both wealth and loss.

He could taste metal—the ghost of it in the air—and realized he was tasting his life's work evaporating coin by coin.

Two rows over, a teenager's fingers shook as he typed I love you into a text box he had never used for those words before. He slid the phone forward with the rest and felt his face burn when a red dot paused between his shoulder blades, then drifted away.

An older woman clutched a silver pendant—a saint with a rubbed face—until gloved knuckles brushed her hand. She flinched but didn't fight. The chain rasped against her skin as it slid away. She folded her hands under her chest so they wouldn't shake where anyone could see.

Two men wrapped rags around hammer heads and drove them into glass, muffling the sound to dull cracks. Display cases sagged inward. Coins spilled like metallic rain onto velvet trays and into gloved hands. Relics—crosses, medallions, ancient paperweights—were swept into sacks without reverence.

At the far end of the hall, beneath banners for a recovered Spanish wreck exhibit, the crew altered course and closed on the display.

The cases here were older, heavier, glass thicker than the rest. Placards spoke of salvage and conservation, of artifacts raised from wreckage and loaned under strict conditions.

None of that slowed the hands that reached them.

They did not strip the display bare. Movements were measured—lifting, weighing, passing over. A chalice was wrapped and set aside; another was left where it stood. Crosses came free with practiced twists, medallions slipped from their mounts.

What glittered was not always what went.

As they were finished, one man reached past gold entirely and lifted a leather-bound volume from its cradle. The cover was warped by salt and time, spine repaired with careful stitching. He did not read the placard. He slid the book into a satchel and sealed it before the sacks were half full.

The crew moved on.

Outside the pavilion, the building shook with denial.

Gunfire cracked—short, deliberate bursts into glass and steel, pinning anyone in the lobby who still believed escape might be possible. People pressed into corners and learned the shape of "stay put" without being told.

More detonations rolled through the nearest parking lot. Then another. Vehicles lifted and slammed down. Alarms shrieked. Glass burst outward. Anyone thinking about reaching a car learned in an instant that cars were no longer refuge.

Inside the pavilion, a child began to cry.

Three voices whispered "shhh" at once.

And the red dots kept moving.

At one table, a crewman whispered numbers under his breath—"ten, twenty, forty"—as if counting could keep his hands honest. Another brushed shards aside with a sleeve before scooping a row of ancient bronzes into a bag, the dull clack of metal on metal oddly tender. A velvet tray bled a stream of dimes into a sack; the zipper rasped shut and somebody's whisper of "good" slid into the dust and disappeared.

At one booth, instinct overcame fear.

Walter Garrison moved an arm, one hand, outstretched as if to shield his niece, Rachael, beside him. His voice never made it past his throat before a rifle coughed once.

The shot hammered him back into the display.

Blood soaked the carpet in a widening bloom.

A second round hissed past Rachael, grazing her arm and searing skin as it cut her down to the floor. Her breath caught. She pressed her cheek into carpet and then she quietly cried in pain and her grief.

The robbery didn't pause. The crew's rhythm was stronger than mercy. Glass shattered. Sacks bulged. Coins clinked against relics in a sound that should not have existed in the same room as death.

Across Cobb County, sirens multiplied—far from the pavilion, closer to everything else. Shouted commands overlapped and canceled one another out. No one agreed on what they were seeing, only that it was already too late to stop.

On both sides of the interstate, red and blue lights flared on vehicles that could no longer move. EMT crews tried to snake ambulances along the shoulders and found their way choked by abandoned cars and the geometry of panic. A paramedic jumped out with a bag and ran, because a bag can run farther than a box can roll.

In the 911 center, calls from the interstate started to eat the calls from everywhere else.

“Multi-vehicle collision—southbound I-75—”

“Northbound too—tractor-trailer jackknifed!”

“We’ve got entrapments—multiple vehicles—”

“Nothing’s moving—units can’t get through—”

The wall of monitors became a wall of fire ants. An analyst dragged a red bar across the interstate map and wrote NO FLOW in a corner box no one had time to read.

And then—over a protected federal channel—a different report cut in. Shorter. Colder.

Not the first thing of the day.

Not the beginning.

An escalation that arrived only after the pavilion had already been turned into a sealed room full of bodies.

At Dobbins Air Force Base, alarms sounded before anyone saw the shooters. Muzzle flashes stitched the perimeter fence, sharp and bright against floodlights. A guard tower hit. Gunfire walked across the flight line and sparked against the fuselage of Air Force Two.

Base security keyed emergency channels at the same instant the flight line locked down.

“Primary air’s not viable.”

“Execute secondary extraction. Now.”

By the time the first unified command post tried to assemble, timelines no longer agreed. Too many scenes. Too many weapons. Too much coordination for coincidence.

No one was ready to say what it meant.

Only that whatever had started in Cobb County was not finished.

Inside the pavilion, people didn't know any of that.

They only knew red dots.

They only knew the taste of plaster.

They only knew the way the air changed when a room decides you don't get to stand up anymore.

The taped guards against the wall made small noises into the tape over their mouths, the kind men make when they are trying to be useful and are not allowed to be. One flexed his wrists against plastic that had decided to be steel.

The other stared at a banner that spelled WELCOME with a cheerful lie and thought, absurdly, about the blister he'd felt coming on earlier. His radio lay in a bin amid a black rectangle of phones and a tangle of charging cords like snakes.

Overwatch's mounted laser scopes waited for their lazy crawl. Not a rhythm yet; that would be polite. A randomness that will feel like inevitability once activated.

Someone tested the air with a word—"help"—and when no shot followed, another voice answered, "Here," and then another,

"Here," until the room was a soft lattice of small declarations that did not change anything and changed everything.

Then, from above, the punctuation came.

Two sharp bursts—downward, deliberate.

One round struck near a cluster of hostages—close enough to make the floor spit fibers and dust. The second struck flesh.

Chapter Three - In Charge

A man cried out, blood spreading dark beside him.

A red dot crossed Walter's back and no one noticed; noticing had learned how to be expensive. Another traced the path of a scarf now pressed into the gut-shot man's abdomen and the woman holding it remembered to breathe because she had almost forgotten.

The scream that followed was immediate, raw, contagious. Panic spiked—but only for a moment. The red dots never stopped moving. The message landed.

Nobody in the room needed to be told what it meant.

Obey, or the room will choose someone else.

The injured man rolled to his side, breath shallow, shock arriving fast. The wound wasn't fatal, but it was bad enough to make time feel louder. Blood darkened the carpet beneath him in a slow spreading stain.

Rachael heard him. She didn't look. She pressed her mouth into carpet and kept counting breaths because that was the only thing she could control. Her arm burned. Her uncle didn't move. The red dot crawled across her shoulder and drifted on.

The room went quiet again.

Not peaceful.

Compliant.

The plunder continued.

Relics were lifted first—crosses, medallions, chalices—wrapped carefully before ever touching a bag. Doubloons followed in handfuls, noisy and fast. The sacks were cinched early and kept light enough to move. What glittered was not always what went.

A woman in a red blazer lay flat with her cheek pressed to the floor, watching sideways as gloved hands stripped relics from her booth. She mouthed the words of a prayer, not daring to voice them, and when the bag closed she felt as if her own lungs had been cinched shut with the string.

Somewhere a dealer tugged a tablecloth too hard and coins rattled. He looked up, embarrassed, and locked eyes with a man whose hand was in a bin. He nodded an apology at a stranger and returned to smoothing cloth, skin prickling for no reason he could name.

The Team Leader moved through the center aisle with energy shaped into stillness. He didn't glance at faces; faces didn't matter. Doors mattered. Hands mattered. Angles mattered. His men were hands. The room was a thing placed under those hands.

The regroup signal came from the Team Leader without words—a tone practiced into muscle.

Outside, the Driver left the cab with the engine still idling and popped the rear bay open, wide, ready for returning hands. Then he moved—quiet, controlled—to the blocking car which had been staged earlier. He eased it out of the parking lot to the last foot into final position, and he would press flush where it needed to press, and made the exit a wall, after the team exits.

Inside, the crew began to peel away in sequence. Bins rolled. Sacks shifted. No shouting. No panic. An orderly withdrawal into the service corridor and out, toward the open truck bay.

Overwatch descended on the lifts with rifles tight across their chests. On the way down, each reached for a taped switch. Rifle-mounted lasers winked off. The mounted units became active.

From the floor, nothing changed.

The dots still moved.

The ceiling still owned them.

That was the point.

The crew melted back into the line at floor level, already back inside their maintenance posture. Bins parked where bins always parked. Mops leaned where mops always leaned. Masks stayed on. The withdrawal looked like labor finishing, not criminals leaving.

Within seconds, the pavilion's heartbeat slowed, leaving only muffled sobs and the hiss of settling dust.

The doors—already sealed, already lied about—held. Adhesive cooled into certainty. The building learned to keep a secret.

No one inside moved. Movement had been redefined as betrayal. Someone prayed. Someone counted screws. Someone found a hand and held it.

And the second injured man—shot for punctuation, kept alive by indifference—lay still, breathing shallowly, the carpet beneath him darkening.

Waiting for help that was already being delayed by design.

The pavilion held its breath and waited for whatever would come through the next door it was allowed to notice.

Chapter Four – Cross Roads

The service corridor swallowed them whole.

Concrete squeezed sound into a close, metallic whisper: the squeak of a wheel that had always squeaked, the soft drum of sacks brushing legs, the thin rasp of breath behind filters. The corridor bent, narrowed, and bent again, forcing the line into single file without ever asking. They moved the way crews always moved when a job was finished and the next one waited somewhere else—no urgency, no pause, no eye contact that might ask a question.

Behind them, beyond sealed doors that no longer remembered how to open, the illusion stayed alive.

Red dots drifted across the pavilion floor in slow, indifferent arcs. They crossed spines, paused on cheeks, slid down arms, wandered away. No rhythm. No response. No correction. From the carpet, it looked as if overwatch still lived above them, rifles steady, eyes unblinking.

That was the point.

There was no one in the rafters anymore. No hands on triggers. No breath behind scopes. The lifts were empty, harnesses slack, motors cooling. What remained was automation—mounted units executing the last instructions they had been given, blind to context, deaf to sound, faithful to nothing but motion.

Inside the pavilion, no one could tell the difference.

They didn't run. Running makes noise. Running leaves memory. They moved the way maintenance crews moved when the shift ended late and another job waited across the building—bins rolling, shoulders loose, posture already disengaging from what had just happened. Eleven men became a line, then a bend, then a corner that erased them.

At the far end of the corridor, the last unsealed door waited.

It opened outward, a narrow mouth onto daylight and service apron. A sedan idled close, already staged, already bored. One by one the men stepped through. Boots scuffed once. Then gone.

When the last cleared the threshold, the Driver re-engaged the sedan. He didn't gun it. He didn't hesitate. He rolled forward until the bumper met steel and pressed. Metal complained. Hinges flexed. The door gave just enough to feel final.

The Driver twisted the key, pocketed it, then stepped out. A bead of adhesive hissed along the seam—bright, wet, then dulling as it set. He smoothed it with his glove, tested the handle with his fingertips.

It answered like a thing that had never been asked a question.

The world beyond that door no longer existed.

Inside the pavilion, the red dots kept moving.

A man near the west aisle lifted his head an inch, then froze as a point of light drifted across his temple and slid away. He lowered himself again, heart hammering, convinced he had been noticed.

A woman pressed her forehead to the carpet and counted breaths because counting felt safer than praying. Someone whispered a name and stopped halfway through it, afraid sound itself might draw attention.

Nothing reacted. That was worse.

The Driver rejoined the line. Ahead of them, the bay door had already been rolled up with the groan of old rollers, opening onto the panel truck's peeled paint and the anonymous promise of a loading lane. Boots climbed. Weight shifted. Eleven bodies filled the dark.

The door thunked down and latched.

A lid on a box that now had only one story left to tell.

The Driver moved to the cab and slid in without hurry. The engine never stopped idling. He eased the truck forward as if the day were a delivery and they were late.

In the mirror: nothing but heat shimmer, a smear of exhaust, empty concrete. He signaled, merged, and became a thing among things in the slow clot of traffic.

Inside the pavilion, time stretched.

The dots continued their crawl. Not responding. Not adjusting. Just moving.

Someone tried to speak and stopped. Someone else shifted a knee and winced, convinced the movement had been seen. The injured man on the floor breathed shallowly, a wet sound catching in his chest. A woman pressed a scarf harder into his side and mouthed words she could not hear herself say.

No one came. The ceiling watched. And then, without ceremony, the truck was gone.

Outside the Conference Center, automated weapons continued to spray the lobby; timed bombs continued to keep people away from the parking areas.

Inside the truck, the first minute mattered more than the next ten. Before anyone reached for a bag, before piles could form, the order asserted itself the way it always did—without discussion. Devices came out together. Phones. Burners. Anything with a battery that could whisper to a tower.

Cases opened with small, final sounds. SIM trays flicked out like teeth. Plastic shells snapped. Screen glass snarled into crazed spiders.

The heap of dead rectangles grew in a corner like a monument to the way modern lives end when you break them into enough parts.

No one spoke. They had learned every job in this hour like liturgy.

SIMs rattled into a greasy paper bag with a sound like rain on a tin roof. Batteries followed into another—heavier, duller. Screens went dark one by one, a constellation collapsing into nothing.

The Driver watched the road and listened. It came quickly. Not sirens. Not radio chatter. Something subtler.

The moment when nothing answered back.

When the last device went dark, the truck took the first turn it had not practiced. Not sharp. Not fast. Just wrong enough. Then another.

The point was not speed. The point was distance between the last signal and the next question. Until this second, the truck had been a probability—something towers and handoffs and automated guesses might chase. The moment the last device died, that thread snapped.

The police were now blind. They did not yet know what they were blind to.

Masks, gloves, coveralls, rags wrapped around hammer heads—anything that might hold a print or a word—went into one pile. The carcasses of phones into another. Palms opened. Pockets turned out.

They checked each other quickly, professionally, without ceremony. Nothing left that could speak, ping, or remember them.

Only then did they sort the weight that was allowed to feel like weight.

Velvet mouths packed with coins and relics made the third pile—wrapped cloth, edges protected. The fourth held what would become money without a mint: rings and watches; rubber-banded stacks of small bills from tills; envelopes with names written in neat, old hands.

And in that same pile sat the thin things that cut deepest—IDs, insurance cards, Social Security slips, credit and debit rectangles. Lives flattened into plastic and paper.

The thin stuff went last. Not for money. Because names travel farther than coins ever will.

Near the rear door, its lid turned down like a modest face, sat a laptop. It looked ordinary the way a knife in a drawer looks ordinary until it isn't.

The man nearest to the laptop eased it open and initiated a program. A blue bar crawled. A routine had begun, wiping the hard drive.

Time was not a thing they planned to gift anyone.

The truck took another turn. The heaviest bag toppled and slid; three hands found it at once and fetched it back, more instinct than care. The Driver kept the speed where it belonged, letting lights and lanes do the talking.

In the mirror: nothing but heat shimmer, a smear of exhaust, empty concrete.

Chapter Four - Cross Roads

Four cars waited nose-out under a thin net of shade. An old contractor's sedan with a ladder scar on the roof. A white hatchback that had always needed washing and never gotten it. A clay-colored SUV with a dent that never asked to be explained. A dull-gray compact whose only opinion was that it started when asked.

The panel truck kissed the crosswise slot and settled.

When the bay lifted, the air beyond felt different—open, sun-heated, flavored with resin and blacktop.

They moved as if the ground itself had told them where to go. Bags found open trunks with soft thuds. Lids closed with polite clicks. No names asked. No names given.

The last man lingered in the truck's bay.

Not out of hesitation—out of habit. The floor held the residue of the morning in ways no one would ever read correctly: streaks of adhesive dulled by dust, a smear where a sack had dragged for half a foot, a partial print set in powder so thin it looked accidental. The kind of mess that meant work had been done and finished.

He tilted the can. The reek built quickly—cardboard, rags, plastic, the polite guts of phones that had already forgotten how to be phones. The air sharpened, became something lungs noticed and did not like. He crouched, touched off a small flame, and set it down for the second it took to believe in itself.

Fire walked. Plastic curled. Glass ticked. Paper blackened. Heat made itself the only subject worth discussing.

He stepped down and hauled the bay door shut. By the time the latch seated, orange leaked at the edges—not dramatic, not fast, just certain. The kind of fire that does not ask permission to become a problem later.

When he climbed into the gray compact, the first car was already a block away.

The white hatchback rolled out, catching a green like it had ordered it. The SUV waited for a delivery van to lurch past, then slipped in behind as neat as a hand moving through water.

The compact sat still long enough for the Driver to look once in his mirror. Not to remember. To make sure he could afford to forget. The truck was fully engaged. Then he pulled away.

Within two blocks, there were four ordinary cars carrying their share of a morning no one would tell rightly for years.

They went to work.

Car One took the slow road. Its cargo did not like to be jarred. Trays of silver lay wrapped like children tucked into blankets, edges protected, weight distributed so nothing would knock itself into a sound that mattered. The Driver stayed in the right lane, ceded on-ramps to people who needed to be first at things, read the road for potholes before his hands felt them. He drove like a man who believed patience could be taught to metal.

Car Two held cash and jewelry. Weight only mattered if you thought about it. He didn't. He took a different route—commercial arteries, stoplights, places where cameras saw too much to remember any one thing clearly. He did not speed. He did not brake hard. He let other drivers be important instead.

Car Three carried identity. Licenses fanned like playing cards. Insurance slips with little crosses in the corners. Social Security paper that looked like nothing and was not. Credit and debit plastics that would become names on ledgers in places that pretended to be far away.

This driver took the third route—the one that crossed neighborhoods where yard signs argued with one another and children rode bikes too close to the street. He stopped fully at stop signs. He waved someone through who did not deserve it. He became invisible by obeying rules harder than anyone else around him.

Car Four carried the laptop. And the small quilt of other people's lives no one else could quite eat: a necklace whose chain had learned a neck so exactly you could almost see it; a wedding ring worn into kindness; a watch that had belonged to someone who had walked on in a story no one would know without the person who had worn it. He did not think about those.

He thumbed the secure handset once.

"River site blown," he said.

"Moving to secondary."

The voice that answered was allowed to be simple.

"Confirmed."

He turned into a shopping center that had never learned what it wanted to be. A nail place. A check-cashing storefront. A vape shop missing a letter. In the far corner, a Goodwill donation box waited, its blue sun-faded to denim, its lid dented like a knee.

He parked where cameras didn't care. Stepped out with a cardboard file box under one arm—the kind professors use to move offices, the kind men use to empty desks when someone else decides their time is over. He lifted the metal lid, felt the hinge complain, and fed the box into the dark.

For a second, plastic scraped steel. Loud enough to be a decision. Then clothes and lamps and old toys took it.

The lid fell. It sounded like something ordinary happening. Which was another way of saying it sounded like what they had counted on.

He walked back to the compact, sat down, and let the car breathe him quiet. He did not look back at the bin. Looking back is a habit you either walk out of or it kills you.

Back behind the trailers where it was abandoned, the panel truck had become a furnace. Paint bubbled and peeled. The windshield slumped with a sound like a tired animal. Smoke fell across the road and lay there, thick enough to taste.

Two boys cut the lot on bikes. The older one pointed. The younger laughed, because smoke looks like a dragon when you're twelve. They pedaled on.

At the strip mall, a woman in a visor lifted the Goodwill lid and found it heavier than expected. She moved it without thinking, dropped her donations, cursed softly, and walked toward the grocery she had come from. She thought about avocados.

On a feeder road, a patrol car ran a red—nearly twenty minutes after the last device inside the pavilion had gone dark.

Not a call from inside. A runner. Breathless. Finding the first radio that still worked.

By midafternoon, the smoke column thinned and gave up. Automation cooled. Glue held.

Four cars became four lives that were not exactly anyone's lives. A truck became a story told later in a room with linoleum and coffee.

Somewhere, under old clothes and a lamp base with a crack you would only see if you wanted to, a laptop went to sleep.

Chapter Four - Cross Roads

They had split the crime so small even God would have needed a magnifying glass to make it whole again. They drove. The country they left behind kept happening.

The men did what they had rehearsed. They vanished into it.

Chapter Five – Captive Audience

The pavilion did not breathe. It only listened.

Red dots continued drifting the way insects do when heat makes them slow—across a shoulder blade, along a neck, pausing at the hinge of a jaw before sliding off into carpet. To the people pressed flat to the floor, those dots were eyes. Overwatch still appeared to live above them. Rifles waited. A thought that might have been hope learned to keep its hands to itself.

No one moved. Not really.

Survival had been reduced to small math—an elbow drawn in a thumb's-width to ease a cramp, a calf flexed once and then forgiven, a mother lifting her child an inch so his breathing found cloth instead of air. The room had rewritten motion. Anything larger than a sigh might be mistaken for rebellion.

Phones were gone—swept into bins and carried off with the men who had stripped the floor. Even the hotel's own lines had gone silent when the PBX died. Call, text, email—it didn't matter. Inside Hilton Pavilion, nothing could reach the world beyond the glass.

The silence was not quiet. It was engineered.

Rachael lay with her cheek against the weave, the smell of dust and old coffee in her mouth. Heat pulsed along her right arm where the round had grazed and torn, wet warmth spreading in a slow comet through her sleeve. She kept her hand flat, fingers extended, pressed into carpet to feel the rhythm of her chest.

In… two-three. Out… two-three. If she counted, she could make time behave.

Walter lay near her. He was still in a way that only one thing is. The red dot that crossed his back did not change anything. A sound in Rachael's throat tried to lift and became a swallow. She slid her left palm until the heel of it touched his sleeve—just once, just enough to know she could still find him in a map made of bodies.

A hand touched her wrist—gentle, precise. A stranger's voice, no louder than breath.

"Don't."

Not unkind. A rule that belonged to everyone now.

Two aisles over, the man who had taken the shot into his belly groaned and then stopped because his body decided the noise was too expensive. His shirt had darkened from pale to the color of dried fruit. He lifted his head once and crawled as far as a forearm and three knuckles before gravity reclaimed him.

A woman further pressed her folded scarf into the wound with both palms. "Stay," she whispered. "Please." She felt his heat, the stagger of his breath, and did not look at the dot that came to rest between his shoulder blades.

The guards against the wall kept their eyes down. Tape had wrenched their hands into usefulness for someone else; the plastic had decided to be steel. One swallowed against a throat gone dry and stared at the banner above the door that still spelled WELCOME with the cheerful cruelty of paint.

A child breathed in little hiccups into a mother's hair. "Is he asleep?" the child mouthed.

The mother—who had run out of words an hour ago—pressed a finger to his lips without thinking about the dot that slid along the part in his hair and blinked away.

The ceiling tile pocked by warning shots dropped new dust in small cascades. It landed on shoulders and sleeves and the rim of a display case like ash. A man who had spent thirty years with tweezers and stamps watched gray specks settle on the old paper inches from his face and decided—without deciding—not to blow them away.

He belonged to the rule now. Everything that was not breath did not belong to him.

Someone began to pray. Not the full prayer—only the shape of it. Someone else counted screws along the baseboard—twelve, thirteen, fourteen—and then lost count and started again because numbness is a kind of mercy if you teach it how.

Dust hung in shafts where overhead lights pretended nothing had happened. Beneath a cart that was no longer a cart, the jammer purred—a sound you could not hear with ears. The body heard it anyway and filed it under this will last longer than you.

Chapter Five - Captive Audience

The room learned patience the way animals learn weather.

Outside the pavilion, the lobby had sorted itself into two kinds of people: Those who ran inward—deeper into a hotel that had never practiced being a fortress. And those who could not stop looking through glass like it was a lake and they might learn a better truth from another angle.

From their side, the pavilion was a painting. Pale ovals where faces were pressed into carpet. Arms outstretched toward aisles—open hands, palms up, emptied. The red points wandered over those backs, and the watchers learned the word sniper with a softness that made it feel less like a word and more like weather.

A crack in the plaster above the vestibule in the lobby popped and coughed dust onto tile. A second chip bit above the concierge's desk. The sconce beside the check-in counter shed its glass throat in a sigh. The devices did not know scale. They only did their job. Those in the lobby did too.

They ducked and scattered and huddled and watched. A woman with a conference badge rattled a handle, got glue on her fingers, and wiped it on her blouse the way you wipe off something you don't want on you.

The front desk clerk lifted the receiver. Nothing. No tone. No click. He set it down hard, heart punching his ribs, and turned toward the lobby.

"Phones are dead!" he shouted. "Everyone down—stay under cover!"

A man in a blazer hit the glass twice with flat fists that made no difference to a thing that was no longer a door.

Chapter Five - Captive Audience

Back in the county's 911 communications room, the boards were totally in the wrong color.

Kennesaw State had been red for seventeen minutes. Northbound and southbound I-75 were both bleeding. Spoof calls—voices that had learned how to sound real years ago—sat stacked beneath the real ones like a trap with a good memory.

"Hilton/Marietta—shots fired—hostages visible—doors sealed," a voice read, eyes skipping across a screen that bent its own reflection into a frown.

"Copy. Any unit free?"

Silence, with voices inside it.

"Negative. Perimeter KSU needs bodies. Interstate is MCI both directions."

"Put Hilton on hold—verify before commit."

The word verify carried the weight of policy. The woman who underlined Hilton — NO INSIDE COMMS in her notebook added a dot beside it that was really a curse. She had learned the sound a cut PBX makes long ago and she was hearing it now without hearing it.

Someone had planned this until planning itself had become a weapon. Then more phones rang.

"Six Flags—Austell—gunfire at the gate—children down—people trampling—"

"Copy—Six Flags—multiple callers—send everything we have west."

"Wellstar ER—shots outside ambulance bay—medic hit—we need—"

"Copy—Wellstar—lockdown—the bay's hot—advise staging."

The map learned two new pains and glowed with them. Hilton was now one voice among many, and the math of the room knew what to do with math: it made numbers larger where they already were.

At the Perimeter, the first patrol unit at Hilton rolled quiet, no siren. He parked nose-out, angled to run if running became the job. He began to walk the perimeter when he heard gunshots, then an explosion, forcing him to try to get under better cover inside, but a door didn't budge, the seam had been touched by some sort of glue.

Working his way to the back of the building, he discovered a car blocking an entrance, leaning its weight into the service door like a drunk into a friend. He tugged the handle. It pretended not to know him.

He spoke softly into his shoulder as if it were an ear.

"Dispatch, Hilton Pavilion. Shots fired and explosions; doors are sealed. No interior contact. Send backup.."

Explosions continued in the parking lots, making their own punctuation every few minutes—commas you could feel in your ribs.

He crept toward the front, staying in the lee of things made of steel. Through the lobby glass he saw people peeling to the walls, hands on panes, faces that had forgotten what faces were for. Through the pavilion glass beyond that he saw nothing he could use—just bodies flattened to the floor, red dots drawing lines no uniform could cross.

He backed off without having to tell himself to.

Bomb squad's got to make the first bad choices. That was the rule too.

"Two-One to Command, perimeter indicates multiple shots still active. Holding until EOD and SWAT arrive for staging."

The gut-shot man, who had rolled onto his side, tried to roll back again but stopped. The scarf pressed into him had become a flag that had given up color. The woman who knelt with her hands on it had her chin in the carpet so hard it hurt the bone.

She put the pain on a shelf and counted his breaths into it.

Rachael's arm burned and then chilled and then did both. She made her mouth into a line because faces are traitors and she would not let hers talk. Walter's sleeve was where her fingers could find it if she let them. She did not.

She pressed her hand into her arm, beneath the place where blood had drawn the fabric tight and held pressure until pressure felt like a decision she had made. A red dot slid across her shoulder and she felt it like heat without warmth. It kept going. She did not test the word luck aloud. She did not give it the dignity of being in the room.

A dealer with a magnifying loupe still around his neck had pressed his face into the carpet so hard the metal ring dug a circle into his cheek and left a print. He would joke about it later if he ever lived long enough to become a man who turned everything into a story. He did not think he would.

A child near the center tried to lift his head the way flowers do when the sun touches them. Three hands landed on his back at the same time and pressed him warm into the floor.

“Shhh,” came from three throats in harmony that was not planned.

No one asked if the lasers were real. They were true. That was enough.

Across the road, the gas station filled with cars that did not need gas. People got out and put hands on roofs the way people do when they look to see carnage.

A delivery driver slowed to read signs with his lips and then sped up because he had never seen so many blue lights in so little space and because the human animal knows when to be a different shape on the road.

A man who planned on attending the coin show, but was arriving late, started to park, but stopped short after hearing gun fire and seeing vehicles on their sides, destroyed. Self preservation took over, and he left the facility before he, too, could become a victim..

Every few minutes, another blast went off near the back of the building. The sound flattened birds from trees and let them remember how to fly three seconds later. Heads turned, then went down.

Phones came up. Phones went down. Everyone here had chosen a different story if they could.

Dispatch was still being swamped with calls.

“Six Flags—multiple injuries—children—”

“Wellstar ER—confirm explosion at ambulance bay—possible device—”

“Hilton calls still unverified. Reports from outside only.”

“Copy. All Hilton units hold warm until EOD. No entry.”

On the map, the pushpins did not have faces. On the floor inside Hilton Pavilion, the faces did not have pushpins. Reality had learned how to be two things at once, and the only people who could fix that were busy holding a rule like a rope.

A voice on the radio that had practiced sounding unexcited said, “Bomb Squad five minutes.”

The officers behind cruisers felt a minute stretch into a different size and decided not to tell anyone, because minutes change shape when you look at them wrong.

Inside the pavilion, the mounted lasers kept doing their job. Not a rhythm—that would have been polite. A randomness that felt like inevitability.

A red dot crossed Walter's back and no one noticed; noticing had learned how to be expensive. Another traced the path of the scarf pressed into the man's belly and the woman holding it remembered to breathe because she had almost forgotten.

Someone on the carpet started to shake—not full panic, just an engine idling too high. The person beside them put a palm between their shoulder blades and left it there.

Here. I am here. Language was too loud to be allowed.

The smell of adhesive lived in the backs of throats and made a letter on the tongue that would not leave for days. The lights above had learned nothing and hummed the same note like insects pinned in a collection.

Rachael closed her eyes and saw her mother's porch—peeling paint, the string of little white lights that had not been little or white for years, the way the rail was smooth where hands always chose to hold it. She told herself the porch still existed. She stored the word behind her teeth.

A man inhaled too sharply and coughed and then froze, waiting for something to happen to him as punishment. It didn't. Sometimes not dying felt like an insult to all the dead things in the world. He forgave himself for feeling that and did not move again.

A coin worked loose from some table found a seam in the carpet and lodged itself there like it had been told to. It leaned into the thread and decided to belong.

Outside, the hotel dressed itself in tape and sawhorses.

Officers spoke into radios in words that do not make good stories—perimeter, warm zone, cold, staging, hold. A fire engine idled, the man on the back step looking at his boots and then at the sky and then at his boots again, as if one of those things might offer instruction.

Inside, the room had chosen its shape and would not be argued out of it by anything less than a different kind of loud.

The jammers began to die. The mobile phones in the lobby suddenly had service again . The red dots inside crawled on. The breathers breathed. The non-breather lay with a dot on his back that meant the same thing every dot meant.

Somewhere in the county, sirens screamed toward children and toward an ER bay and away from this building for a little while longer. Distant and close did not know how to be different things.

Time did not pass. It pooled. It lay where it was and waited for someone with the right tools to push it into shape people could live in again,

The man with the gut wound drifted in and out, a tide with no shore. Each time he surfaced, the world was the same: carpet fibers in his eyelashes, the woman's scarf pressed hard into him, the heat and the cold arguing about which one owned him.

He stopped making noise because his body learned the price.

The woman did not stop counting. She had not planned to become a clock, but the room had appointed her one.

Rachael's arm had gone numb around the burn, the edge of pain retreating into a dull ache that let her think again and punished her when she did. She did not move her hand from where it pressed her thigh. She had decided that this pressure was the one thing she could choose.

Walter lay the way he lay. Still. Unnegotiable. The dot on his back slid and slid again, indifferent to the fact that it had nothing left to enforce.

A guard against the wall swallowed and tasted copper. The tape had pulled hair from his wrists and the sting gave him something to hold on to that was not the thought of a radio he could hear hissing from inside a bin ten feet away. He stared at the banner that spelled WELCOME and wondered when letters had learned how to lie.

Another guard found the blister on his heel again with his mind and used it like a nail to hang his focus on. Training told him to catalog exits. There were none. Training told him to breathe. He did.

A child's hiccuped breath softened into sleep against a mother's shoulder. The mother did not allow herself the luxury of believing that sleep meant safety. She allowed herself the luxury of not waking him.

Dust continued settling from the wounded ceiling, a light snowfall that landed on sleeves and hair and paper and made everything look older by an hour. A man with a loupe still biting his cheekbone watched the dust settle on ink and decided not to blow it away. He belonged to the rule now: breath mattered; nothing else did.

Someone prayed again—smaller words this time, ones that asked less and offered more. Someone else counted screws along the baseboard and reached the same number twice and decided that meant something good.

Across the street, the gas station's canopy lights buzzed like insects that did not know what to do with themselves. Cars still idled with doors open. Peoples' hands on roofs, on hoods, on one another's sleeves, as if touching anything solid might teach the world to hold still.

A woman in a visor paced a tight circle and said into her phone, "I can't tell," over and over, until the words lost meaning and became sound. She did not notice when her keys slid from her palm and came to rest under a trash can. She would find them later and be surprised by how heavy they felt.

A delivery driver slowed, read the signs with his lips, and then sped up because he had learned the shape of places that want you gone.

A man with a badge walked toward the front doors with purpose until a uniform raised a flat hand and turned him back without words. He obeyed because the hand was the same shape as the ones on the other side of the glass and he had learned something from their shape.

Every few minutes, another blast went off near the back of the building. Birds fell from trees and remembered how to fly three seconds later. Heads lifted and then went down. Cameras came up and then went down, too.

Everyone here had chosen a different story if they could.

Dispatch.

"Hilton still no inside comms."

"Copy. Bomb Squad three minutes."

"Six Flags update?"

"Multiple transports en route. Children accounted for."

"Wellstar?"

"ER secure. Secondary bay closed."

The board did not care about sequence. It cared about saturation. Hilton sat in the middle of a mess big enough to hide inside.

"Hold Hilton is still hot," the supervisor said again, because repetition is what you do when policy is the only rope you have. "No entry until EOD."

The map obeyed.

Behind cruisers, officers adjusted vests and checked watches that were lying to them. One leaned on a door and felt the thump of an explosion in his chest and decided not to look at the back of the building again yet.

Bomb techs rolled in quiet, cases heavy, faces unreadable. They did not hurry. Hurry belongs to the untrained. They staged and waited because the building had told them it would punish impatience.

A lieutenant spoke into a radio in a voice he had practiced to sound calm. "All units, maintain perimeter. No interior movement. Let the room tell us when it's done."

No one laughed at the sentence, even though rooms do not talk.

Back inside, the mounted units continued their crawl; the red points drifting without pattern, patient and merciless. From the floor, it was seamless. The ceiling still owned them. A red dot traced the edge of a scarf, then wandered off. Another crossed a shoulder and slid away. No one tested them. No one needed proof anymore.

Someone on the carpet shook again, a small tremor that stopped when a palm landed between shoulder blades and stayed there. Here. I am here. Language remained too loud.

Rachael closed her eyes again and thought of the porch one more time—the rail, the lights, the place hands chose. She told herself the porch would wait. She counted.

The gut-shot man's breath grew thinner, then steadied, then thinned again. The woman with the scarf decided that praying was the best job for the moment.

The room had learned how to be smaller than fear. It had learned how to be still without calling it peace.

Waiting outside, tape fluttered. Radios crackled. A fire engine idled. A medic knelt and stood and knelt again because that is what medics do when they are not yet allowed to do more.

Inside, the non-breather lay as he lay. The breather breathed. The red dots crawled on.

Time did not move. It waited.

And everyone on the floor learned how to hold that waiting without letting it become a thing that broke them, until someone with the right tools, the right suit, the right patience, told the room it was allowed to change shape again.

Chapter Six – Reality Strikes

The screen showed a still frame: the shattered north gate at Dobbins Air Reserve Base, smoke billowing, a guard shack torn open like a toy. Red text at the top read:

DOBBINS ARB – 11:37 HRS – EXPLOSION EVENT

FBI Atlanta Field Office - 11:38 a.m.

The elevator doors didn't just open; they spat people out.

Agents moved fast down the hallway, sidestepping one another, coffee half-forgotten in their hands. The building had a sound on mornings like this—a higher pitch in the air, like the hum inside a power line. Special Agent Sloane Carver felt it in her teeth as she cut toward the Joint Operations Center.

"Carver!" someone called. "Ops two!"

She followed the voice.

Inside Briefing Room Two, half the field office was already there—Counterterror, Criminal, Intel. The projector washed the far wall in harsh light. Assistant Special Agent in Charge Richard Keene stood at the front with his jacket off, tie still knotted, posture tight.

Keene didn't waste time.

"Take your seats," he said. "This is real."

Sloane slid into a chair near the front. Ellis dropped into the seat beside her, notebook already open, pen tapping too fast.

Keene clicked his remote. The next slide showed a map of Cobb County—I-75 running like a spine through the center, three red icons blinking along it.

"At 10:51," Keene said, "Cobb County Dispatch began receiving calls about explosions along I-75 northbound. Overpasses. Shoulders. A few minutes later, this—" he gestured toward the Dobbins gate image "—hit the feeds."

He clicked again. Another image: the west perimeter fence along Dobbins, folded inward. A Humvee listing on flat tires, its windshield spiderwebbed.

"Two perimeter breaches at an Air Reserve Base," Keene said. "Simultaneous with multiple explosions along the primary interstate corridor as the Vice President is in this city."

The room held its breath for half a beat.

"Where is she now?" someone from Counterterror asked.

Keene flicked to the next slide: a schedule block.

VP VICTORIA HALE – MIDTOWN POLICY FORUM

REMARKS: 12:00–1:35

HOLDING LOCATION: BACKSTAGE

"Still downtown," Keene said. "Secret Service has her locked in the venue. Motorcade movement is frozen."

"And Dobbins?" Sloane asked.

"In lockdown. OSI and Security Forces are treating the perimeter as hostile."

Ops Specialist Nguyen spoke up from the back. "Cobb is calling in every warm body. APD is backfilling corridors inside the perimeter. GSP is sealing exit ramps. It's a mess."

"All right," Keene said. "Here's what that means for us. Until HQ tells us otherwise, Atlanta FBI is supporting the Secret Service and bridging to local command. We are not in charge, but we are on the hook."

He drew three big letters on the whiteboard: WHY NOW.

"Someone either wanted to hit Dobbins itself—or they wanted to force changes in the VP's movements. Both are bad. Both involve us."

He turned back to the room.

"Carver, Ellis. Make the calls."

Sloane straightened. "Secret Service or Cobb first?"

"Both," Keene said. "Carver, notify the Service that we agree the Cobb and Dobbins explosions as possibly shaping operations, not random. Ellis, patch into Cobb County Command. Tell them the Bureau is monitoring and we want signatures on those devices as soon as EOD has them."

Ellis scribbled furiously.

"And one more thing," Keene added. "We split our response now, not later."

He wrote on the board:

TEAM A → Dobbins ARB

TEAM B → Midtown (VP Site)

"The Service is stretched," he said. "We're sending a unit to cooperate with OSI and a unit to attach to the VP's site lead. Carver, you're running Team B."

Sloane felt her chest tighten once, then settle. "Understood."

What no one yet understood was that the calls were not sequential. They were concurrent—threads pulled tight at the same second across the metro.

Keene's gaze swept the room. "Nobody freelances. Nobody chases their own rabbit. You see something that might matter, you bring it back to the board.""We have to treat this as a potential leadership threat," someone said. "These county hits are capable of forcing movement."

No one in the room challenged it. It was the assumption protocol demanded.

Nguyen raised a hand. "Do we have any chatter tying this to foreign actors?"

"No," Keene said. "Domestic indicators only—for now. We're not putting the T-word in any reports until HQ blesses it. Call it a coordinated attack until told otherwise."

He closed the laptop with a soft click. "Move."

Chairs scraped. People surged for the door. Sloane grabbed the edge of the table for half a second, grounding herself, then reached for her phone.

12:11 p.m. – FBI Ops Desk

She dialed the Secret Service Protective Operations line from the wall phone so the audio could be routed straight into the threatboard log.

“This is SA Carver, FBI Atlanta,” she said. “We’re running local support. We have multiple explosions in Cobb County, including Dobbins ARB. Our assessment affirms your expressed concern that these events are being orchestrated to effect VP movement, not just disrupt traffic.”

“Copy, Carver,” the operator said. “Stand by—protective lead patching in.”

A new voice came on—a man with no time for niceties.

“Carver, this is Kellerman, Protective Detail. You’re confirming the overpass hits and Dobbins could be prelude for something aimed at Hale?”

“I’m saying,” Sloane replied, “that if I wanted to control where she could or couldn’t go, this is roughly how I’d start.”

Silence. She could almost hear him nod.

“We’re holding her at Midtown for now,” Kellerman said. “We scrubbed the primary route back to Dobbins. We’re building an alternate to Peachtree–DeKalb. If you get anything that says Cobb is part of a larger play, I want it yesterday.”

“You’ll have it,” Sloane said.

She hung up, then punched a new sequence.

12:14 p.m. – Cobb County Police Command

The line crackled once and settled into the flat noise of too many radios bleeding into background.

“Cobb County Unified Command, Captain Laird.”

“Captain, this is Special Agent Sloane Carver, FBI Atlanta.”

A beat.

“Go ahead, Agent.”

"We're monitoring your situation along I-75 and at Dobbins," she said. "We don't have a federal seizure here—yet—but we are highly interested in signatures and timing."

Laird let out a breath that sounded like he'd been holding it since dawn. "We've got overpasses blown in both directions and a guard shack that's now confetti," he said. "Traffic's stacked, and we're getting calls about at least one explosion near the Hilton Pavilion. I've got SWAT deployed in three directions and EOD juggling more calls than I have fingers."

"Anyone claiming responsibility?" Sloane asked.

"Nothing," Laird said. "No calls, no manifestos, no chat. Just boom."

"All right," Sloane said. "Here's what I can share: the Service is worried your events could be part of a coordinated attempt on the Vice President. That means two things: one, you're going to get federal attention even if you didn't ask for it; and two, the faster we get basic forensics, the more chance we have of knowing whether this was meant to hit you or push her."

Laird swore softly under his breath. "Jesus. Okay. We'll prioritize device signatures and timers. You getting on the ground?"

"Team A is heading to Dobbins," Sloane said. "My team is going to the VP's location downtown. Later today, someone from our shop, and probably GBI, will likely show up at your Hilton command trailer to talk through timelines."

"That trailer's already overloaded," Laird said. "But if this is tied to Hale, I get it."

"I appreciate it, Captain," Sloane said. "We're not here to take the case away from you. We're here because someone may be using your county as part of something bigger."

"We'll keep a corner open," he replied. "Barely."

She hung up.

12:22 p.m. – FBI Motor Pool

The garage ramp echoed with engine noise. Two unmarked Chevy Tahoes idled side by side, red-and-blue dash strobes off, for now.

"Carver," Keene called from the edge of the loading area. "Team A's wheels-up to Dobbins."

She saw them pull out—two SUVs, an EOD van, and an OSI contact riding shotgun.

"You and Ward are Team B," Keene said. "Midtown."

"Ward?" Sloane asked.

"GBI assigned a liaison," Keene said. "Major Crimes. She's solid. And if Cobb keeps bleeding into this, I want someone state-level who knows the terrain and the politics."

As if summoned, Special Agent Alicia Ward emerged from behind a concrete pillar, GBI credentials clipped neatly to her jacket. She carried a slim folder and looked like the sort of person who remembered everything and talked about maybe half of it.

"Agent Carver," she said.

"Ward," Sloane replied. "You draw the short straw today?"

Ward's lips curved briefly. "I'm the courtesy call that keeps the locals from thinking the Bureau drove a tank over their toes."

"She's underselling it," Keene said. "Ward's people have been looking at some fringe activity along the Cobb corridor. Nothing has been chargeable yet. This might be nothing. Might not."

"Might be useful once the dust settles," Ward added. "If there's overlap."

No one said terror. They didn't need to. The map upstairs was doing that quietly on its own.

Keene checked his watch and then looked at Sloane.

"Get to Midtown," he said. "Meet the Service's site lead. If they reroute her, you'll hear it in their voices before you see it on the board."

"Copy," Sloane said.

"And Carver—" he added.

"Yeah?"

"If this turns into the kind of day I think it might, everybody's going to ask why we did or didn't immediately connect what happened in Cobb to the VP. I want our notes to be too clean to punch holes in."

"You'll have them," she said.

12:39 p.m. – Midtown Civic Center Perimeter

By the time Sloane and Ward arrived, the rally site looked like someone had overlaid a football stadium security plan on a neighborhood block.

APD cruisers blocked the cross-streets. Metal barricades funneled foot traffic. Secret Service agents in suits walked purposeful loops, eyes scanning faces, rooftops, windows.

Sloane held her FBI credential case up as they approached the inner checkpoint. Ward did the same with hers.

The agent on the line glanced at both IDs and tapped his earpiece. "Carver and Ward, FBI and GBI," he said. "Advance wants them inside."

He stepped aside. "You're late to the party," he said. "But the DJ's still warming up."

Inside, the air had the damp electric feel of a room about to fill with people and cameras and potential energy.

They found Kellerman, the Secret Service site lead, at a table cluttered with route maps, screen printouts, and three cups of coffee in different stages of abandonment.

“Agent Carver,” he said by way of greeting. “You’re the one who called us about Cobb.”

“Yes,” Sloane said. “This is Alicia Ward from GBI.”

“Agent,” he nodded.

He jabbed a finger at the maps.

“Primary return route to Dobbins runs through sectors where devices have already gone off,” he said. “We’re scrubbing those lines. For now, Hale stays here until we decide whether to push her to Peachtree–DeKalb or bring her out by ground.”

“Any threats specific to the venue?” Ward asked.

“Nothing we’ve picked up,” Kellerman said. “But Cobb changes the lens. We have to assume any visible route could be exploited.”

He looked at Sloane.

“You called this shaping,” he said. “You still think that?”

Sloane wanted to say no. Wanted to say it was coincidence. Wanted to say it would all shake out as some idiot with homemade fertilizer and a grudge against overpasses. She didn’t.

“It fits,” she said instead. “Blow the highway. Hit gates around an airbase. Force law enforcement and military into one theater while you pick your moment in another.”

"And the other theater," Kellerman said, "is where the VP stands behind a podium."

"For now," Sloane said.

They held each other's gaze for a second longer than was comfortable.

Then Kellerman straightened. "You're attached to my perimeter units," he said. "If anything about the movement pattern feels wrong, I want to know it before it hits my radio from upstairs."

"We'll walk the lines," Ward said.

Sloane nodded.

They turned toward the exit.

1:02 p.m. – Outside the Rally Doors

The roar of the crowd inside had a rhythm—the murmur of intros, the crest when the Vice President stepped to the microphone, the first burst of applause.

Sloane stood on the far side of the wall, reading nothing and hearing everything.

She glanced at Ward. "If Dobbins hadn't gone hot," she said, "she'd be on her way back to the airfield already."

"Instead," Ward replied, "she's a fixed point in a bad equation."

Sloane didn't call it a trap. She didn't have to.

The blasts had already started writing the math.

And somewhere else, people with a different map were waiting for the next digit to fall into place.

He didn't introduce the task. He didn't have to.

"Review," he said.

The men responded as one.

"Looked well organized and dedicated."

Thick pencil strokes traced the perimeter of the Vice President's designated airfield. No names. No insignia. Just geometry and timing.

Another man—older, jaw tight, shoulders boxed from work—pointed at the long stretch of fence sketched along the page. "Treeline?"

"Three hundred meters from the west service road," answered someone at the back. "Slope shallow enough for a crawl. Cover adequate."

Another nod.

"What time?" the Leader asked.

A third voice: "I was done at shift change. When eyes are tired and heads are full."

He turned the page. The next sheet showed the flight line—not labeled, not precise, but recognizable to anyone who had watched news footage of arrivals and departures. Lines drawn not to scale but to meaning. Arrows indicating movement. Numbers counting seconds and meters.

A man near the front clenched his gloves once, soft leather against palm. "Confirmation?"

The Leader tapped the corner of the page. "Two sources. Both reliable."

Not intelligence services. Not insiders. Just the compound's strange network of watchers—news cycles, published schedules, transportation chatter, the invisible tide of information that drifted through open channels. It wasn't sophisticated. It was disciplined.

A man in the second row lifted his chin. "What about the interim?"

The Leader slid a fresh page out and placed it down. This one carried a simple layout: a rectangle for a stage, a smaller rectangle for a podium, squares for exits. A rally hall.

"Contingencies," he said.

They studied the sheet the way a chess player studies the board long after the pieces have been set. It wasn't about the rally itself. It was about movement. Where people funneled. Where crowds choked. Where exits clogged. How teams moved when they thought they were in control of the moment.

A hand raised. "Which scenario is primary?"

"Airfield had to go first," the Leader said. "The public event is ancillary. The first waves were designed to stretch resources and their response."

"So we created noise," a man said. "Enough to force a split."

Enough to make the real objective vulnerable.

The Leader gave another nod. "Noise first. Movement second. Timing always."

Timing meant more than clocks. It meant listening for echoes they would never hear—sirens, radios, crowds—responses unfolding elsewhere, unseen but counted all the same.

One man—older, slow-moving, face cut with lines at the corners of his eyes—studied the maps longer than the others. He wasn't the Leader. He wasn't even high in the hierarchy. But he was something close to an archivist. He remembered things the way other people remembered birthdays or smell. When he finally spoke, he did so with quiet certainty.

"This is the biggest one yet."

The Leader didn't lift his gaze. "It is not big. It is required."

A shift moved through the room—not fear, not excitement, but alignment. A collective tightening.

Someone at the back asked, "Any word from the spotters?"

The Leader didn't stop his hands. He didn't lift his head. He ignored the comment.

"Time," he said.

The men filed out, not in procession, not in ritual—just in quiet, efficient rows that dissolved into the yard. Dawn crept over the pines in thin, white slices. Smoke from breakfast fires drifted upward. The rest of the compound was beginning its day—chores, prayers, drills. Ordinary tasks for ordinary lives.

But these men did not join them.

Instead, they split into three groups.

Group One walked toward the treeline, voices low, steps measured. They would scout the staging point again—path, cover, crawl distance, exit route. They knew it already. They would learn it again.

Group Two moved toward an equipment shed, where crates were unlatched and repacked—not with weapons, not yet, but with tools that could be mistaken for tools until the moment they weren't.

Group Three stayed in the yard, kneeling on the packed dirt, drawing lines with fingertips—approach, retreat, diversion—and then wiping them away so memory had to do the work.

Not drills.

Rehearsals.

Not violence.

Choreography.

They were the unseen half of the story that would play out soon. The coin-show attack had required precision. The airfield sequence would require something more: belief and synchronization.

Noise to confuse. Movement to fracture. Pressure to open a window that was never supposed to exist.

The choreography stayed beneath the surface—quiet, measured, ready.

Chapter Seven – High Value Target

The VC-32A shimmered in the Georgia noon, UNITED STATES OF AMERICA painted in proud blue along her fuselage. To people who waved at planes, she was just a sleek jet on a hot ramp. To the men crouched behind concrete at Dobbins Air Reserve Base, sweat tracking down their spines, she was an oath turned into aluminum and composite—and a bullseye.

The first explosion had unstitched the north gate.

Sound slapped the airfield like a giant hand. Windows coughed glass back into rooms. The guard shack leapt, came apart, and scattered itself into the day. For a second the ramp went white and ringing, and then the radios found their voices like survivors.

“Gate One’s gone—possible VBIED—casualties—”

A second blast walked down the west perimeter, folding chain link toward the runway, posts snapping in hot little pings. A Humvee rocked up on two wheels and slammed down. Its horn caught in a single idiot note and would not stop.

Then the gunfire started.

At first it were feelers—three, five, seven rounds—just enough to make the mind hunt angles. Then it lengthened into steady volleys, careful as breath, chewing plaster off the motor pool’s cinderblock wall and flicking sparks from the ribcage of a light pole. From the dark line of trees to the west, rifles spat a rhythm as clean as a metronome. Nothing in the shadows moved. Nothing had to. The weapons were emplaced under brush nets, rigged to fire on intervals, batteries humming.

"Lock it down!" a Secret Service supervisor barked into his sleeve. "Principal is downtown. Ramp integrity only."

Security Forces dove and returned fire in pairs and singles, rounds walking into green that refused to offer a silhouette. An OSI agent slammed into the lee of a Jersey barrier and worked his breathing down. A CAT operator popped the latches on a matte case, yanked a carbine free, and cursed because all he could put rounds on was sound.

Heat lifted off concrete; the air stank of cordite, burnt rubber, and the sweet chemical edge of fuel. Debris pattered back to earth. The base PA choked once, barked the first half of intruder alert, then died into a smear of static.

Senior Airman Kaleb Ruiz pressed his cheek into the ramp's hot concrete and tried to breathe through the ringing in his ears. His sergeant's voice came clipped and cold through the radio: "Hold your sector. Do not chase noise." Ruiz nodded at nothing. He thought of his daughter's birthday cake, pink icing cooling in a kitchen, and told his heart to count to sixty. To his left, a medic dragged a bleeding guard by the armpits, boots scraping across the asphalt, leaving a dark smear behind. Another burst rattled against the fence, showering them with splinters of metal and rust.

Through the cockpit glass, one of the pilots saw everything from his high perch—plumes of smoke, scattered defenders, the insane brightness of sunlight cutting through chaos. He gripped the yoke though the plane wasn't moving, telling himself it was control. In the cabin behind him, staffers had buckled into jump seats, peeking through shades they weren't supposed to touch, listening to the muffled rhythm of gunfire and asking each other questions no one could answer.

Chapter Seven - High Value Target

The jet gleamed white and blue, pristine and obscene, like a wedding cake dropped into a battlefield.

In a bare room miles away, voices moved across a different net—calm, clipped, ex-military.

"Dobbins contained."

"Timeline green. Proceed Phase Two."

"Solid copy."

No excitement, no chatter. Just call-and-response, confirming chaos as if it were another drill.

Downtown Atlanta, Victoria Hale's voice carried in warm, steady lines, the practiced cadence that made hard edges sound like soft promises.

"…and together we will write the next chapter of justice—"

Applause rolled over her like weather. The candidate at her side nodded one beat too late and smiled too wide. Camera shutters ticked like insects.

In the wing, a phone buzzed. An agent's face went still. He leaned to the site lead, cheeks not moving, breath making the words work without the mouth.

"Explosions at Dobbins. Multiple gates. Ramp hot."

The site lead did not even cut his eyes. "Lock elevators. Freeze the garage. Double the motorcade."

Another buzz. Another eye-flick. "They're calling it a storming assault. Treeline fire, multiple secondaries."

“Peachtree,” the site lead said, voice a gavel. “Backup’s fueled. We hold her until the corridor is cold.”

On stage, Hale smiled the smile she used when jokes landed and teams worked and she wanted you to feel included. Nobody out front knew the day had tilted under their feet.

The applause faltered as a muffled boom rolled through the floorboards. A second later the crowd’s noise twisted into confusion, then fear. Folding chairs toppled. A mother snatched her child by the armpits and ran without knowing where. A cameraman tripped, his rig still rolling sideways as it filmed ankles and spilled banners. Secret Service agents surged into a diamond, shouting, “Move! Move!” as they muscled Hale offstage.

Reporters tried to cling to their equipment, some narrating into dead mics, others ducking with eyes wide. A local TV crew went down in the crush, their boom mic dragging across the floor as if trying to record panic itself. The applause that had filled the room only moments before was gone, collapsed into a chorus of shouts, cries, and the high keening edge of panic.

Through it all Hale did not quicken her step; she allowed herself to be moved, her face set, eyes steady, as if she were refusing to loan her fear to the moment. One agent barked, “Ma’am, eyes down, hands in,” and she obeyed, calm enough that staffers nearby took cues from her stillness.

Two rows over, Atlanta’s mayor had already been lifted from her chair by her APD dignitary protection officers. They moved her in parallel with the Service, hustling her toward the same secure corridor, their movements practiced, coordinated. In the agents’ comm net, a clipped confirmation: “Primary secured. Secondary protectee secured. Both moving west corridor.” The distinction was clear. Hale was the mission; the mayor was safeguarded as part of the larger shield.

On the compound's intercept gear, the same call spilled through in frantic Service cadence. The men heard it in real time.

"Primary secured. Secondary secured. Moving west corridor."

Their reply was quiet, flat.

"Copy west corridor. Corridor denial active. Hold Phase Three assets."

Hours earlier, the corridor to Peachtree-DeKalb had been turned into an equation and solved.

Bomb techs in Nomex walked the outbound blocks with mirrors and poles, knees dusty, eyes tunneled. K-9s dragged handlers toward the wet smell of culverts and the sour metallic breath that hides under trash. Manholes were secured shut, welded down to stay that way. State troopers posted on overpasses, forearms on rails, scanned guardrail seams, drainage mouths, sign posts.

A box truck that didn't quite match its paperwork coughed up a polite driver, a clean bumper, and two taps from a gloved hand anyway. A pilot car ran the route three minutes ahead, voice purposely bored into the radio:

"Courtland to 85 north sterile. Lenox overpass clear. Surface approaches sterile. PDK ingress green."

At every cross street a cruiser idled. Motors strung lanes in a dotted line of chrome and plastic. From above, the corridor looked like a strip of silver tape pressed across the city.

Inside the rally hall, an agent touched his earpiece. "Route is green in full. We're a go."

Outside, engines woke as one. The rumble set beer signs trembling two blocks away. The instruction slid through microphones and into muscles: Peachtree is hot. Load in two.

The world folded in half.

The first device detonated under an overpass the sweep team had cleared fifty minutes earlier. The blast rolled inside concrete like thunder in a culvert, spat dust and grit into sunlit air.

The second lifted water out of a drainage ditch and threw it across lanes with a skirt of gravel.

The third cracked near a barricade line two blocks from the rally and made shopfront glass flex before it remembered how to be glass and settled into place with a sound like ice.

"Route Bravo compromised!" the motorcade commander snapped, voice clipped into pieces by adrenaline. "Multiple devices—timed and staggered—freeze the principal, freeze the corridor—do not roll!"

The Suburbans rocked on their springs; drivers' hands locked at ten-and-two. Doors stayed shut. Engines idled with the hostility of animals told to heel.

In the service corridor, the agents' diamond tightened until shoulders touched. "They placed after the sweep," one agent hissed. "They anticipated PDK."

Staffers backed into cinderblock, white-knuckle phones pressed to chests. Beyond the doors the crowd surged the outer barricades in dumb, tidal thinking. Dust webbed down from ceiling tiles onto suits and hair.

Hale sat on a gray metal chair dragged from a closet. She crossed one knee, folded her hands, and looked at the site lead. The applause she had stepped off of still rang; the smell of perfume and hairspray and fresh-printed signs didn't know yet it had been replaced by the smell of fear.

"Ma'am," the site lead said, crouching into her eye line, sweat shining at his temple, "we are holding you here until we clear another corridor."

"Then we hold," she said. No tremor. No complaint. The detail lead was already on his mic, voice sharp: "Command, alternate corridor. Standby for rotary evac if Bravo stays hot." Her composure didn't change the plan, but it steadied the room.

Beside her, the mayor pressed her hands flat on her knees, eyes fixed forward. Her detail clustered near the door, radios tight against their ears, waiting on instructions that would come from someone else's chain of command. She said nothing to challenge the silence, only leaned toward a panicked aide and murmured, "If the city can survive fire, it can survive this. We hold." Her words weren't orders—they were balm.

Another blast rolled heat under the door; the floor ticked, a sound like the building cracking its knuckles. A staffer clapped a hand over her mouth and made a sound she hadn't known her throat could make. Hale didn't move. The mayor didn't flinch. Two women, one federal, one local, calm in different ways, anchoring a room that wanted to shake apart.

On the compound intercepts, the Service net screamed. "Route Bravo compromised. Freeze principal. All units hold position!"

The reply came cool, measured.

"On schedule. Bravo locked. Phase Four set."

Phones all over Atlanta vibrated at once. CodeRED crawled up screens:

EMERGENCY ALERT: SHELTER IN PLACE. MULTIPLE COORDINATED INCIDENTS. NATIONAL LEADERSHIP TARGETED. AVOID TRAVEL.

Interstates seized. Ramps closed behind glittering lines of bikes. Horns layered into a single unbroken scream.

The FAA widened the ring over the city; commercial flights banked for Nashville, Charlotte, Birmingham. News drones were grounded. Only the CAP fighters drew white loops into blue and the small gray hummings of law-enforcement UAVs stitched quiet zigzags above rooftops.

Every channel cut in.

CNN: BREAKING: EXPLOSIONS NEAR AIR FORCE TWO – ATLANTA. Fox split-screened Dobbins smoke with I-75 wreckage and medics sprinting at Wellstar. An MSNBC anchor said, softly, as if trying not to scare anyone, “This feels like our 9/11.”

WSB’s drone feed shook, showing smoke columns crooked against grid streets. “These are live drone images,” the anchor kept saying, as if the word could be a reassurance. Cell videos looped on TikTok and Twitter; shaky captions crawled: “stuck on 75 bc VP then BOOM,” “white plane at Dobbins and smoke???” Push alerts hammered phones: BREAKING—Atlanta Under Attack.

Guests stacked onto panels like a wall. A retired general said, “This has all the hallmarks of a coordinated assault on national leadership.” A former FBI counterterror chief said, “Multiple sites, timed devices, jammers—post-9/11 tradecraft.” An ex-Secret Service agent said, “You freeze the motorcade until the corridor is sterile. She is not moving until the city belongs to her again.”

On CNBC, the crawl under green and red arrows read: MARKETS SLIDE ON ATLANTA ATTACKS – VP BELIEVED SAFE.

Local Atlanta channels cut between live reporters who contradicted each other by the minute. One breathless WSB anchor shouted over sirens behind her, "We can't tell if this is centered on the Vice President, but people are terrified—people are saying terrorism—" before a producer yanked her into cover as another distant blast shook the shot.

Social media lit up with shaky livestreams. Some filmed empty roads under blue skies. Others captured smoke rising over Dobbins. One popular clip showed a sobbing woman screaming into her phone, "They're trying to kill the Vice President!" and the phrase became a trending hashtag within minutes.

In the compound, a man with headphones leaned back in his chair. The Service net was still pouring frantic orders. "Federal override. No breach. Hold perimeter." He copied it down in neat block letters.

The reply into their own net was calm.

"Hilton contained. Delay achieved. Phase Five hold posture until exfil sync."

At the Hilton Unified Command trailer, radios hissed and bit. On a whiteboard, someone had written DO NOT BREACH UNTIL LOT COLD. Someone else had underlined it twice as if that could make patience easier. On a folding table, paper cups of coffee gathered skins.

SWAT stacked by the door like geometry turned to muscle: shields up, rifles at low ready, hands quiet. Behind them, medics paced with gurneys, the plastic wheels squeaking because something always squeaks no matter how you plan.

"Command, they're bleeding in there," a medic said into the radio and into the room and into the parts of the day that still took messages.

"Hold," the command voice said. "Federal override. VP is cold. No breach."

"They'll die on that floor," the medic said—not an argument, an observation.

"They'll die either way," the command voice said, not unkindly. "Orders stand."

Another medic leaned close to his partner and muttered, "We've got two minutes, maybe three, before that chest wound goes dark." His partner nodded without lifting her eyes. A SWAT operator kicked gravel against the wall, then hissed through clenched teeth, "We train for entry, not babysitting asphalt." His teammate answered back just as quietly: "Orders are orders.

Doesn't make it less bullshit." The commander kept his face blank, writing notes into a logbook no one would ever read, because recording the waiting was all he had to offer.

Outside, another timed blast rattled windows. Everyone froze, listening for screams that did not come, then went back to pacing the same grooves into the gravel.

One operator kept his eyes on the pavilion's glass façade. "Movement inside," he murmured. "They're still down, but they're alive." It wasn't hope so much as data, but even data steadied nerves for a moment.

Far away, the compound net stayed calm. "Hilton perimeter static. Federal override confirmed. Delay sustained."

"Copy Hilton. Timeline holds. All assets stand by Phase Six."

Backstage at the rally, the site lead's phone buzzed again. "Alternate corridor sweep in progress. Rotary assets under consideration." He said it into the net like reading ingredients off a jar.

Victoria Hale hadn't moved except to uncross and recross her ankles. The calm inside her made other people's fear look loud. Agents whispered into wrists; reporters cried without the dignity of noise; staffers stared at a word on a phone that said shelter and felt personally indicted by it.

"Next plan," she said again.

"Yes, ma'am," the site lead said, which is what you say when the only answer to a problem is time.

Beside her, the mayor remained silent, hands folded in her lap now. She gave the room nothing but steadiness, the same quality Hale radiated but at a civic scale—local leadership forced to be a passenger in someone else's chain of command. It was enough.

Atlanta was frozen. Roads sealed. Airspace dead. On screens, anchors used the word terrorism because vocabulary has to go first and the rest of life follows. In a service corridor, the Vice President sat calm while a city trembled.

The mayor sat beside her, lips pressed thin, calm in her own way. Inside Hilton Pavilion, hundreds lay face-down on carpet that smelled of dust and glue and yesterday's coffee, convinced the men who had stolen their breath were still above them because red dots had convinced them and fear is a better storyteller than truth.

Outside, smoke curled and thinned and fattened again, writing a story nobody yet knew how to read.

Chapter Eight – Breach

They were told to hold.

The order came from a voice on the federal net that never sounded out of breath. Primary protectee is elsewhere. Do not escalate. It came again after a pipe bomb thudded between cars and threw safety glass across hoods like a glitter storm. It came a third time while red dots kept crawling across the pavilion's blackout panes and every cop at the perimeter stared at the windows, convinced rifles were still waiting above the hostages.

Hold—while the lot stank of burned rubber and adhesive.

Hold—while radios overlapped into a single electric hiss.

Hold—while time wrote itself in blood on the far side of sealed steel.

The Cobb incident commander stood in the thin shade of a mobile command trailer and ground grit between thumb and forefinger. The grit was plaster shaken from beams and fibrous dust the carpet had saved for bad days. Down the block a siren climbed and flattened as another unit kissed the tape. Ten yards right, a bomb tech's respirator hissed in and out with the steadiness of a sleeping animal. Far off, another device popped with manners too polite for what it did.

He looked at the liaison in a navy windbreaker. She listened into her earpiece, nodding to someone who lived inside it. When she met his eyes she said it again without apology. "Primary is cold. You do not move until the exterior is cold."

The heat rose up his throat like a bruise. Enough.

He thumbed his mic. "Snipers—take the outer perimeter. Clear them."

On the parking deck, the countersniper let the world shrink to a flash of glass. The rifle smelled of oil and ozone. He rode half an exhale. Press.

Crack.

The mounted emitter popped like a bulb and spun off steel. Two other rifles answered from different angles—crack, crack—and the big room swallowed the echoes.

"Perimeter one neutral," he murmured, cheek glued to the stock. Another glint, a second squeeze. Crack. He worked the bolt and felt the mechanical comfort of parts doing what they were made to do. Treeline shooters quiet."

Inside, dust salted faces pressed to carpet. Even with eyes clenched, the flash painted eyelids white. Someone hissed, "They're back," and the whisper crawled through two hundred bodies like a small, frightened animal that needed to be held.

A red dot moved off the small of Rachael's back and lit someone else. Her cheekbones were tender where carpet had imprinted them. Her mouth tasted like chalk and pennies. Counting helped—numbers were honest when nothing else was. In…two…three. Out…two…three. Her sleeve had dried into her skin; when she flexed, the wound tugged. She told it to wait.

"EOD," the incident commander said. "Status."

"South and east lanes cold," came through the muffling of a mask. "North lane residual shards. Blocking car adhesive only. Tow staged."

The IC stared at the rear service doors. He could smell resin even from here—sweet and wrong, like burned candy. He keyed the net before his temper shouted first. "Front team—rear team—simultaneous breach. Go."

Front—lobby doors.

Ram up. Boom—clang. The hit rang metal like a bell. Shock climbed through gloves and wrists into teeth. Resin groaned and laughed. Halligans bit. The seam flexed, then settled into stubbornness.

"Again." Boom—clang. Sweat crawled under sleeves; the operator tasted metal at the back of his tongue, adrenaline turned to pennies. The door took what it was given and kept being a door.

"Front negative," the team leader clipped. "Bonded shut."

Rear—service doors.

Ram again. Hinges screamed; resin smoked and stank like burned plastic and cheap glue. A quick strip charge snapped at the latch. Concussion slapped armor and white dust leapt like startled fish. Hinges buckled a finger's width, then froze, insult made metal.

"Rear negative," their leader said, breath level by training and rage. "Sealed solid. No purchase."

Silence held the net across three hearts. Then someone half-off-radio muttered, "They glued the goddamn building shut."

In the monitoring van, the comms tech tapped his mic twice.

"Front negative. Rear negative. Both breach teams failed. Time index 12:41."

The reply came back on a separate channel, Vehicle Two's driver holding a position on a feeder road.

"Copy. Holding south approach. Confirm no units on the bypass yet?"

"Affirmative. No law-enforcement presence east of the interchange. Maintain stand-by until route update."

Inside, the pounding traveled through floor into ribs. The carpet hummed. The room learned to be a drum. To the prone bodies it wasn't rescue. It was men with guns trying to come back through the skin of the world.

A woman set her face on her forearms and whispered a prayer into her own skin. A child burrowed his nose into a sleeve that smelled like laundry and fear. Rachel clenched her teeth until blood slicked her lip to give her mouth a job that did not include screaming.

The IC stepped out from the trailer's shade and slammed his helmet into the panel so hard the radios inside stuttered. Pain barked in his knuckles. He welcomed it.

"We train for doors," a shield whispered, not quite off-net.

"Today glue wins," the breacher muttered, eyes on the seam that had refused to be seam-like.

The IC keyed up, jaw tight. "Rescue Group—your door. Bring every tooth you've got."

He hated saying it. Hated that in a story told later someone in Nomex would be in paragraph one. Hated that his people would hold shields over carpenters.

"Copy, Rescue," said a voice that smelled of diesel and sweat. "Left flank in thirty."

Saws shrieked, diamond teeth making bright pinwheels off resin and steel. The smell punished—burned glue, hot metal, the sharp bite of ozone where the blade arced. A spreader groaned in like an old animal; the seam stretched in glossy white ligaments, snapped, stretched again.

SWAT stood over the work with shields high and rifles threaded through noise. The shield's faceplate vibrated to the saw's keening. To them this felt like guarding carpenters. To the firefighters it felt like surgery—keep the cut clean, keep the patient breathing, keep your hands where they belong while someone else holds a gun on the ceiling.

Inside, the new sound was worse than the pounding: a banshee caught in a pipe. It vibrated fillings; it tickled ribs. Sparks threw stars across the room. Dust found new lungs.

“Almost,” a firefighter grunted. He levered the Halligan and felt the glue give like tendon. “Set. Again.”

The scream of saws leaked faintly through the scanner feed. The operative in the van didn’t flinch.

“Rescue Group forward. Tools on doors now.”

He shifted channels. “Vehicle One, adjust northbound two blocks—Cobb PD setting cones at Barrett Parkway. Use secondary. Time window under five.”

“Copy, Vehicle One. Rerouting now.”

“Tow it,” someone said behind the building, and a diesel coughed. Chains clanked against the blocking sedan’s frame. The tires squealed and laid black arcs. Adhesive fought, then tore—white threads snapping back like punished spiderwebs. The car jerked free and skated to a sulky stop.

Behind it the service doors still blushed white at their seams. Testing the handles was like pulling at bones. No back door. Everything was front.

“Stack,” the team leader whispered, and a line of people turned into geometry.

“Bang-bang-bang—go.”

Flashbangs sailed. They popped with thunder. Light turned into pressure and slapped eardrums. Carpet shook. Hostages shrieked into fibers and tried to make their bodies thinner than anatomy allows. Someone vomited—acrid and sharp.

Then black moved—shields, rifles, cadence.

"Police! Do not move! Hands where we can see them! Hands only!"

"Left clear!"

"Right clear!"

"Rafters!"

Two rifles threw short, impolite bursts into the last little glass eyes clinging to beam and bracket. Shards pattered down. The red ghosts that had been crawling all morning finally died. Silence rushed in, jagged at the edges but real.

The number-one shield could feel his heartbeat in his palms through the grip. He tasted the sour after-smell of the bang—the way it turns air into a thing you can drink and hate. Training drew his muzzle through its arc without asking opinion: corners, angles, then bodies—so many bodies—flat and obedient and trembling.

Behind him, a medic's knee hit tile and he swore at the jolt in his spine and then forgot pain because the world in front of him needed hands.

"Pressure there," he told a stranger, moving their palm into warmth at the gut-shot man's belly. "Don't lift. You're the weight."

"Immediate," another medic barked, hand already feeding gauze into a wound that drank. "Two large-bore, hang one." A bag hissed into life. A cuff wheezed. Plastic crackled. The language of survival is ugly and efficient.

Rachel found a voice small enough. "My—" She swallowed dust. "My uncle."

The medic followed the line of her eyes. Walter lay in a glitter field of velvet shards. A gray stillness had taken his face. The medic placed two fingers on his wrist for ritual, not hope, and then set a hand on Rachel's for exactly one second. In that pressure his palm said I see you and I see him and we will keep you in this world.

"Chest wound, no pulse," a tac medic called from the aisle. His voice was gentle and square at once. "Expectant."

"Tag him," came the answer. Tags rustled—plastic and paper that felt indecent and necessary.

"Command," the team leader said. "Pavilion secure. No shooters. Mounted devices neutral. One deceased confirmed. Multiple criticals."

"Copy," came back flat. Relief, here, was math.

The headset picked up EMS chatter too fast for civilians to follow, but the operative spoke the code fluently.

"Multiple red tags. One black confirmed. Homicide spin-up in progress."

He pressed another key. "Vehicle Three, avoid Chastain Road. Roadblocks forming east and west. Use Pine Ridge connector, repeat Pine Ridge."

A driver's calm voice answered, "Vehicle Three copies. Pine Ridge. Standing by."

Outside, the corridor remembered how to be a hallway. Gurney wheels squealed in their particular language. A patrol sergeant walked a line of uniforms toward a white tent breathing in Lot B and slapped his clipboard against his palm like a gavel.

"Everyone gets logged," he told the civilians they funneled into folding chairs that felt like pews. "Name. Number. Where you were. Don't trade stories. Don't tidy what you saw to match your neighbor. We need the mess. We'll find the truth in it."

The air under canvas tasted like plastic and dust. A woman held her hands flat on her knees because if she lifted them she might never stop shaking. A teenage boy stared at the grid of the tent fabric and counted intersections because numbers held still. A guard with tape marks on his wrists stared at his empty radio clip; when a detective asked, "Where's your radio?" he nodded once like a man confessing to something he wished weren't true.

Beyond the tent flap, a saw wound down at last with a tired whine. The smell of resin lingered like a bad decision.

Firefighters wiped glue smoke off face shields. SWAT still bristled, helmets low. The IC did not look at either. His jaw pulsed. Pride had a taste; he swallowed it.

Inside, Rachel went onto a gurney on a count—"one, two, three"—and let hands own her weight. The ceiling above her finally remembered to be ceiling. As they rolled, the stretcher kissed a crack in the floor with a squeal, and she laughed once—not because anything was funny, but because the body sometimes chooses a sound at random.

They passed a shape under a gray blanket. She knew its outline was a sentence with a period. She looked past, fixed her eyes on the exit where light waited.

In the aisle, an officer whose muzzle now pointed at tile instead of sky found the team leader's eyes and shook his head: negative. There were only ghosts here.

A detective at the threshold lifted his radio. His voice had the weight of ritual. "One fatal. Multiple shot and injured. Notify Homicide. Medical Examiner notified."

Dispatch answered with the sound of a throat clearing. "Copy. Homicide en route."

The van's interior glowed with the muted green of radio LEDs.

"Dispatch confirms: Homicide en route. Scene has transitioned."

He keyed the secure line. "Vehicle Four, you are the primary load. Avoid perimeter south—Georgia State Patrol moving units in. Take the alternate west exit. Window clean for now."

A beat of static, then: "Vehicle Four copies. West exit. Moving on schedule."

The operative logged the last line, closed the ledger, and leaned back. Calm as stone.

Someone in the tent muttered to a partner, "Poor bastard who draws this one." The partner made a noise that could have been sympathy or humor and lifted his pen for the next name.

Inside, a medic smoothed a gray blanket over Walter up to the chin. The blanket made a clean line the eye couldn't help but read. Dust hung in the grid of light like the room's last sermon. A CSU van's taillights eased toward the perimeter, red cubes in exhaust haze.

"Inner scene preserved," a voice said to the log. "Entry log active. No movement around expectant until Homicide and ME arrive."

At the command trailer, the IC stepped back from the map on the whiteboard; the federal liaison said something into her ear that did not change the air; the word investigation replaced the word rescue without anyone saying it out loud.

By the time the detective arrived, the chaos of saving lives had begun to ebb, and what remained was a room that belonged to the dead.

Chapter Nine – Net Loss

Cobb County Police Headquarters – Homicide Division

The radio dispatcher's voice came across the room with no room for hope.

"Hilton/Marietta Pavilion—confirmed fatal. Multiple wounded. Notify Medical Examiner and CSU. Homicide to respond."

Chairs stopped squeaking. Pens froze midstroke. The bullpen inhaled and didn't exhale.

"Not it," someone said without humor.

"Dark hole," another muttered. "You'll drown in witness statements before you touch a lead."

No one volunteered. The supervisor didn't ask. He scanned faces he'd known for years and stopped on the newest one—pen still hovering over a notebook like it could hide her.

"Whitaker. You're lead."

The sound in the room changed; not louder—sharper. Tara felt the weight of eyes. She wasn't part of the barstool fraternity or the war-story circle. Six months in homicide; before that, robbery; before that, South Precinct nights where your coffee went cold before the call ever did. She closed her notebook and stood because her legs knew the choreography her stomach didn't.

"Yes, sir."

Across two desks someone let a breath out through their teeth and pitched it just loud enough. "This homicide's gonna kill her career."

Tara slid her badge into her jacket pocket and wrapped her fingers around her keys. The knot in her throat didn't make it into her voice. She was already moving.

Hilton/Marietta Pavilion – Incident Commander's Net

Inside the pavilion the call had gone out seconds earlier.

"One confirmed fatal. Notify Homicide. Notify Medical Examiner. Request CSU. Scene is sealed. Entry log active."

Yellow tape bloomed across entrances. A sergeant tore open a new logbook and wrote the time with a heavy slash. Two officers took positions over the sheet that had been pulled to Walter Garrison's chin. Their rifles were slung but their faces had the locked look of men guarding something sacred and broken.

This was the moment the scene stopped belonging to the gunmen and started belonging to the people who would have to name what was left.

Medics kept their rhythm. Frank Harper lay pale and sagging, chest hitching under the fogged mask.

"BP crashing—forty systolic—hang another liter! Two wide-bore!"
Gauze disappeared into a wound that refused to obey.
"Charging—clear!"

Frank's body jumped against the carpet; glass gritted under the gurney frame. For a breath the monitor held a flat, unnerving tone, then stuttered back into a weak, uglier life. The air smelled like ozone and iron and resin—the chemical sweetness of glue turned sour by heat.

"Move—load and go!"

The stretcher rattled over shards and into the bright rectangle of the lobby, boots and knees making a narrow corridor that existed only for him.

Rachael Garrison's arm throbbed as the medic tightened the bandage. "Grip my hand," he said, calm substituting for hope. She did, because it gave the hand a job.

Her eyes would not unhook from the cloth two booths away. Walt's shoulder made a blunt hill beneath the sheet. She reached toward that hill and the medic caught her wrist and returned it to her lap. "We'll get you out. Breathe with me. In—hold—out."

Around them the scene split itself into smaller, human problems. A teenager with a bandaged temple blinked against the sting of antiseptic; a medic snapped a green tag around his wrist. A woman hissed as her swollen ankle was cradled into a splint; yellow band tugged tight. A man touched his ear where shrapnel had kissed it and stared at the blood painting his fingertips. Somebody vomited into their own hands, shock arriving late and rude.

"Names," a patrol officer said to survivors who could stand. "Phones. Where you were. We'll move you to the tent outside."

A bellhop who had spent the morning on the other side of a different counter held a clipboard like a lifebuoy and tried to remember how spelling works under pressure.

The room's volume dialed down as gurneys squealed away. The voices that remained were clipped, purposeful. The hum left by emergency lights put a thin thread through the silence.

The pavilion took inventory of itself. Blood pooled where the floor dipped. Coins glittered in constellations where glass had surrendered. Phones lay in a heap against a wall, as if surrender had a geography. At the back wall, trash bins stood in a line so straight it read like handwriting—wheels streaked with adhesive, lips nicked by cases they had swallowed with no one noticing, now mute evidence of what precision looks like when it pretends to be ordinary.

Outside, Perimeter

Word outran tape. Cars nose-dived against curbs; doors were flung; people ran to the line and hit the wall of uniform and outstretched palm.

"Ma'am, you can't go through. Who are you here for?"

"My husband. He texted 'down' and then nothing. His name is—"

"Write it here," an officer said, pressing a clipboard into hands that shook. "We're working reunification across the street."

The hotel had given up a ballroom. It had rows of chairs now, a folding table with stacks of paper, a chaplain who looked too young, a PIO who had an expression built for saying no comment in a way that felt like care. Families handed over names, descriptions, photographs held up on phone screens with fingers that wanted to break the glass.

"My son—fifteen—he went with his grandfather."

"My wife is wearing a blue cardigan; she has asthma—if she's in there she—"

"We'll seat you," an officer said, the tone taught to make people sit. "When we have news, you'll hear it first."

The air inside the ballroom tasted like coffee that no one drank and sweat that nobody cared enough to hide. People clutched each other because that's the thing hands do when they can't do anything else.

The Pavilion Freezes

With the last gurney out, quiet arrived as a presence, not an absence. It had weight. It made every step loud. It made breathing sound like disobedience.

Patrol spread to the tape and the tent. The logbook at the door grew more names. Every entry was a promise and a liability.

Someone pulled the adhesive placard at one door and it tore against its glue and then remembered the day and stopped being a sign and became evidence. A CSU tech knelt in the doorway and photographed the glue seam like a wound.

The smell settled into layers: resin, iron, old dust, sweat turned cold. The taste of plaster fixed itself into the back of throats and refused to leave.

CSU and ME

The Crime Scene Unit arrived with tripods and cones that rattled against each other like the bones in a mouth. Cameras were slung; scale rulers and evidence bags and gloves came alive under practiced hands.

Wide-scene photographs first—booths to banners to bins to adhesive-sealed doors. Then closer: casings marked with bright numbers that looked obscene; impact points circled; coins chalked around as if drawing a ring could keep them from rolling out of the story. A tech paused to shoot the neat line of trash bins from low angle, the adhesive streaks on their wheels catching light. He wrote transport path in his notebook and underlined it twice.

The Medical Examiner's investigator moved like someone who had learned not to hurry for the dead. She crouched beside Walter and peeled back the sheet only enough to see what needed seeing: wound, posture, pooling. She dictated in shorthand: "Male, late fifties. GSW torso. Pronounced at scene. Body cool, lividity dependent, early fixed. Photograph set B, frame one." The sheet came back up, smoothed with the kind of care that is love's cousin.

No one touched him yet. Paperwork had to materialize—photographs, forms, the slow bureaucracy of the end of a life. A CSU tech placed a small tent over a casing that had been flirting with a crack in the tile.

Witness Tent – Lobby Voices

Under the white canvas, heat pooled low. Chairs squealed against scuffed ballroom floor. Patrol moved through the rows with clipboards and the kind of softness good cops learn to borrow for an hour and pay back later when nobody is looking.

"My booth was near the center. I heard two shots, then more."

"I counted five—no, seven. The banners waved when the ceiling dust fell."

"Someone said they weren't in here anymore, but the dots kept moving."

A father rocked on the edge of his chair, his hand on the back of his teenage son's neck. "He just…stopped answering," he told the officer writing his wife's name into a ledger like it would commission a miracle. "He said 'down' and then…nothing."

"We'll find your people," the officer said, not promising, promising anyway.

A bellhop sat with his hat clamped in his hands and told the same two sentences three times to three different people and nobody minded. "I saw the glass flex. I thought it was going to explode. I thought the whole wall would breathe."

Vendors Pulled Aside

Before the last of the vendors were herded to the tent, two detectives peeled a handful from the stream to catch fresh recollections that would curdle by morning.

"What did you have in your case?"

"Morgans, slabbed—forty pieces. Two proof sets. A 1909 Lincoln VDB. Insurance lists this row at four hundred grand." His voice climbed in small steps and looked down to see how high it had gotten.

"And you?"

"Bullion Eagles—full trays. I can't tally until I… until—" He swallowed and found anger to stand on. "Hundred thousand? Two? It's gone."

The woman in the museum blazer didn't look at the ruined Plexiglas when she spoke. "Display pieces only. On loan. Spanish colonial gold—shipwreck recovery." She named the insurance figure and made a detective look up, which is difficult to do when grief is in the air. "Two point five million. One was a cross with emeralds. It was supposed to go back next week."

"Million?" the uniform asked, pen pausing midair. "With an M?"

She nodded once, apologizing to the air for the number.

Another vendor said, voice flattening to keep it from cracking, "Byzantine reliquary. Fifth century. From a church, not cataloged for sale. You can't put a number—but if you have to, it's better to lie low than high."

A whisper moved through uniforms. They had expected jewelry, loose bullion, rare dimes carried carefully. They had not expected a museum catalog written into the losses.

“This isn’t a heist,” one detective muttered to his partner. “It’s a war chest.”

Across the aisle a dealer thumbed through a plastic sleeve of insurance forms with hands that kept forgetting their instructions. “This row alone?

Ten million insured.” He sniffed, a sound like anger apologizing to grief. “If you add the relics…fifteen? Twenty?”

The numbers sat like a new kind of weight. A CSU tech photographing the coin constellation near his knee stopped clicking long enough to stare.

On the drive Tara’s radio crackled with neutral facts. CSU on scene. ME investigator on scene. Scene frozen. Witness tent active. Family holding established. The mutter from the bullpen came back uninvited—This homicide’s gonna kill her career—and she turned the wheel before the thought had a chance to pick a seat.

She remembered a set of South Precinct nights when no one had remembered her name at shift change. She remembered a robbery victim who had thanked her for listening like that was a service you had to request. She told the steering wheel that this would not be the day she gave anyone a reason to forget her again.

The Pavilion – Tara’s Arrival

Blue lights painted jittering squares on glass. She ducked under tape and wrote her name into the entry log. The officer wrote “Whitaker” like he was writing responsibility and not a name.

The smell inside found her and made itself known: resin first, sweet and wrong; then iron; then sweat flattening into something like sadness. The hush was not empty—it was full of camera shutters and the soft squeak of cones against tile and the scratch of pens against paper.

CSU flashes made a stuttering day out of the room. Each burst froze the universe: coins bright as stars; the neat line of bins like a diagram of the theft; the adhesive seam at the door photographed like a wound; phones piled like surrender under a wall; Walter's shoulder under the sheet, a blunt geography that the brain will insist on naming even when the mouth is not invited.

Patrol nodded as she passed. Not welcome—acknowledgment. The kind that says we all know who has to carry this thing now.

The incident commander met her halfway down the center aisle. "Detective Whitaker. Scene's yours."

She nodded once. The bullpen sentence came back and stood beside her. She didn't tell it to leave. She just spoke over it. "Who's your best initial on witnesses?"

"Security guards left inside. Some vendors with closest proximity—we held a few before the tent. The niece is en route to the hospital—arm wound, stable. We'll tag her for later."

"Good," she said, and her pen already had a date and time on a page it hadn't existed on five minutes ago.

She let herself do the slow circle because this is what you owe the dead: a first pass that is a seeing, not a touching. Booths broken. Banners torn. Coins like constellations someone named out of grief. Adhesive seam photographed and logged. Bins lined like a drill team. Shell casing tents bright as children's toys in a room that had no patience for children. The sheet that made a field and a hill at once.

She did the thing you do when you make the world behave by turning it into words.

Body position—center aisle. Pooling consistent with angle of fall. Note adhesive seams and lined bins—organized exit path. Gather vendor loss figures—note museum pieces. Locate security guard statements—radios removed, pistols retained. She underlined reliquary without telling herself why.

The ME investigator rose from her crouch and said what needed saying: "We'll need your okay before we move him."

"You'll have it after CSU finishes the primary pass," Tara said, her voice doing its best imitation of someone else's certainty, and it worked enough to move the next minute along.

In the doorway a CSU tech waited, tripod underarm. "Detective? We haven't touched the phones or the wallets pile. Do you want wide shots only until you've walked it?"

"Wide only. Don't breathe on those until I bless them," she said, and heard her old sergeant from robbery in her mouth and made peace with borrowing his spine for an hour.

She made herself not look toward the sheet again and failed. She made herself walk toward it and succeeded.

They thought this case would bury you, the bullpen voice said, stubborn as a stain.

She opened her notebook. The top line turned into a sentence. It was not poetry. It did not need to be. It was a list of things the dead had earned.

"Garrison, Walter," she wrote. "Homicide #1."

Then she kept going.

The headset picked up EMS chatter too fast for civilians to follow, but the operative spoke the code fluently.

"Multiple red tags. One black confirmed. Homicide spin-up in progress."

He pressed another key. "Vehicle Three, avoid Chastain Road. Roadblocks forming east and west. Use Pine Ridge connector, repeat Pine Ridge."

A driver's calm voice answered, "Vehicle Three copies. Pine Ridge. Standing by."

Outside, the corridor remembered how to be a hallway. Gurney wheels squealed in their particular language. A patrol sergeant walked a line of uniforms toward a white tent breathing in Lot B and slapped his clipboard against his palm like a gavel.

"Everyone gets logged," he told the civilians they funneled into folding chairs that felt like pews. "Name. Number. Where you were. Don't trade stories. Don't tidy what you saw to match your neighbor. We need the mess. We'll find the truth in it."

The air under canvas tasted like plastic and dust. A woman held her hands flat on her knees because if she lifted them she might never stop shaking. A teenage boy stared at the grid of the tent fabric and counted intersections because numbers held still. A guard with tape marks on his wrists stared at his empty radio clip; when a detective asked, "Where's your radio?" he nodded once like a man confessing to something he wished weren't true.

Beyond the tent flap, a saw wound down at last with a tired whine. The smell of resin lingered like a bad decision.

Firefighters wiped glue smoke off face shields. SWAT still bristled, helmets low. The IC did not look at either. His jaw pulsed. Pride had a taste; he swallowed it.

Inside, Rachael went onto a gurney on a count—"one, two, three"—and let hands own her weight. The ceiling above her finally remembered to be ceiling. As they rolled, the stretcher kissed a crack in the floor with a squeal, and she laughed once—not because anything was funny, but because the body sometimes chooses a sound at random.

They passed a shape under a gray blanket. She knew its outline was a sentence with a period. She looked past, fixed her eyes on the exit where light waited.

In the aisle, an officer whose muzzle now pointed at tile instead of sky found the team leader's eyes and shook his head: negative. There were only ghosts here.

Chapter Ten – Under the Lights

They tagged him red before he knew the color existed.

Hands pressed hard into Frank Harper's belly—heat and weight and a voice saying, "Hold here—both palms—don't lift." Tape ripped, scissors rasped along skin, plastic crinkled. Someone shouted for a second line and the second line appeared, stainless flash of a needle burying in his arm, a river forced open.

"GSW midline—hypotensive—tachycardic—two large-bore wide open—O_2 by mask," a medic rattled, head tilted toward a lapel mic. "ETA three to Cobb General—spin Trauma One."

The information fell onto Frank's face like rain. His world narrowed to the hot-iron taste inside his mouth and the scrape of air stealing through a mask that smelled like plastic and bleach. The ceiling above him was not a ceiling. It was a field of humming light that refused to hold still.

"BP sixty over palp," another voice cut in—female, urgent and steady at once. "Radial's thready—he's dumping."

They lifted him and the floor dropped; his spine rattled against the stretcher frame. He tried to say something and coughed instead, red bubbles blotting the clear mask.

"Don't talk," the medic said. "Breathe for me. Stay here."

Three feet away, Rachael Garrison's gurney sat against the wreckage of a display case, her sleeve soaked the same color as her uncle's sheet. When the first medic saw her, he had swiveled with controlled panic. "We've got another—" he started, but he was already moving—hands on Rachael's shoulders, tipping her back, eyes measuring how much blood belonged to her.

“Through-and-through graze—upper arm,” the second medic said after two seconds that lasted ten. “Bleeding controlled. Tag yellow.”

The way the room tilted for two different people—one into a storm, one into a holding pattern—made its own kind of weather. Rachael nodded to things she could not see, felt the bandage bite, hissed at the sting, and found her eyes again snagging on the white sheet laid a few yards away. Walt’s shoulder made a blunt geography under the cloth. She reached toward it. A gloved hand redirected her wrist gently back into her lap.

“Look at me,” the medic said, kneeling into broken glass with the careless grace of a person who has forgotten how to worry about their own knees. “Name?”

“Rachael Garrison.”

“Allergies?”

“None.”

“Medications?”

She shook her head.

“When did you last eat?”

“I don’t know. Breakfast.”

“You’re okay,” he said. The sentence was both true and a lie. “We’re going to move you. Stay with me.”

Across the aisle, someone shouted “Clear!” and Frank’s body jerked from the first shock. The smell of ozone cut through blood and resin; the monitor changed its song from a long unkind note to a ragged rhythm that felt like it hated work.

“Load—go now!”

They ran him toward daylight; they rolled her after him, slower.

The first rig slammed its doors and was already rolling when Rachael's gurney kissed the lip of the second. Sirens drilled into the day as the ambulance bucked over a curb and grabbed the street.

Inside Frank's box, there was nothing but contingency. A paramedic leaned into his face and spoke through a plastic shield that fogged and cleared, fogged and cleared.

"Frank, can you hear me? You're going to the hospital. We are three minutes out. We need you here."

His skin felt too big. The mask shoved air into him in greedy handfuls. He felt fingers tap an artery at his wrist, felt the head shake he hadn't earned.

"Two large-bore, both running. Pressure bag it—let's go," the medic said. "Give me a second liter—no narcotics—no."

"Cobb General, Medic Eight," the driver said into the radio. "GSW abdomen, male, forties. Hypotensive—BP fifty-eight systolic, HR one-forty. Two large-bore IVs, normal saline wide open. O_2 on mask, sats in the seventies, dropping. Distended abdomen. FAST likely positive. ETA two minutes. Spin Trauma One."

A voice came back tinny and calm, practiced over a thousand bad days. "Trauma One is yours. MTP activated. Blood bank notified."

The words did not reach him as meaning—only rhythm.

Rachael's ride had a siren, too, but inside it the air felt thicker with quiet. The medic at her shoulder wrote in small, sharp letters onto a triplicate form that would become her first recorded version of the day.

"GSW, upper arm, through-and-through. No deformity. Bleeding controlled. Yellow tag." He glanced at her face. "Pain zero to ten?"

She looked at him without understanding the math. “Three,” she said, because it gave him something to fill the box with.

“Allergies? Meds?” He ran through the list again, his tone a calm boat in rough water. “Any history of bleeding disorders? Pregnant?”

“No. No.” The words felt like she’d borrowed them from someone else’s mouth.

He checked her pupils with a small light. He checked her fingers under the bandage. He checked her pulse at the wrist and nodded to himself and wrote something else. The gurney’s vinyl stuck to her back. The air reeked of sanitizer and, beneath it, the cruder truth of iron. Walt’s blood had dried in her sleeve and clung to the crook of her elbow in flakes that did not belong on her skin.

She asked once, small and flat: “Is he—my uncle…?”

The medic’s eyes lost focus for one second the way people’s eyes do when they look for a gentle place to set down a hard thing. “I don’t know,” he said. It was the kindest sentence he could say where a lie might have hurt more later.

Her rig slowed as the turn came up. Through the small rear window she glimpsed a square of bright like a door opening. The other ambulance’s lights vanished past that square.

“Trauma team—let’s go!” A voice rose inside the doors and the hospital answered with movement.

“GSW abdomen, midline entry, unstable—BP fifty-eight, HR one-forty, sats seven-two—two large-bore—fluids running—FAST likely positive!”

They drove Frank through double doors that banged against walls and delivered him into fluorescent dusk. Hands latched, ripped, slashed; scissors made a chattering sound as fabric surrendered; the mask disappeared to be replaced by a tube that someone held in one hand like a compromise made with the throat.

"Tube—seven-five—etomidate—sux," an anesthetist said, and the tube slid, and the bag connected, and the chest rose in a way that felt like a thing being convinced against its will.

"Good chest rise—confirm CO_2—secure the tube."

The surgeon's voice was a metronome in a hall full of drummers. "Two units O-neg now—give me the rapid infuser. Plasma with it. Get blood bank here." He pressed his palms against the wound and leaned with the embarrassing intimacy of a man trying to keep another man's blood inside him by force.

"FAST exam," a resident said, moving a probe across the abdomen. Gel bloomed glistening on gray skin.

"RUQ positive—free fluid—he's bleeding."

"Prep for laparotomy—OR now. Call anesthesia—running table in ten," the surgeon said. He didn't have to raise his voice. The room bent around him anyway.

"BP forty—he's fading!"

"Epi in. Calcium in," the nurse at the crash cart said, hand flipping vials like cards. The gurgle of suction joined the music, and the slurp would later be the only sound Frank remembered exactly.

Someone said, "Stay with me," into the part of him that had sunk. He could not decide which direction the voice came from. He tried to climb toward it and his arms did not answer.

Rachael's gurney took a right where Frank's had gone straight. The noise became architecture, then memory. A curtain on a track whispered shut and made a small white room around her.

"GSW to left upper arm, graze—through-and-through, bleeding controlled," a nurse said, sliding a tray closer with a practiced hip. "Let's clean it up."

Betadine burned like a complaint against the surface of her skin. Saline poured from a squeeze bottle—cool, insistent, washing the wound clean. A syringe stung; she watched the skin pull taut under the wheal, the way it always looks wrong when you know it will make a right later.

"Lidocaine. You'll feel pressure, not pain," the nurse said. "We'll irrigate, redress, then you'll go for an X-ray to rule out bone and fragments."

Another nurse tugged at her blouse. "We need your clothing for evidence," she said, gentle like she was asking permission for something that didn't need it. The blouse slithered off with an ugly sound. Someone slid it into a brown paper bag, sealed the top with tape, and wrote in block letters: R. Garrison – GSW – Clothing. The second nurse signed the tape and looked Rachael in the eye. "Chain of custody," she explained, because dignity sometimes sprinkles itself in the form of information.

A social worker appeared in the space the blouse had left and sat on the edge of a rolling stool. "Rachael? I'm Mariah. I'm here to sit with you," she said. Her voice made a small, warm room inside the curtain. "Do you have family we can call?"

Rachael thought of a phone she had thrown away from her body when a voice said Down! inside another building. She shook her head, then nodded, then stared at her hands because hands at least will tell you exactly what they are doing.

"Walt," she said. The name fell into the sterile air like a mistake in a clean equation.

Mariah's eyes did the thing good eyes do. They did not blink. They did not look away. "We'll help you reach someone," she said. "You are not alone."

On the other side of the curtain, someone shouted "Ten blade," and a metal tray answered with a clatter that Rachael felt between her teeth.

They warmed his blood because cold kills; they covered him with blankets because the body fights by giving up what it thinks it can spare. The anesthetist watched a monitor and the monitor watched a cliff.

"OR says five minutes," a nurse said, breaking her sentence into four pieces with the speed of her need.

"He doesn't have five minutes," the surgeon said—modern, not cruel. "Pack him. Keep his brain perfusing."

"Packed—lap pads x six," someone answered, their hands moving like the inside of a machine.

"BP thirty-eight," the recorder said, pen racing and not fast enough. "Pulse is thready. Sats sixty-seven."

"Epi again. Push calcium. Push."

Frank slipped when the room got too bright. He fell toward a place that smelled like the first warm day of a summer he would have otherwise forgotten. Someone said something into his ear that sounded like church. He came back angry, dragged by the bag on his mouth and a pair of hands that refused to think of hands as violent instruments.

"Almost there, Frank," a voice said, and this time the voice had a place. It lived in a woman's face half-hidden by a shield. Her eyes were brown and insistent. "You stay with me, you hear? Look at me. I'm not letting go."

He understood that he existed because someone else refused to be done.

They wheeled her to X-ray and the hall went on forever. The tech spoke with the same careful kindness as everyone else. "We're going to take a picture of your arm," he said, and the verb made her want to tell him not to call it a picture.

The machine radiated its small act of faith, and the screen made bones appear like secrets that had accepted their fate. "No fracture," the tech said, returning her to the small white room and the nurse with the new bandage.

A police liaison appeared through the curtain like someone materializing in a story. He didn't ask questions right away. He asked for her name again, and whether she wanted water, and whether she would prefer to wait for a plainclothes detective. "We'll need a statement later," he said. "Not now. Later."

His eyes flicked to the paper bag with her blouse inside and he wrote something in his notebook that looked like time.

Rachael stared at the new white bandage and the way the red was already figuring out how to be itself again. She lifted her hand and discovered it wasn't shaking now; it was empty. Nothing that mattered could be put there without the hand lying to her.

Through the curtain the trauma bay flexed its voice again. "BP forty-two—he's circling—OR, now!"

Silence afterward sounded like a verdict that refused to explain itself.

Hospital security had shut the sliding doors to the trauma hall and posted a guard. Family members had begun to arrive, drawn by television noise and the kind of text messages that write a person's heart the word down and then quit. A patient advocate moved among them with a clipboard that could not, in the end, help.

"My husband is in there," a woman said, and the advocate nodded as if the mere act of nodding could change anything except the comfort it offers.

"My grandson—he's fifteen—his name is—" A man held up a phone with a photo cupped in both hands, as if presenting it to the air could teach the doors to be polite.

"We have a process," the advocate said, the phrase softening itself against its own hardness. "We will tell you as soon as we can tell you something true."

A chaplain stood with a hand around a cup of coffee they did not drink.

Inside Trauma One, the surgeon lifted his hands. "Move," he said, and the team moved with him. The gurney surged forward and the bay emptied toward a brighter light. The doors to the operating room sighed open and swallowed everything.

Rachael watched the ceiling tiles in her small white room and tried to will them into telling her what becomes of a man whose name was Walt when names still mattered. The bandage held; the sling cradled; the nurse documented; the social worker remained seated with her like a promise.

"Do you have someone we can call?" Mariah asked again.

"No one," Rachael said, and it felt like borrowing an earlier day. "My Uncle was with me, but he was shot, too…"

"I can get the hospital Minister to drop by, if you like," Mariah said. "Not now. When you're ready."

Rachael nodded, and for the first time since the breach, her hands found each other and held.

A uniform stood at the foot of her bed for one formal minute and then left, satisfied that the chain of custody for what she wore would hold, that her pulse would hold, that her name would hold. He closed the curtain with a courtesy she did not have the energy to thank.

Outside, a portable TV above the nurses' station scrolled red banners across a news anchor's mouth. BREAKING: ATLANTA UNDER ATTACK. The sound was off. The words were loud. Somebody had paused the world and given it captions.

Rachael leaned back and closed her eyes and saw, not relief, not safety, but a white sheet and a hill that was no longer a shoulder. She opened her eyes again because the ceiling was easier even if the ceiling wanted nothing to do with her.

From this point on, survival would answer to paperwork.

A nurse parted the curtain and looked over her shoulder. "Detective Whitaker?" she asked the hall. "Your shooting victim is in Bay Six."

Tara stepped through, the air here different from the pavilion—cleaner, colder, recorded. She introduced herself with a voice that had learned how to carry grief without dropping it. "Rachael? I'm Detective Whitaker. I won't keep you. I just need to tell you—" she saw the social worker's eyes, adjusted— "I'm here. When you're ready, I'll take your statement. Not now."

Rachael nodded once. Phrases had become too expensive.

From down the hall, a voice, practiced and relentless: "Notify OR they're rolling." The words pushed through the thin wall and made themselves a room in Rachael's chest.

Tara stepped back and let the curtain kiss shut behind her. She looked down the length of the emergency hall—toward the trauma doors, toward the cluster of people who had learned how to stand in the way of bad news until it asked permission to pass. Her notebook was already in her hand; she hadn't told it to be there.

"Body of Evidence," she wrote at the top of a new page, because names mattered and the dead deserved titles too.

Beyond the swinging doors, the operating room took a breath and held it, and then the day rolled forward under lights that did not care who lived beneath them—only that they shone.

Chapter Eleven – Body of Evidence

By the time the last ambulance pulled away, the pavilion's heartbeat had slowed to something grim but steady. The roar of panic was gone, replaced by the metallic click of cameras and the low murmur of officers marking evidence. Yellow cones sprouted across the floor, tiny flags planted in rivers of glass and pools of blood. The air still smelled of powder and fear, but it was tempered now by the sterile bite of fingerprint dust and chemical sprays.

Patrol officers who had stormed in with rifles were redirected to the tape line, replaced by CSU techs moving like careful gardeners through wreckage. Every boot print in plaster dust was photographed, every shell casing bagged, every shattered booth frame tagged. The chaos of the robbery was being rewritten into order—one chalk line, one photograph, one page of notes at a time.

Detective Tara Whitaker walked the aisle with her notepad open, jotting in quick strokes, eyes scanning for details that could vanish if not claimed immediately. What had been a battlefield minutes earlier was now her responsibility. What remained was the story left behind, and it was her job to make sure it spoke clearly.

Dr. Carolyn Holt moved with her recorder already in hand, latex gloves snapped tight at the wrist. Her voice was steady, clinical, a low monotone that laid a spine of facts through the room: "Male, identified as Walter Garrison. Gunshot wound, anterior chest. Pronounced dead at scene…" Each word dropped into the recorder with the finality of nails into wood.

Tara kept pace, pen scratching, eyes flicking to the places where the room offered its quiet testimony—broken cases, coins scattered like stars, adhesive strings still clinging to the service doors. She didn't interrupt Holt's process; she mirrored it, sketching quick arrows and underlines, letting the clinical and the investigative braid into a single narrative.

When Holt bent, one knee sinking into carpet still damp with blood, Tara shifted to block glare from a flash. Holt's gloved hands hovered—never touching—pointing out stippling absence, the downward trajectory. Her gaze lifted once toward the rafters before returning to the wound.

"Trajectory downward, right to left. Consistent with elevated shooter," Holt narrated.

Tara underlined it twice.

A CSU tripod snapped open near the center aisle. A tech set a laser in a metal cradle; a tight green line lanced upward through dust, stitching floor to ceiling. A second beam speared cleanly through a spidered hole in plaster and kept going, painting a stripe across steel webbing above. From the floor it looked like the robbery again—light crawling the rafters—but the meaning had twisted. The criminals' red dots had frozen people into obedience; the investigators' green lines turned terror into geometry.

"Angle seventy-eight feet from impact—downward slope consistent," the tech murmured for his recorder. A camera popped and whined, capturing the beam and the numbered cone together. Tara felt the echo chill her: same ceiling, same beams, opposite ends of human intent.

"Document the adhesive seam with placard," she said, nodding to a MAXIMUM OCCUPANCY REACHED sign still wearing a collar of cured glue. The tech set a scale beside the seam, shot it wide, then stepped in for macro until ridges of glue looked like glaciers.

Glass glittered in pale dunes against stripped cases. A trace specialist hunkered at a velveted ledge, lifted a filament of torn nitrile with tweezers, and let it fall into a paper bindle. Label, seal, date, initials. Another tech teased fibers from a splintered frame with a micro-vac; the device hummed softly, collecting dust the eye wouldn't dignify with a name.

"Scissor-lift tracks," someone called. Twin arcs scarred concrete under a beam bay, looping from a service door to the first ceiling impacts. Tara jotted without looking down. Lift to rafters—overwatch position—no brass aloft (collect below).

Outside, the witness tent had the sound of a church basement after a funeral—voices kept low out of respect for a thing that had already happened and would not be persuaded to unhappen. Vendors sat with wrists still red from tape, faces shallow from adrenaline drain. Family members pooled at the periphery, pressing names into officers' hands as if syllables could become keys.

"They took every relic case on this side," a dealer told a patrolwoman with a clipboard. "Forty booths? More? It's millions. The museum-on-loan stuff alone could be past ten."

"I saw a white panel truck backed to that service door before we opened," another vendor said. "Didn't look out of place—looked like janitors. They rehearsed the way boredom looks."

Tara moved aisle by aisle, catching fragments and writing them in block letters. A teenage girl asked the same question three different ways—have you seen my father; is my father okay; will someone please tell me about my father—and a patient officer answered the same way three times—we don't know yet; we'll tell you when we do; we're not forgetting him—and the tent felt like a waiting room for a verdict no one wanted to deliver.

A sergeant caught Tara at the trailer door and pressed a damp slip into her hand. "You'll want this," he said, voice pitched low. "Panel truck. White. Fully involved when fire rolled up. Same make folks here are describing."

"Where?"

"Industrial spur off Delk. We had to wait for FD to knock it down before stepping in." His mouth tightened. "Just like the breach. Glue, then saws. They planned our schedule as well as theirs."

A scene wrote itself in Tara's mind: foam seething over a blackened shell, heat shimmering off bowed metal, firefighters carving steam from flame while cops watched clenched behind tape. When the water stopped hissing, what remained was a steel coffin—puddled plastics, warped framing, purpose reduced to ash. Nothing unburned enough to speak, which was exactly the point.

She folded the slip into her notebook. Truck burned—secondary scene—no lift, no prints. Plan includes fire. Through the open door she stared at the pavilion's wide mouth, cones planted like small gravestones, and felt the case grow teeth.

Inside the command trailer, detectives hunched over maps under jaundiced battery light. Channels hissed and overlapped. Someone, too loud, said what others were being paid not to say. "No one wants this. Four hundred witnesses, a dead dealer tied to half the tables, half the county watching the news crawl. This'll bury whoever takes it."

"Rookie's got it," another voice said, low and mean. "Watch her drown."

Tara wrote three names where they couldn't see: Walter Garrison—DOA. Rachael Garrison—GSW, stable. Frank Harper—GSW, critical. She underlined each once and added a fourth: Unknown Crew—airtight. She capped her pen, uncapped it again, and stepped back into the bright wreckage.

When Holt gave her final nod, the men who had stood guard unfolded a dark bag on the carpet. Plastic sighed. They lifted Walter at shoulders and knees. The sound he made as weight shifted—the ordinary grunt of a body being moved—felt obscene for its normalcy. The zipper rasped, teeth catching perfectly, and the room stood still long enough to prove that silence could be a kind of procession.

They rolled him along the center aisle. Vendors at the tape line bowed their heads without being told; a CSU tech lowered his camera for one full breath and then lifted it again. A banner with the coin club's name sagged under a ventilation draft as the stretcher slid beneath it and out into the light.

Frank had left in sirens and urgency; Rachael in quiet and cotton and iodine. Walt left in a hush that felt heavier than either one.

The doors to the coroner's van closed with a hollow metal report. It sounded like a period.

"Footwear impressions along aisle seven—dust before anyone breathes on it," Tara said as CSU returned to their kneeling. "Fiber pulls from that case lip. Get me the macro of the occupancy placard with the adhesive seam—one wide, one detail." Her voice carried just far enough to find the hands that needed instruction.

Evidence markers sprouted in fresh rows: brass, glass, adhesive smears; a gouge in tile where a ram had struck; a scuff where a shoe had failed to find purchase. A tech used a micro-vac on a strip of velvet; another placed a scale beside an impact point and took three clicks, stepping in closer with each shot. The green lasers kept drawing their clean lines across the rafters as if stitching the room shut.

Tara stood very still and let the scene talk. The pavilion felt like a body under autopsy: incisions becoming explanations, organs labeled, cause of death walking itself toward a report. Holt would do it later on a stainless table under buzzing lights; here, in a room where grief still smelled like iron, CSU did it with paper and light.

She wrote a single line down the margin. The living left in sirens. The dead left in silence. The criminals left nothing. She closed her notebook and opened it again, unwilling to be finished.

Back at the pavilion, the lasers nudged their last degrees and snapped off. The rafters went ordinary again, pocked only by the holes that had started this. Holt straightened and clicked off her recorder. CSU zipped bags. The logbook at the door took one last name with a blunt pen.

Tara swept the room and felt the shape of the next chapter settle. The pavilion had been opened like a body and named like a map; she and Holt had taken what they could from it without moving what could not be moved.

Holt would soon be doing to Walter Garrison what CSU had done to the room—gloves on, steel under light, the careful language of cause and effect. The dead could not speak, but silence could be turned into evidence if a person was careful enough with it.

And tomorrow the living would begin to speak, too.

She closed her notebook. The hum of the lights pressed against the quiet and held. Then she stepped toward the tent and the long night of whispers and reports waiting on the other side of the tape.

Chapter Twelve – Cold Cuts

The ER bay smelled faintly of bleach and warmed plastic, the curtain walls doing little to block the noise from other patients and staff outside. Rachael Garrison sat propped against pillows, her left arm wrapped tight in fresh gauze, IV tubing capped but still snaking into her hand. Her skin looked pale under the fluorescent wash, her eyes rimmed red not from pain but from the shock still anchoring her to the moment Walt had fallen.

Monitors pinged nearby, each tone reminding her body where it had been and what it had lost. A television mounted high on the wall whispered muted news coverage of the robbery, closed captions crawling with speculation. She looked away from it every time her eyes wandered.

Detective Tara Whitaker pulled a chair close, setting a small recorder on the tray table beside a cup of water gone lukewarm. She kept her tone soft, low enough to feel like a conversation instead of an interrogation. Her notebook was open, pen ready, but her body leaned forward with the posture of someone listening, not prying.

"Can you tell me what you remember?"

Rachael blinked slowly, her gaze fixed on a point just above Tara's shoulder. Words came in halting bursts: dust sifting from the ceiling after the first volley, the crowd slamming to the floor, the red dots swinging across bodies. She described the press of Walt's hand pushing her down, his body shifting between her and the gunmen, and the burn along her arm as a round seared past.

She whispered that she could still feel the warmth of his palm, even after it had gone slack. Her voice cracked but never broke; she spoke as if holding her uncle's dignity together required her not to cry. Every so often she swallowed hard, staring down at the blanket as though steadying herself against a wave.

Tara didn't press when memory faltered, only nodded and scribbled notes. Evidence was being built, but the interview was more than that—it was grief finding its first words. The monitors in the hall chimed at odd rhythms, shoes squeaked on waxed tile, and somewhere down the corridor someone cried out in post-op pain. Rachael seemed to flinch at every noise, her mind replaying the pavilion. Tara saw the tightness in her jaw, the tremor in her fingers when they brushed the blanket, and she understood the wound went deeper than the through-and-through along her arm.

A nurse stepped in briefly to check Rachael's IV, glancing at Tara as if to ask whether this should wait. Tara shook her head gently, pocketing her pen until Rachael nodded that she could continue. The conversation resumed in fits, but each fragment added to the whole. When the words ran out, Tara closed the notebook and slipped the recorder back into her bag. She told Rachael she would check on her again the next day, then touched her shoulder lightly before stepping out into the corridor.

The hospital smelled of antiseptic and burnt coffee, of overworked machines and the faint trace of flowers delivered by relatives who didn't know what else to do. The waiting areas were full of quiet bodies—families leaning forward, staring at linoleum as though it might answer their questions. An old television droned in the background, anchors speculating on motives, tossing phrases like "domestic terrorism" and "well-coordinated assault" into the air with no evidence to back them. Tara slowed as she passed, feeling the weight of words spreading before facts had even been logged.

She checked at the ICU desk about Frank Harper. The nurse shook her head: he was still under heavy sedation after surgery. "Maybe later tonight, maybe tomorrow," she said. "We'll page you when he can tolerate questions." Tara nodded and signed the log, leaving her cell number in block letters. It was going to be a long wait.

She spent part of the afternoon moving between the cafeteria—where a burger shriveled under heat lamps—and the chapel, a small square of stillness where votive candles flickered against glass. The hours crawled. She returned again to the ICU desk, and at last, near dusk, a nurse waved her in.

The ICU hummed with the rhythm of machines—pumps sighing, monitors beeping in uneven cadence, oxygen hissing softly with each breath forced into Frank's lungs. He was propped slightly upright, chest bound in heavy dressings, sweat slicking his forehead despite the cool of the room. Every word cost him, his throat raw, voice thin as thread.

Tara stood at his bedside, notebook closed in her hand. She didn't want him watching her pen, measuring his answers against how quickly she wrote. "Frank," she said gently, leaning closer, "tell me what you can."

His eyes flickered open, unfocused. "Noise… first," he rasped. "Ceiling… coming down. Dust." His chest hitched with the effort. A nurse at the monitor shot Tara a look, but didn't interrupt. Frank swallowed, licked cracked lips. "Red… lights. Dots. Pain. Then… nothing."

Tara nodded once, voice low. "That's enough. You've helped more than you know." She didn't ask for faces, didn't press for detail. What he had given was fragmentary, but it was clean—the outline of a nightmare, offered by a man still balanced on its edge. His monitors kept bleating in uneven rhythms, a fragile choir.

Tara listened until she was sure his words had steadied into silence, then backed away. She left him with the nurse, steps quiet as though anything louder might break him further.

The morgue was colder than it needed to be, the kind of cold that seeped into knuckles and slowed handwriting. Fluorescent lights hummed faintly, their steady pitch broken only by the compressor's low rumble from the cooler. Stainless tables gleamed under the glow, reflecting thin echoes of every movement. Even the air smelled metallic, like old coins rubbed between damp fingers.

Dr. Carolyn Holt stood with her recorder already running, gloved hands steady as she pulled back the sheet. "Body received, male, identified as Walter Garrison. Age sixty-two." Her voice was flat, precise, shaped for a transcript rather than the living.

The gunshot wound was exposed, a dark oval against pale skin. Holt leaned slightly, eyes narrowing, careful not to touch as she noted details aloud. "Single entry wound, anterior chest, approximately midline. No stippling observed. Surrounding tissue intact." She paused only long enough for her assistant to scribble, then continued, "Trajectory appears downward, right to left."

The clicks of the recorder and the scratch of the pen were the only sounds in the room. Where others might have seen only blood and loss, Holt spoke in the language of science, stripping emotion until only evidence remained. Behind her, a CSU photographer fired a laser across the wound, recreating a trajectory line that mirrored the criminals' own red beams in the pavilion—ghosts of technology used for opposite purposes.

Holt stopped before the internal exam, covering the body again with the sheet. "Pause external. Resume after sample prep." She clicked off the recorder and peeled her gloves carefully, eyes already moving to the clock. The room exhaled with her silence, leaving only the cold.

Later, after the bone saw had finished its shrill work and specimens were bagged, Holt leaned toward her recorder once more. "Cause of death: high-velocity projectile wound of the chest. Homicide by gunshot wound." The finality of her tone made the fluorescents seem louder, the air colder. She pressed the stop button, gloves snapping free of her wrists, and left the room to its quiet.

Miles away, heavy gates closed behind four vehicles. The convoy's engines ticked as they cooled, paint flecked with dust from back roads. The compound looked like a farm—corrugated barns, weathered fencing, a lean-to stacked with hay. But every line of it was deception. Cameras hidden in birdhouses tracked every angle. Ground sensors buried in gravel fed signals back to a windowless hut. If anyone crossed the wrong patch of earth, someone in that hut could decide what happened next. Self-sufficiency was cover; survival was the core.

The men unloaded with calm precision. Sacks thumped onto long wooden tables, coin trays sliding free of velvet with faint metallic sighs. Relics wrapped in cloth were laid in rows, tags scribbled by gloved hands. Wallets stripped of cash, IDs stacked into neat piles, credit cards banded with rubber. Watches and jewelry glittered in one tray, their value undeniable even before appraisal.

One man read aloud in clipped tones, a report more military than criminal. "Phase One: diversions successful. KSU engagement cleared in under three minutes. I-75 north and south lanes neutralized. Devices detonated as planned. Phase Two: pavilion entry. Guards neutralized. Doors sealed. Loot extracted—forty-two vendor booths cleared. Items include coinage, gold bars, relics, personal property. Estimated total haul:

in excess of ten million U.S. Phase Three: exfiltration successful. Truck destroyed, assets split four ways. All teams accounted. No loss of life or injury to personnel."

The man at the head of the table nodded once. He never gave his name. "Logged. Catalog by dawn. Loose items dispersed in forty-eight hours. Rarities retained for directive. Blocker car destroyed. Truck burned. Laptop discarded." His voice was calm, stripped of anything but authority. The men around him bowed their heads slightly, acknowledging both the order and the weight of it.

The cataloging stretched through the night. Bags of coins were stacked against one wall, trays of relics secured in crates, smaller items—jewelry, IDs, credit cards—sealed in envelopes. A scribe recorded each category by hand, block letters precise. "Gold: thirty-four pounds. Silver: two hundred sixteen pounds. Currency: approximately three hundred thousand. Relics: nine crates, mixed origin. Personal property: sorted." The words sounded like scripture, a litany of theft turned into order. A young recruit miscounted a stack of bills and earned a sharp correction from the man beside him; discipline extended even to the math of crime.

Men moved through the barn-turned-warehouse with the ease of farmers tending crops. Outside, irrigation pipes glinted in sunlight. Inside, they sharpened blades, checked rifles, prepared for the next phase. Nothing here was accidental. Not the produce fields.

Not the solar panels angled toward the sun. Not the small herd of cattle grazing nearby. Everything looked ordinary from the road, and that was the most dangerous thing about it.

"Phase complete," the leader said at last, closing the ledger with a soft thump. His men stood in silence, the weight of success heavy in the room. Then he dismissed them with a single nod, and the barn went back to looking like a place where hay should be stored.

The pavilion itself wound down more slowly.

By nightfall, the Hilton lot looked like a battlefield tidied for inspection. CSU techs crouched for their last photographs, angled flashbulbs flaring against shards of glass. Yellow cones and numbered placards sprouted everywhere, but now gloved hands plucked them up one by one, tucking them into plastic bins. Evidence crates—shell casings, fibers, blood swabs, even scraps of laminated signs—stacked on dollies and rolled out under escort.

At the tape line, a sergeant checked names against the log before signing custody over to Homicide. The clipboard shook a little under a light breeze; his initials turned the day from scene to case file. A detective in plain clothes muttered that the press would be circling like vultures before sunrise. His partner only nodded, eyes on the bins going into vans.

Inside, the room had been drained of its chaos. Booths were husks, cases shattered, carpet stained in wide brown blooms. The air smelled of plaster dust, adhesive, and bleach where techs had cleaned sampling tools. The noise dwindled to a few last shutters, the rip of tape, the squeal of wheels fading into distance.

Finally, the last team backed through the service door, pulling the tape tighter behind them. The pavilion was left silent, sealed under watch. From the outside it looked like a hotel ballroom asleep after a convention. From the inside it was a tomb, frozen until the courts called it awake again.

Tara sat at her desk that evening, the bullpen buzzing faintly behind her. Phones rang, detectives laughed too loudly about smaller cases, the smell of burnt coffee drifted from the break room. In front of her lay the case file: thin, fragile, already marked as trouble. She flipped it open anyway. CSU reports listed casings, footprints, adhesive residues. Witness statements stacked, some coherent, some broken. Photographs of shattered cases, blood-stained carpet, and laminated signs with glue still clinging at the edges stared back at her.

She read through Holt's report again: Cause of death: high-velocity projectile wound of the chest. Homicide by gunshot wound. Walt Garrison, sixty-two, coin dealer, uncle, familiar face on the circuit. Nothing unexpected—except one small line in the margin: an old, faded tattoo near the ribs. Holt had noted it clinically, but Tara found herself staring. Walt had never struck her as the type. It might mean nothing. It might mean everything.

She turned to CSU's technical summaries: adhesive used to weld doors shut, laminated signs staged in advance, rifles rigged to remote triggers, lasers mounted to sweep hostages even after the gunners had gone. Devices with simple but reliable timers, jammers blanketing cell towers, spoofed calls to overwhelm 911. Each report was clinical, but together they read like choreography.

She made her own list in block letters across a legal pad:

Walter Garrison—DOA.

Rachael Garrison—GSW, stable.

Frank Harper—GSW, critical.

Unknown offenders—eleven, military precision.

Collateral victims—multiple, sites spread.

She underlined each name hard enough to etch the paper.

Her eyes drifted to the timeline pinned on the whiteboard: pavilion robbery, KSU shooting, I-75 shutdown, Dobbins explosions, devices outside the hospital. Cobb County had been forced to its knees. The Secret Service had rerouted the Vice President to another airport because Dobbins was compromised.

Was that coincidence? Or had the robbery been one more spoke in a larger wheel?

Tara didn't write the question down. She just sat with it, the way you sit with a word on a crossword you're not ready to ink. The evidence whispered theft. The pattern murmured politics. If the day's chaos was designed to pull protection in every direction, then the pavilion may never have been the main target at all.

She tapped her pen against the desk, staring at the puzzle in front of her. Somewhere, under a barn roof, men congratulated themselves on millions in coins and relics. Here, under bad lighting and old coffee, Tara wondered if the shortest line in the puzzle ran straight at the Vice President.

Chapter Thirteen – Pariah

The turnoff looked like a hundred others that never make maps—packed dirt, weeds pressed flat by tires, a gate that lifted and fell without comment. Nothing here announced purpose, and that was the design. Places like this were not destinations; they were filters.

A white sedan rolled in first, slow enough to look lost. Ten minutes later another vehicle followed, then a third. No pattern close enough to notice, no rhythm that would survive a second glance.

Inside the structure—once meant for feed, now meant for nothing in particular—canvas sacks thumped onto folding tables. No greetings. No recounting. Inventory began immediately.

"Coins left. Relics center. Jewelry right. Cards and IDs separate."

It wasn't cruelty. It was process.

Velvet trays emptied their contents into light that didn't care what it revealed. Gold stayed silent. Paper stacks made heavier sounds than they should have.

"Coveralls burned with the truck."

"Masks and gloves too."

"Laptop?"

"Disposed. No linger."

A carpenter's pencil scratched lines through a ledger that never asked for explanations. When the last item was logged, the tables were cleared, the sacks folded, the room returned to its original lie.

By the time the vehicles left—never together—nothing remained that could explain what had passed through, only the certainty that it had not been meant to stay.

What mattered wasn't what had been taken, but how quickly it could be made to disappear.

The compound gates shut with a patient, practiced clunk. Dust lifted in soft veils from the gravel track and drifted across a yard that pretended to be a farm—rows furrowed straight as a ruler, a feed shed with paint flaking into curls, a windmill turning lazy circles above a row of solar panels. Up on the ridge it would pass for self-reliance. Inside the fence, it was process.

Engines ticked as they cooled. Men moved in calm lines, boots quiet on swept concrete. Long tables draped with tarps waited like staging areas. Sacks thumped onto them, one after another—the sound of weight and purpose. Coins made their small metallic weather when velvet trays came free; relics—crosses dulled by fingers long gone, medallions, a bone-handled knife scratched with shallow runes—were unwrapped and laid in rows. Wallets surrendered cash to envelopes, IDs to neat stacks, cards to rubber bands. Watches and rings fell into a bin where their faces caught the barn's fluorescent light and held it like tiny suns.

The Leader stood at the head of the room, hands clasped behind his back. He gave no speech, offered no congratulations. He simply turned his chin a fraction. "Reports."

"Diversions," said a voice three men down—a pale man with a shaved head and a scar that ran an unremarkable line along his jaw. He didn't glance at anyone else. He spoke to the Leader and to the ledger a scribe held at his elbow. "Kennesaw State. North and south lots. Rifles discharged, tires shredded, vehicles disabled. Time on target under three. Exfiltration clean."

The Leader inclined his head by the width of a coin. "Interstate."

"I-75 northbound and southbound," another man said, a farm boy's tan on a face that didn't remember laughter. "Jackknifed semi, secondary collisions. Devices set in culverts, staggered detonations. Gridlock achieved. Exfiltration clean."

The Leader's gaze moved on. "Pavilion."

"Entry as rehearsed," the operational lead said. "Guards neutralized. Doors sealed. Overwatch in rafters. Forty-two booths cleared—coinage, gold bars, relics, cash. Four teams split loads. Truck destroyed."

The words stacked in air like crates. "Losses."

"None."

A breath traveled the room and went dormant again. The Leader gave a nod so small only men who lived on the weight of nods would have noticed.

"Electronics," he said.

The youngest of them stepped forward. His shoulders tried to square and failed. "Devices stripped from victims. Phones destroyed. SIM cards retained for burn. Laptop deposited per plan. Erasure run."

"Ops laptop," the Leader said, and let the two words sit like a test.

"Administrative unit recovered in error," the young man said. His voice was steady because he made it that way; his throat worked like a man drinking something thick. "Partition wipe executed before deposit."

The ledger scratched; a pencil underlined. The Leader's chin neither rose nor fell. "Administrative. Records."

Silence collected in the rafters and listened to itself. The men toward the back suddenly found the business of their boots. The Leader's eyes held the young man like a pin holds an insect in a glass case.

"Step forward," he said.

The operative obeyed. His boots made the wrong kind of noise on concrete—too loud, too singular. The Leader's questions were not questions; they were prompts.

"Role."

"Electronics support."

"Action."

"Retrieved laptop. Deposited at designated site."

"Wrong. Laptop."

No anger, no volume—only grammar bent into judgment. Two men stepped from the side of the room, lifted the young man by the elbows, and carried him the way men carry things that must be moved. He didn't struggle. Everyone in the room knew there was no appeal attached to the word that had already been said.

"You are a pariah," the Leader said, turning back to the tables, to the sacks, to the ledger. "Catalog by dawn. Crates secure. Rarities retained. Loose items dispersed forty-eight hours."

In the corner, a small burn barrel sat with blackened plastic still soft at its rim. Masks and gloves had gone up there hours ago; SIM cards would follow. Near it, on a mat where dust had drawn its own geometry, a laptop sat with tape on its lid. It would leave with the next truck—to the place where cast-offs went.

Process resumed. Coins sounded like rain. Paper made its dry sigh. The room relearned the discipline of pretending not to notice what discipline demands.

Across the county, a forklift whined along a cracked concrete floor, horn tapping warnings as it swung. A dock door rolled up slow, turning daylight into a rectangle, then a square. Heat pushed into a space that stank of cardboard, old cloth, and machine breath. A radio tried to be cheerful from a nail in a post. Dust took that suggestion and coughed.

A bin rattled onto the dock. Plastic toys, paperback romances, a printer with its glass spidered. The bin lurched when a wheel hit a ridge in the concrete. Something slid and thumped: a laptop with a hinge that had learned patience, its lid scuffed pale in two corners. It wedged itself under a strand of Christmas lights coiled like a snake in summer and waited.

"Three pallets by lunch or we're here all night," a supervisor said, not cruel, just tired. A worker in a neon vest wiped his forehead and looked into the bin like it was a personality test.

"People donate the nastiest—" he began, and his buddy laughed and finished it for him while tugging free a toaster that had dreamed bigger. They sorted what could be sorted and gave up on what couldn't, building two piles: maybe and no.

The laptop came free on the second pull. The worker held it one-handed, thumb testing the hinge without caring about the result. "Tag it," someone said, and the man with the masking tape wrote a number that meant nothing to anyone and stuck it to the lid. It squeaked just a little when he pressed. He set the machine on a metal shelf that rang a small note and moved on.

Hidden in plain sight, it learned a new kind of waiting.

The homicide bullpen had its own music—the faint ring of half-answered phones, the scrape of chairs, detectives trading gossip louder than the details of their cases. Tara Whitaker sat at her desk and watched men build shelter out of small talk.

The captain's door opened. He crossed the room without preamble, shoes scuffing tile, and set a folder on her desk so thin it could have been a joke if anyone here remembered jokes. "Pavilion homicide is yours." It wasn't new information; she'd been carrying it since the night it cracked the city open. But saying it made it official enough for the ledger, and you have to respect ledgers in rooms like this.

The room shifted around the words. Conversations stalled. Chairs squeaked. Heads tilted to listen and then tilted the other way to perform not listening. High profile. Low probability. A career sinkhole with a badge around its neck. Tara looked at the folder, then at the captain's mouth in case it knew anything his words didn't. It didn't.

She didn't open it yet. She rested her palm on the cover the way you press a card onto a table to make it lie flat and let the quiet gather under it. The case was hers. Nobody here wanted it solved.

An hour later, the conference room smelled of burnt coffee and dry-erase markers, of men who would rather be elsewhere. Detectives squeezed around a scarred table and paged through notes they would not own, eyes on the big wall clock more than on the small slide deck someone had begged into existence. A blurry body-cam still of the pavilion floor. A shot of the sealed doors with placards glued shut. A press photo of Walt Garrison under a white sheet. Each image hung on plaster for seconds too short to matter.

“Scene secured, SWAT clear, coroner logged, victims in hospital,” the captain said, tone flat as groceries. No questions. No strategy. Another slide of a problem nobody wanted.

When the briefing ended, chairs scraped back, papers shuffled, and the room filled itself with conversations about traffic, kids, ball scores—everything but the thing that had emptied a ballroom. Tara stayed alone with the blank wall. One of the veterans walked past the door with another at his shoulder and staged a whisper meant to be heard. “It’s Whitaker’s now. Sink or swim.” The other man chuckled in a way that had nothing to do with humor. She pressed the edge of her notepad until the cardboard bent and stood.

Back at her desk, the air had a shape. Detectives who usually leaned on her chair to trade gallows jokes found sudden reasons to walk the long way around. Conversations that used to drift over her shoulder dropped to whispers when she came within earshot. The file wasn’t paperwork anymore. It was a quarantine sign.

She opened it anyway. The pages were thin: a scene log with ink that already looked tired, a handful of names scrawled hastily, photos that felt like they were going wrong in the chemical even as she held them. It was a skeleton, not a case. She flipped to a blank sheet and wrote her own list in block letters steady as a heartbeat: Walter Garrison—DOA. Rachael Garrison—GSW, stable. Frank Harper—GSW, critical. She underlined each once, pressing hard enough to score the paper beneath.

She turned one more page and found Holt's notes: trajectory downward, right to left. No stippling. Another margin held a small clinical note about an old tattoo near Walt's scapula, crude and faint. It snagged at her. She circled it lightly and let it be.

The bullpen buzzed with phones and the muted laughter of men circling smaller, safer cases. Tara shut it out. The file might have been an anchor to everyone else, but to her it was fuel. If they expected her to sink, she would find out how deep the water went.

By evening, the captain called her back into his office. The blinds were half-closed, the only light from a desk lamp that threw hard shadows like bars. He didn't sit; he leaned against the desk with his arms folded across a chest that advertised the gym and a calendar. The pavilion folder was in his hand because theater matters.

"You'll hand the case off to Cold Case," he said. "Effective immediately."

There was no explanation on the plate with the sentence. There rarely is. Cold Case is where files go to retire without a party. Tara set her face and nodded once, clipped and professional, because the worst thing you can give a man who expects you to flinch is satisfaction.

She walked back through the bullpen that was not a bullpen anymore and slid the folder into her bag. Officially, the case was gone.

Unofficially, it had just put her name on its chain of custody in a new way.

She returned to her desk without sitting and flipped through a stack she should now pretend not to own. CSU's technical summaries: adhesives used to weld doors shut; laminated signs staged like props; rifles mounted to throw the memory of red light along rafters long after the men had left; devices with cheap, righteous clocks; jammers; the way the 911 console had been turned into a siren that wouldn't stop eating itself.

She set Holt's final sentence over all of that—homicide by gunshot wound—and the shape of the day offended grammar. Coins screamed from empty cases and trays, but the pattern whispered something worse.

Did this read like greed or choreography? Cobb County had been turned into a net; the Vice President's detail had been forced to cut and run. Tara owned no answers yet, only questions. She didn't write the biggest one on paper. She held it like a word in a crossword, kept to herself until she could prove it and survive the day it would cost her.

"Whitaker," someone said from behind her, the tone built to be neutral. "You forget something?" She looked at the Cold Case detective holding the empty smile designed by HR and gave it back in kind.

"No," she said. "I'll bring it by."

When he was gone, she took a breath deep enough to hurt and closed the folder without closing it.

Back at Goodwill, the refurb benches hummed with machines. Dust breathes when it's warm; it breathed now in shafts of light from high windows. The place smelled of heated plastic, faint solder, and the electric pennies of ozone where fans blew out years.

The worker at the third bench from the end plugged the scuffed laptop into a universal power brick, waited for an old BIOS screen to shiver its way up, clicked through to a diagnostic suite he could run blind.

"Wipe," he said—to himself and to the screen.

The program did its plodding crawl—sectors, partitions, percentages—making small beeps when it reached places that used to be files. The worker leaned back on a stool and traded gossip with the woman at the next bench about how the foreman never stopped talking and how the break-room coffee could legally qualify as a different category of fluid if only the EPA would take their calls.

The software chirped again; the worker turned back. "Clean," he said, and meant only that the program told him what to think.

He dropped a small suite of free office software and a trial antivirus onto the drive, watched bars climb and consolidate. He typed the date and an intake code onto a strip of masking tape and pressed it across the lid with the side of his thumb. The adhesive squeaked the way adhesives do when you know the building's age by smell.

He carried the machine to a shelf that had learned to carry a hundred other machines and settled it into a row by size. From the aisle, all the machines looked the same: neat, anonymous, adoptable.

At the compound, a man had been walked out of a barn in silence for the sin of choosing it. Here it had been weighed, tested, wiped, clothed, and given a number that promised a second life. Both facts were true at once. Inside its partitions, a ledger slept.

And across town, at a desk under bad light, a detective who had just been told she was no longer needed refused to put down her pen.

Chapter Fourteen – The Vault

The office park could have belonged to anyone: an insurance agent, a dentist, a mortgage broker. Glass doors threw back the morning sun; HVAC units droned behind the building. On one of those doors, etched in modest lettering, was a single word:

Cylentra.

The name wasn't clever branding. It was a promise Marcus Raines had made to himself long before the concrete was poured. His mother, Cylen, had raised him alone. When she was dying she told him not to mourn her—"Do something nice for a child." Cylentra carried her forward: Cylen plus tra, for transformation. People saw a company. Marcus saw her name—and learned early that doing good work meant being trusted with things other people couldn't handle on their own.

He built this place himself, not a strip-center lease or shared suite but a quiet, stand-alone facility in Alpharetta, tucked behind tall hedges and young trees. The plantings weren't just pretty; they broke sight lines from the road. The entire ground floor hid behind green, its walls reinforced block and steel. Sunlight poured across the second-story glass like any modern office; at street level the hedge drew a curtain over the truth.

Alpharetta was the right choice. The city was booming, its skyline a patchwork of tech headquarters and cranes. Cylentra belonged here: a boutique firm that felt at home in the corridor and solid enough to be trusted. The building made its own quiet statement. It looked modern, polished, successful—yet carried an undercurrent of permanence, as if it had grown into the landscape rather than been dropped on top of it.

Visitors rarely noticed the subtler cues on approach. Parking bays fanned just so, leaving gaps that let cameras cover every angle of the lot. A dome tucked into a light standard watched the curb; a rectangle high on a wall hummed softly at night—vibration and acoustic sensors listening to concrete. The trick was never to look secretive. The trick was to look like a place with nothing to hide.

Marcus moved through the space with the calm authority of a man who had already lived two lives. At six-four and lean from discipline, he still carried the memory of Georgia Tech's linebacker days and the bruising years with the Cowboys. His mother had raised him to be risk-averse, to think about the years after the lights, to prize humility and prudence over impulse. That's why he managed his money carefully, why he built rather than rented, and why every stone of Cylentra carried the weight of his promise to her: be proud, be self-reliant, never reckless.

Inside, visitors stepped into a bright atrium. A guard station sat just inside the doors—not a turnstile or a barked demand, just a desk with a watchful eye. IDs were checked; badges printed; names logged. It felt professional rather than suspicious, the way a hospital lobby feels when you realize someone thought about safety before you arrived.

From there, most rode the elevator up.

Upstairs, the public face of Cylentra looked closer to an Apple store than an office. Cool light washed across polished floors. Laptops, tablets, and small networking gear sat on clean counters, cabled and powered, easy to try without asking. A receptionist greeted visitors with polite warmth, logged them in, and steered them to the right counter.

The service desk—Cylentra's hub—moved in ordered motion: techs in tidy polos diagnosing machines, opening tickets, staging returns. At the far end, a pickup area handled refurbished releases. No one left carrying a device until they'd spent twenty minutes in a small training room off the lobby—setting up accounts, securing files, learning updates. To Marcus, dignity wasn't just handing someone a machine; it was teaching them to own it.

Along one glass wall, a small academy pulsed quietly. Georgia Tech interns moved from chair to chair while children and teens pecked at keyboards—typing games, scratch-code loops, first scripts that worked on the third try. Marcus had built this wing for Cylen as much as for the kids. If he wanted to honor her, he would do something nice for a child—and keep doing it.

The outreach didn't stop at the building. Cylentra ran a traveling academy—a trailer outfitted with computer banks and a hospitality counter. It parked in underserved neighborhoods where kids could climb aboard, learn basic coding or office skills, and leave with certificates. Some went home with refurbished laptops. A handful earned scholarships to keep going. When his schedule allowed, Marcus went with the trailer. Parents remembered him from Saturdays at Bobby Dodd or Sundays on TV; children stared at the giant who shook their hands with gentleness. He let the old notoriety open doors and then talked about what mattered—about a mother who worked two jobs and taught him that books outlast trophies.

"I came from the same place you did," he told the kids. "What made the difference was love, work, and people who believed in me. That's why I'm here—to believe in you."

The work upstairs looked simple. What made it complicated—and trustworthy—was what happened to every device before it ever touched those counters.

Trade-ins came from everywhere: schools with tired labs, charities upgrading offices, families with old laptops, small businesses clearing back rooms. Every drive was treated the same. Disks were scanned surgically, line by line. If an intake scan surfaced family photos, tax returns, or confidential spreadsheets, Marcus called the donor himself. Did they want it back? Was it all right to destroy? He didn't delegate those conversations. Government or charity, school or private citizen—everything was handled with the same care.

The upstairs made the promise with glass and light. The ground floor kept it.

To most, the elevator was boring—brushed steel with a tidy panel. You swiped, pressed 2, and rose. But when the right card met the reader, the car behaved differently. The front doors slid shut as usual. The cab didn't move. A soft chime sounded. Then the rear panel—which a casual visitor would have taken for decorative steel—whispered open onto a short, silent corridor. From the lobby, nothing looked unusual. To the person inside, a second world had appeared.

The first time a guest rode it, there was always a pause—the instinct to wonder if the car had stuck, the way silence pressed like a hand to the chest. Air from the corridor felt cooler, drier, tasting faintly of ozone. By the time they stepped out, they already understood: they were somewhere else now.

A second guard station waited there—reinforced glass, ID scanners, overlapping camera feeds. Photo ID was checked again. The appointment—time, room, escort—was confirmed against the log. No exceptions. Even repeat clients sat for a minute on a row of chairs until the red light over the interior door clicked to green.

Beyond that door lay what staff and cleared clients quietly called the Vault.

It didn't try to dazzle. A compact lounge held a few low chairs, a long console with coffee and water, a private bath behind a sliding panel. There were no windows. Here the light was lower, the air still; voices fell to a hush out of respect as much as discretion. Three SCIFs branched away—secured, windowless, rooms built like vaults inside the vault. Glass went opaque at a button. Each was soundproofed and self-contained, with its own refreshment nook so no one broke chain-of-custody mid-task. Carts and sealed cases waited at thresholds, wheels wrapped in antistatic sleeves.

At the very back, away from lounges and clients, the building's skin changed again. Floodlights bathed a recessed loading bay that faced the inner drive rather than the street. Scheduled deliveries arrived there, not through the atrium. Manifests were checked the night before by phone; IDs were matched to the schedule; signatures confirmed against the book.

Only after that did the call go out—to the sealed room.

No outside hand moved classified hardware once it crossed that line. Marcus' son, Daniel, the single custodian—gloved, quiet—came to the bay and took the cases himself. The handoff happened in view of cameras while Marcus stood with the paperwork. Couriers eased metal cases onto a waiting cart. From there the custodian wheeled them down the short corridor to the biometric gate of the enclave. Retina scan. Hand geometry. Passphrase. The door acknowledged one identity and no other. Marcus never crossed it. No client ever had. That was the point.

The enclave reflected its keeper. Cables coiled in perfect loops. Racks blinked with quiet regularity. The silence felt deliberate—sound-dampening panels swallowing even the scrape of a chair. Paper never left the room. What came out were only encrypted synopses through a pass-through slot—thin, numbered printouts that read like ledgers.

Every intake passed through that node first. Drives imaged. Partitions mapped. Anomalies flagged. If something surfaced—hidden caches, odd partitions, labels that didn't fit—the system generated a thumbnail synopsis, stamped time and hash, and slid it through the slot into the Vault's outer air. Only then did the wipe begin. Only then did a clean operating system go down, and a green light send the machine upstairs to the refurb floor.

It was a routine—impersonal by design—that turned trust into a process.

On an ordinary morning, another laptop rattled onto the intake table. Its plastic was scuffed; the hinge pulled a little left; no power cord. It looked like a cast-off from a dorm or a small office.

The diagnostic cable clicked into place. Lines of data crawled across a screen—partition counts, storage maps, a thin forest of folder names. Then the trees parted. Extra volumes nested inside one another like rooms inside rooms. Folder labels surfaced that didn't belong to homework or PTO minutes: haul. transfer. loadout. Cold words with logistics baked into them.

A single-page synopsis rattled through the pass-through slot. Marcus took it in the quiet of the Vault and read. Rows of counts. Dates. Labels that didn't matter until they did.

Then the line that pulled his chest tight:

MARIETTA – JUNE 6, 2020.

This wasn't residue. It was accounting.

He stood with the page in his hand while the Vault's hum filled the silence. It was nothing more than black ink on white paper. But it carried a weight he could feel in his sternum. The oath of confidentiality that had built this place warred with headlines burned into memory—diversions and explosions, a hospital bay gone hot, a pavilion emptied of sound except for the noise grief makes when it runs out of breath.

The laptop itself never left the enclave. It sat logged and locked like a dozen others waiting for the wipe. Nothing about the chassis set it apart. Only the paper in his hand had weight. He pressed his thumb into the margin and left a pale crescent. The choice was simple to name and hard to live with: keep the promise—or bring someone else in.

For the first time since he poured the slab for this building, Marcus felt the ground tilt under the Vault.

It would not stay buried.

Chapter Fifteen – Cache

The compound lived beneath the canopy of pines like a secret kingdom, hidden from the road by distance, timber, and deliberate design. To the casual driver, it looked like an ordinary farm: barns and silos, fields of corn and beans, cattle drifting under the fence shade. A windmill creaked. Smoke curled from a chimney where women baked bread. A tractor moved along a furrow, the driver lifting a hand in greeting to no one but the sky.

Up close, the disguises parted and the order showed itself. Rows of vegetables ran like ruled lines to the tree line; irrigation popped and hissed on timers. A long, low barracks sat behind the equipment shed, its cots made tight enough to bounce a coin. Next to it, a washhouse steamed in the early light, boots ranked on racks outside to dry. The mess hall took the shape of an old tobacco barn—long tables down the middle, benches polished by years of use, a coffee urn that never went cold. A small infirmary kept to the shade, two cots and a cabinet of antibiotics and gauze inside. A root cellar and smokehouse shouldered the kitchen's back wall. A chapel had been repurposed into a meeting hall: plank benches, a wide plank stage, banners hung from rafters. The torch-in-ring emblem appeared everywhere—painted, stitched, carved.

Men patrolled the perimeter in pairs, rifles slung loose but ready, dogs padding at their sides. The kennel held nearly fifty animals—shepherds and mastiffs mostly—trained to guard and, when told, to break a man. Beyond the barns, hog pens sprawled wider than a visitor might expect. The animals grunted and churned the dirt with their snouts. To outsiders, the elders had Scripture at the ready: "And the swine, though it divide the hoof, yet cheweth not the cud, it is unclean to you: ye shall not eat of their flesh, nor touch their carcass" (Leviticus 11:7). Inside the fence, the explanation was plainer and not for strangers: hogs ate what needed to disappear. They were nature's garbage disposals.

Other work filled the shadows. One shed had been converted into an armory, walls lined with rifles and pistols, crates of ammunition stacked waist high. Another housed workbenches where bomb casings lay open, their bellies wired with timers and triggers by careful hands. A long building with blacked-out windows served as a garage, mechanics bent over an odd fleet: battered panel vans with service logos, hay trucks with false compartments, a half-dozen heavy military transports sleeping under tarps.

There was even an airstrip—a thin scar of asphalt cut into the trees, just wide enough for private planes and helicopters. At dawn, engines sometimes coughed to life and lifted parcels that never appeared on any ledger.

Peacocks drifted along the edges of the farm, tails catching sunlight as they stepped across fence lines. To the drivers passing on the county road, the birds looked like decoration, a farmer's indulgence. The Hands treated them as holy. "That's the Lord's alarm system," the elders said. "Beautiful in appearance, but a reliable warning for people of faith." The men trusted peacocks more than cameras or tripwires. Electronics could be blinded. Dogs could be poisoned. But nothing silenced a peacock's scream when something moved in the trees.

Life ran by rule. The men—the Hands—trained, patrolled, and carried out raids. The women—the Keepers—cooked, washed, kept quarters, and raised children—Sparks, they called them—who learned their letters with scripture and their numbers with cartridge counts. Every morning began with shouted call and response: "The Hand burns for Him!" answered by "The flame cleanses!" Indoctrination was constant. Torches appeared everywhere: murals painted on the sides of the barns, banners stitched and hung in the meeting hall, the emblem carved into the chapel posts by knives that left their kisses in the grain.

On this morning, the benches of that hall were full. The recruits stood at the front with their heads bowed. The Trial by Fire was about to begin.

Before a man could be branded, he had to be tested. Weeks earlier, each had been handed an assignment that made no sense to him. One was ordered to steal a battered tin wind-up toy from the back shelf of a pawn shop and leave the cash drawer untouched. Another was told to lift an old coin—a tarnished gold piece under glass—from a collector's booth at a county fair, walk past velvet and eyes, and make it disappear.

A third had risked arrest slipping a century-old book out of a library archive, the librarian's stamp still browned into the flyleaf. Others carried home oddities that sounded like dreams when they were whispered in bunks: a brass candlestick with a dent in its base; a fragment of stained glass pried carefully from a church basement window; a cracked chalice; a coin scale; a ledger page torn from a forgotten safe.

They were never asked to steal cash or weapons or things the world agreed were valuable—only peculiar objects that seemed worthless to everyone but the elders. That was the test. Obedience without explanation. A man willing to risk jail for what looked like nothing could be trusted with something that mattered.

Some of what they brought vanished into storage; some was tagged, cataloged, and never spoken of again.

They had delivered exactly what was demanded. The prizes were long since handed up. Now they stood straight in their shirtsleeves, waiting for what came next.

The iron hissed when it touched the flame, glowing orange, the torch-in-ring emblem shimmering against the coals. The first recruit stepped forward. His shirt was stripped away, his chest heaving. The iron pressed to his forearm; the room filled with the stink of burnt flesh. He did not cry out. None of them did.

When the iron lifted away, the leader placed something cold into each man's palm: a bar of gold, no larger than a thumb, stamped with the same torch-in-ring that now marked his skin. Flesh and metal. Pain and prize. One mark could never be taken away; the other was proof he belonged.

The congregation roared, fists lifted like a field of black saplings in a wind. The recruits had been tested, scarred, rewarded. Now they were Hands.

Miles away, in Alpharetta, Marcus Raines sat behind his desk inside his own kind of compound—steel and glass instead of timber and tin, but built on the same principles: discipline, secrecy, trust.

The printout Daniel had passed through to him lay square on the blotter. Black ink on white paper—columns of file counts, labels, dates. Ninety-nine times out of a hundred, these synopses were routine: general files, photos, spreadsheets—things forgotten before a machine was traded in. This page was not routine. It began with a single header, stark in its simplicity:

MARIETTA – JUNE 6, 2020.

Marcus stared at the words, the date burned into his memory. And from the small thumbnail Daniel had included, the directory beneath it did not look like homework or household books. It looked like the bones of a plan.

He leaned back and watched dust drift in a shaft of morning light. Cylentra's oath of confidentiality played itself back in his head—the words he'd given churches, schools, businesses, federal clients. Break it once and the vault would never mean anything again. But what did it mean to keep quiet when the paper in his hand stared back with that kind of deliberateness?

The laptop itself sat on a cart outside the secure room, tagged and waiting like any other device. Nothing about the chassis was different. Only the paper in his hand had weight. He pressed his thumb into the margin and left a faint crescent. The choice was simple to name and hard to live with: keep the promise—or bring someone else in.

Now, with the synopsis on his desk and the oath pressing on his chest, he knew who to call. Outside his family, there was one man he trusted with both law and conscience: his oldest friend, Tyler Mathis.

Their friendship stretched back further than most people realized. Long before Cylentra, before the NFL or law school, there had been Valdosta—two boys raised by single mothers who worked too many hours and still found a way to put cleats and books in their hands. On Friday nights, Marcus was the enforcer at linebacker, the ground-tilter. Ty lined up at wide receiver, but made his name on special teams—returning punts and kicks with the kind of vision that could flip a game in ten seconds flat.

When Georgia Tech's coaches came south to recruit Marcus, their eyes kept drifting to the wiry return man fielding punts with impossible balance. Back in Atlanta, those coaches and fans murmured that he felt like a modern echo of Ray 'Razor' Hinton, the seventies return man whose highlights lived longer in memory than on film.

Both earned scholarships north—Marcus anchoring Tech's defense, Ty stretching fields and flipping momentum as a returner. Then their paths diverged: Marcus to the NFL; Ty to the Georgia State University College of Law. After the bar—passed as smoothly as he once juked tacklers—Ty clerked for a federal judge, then joined a firm specializing in intellectual property and computer law. When Marcus sketched the first lines of Cylentra, Ty was the one who said: don't be a shop—be a vault. Build it so even the government will trust you.

Now Marcus needed him again.

The request went out quietly. No lobby call, no front-desk hello. When Ty arrived, he tapped his card at the elevator's brushed steel panel. The front doors slid shut; the car didn't move. With a muted chime the rear panel whispered open onto a guarded corridor. Credentials were checked, the log took his card number, the red light over the interior door turned green. Down here there were no casual visits. As Cylentra's registered agent and counsel—and Daniel's godfather—Ty's badge didn't read GUEST. It gave him senior-staff access.

Marcus was waiting in the private conference room. He slid the printout across the table without a word. Paper rasped against laminate and came to rest in front of Ty. Ty read it with a lawyer's eye—two lines at a time, structure rather than sentences. Halfway down, his jaw tightened. At the bottom, his knuckle tapped twice against the margin.

"Marietta — June 6, 2020," he read aloud. He looked up. "Jesus, Marcus… this wasn't chaos. It was about the money—the heist, and the Vice President; they were connected after all."

"If you turn it over," Ty said a beat later, "you break the promise you built this company on. If you don't, you make yourself custodian of a crime."

Silence stretched.

Ty slid the page back. "You don't move the hardware. Ever. You keep it logged, exactly as it came in. No one touches it but you and your process. What you can share is the information—not the machine, not the image, not the drive. The synopsis. The paper. That's what we hand off, and only through me, under attorney–client privilege. If it's challenged, you can still swear you never broke your oath."

"So the vault stays intact," Marcus said, rubbing his jaw, "and you carry the burden."

"That's the only way it survives."

The room went quiet again. Marcus stared at the paper. The only thing worse than stepping onto the narrow bridge Ty had laid out was standing still. The vault had been built on promises; the day was asking what those promises were worth.

Ty rested his fingertips on the page, then folded it into his briefcase and slid it in as if it were evidence already. "We can't sit on this alone," he said. "We need someone who carried it when it was fresh and has nothing left to lose."

"Who?"

"Tara Whitaker."

The name had its own gravity—not for Marcus, but for Ty. He remembered her from the first days after the pavilion murders, standing in front of microphones that seemed to be waiting for her to fail. She'd been young then—about thirty-two—and already wearing a homicide badge most don't earn until later. Army MP before coming home; Savannah-born; Georgia Southern for criminal justice; a fast ascent into Marietta PD's homicide unit. Five-seven, fit, strong; olive-toned skin; dark hair pulled back tight; hazel eyes that didn't blink at cameras. Blunt. Sardonic. Unafraid.

"They buried her when the case went cold," Ty said quietly. "Made her the face of the failure so they didn't have to wear it. She's mid-thirties now—older, sharper. If we show her this, she won't let go."

Marcus exhaled. Bringing her in meant trust, and trust was currency he didn't spend lightly. But Ty's certainty was the kind forged on fields and in courtrooms.

"She sees this," Marcus said, "and she'll never let it go."

"That's exactly the point."

Hemingway's, Marietta Square

Ty chose a corner booth away from the windows, where the murmur of lunch traffic covered anything that needed covering. He set his phone on the table, angled just enough so she could see the screen.

A file header appeared: **MARIETTA – JUNE 6, 2020.**

Tara's breath caught. "That's mine," she said quietly.

"Keep watching," Ty told her. Then, into the phone, low and even: "Proceed."

The person on the other end scrolled. Another page appeared. Then another. Each marked the same way—structured, deliberate, nothing like junk data.

"Show her more," Ty ordered.

The pages kept turning until Tara raised a hand. "Stop. That's enough." She leaned back, pulse ticking in her throat, eyes locked on the screen. "This is definitely my case—and it's new information."

Her voice thinned to focus. "Is there anything else?"

"Show the directory," Ty said.

The screen shifted to a scrolling list of file headers. Line after line carried dates and place names, each structured like the Marietta entry. Dozens of them.

Tara's jaw clenched, her eyes sweeping the list. "There's no way… all of these?"

Ty said quietly, "Before I contacted you, I pulled a dozen at random. Every one of them tied to a violent crime and/or a theft. Not just here. Across the southern states. Robberies. Assaults. Killings."

She sat back hard, the decision already taking shape. "Then it stays small. Off the books. A joint task force we handpick."

Ty didn't argue. He rose, folding his jacket over one arm. "Call me back with their names tonight. Tomorrow morning—nine a.m. I'll send the address. Bring them."

The phone went dark.

For a long beat, Tara watched her reflection in the black glass and listened to the room's noise creep back. Five years ago, the case had been taken from her hands and buried.

Not this time.

She started dialing.

One by one, the calls went out. Holt answered first, brisk and professional. Sloane's voice carried quiet surprise but no hesitation. And when Rachael heard, her reply was immediate: "If it's about my uncle, I'm in."

When the last call was finished, Tara exhaled and pressed Ty's number. He answered on the first ring.

"I've got the names," she said. "They're all in."

"Good," Ty replied. "Then their badges will be waiting. Nine a.m., sharp."

The line clicked off. Tara set her phone down on the table, the weight of the day finally still in her chest,

For the first time since the pavilion, she felt the case wasn't hers alone.

Chapter Sixteen – Task Force One

Each of them noticed something different as they pulled into the lot.

Tara thought about how much downtown Alpharetta had changed—restaurants, shops, and streetscapes polished into something unrecognizable from years back. The location felt more like a business lunch destination than the start of anything serious.

Sloane caught herself admiring the landscaping. The hedges and pines looked deliberate, chosen to soften the modern lines of the building. She made a mental note that it was the kind of upkeep her own office could never budget for.

Rachael's eyes lingered on the glass façade. Not a skyscraper, not even tall by suburban standards, but it fit. Sleek without being flashy, the kind of place you'd expect to see in Alpharetta's tech corridor.

Holt, walking in behind the others, was already wondering what the inside looked like. She liked the outside well enough, but her mind was on chairs, tables, and whether there'd be space to spread out her notes.

Whatever they had expected, it wasn't this. The building belonged here—comfortable in its surroundings—and that made it harder to guess why they were meeting inside.

The lobby was quiet, polished, almost too ordinary for what it would soon host. A wall bore the company's name in brushed steel letters, understated but impossible to miss.

A small café glowed from one corner, the scent of coffee drifting across. Bathrooms sat behind frosted glass doors, clearly marked, another touch that made the space feel normal.

Beyond the atrium, frosted glass walls suggested depth without invitation—conference suites, offices, and support rooms receding out of sight. Directional signage pointed toward Client Services, Training, and Administration, the kind of labels that reassure visitors they are in a real place with real work happening just beyond the public edge. Nothing about the layout felt truncated. The building offered enough to satisfy curiosity—and no reason to look further.

Tara Whitaker arrived first, posture stiff, a folder tucked under her arm. She gave her name to the guard, who checked a list and asked her to wait. Sloane Carver came next, her FBI credentials hanging at her hip.

Holt followed, recorder bag on her shoulder, eyes sweeping every corner of the lobby like she was already logging details. Rachael Garrison was next, stepping carefully, her expression set but her eyes betraying nerves. A final figure stepped in behind Rachael—a woman with a GBI badge clipped to her belt.

Tara blinked. She hadn't expected anyone to actually follow through. Tara nodded toward the woman she'd seen that morning in the lobby, now standing with quiet, steady confidence near the far end of the table.

"Special Agent Alicia Ward, Georgia Bureau of Investigation - Major Crimes Division. She was handling the administrative side earlier. This is the real reason she's here".

The GBI agent gave Tara a small nod.

The rest exchanged only quick nods. No one wanted to break the silence.

The guard picked up the phone, spoke a few clipped words, and hung up. A moment later the elevator doors slid open.

Tyler Mathis stepped out.

Sloane recognized him immediately. “Ty,” she said under her breath, half-surprised, half-relieved.

He greeted them warmly, not as an attorney or a former athlete, but almost like a tour guide welcoming honored guests. In his hand was a small stack of badges.

“One for each of you,” he said, moving down the line. “You’ll need to wear these personalized access cards the entire time you’re in the building. Thanks to Sloane for getting me all of your names early.”

Each card carried their photo and name, already printed, already laminated. The detail made them pause. Rachael turned hers over twice, wondering how Ty had gotten her picture without her ever posing for it. Holt slid hers into her pocket with a clinical nod. Tara clipped hers immediately, hazel eyes narrowing as if she were already calculating the implications. Sloane studied hers, impressed despite herself.

“You’ll need to wear these at all times while you’re in the building.”

He led them to the waiting elevator. The brushed steel doors slid open.

"If you don't use your badge," Ty told them, gesturing toward the reader panel, "this car takes you nowhere. It'll just sit here." He tapped his own badge against the sensor, demonstrating the faint green glow. "Every card is coded. Only yours works for you."

The four stepped inside. Ty followed, but instead of taking a place in front, he lingered near the rear panel. The front doors closed smoothly, just as expected.

Then he said, calm as ever: "This way, please."

The rear panel whispered open.

Instead of another floor, a short, controlled stairwell descended into cooler light—reinforced concrete, sound-dampened walls, the air tasting faintly of ozone and steel.

Only then did it register: the elevator hadn't taken them anywhere at all. It had simply let them through.

They filed out slowly, walking down the stairs, glancing at each other. One muttered, "What the hell…?"

At the foot of the stairs waited a reinforced glass checkpoint—lit low, designed to stop momentum.

The guard behind the glass checked IDs, logged each name, and directed them to secure their belongings.

The buzzer sounded. The inner door unlocked.

The group stepped forward into another lobby, this one quieter, more private. Marcus Raines stood waiting, tall and broad-shouldered, arms folded loosely across his chest.

"Welcome," Marcus said evenly. His voice carried calm authority, steady without edge. "We'll talk inside."

He gestured toward the card reader beside the final door. "This is where you'll be setting up," he explained. "Each of your badges will give you entry."

Tara stepped forward first, swiped her card, and watched the light turn green. The door unlocked with a low hiss.

Together, they walked into the war room for the first time.

What lay beyond was unlike anything any of them had seen inside law enforcement.

The ceiling rose higher than expected, humming faintly with hidden servers. Two walls glowed with monitors, some streaming live data, others frozen on stills tagged in quiet green or red. A third wall held glass-fronted evidence bays, each slot digitally stamped with a status light. At the center, a matte black table dominated the room, its surface smooth except for embedded screens that flickered awake as they entered.

To the right, a refreshment area offered more than any precinct break room ever had: a sleek automated coffee maker with options scrolling on a touch screen, baskets of fruit, a spread of snacks, and a fully stocked refrigerator with water, sodas, and sandwiches. A microwave and freezer sat beneath the counter. Beyond that, a private bathroom was tucked behind a frosted panel door.

On another wall stood a secure bin for paper reports—updates to be scanned in overnight by Daniel. Next to it was a rack of trays for physical evidence, each digitally logged when items were deposited. None of the newcomers realized yet that anything they left would be properly scanned and filed into the system by morning.

Marcus pointed to the desks that ringed the room, each already set with a monitor and login screen. "These are yours. First time in, you'll change the password. Then you'll have access to the full preloaded database—every hidden file we've uncovered. It's simple: select what you want to review, pull up data, add what you find. Anything you log becomes part of the record."

Each desk also had a slim, advanced mobile device resting in its charger. Marcus gestured toward them. "Your phones and laptops stay locked outside. These are your secure lifelines. They can call or text only within this group—speed dial to every name you see, group messages if needed, camera and scanner functions if you're in the field. Nothing goes beyond us."

For a long moment, no one spoke. Tara's eyes swept the bays, Holt's hand drifted toward the evidence cabinet, Rachael glanced at the fridge as though startled by its normalcy. Sloane let out a quiet breath she hadn't realized she was holding.

Finally Tara asked what they had all been thinking: "Where in the hell are we?"

Marcus gave them his elevator speech, steady and practiced. "This facility was designed to be more secure than anything outside Fort Knox. The NSA has authorized us to handle their most classified documentation. If there's a place you can work without fear of compromise, it's here."

Rachael looked at the others, her voice firm. "Then chain of custody isn't a problem. Based on what we just heard, this place is more secure than any police department or FBI office I've ever seen."

Holt muttered under her breath, "Finally feels good to come to work again."

Introductions

Marcus went first. He told them how Daniel's process had flagged something unusual, how the synopsis landed on his desk, and why he'd called Ty—his oldest friend, attorney, and the one person he trusted to help him balance his oath of confidentiality with what the document suggested. Ty exhaled once, slow, steady. Not nerves — the weight of every case where the truth came too late. This time, he promised himself, they would get ahead of it.

Ty followed, introducing himself as Marcus's counsel and longtime friend, explaining his background in intellectual property and technology law. He described how he vetted the information and made the call to Tara—not as a favor, but as the legal proxy to protect Marcus's company while ensuring the evidence didn't die in silence.

Tara introduced herself next. She didn't waste words, simply outlining her career—Army MP, Savannah native, Georgia Southern for criminal justice, and a homicide detective in Marietta. She explained how the case had been shelved, how she had been branded as the failure, and why she agreed immediately when Ty reached out: because she had promised herself she'd never let it rest if new evidence surfaced.

Then Tara turned to the others.

"Dr. Carolyn Holt," she said, gesturing toward the medical examiner. "When Ty told me some of these files tied directly to homicides, I knew I needed her. Holt documents everything—no shortcuts, no pressure bending her reports."

"Agent Sloane Carver," Tara continued. "FBI, Atlanta Field Office. I trust her. Cases crossing state lines are coming, and when that happens the Bureau will claim jurisdiction. Sloane's the one I want already inside the circle when that day comes."

The others heard "FBI" and "liaison" and accepted it at face value. Sloane heard the quieter truth of what it meant: outsider.

Her whole career had been lived in the space between. She came out of Quantico convinced the Bureau's creed—mission, justice, integrity—would be enough. It hadn't taken long to learn that cases didn't move on creed alone; they moved on optics, capital, and who could sell a narrative at the podium.

Sloane didn't play the club game. She didn't smooth over gaps for reporters or court politicians in the office. She wrote warrants that were tight, preservation letters that judges could sign without lifting a red pen, and subpoenas that survived cross-examination. Supervisors respected her work, but they didn't invite her to the inside table.

Her ASAC, Richard Keene, made the arrangement clear. He trusted her paperwork—cold, narrow, admissible. But when an operation had a microphone attached, he assigned someone else. When resources were thin, her cars were cut so another agent could cover a flashier case. She'd written the packet that cracked a fraud ring two years back, but she'd watched another agent give the press conference, smiling behind a lectern with the words our findings on his lips while she sat two rows behind with the returns that had made the finding possible.

That was her rhythm: necessary but invisible, reliable but peripheral. Locals saw her badge and never her name. Headquarters saw her output but not her face. She became the one sent as "liaison" when no one else wanted the seat. The one whose job was to keep the paper clean while others played the politics.

It didn't bother her most days. It was the weather she lived under. Keene wasn't malicious—just steady, high pressure, indifferent to individuals. He cut her requests for resources not out of spite but because another chart needed to look better upstairs. He once told her, almost kindly, "You're reliable." She'd understood exactly what that meant in his mouth: essential, unglamorous, and never in the picture.

Which was why this room didn't feel foreign. It wasn't Bureau and it wasn't local. It was somewhere in between—her natural ground. Off the books sounded like liability to most; to Sloane it sounded like honesty. Nobody here wanted a podium. Nobody here was playing for headlines. They wanted a case that could breathe in court and survive chain-of-custody. That was her kind of work.

She glanced at Tara, saw the wary nod of another woman who lived outside the circle, and gave a small nod back. They wouldn't waste each other.

Tara nodded toward the woman who had been standing with quiet, steady confidence near the far end of the table.

"This is Special Agent Alicia Ward, Georgia Bureau of Investigation — Major Crimes Division."

Ward stepped forward, her hands linked loosely in front of her. Her voice carried the calm authority of someone used to briefing sheriffs, judges, and legislators in the same week.

"GBI handles the cases that spill across county lines or grow too big for one department to hold," she said. "For the last decade, that's been my world — multi-site violent crimes, organized crews working across the state, and joint operations with both the Bureau and local agencies."

She glanced briefly at Tara, then Sloane.

"When a case crosses State jurisdictions, someone has to make sure no one is blindsided — or blocking the very people trying to solve it. That's why I'm here. To keep agencies aligned, to coordinate resources, and to ensure this task force has full access to state investigative authority when the ground starts shifting."

She stepped back into the semicircle without flourish.

No ego, no apology — just a quiet promise of competence.

Finally she looked at Rachael. "And Rachael Garrison. You all know her name from the news five years ago. She was there in the pavilion with her uncle. He didn't survive. When the case was dumped into cold storage, I promised her that if anything new surfaced, she'd hear it first. I made the call, and she insisted on joining us—not as family seeking revenge, but as a prosecutor. She'll be our guardrail, our legal sounding board when it comes to warrants, filings, and admissibility."

Rachael hadn't planned on carving her life around courtrooms. That changed the day her uncle was killed. She'd thrown herself into law school and then the DA's office the way some people throw themselves at grief—hard, focused, determined.

Two years in Violent Crimes had sharpened her instincts; she learned to dissect affidavits, build cases that could survive hostile judges, and speak the language of warrants with a fluency born of purpose, not ambition.

Rachael's voice was calm when she spoke. "I'm here to make sure his death isn't in vain. And that the work we do survives the system."

Rachael could move through warrants and affidavits with practiced ease, flagging weak language before it could become a problem. It wasn't ambition—it was habit. She knew where judges hesitated and where procedure collapsed, and she could correct both before anyone asked.

The group spent the next hour exploring the room. Each sat at their assigned desk, logged into the preloaded database, and changed their passwords. The system was designed to be simple: scroll files, search by tag, pull up a record with a few clicks. Holt quickly gravitated to the medical files, Sloane tested cross-state incidents, Tara pulled open the Georgia-specific folder. Rachael stayed near Ty, reading procedures and flagging legal traps.

They discovered the refreshment area soon after. Tara poured a black coffee, Holt grabbed water, Sloane tried the touch-screen cappuccino. Rachael and Ty ended up side by side at the machine, where Rachael quietly admitted she had once sat in on one of Ty's CLE lectures.

She said she'd meant to thank him for his insight into digital forensics and how useful it had been for prosecutors. Ty grinned, surprised, and they shared a few easy jokes—including Rachael's crack later that at least his advice would keep him out of one of her office's "complimentary orange suits." Ty deadpanned back that orange was never his color anyway.

The atmosphere loosened, briefly human.

But when Tara called them back to the center table, the weight returned.

She laid out their lanes: she would lead investigations within Georgia, Sloane would monitor interstate cases, Holt would document deaths, Rachael would advise on warrants and admissibility, Ty would bridge the legal-technical divide. Holt would speak for the dead. Rachael would guard admissibility. Sloane would watch the interstate. Tara would lead the hunt inside Georgia.

“This isn’t an assignment anymore,” Tara said finally. “It’s ours. And if we take it, we don’t give it back.”

The war room went quiet again.

No one added a word. The work began.

Chapter Seventeen – Sense Out Of Chaos

The war room was quiet except for the steady hum of servers. No one rushed to speak. The evidence files had been laid out on the central table in neat stacks, digital folders mirrored on the wall screens. For the first time since the robbery, the fragments of chaos were all in one place, waiting.

Tara stood closest to the board, arms folded, her eyes scanning the icons as though sheer will could force a pattern out of them. Holt adjusted her glasses and hovered over the stack marked Medical, her hands itching for the sterile discipline of autopsy notes. Sloane pulled files into a neat pile and began scanning them for logistics: dates, locations, timing. She sketched quick columns in her notebook, tightening them into order.

"We don't chase theories," Tara said quietly. "We start with buckets. Robbery. Murder. Victims. Forensics. Legal. We build the skeleton first. The story will come."

The others nodded, and the rhythm of the room shifted. The silence wasn't hesitation anymore. It was concentration, the collective intake of breath before the real work began.

The table filled quickly as each person claimed their lane. Holt drew the autopsy reports and ER summaries toward her side, stacking them in precise piles. She circled entries, underlined trajectory notes, and began sketching diagrams. The dead spoke cleanly to her, and she was fluent in their language.

Tara pulled witness statements and began separating panic from precision, underlining words that carried consistency across reports. Her pile grew messy, but her pen strokes carved hard edges through the noise.

Rachael stayed quiet, her chair angled slightly away from the table, her bandaged arm cradled against her side. When a file was mishandled, she leaned forward and tapped it with her pen.

"Stop. You can't split that report."

Holt looked up, eyebrow raised.

"Autopsy summaries have to stay whole," Rachael said. "If you break them into pieces, defense will argue mishandling. One chain, one document. If you need cross-reference, you build it from the original, not from fragments."

Tara gave a short nod. Holt muttered, "Fair," and returned to her diagrams.

Rachael's voice stayed even as she added, "Same with warrants. Any digital record mirrors back to me, nowhere else. If a file touches two hands without a log, it's broken chain. And a broken chain is the end of this."

Later, when Sloane suggested moving on a lead, Rachael pushed a draft affidavit back across the table.

"Judge won't sign this. Scope's too broad. Narrow it to the specific items we've already documented."

Sloane bristled. "Every time we draft one of these, you cut it down. We're burning daylight."

"Better to lose daylight than lose admissibility," Rachael replied, calm as ever.

Sloane's jaw tightened. "We'll never stay ahead of them at this pace."

Tara looked up from her witness stack, sharp. "She's right. I've seen airtight cases collapse because somebody wanted speed over procedure. If we want convictions, we play inside the lines."

Across the table, Ty finally lifted his head. He hadn't touched a file all morning, but the legal threshold caught his ear.

"She's not wrong," he said evenly, his voice carrying the weight of courtroom experience. "Federal judges kill warrants for less. A clean affidavit is insurance—if it holds in this room, it'll hold in court."

Rachael gave a small nod and returned to her notes.

By mid-afternoon, fatigue was showing. Tara gnawed absently on the end of her pen, teeth marks notched into the plastic. Holt kept aligning her stacks of medical notes by millimeters, a ritual she returned to every few minutes as though order on the table could fight the chaos in the files. Rachael wrote in her tidy script, her fatigue hidden in precision. The smell of coffee long gone bitter hung over everything.

"This would be a hell of a lot easier if we had a search engine," Sloane said at last.

What she meant wasn't a Google query, but the kind of federated indexing system only a handful of government contractors were even allowed to build.

The others nodded in agreement. One of them told Ty to see if Marcus could get it added. Ty rose, gathered his notepad, and stepped out.

As the door began to re-open, the wall screens flickered. When the display settled, a new search bar stretched across the top of everyone's open screen.

By the time Ty walked back inside, Sloane was already staring at the new icon pulsing in the corner of the display. She turned to look at him, waited a beat, then said, shaking her head, "Okay. Pick my lottery numbers next."

A bit confused but game to help, Ty pulled out his war-team device. Seconds later Sloane's unit buzzed. She glanced down, saw the random digits he'd sent, and burst into laughter so sharp it bent her forward in her chair.

Tara frowned. "What's so funny?"

Sloane, still gasping, forwarded the message to the team. Holt snorted first, Rachael let out a startled laugh, and even Tara cracked as the sound spread until the whole room dissolved in it.

Ty looked around, acting baffled. He checked his zipper, his shoes, even turned sideways to catch a glimpse of his back in the glass. "What—what is it? It's some kind of code that there's something on me that I didn't notice?"

That did it. Holt doubled over, Rachael's laugh broke loose again, and Tara had to cover her face with her hand. The sound rolled through the soundproof room, bouncing back at them until they were gasping for air.

When it finally ebbed, Sloane pointed at the screen. "The search engine. It was there before you'd even shut the door. The lottery thing? It's just what people say when somebody makes the impossible happen instantly."

Ty pocketed his device, still red around the ears. He had done exactly what she asked, word for word.

Sloane stayed at her station, curiosity sparked now. She typed: Detailed map of the United States.

The map appeared instantly, sharp outlines and relief shading as if it had been waiting for her to ask. Sloane blinked once, then leaned closer.

Her fingers hovered again. She typed: Superimpose all database file-header cities on the map.

The screen refreshed with a dry, clinical click, like a slide locking into place.

She pressed enter.

In a blink, small points of light dotted the country. They weren't random—some were clustered, others strung in crooked lines, a few scattered wide.

"Everybody," Sloane called. "Over here. Big board."

They gathered at the workstation, and with a tap she transferred her screen to the wall display. The map filled the room, pins glowing against the outline of the states.

"First request was just a U.S. map," Sloane explained. "Second—overlay every city from our file headers. This is what came back."

Tara stepped closer, following the line of dots with her finger. Holt narrowed her eyes and began sketching the groupings into her notes. Ty crossed his arms, studying the distribution. Rachael wrote the time and request into her log.

No one spoke for a moment, each processing what they saw in their own lane. It wasn't drama. It was data.

As the search engine settled into place, the team began feeding it. Each case file was tagged electronically: robberies by date, murders by jurisdiction, medical by wound type.

Tara handled the witness statements, splitting them into two categories she labeled panic or precision. If testimony wavered, contradicted itself, or sounded like fear rewriting memory, it went under panic. When a witness repeated details with the same cadence across interviews, Tara tagged it precision. The distinction was crude, but it helped the system separate noise from signal.

Holt worked in parallel, cross-loading medical files. She flagged every diagram, ER note, and autopsy report that didn't look right when compared against crime scene photos or field notes. If a wound angle in a report didn't match the trajectory she'd measured, she logged it as discrepant. Those became their own folder, a silent catalog of details that might prove patterns later.

Sloane took the geographic data, methodically entering each incident by city, county, and GPS coordinate. She layered in time stamps and drew cross-links between robberies that landed too close in both date and location to be coincidence. Her shorthand read like a transit map of crime—nodes and connections, routes and collisions.

Rachael kept her chair slightly apart, reviewing every affidavit draft and evidence log before it was uploaded. Her initials became the gatekeeper's mark, ensuring nothing entered the system that couldn't survive a judge's scrutiny. If language was sloppy or scope too broad, she bounced it back across the table without apology.

Together, their work reshaped chaos into something navigable. The system pulsed brighter with each entry, files tightening into a structure that could be searched by day, week, year—or by a single word buried in a paragraph. It was the first time the task force felt like it was fighting with order instead of drowning in fragments.

As the evening wore on, Ty glanced at the clock and said what everyone had been avoiding. "We need to talk about something practical. Travel. Meals. Lodging. We can't expect people to keep paying out of pocket."

No one argued. Holt straightened her stacks. Sloane capped her pen. Rachael set her pad aside.

"I'll take it up with Marcus," Ty said. "He's the only real business mind in the building. If anyone can find a way to keep this afloat, it's him. We're finally getting traction—I don't want this to stall because of hotel receipts."

Later, in his office, Ty laid it out for Marcus. "We can't keep asking people to donate their time and money. Can you talk to your contacts? See if there's a way to cover us?"

Marcus listened, then nodded once. "I'll see what I can do."

He made the call that night. He explained the problem and the progress. His NSA contact put him on hold, came back a few minutes later, and said, "It's authorized. As of morning, this task force is designated as a pilot program under NSA oversight. Credentials, cards, reimbursement procedures—courier in the morning."

The next day, Marcus appeared at the war room door with a stack of sealed boxes, still warm from delivery. He set them on the table one by one.

"Ty made a persuasive case," he said simply. "I ran it past my friends at NSA. They moved fast. These are yours."

They opened them. Inside were NSA credentials with their names and photos, a packet of instructions, and a government-issued credit card.

"All costs for this pilot program are covered," Marcus said.

"Reimbursements go through the secure portal on your devices. If anyone presses you about what you're doing, there's a contact number in there. It routes to the President's Chief of Staff. That's your cover. Use it if you need to."

He paused at the door. "If you need anything else, let me know."

They sat with it for a moment. The room felt heavier. Official.

The long day bled into evening. Files were stacked, the search engine still glowing faintly across their screens, but the air had thinned into fatigue. One by one, the team pushed back from the table, murmured goodnights, and drifted out.

Rachael lingered at the refreshment counter, pouring the last of the coffee. Ty was already there, rubbing his eyes and reaching for bottled water.

"You probably don't remember," Rachael said lightly, "but like I said, I sat in on one of your CLE presentations a few years ago."

Ty blinked, then chuckled. "I do at least one a year. Which one was that?"

"Atlanta Bar Association," she said. "Technology in courtroom evidence. About three years back."

Recognition flickered. "That was a big turnout. You were there?"

"I was," she said. "I actually wanted to ask you something afterward, but I didn't get the chance."

Ty grinned, leaning back against the counter. "Too bad. I love real questions. Most of those rooms are full of lawyers who either don't want to be there or just want to show off. Which category would you have fallen into?"

Rachael raised an eyebrow. "You really want me to answer that?"

"No need," he said, giving a quick wink. "I've been watching how you work here. You'd be in the quality category."

The moment stretched just a little too long, both of them laughing softly against the hum of the servers. It felt different—less like relief, more like something that had been waiting its chance.

Over the next week, the small breaks became routine. They compared war stories from cases, traded dry humor only other attorneys would find funny. By Thursday, Rachael suggested coffee outside the building. By the weekend, it was dinner—her joking that the DA's office never picked up the check, him countering that his expense account made everything deductible.

The rhythm accelerated, the way it often does when people are locked in a pressurized space and decide not to waste time. Coffee turned into dinners, dinners into lingering goodbyes, and one night a kiss that didn't stop at the cheek.

When Rachael invited him over for a home-cooked meal the following week, Ty assumed it was just another evening to talk shop. Instead, they found themselves cooking side by side, bumping shoulders, laughing when flour dusted his shirt. By dessert, formality was gone.

By the time Ty carried her laughing into the bedroom, following her lead through hallways he'd never seen before, formality had been left at the door.

A soft chime rolled across the investigators' desks—Tara's, Sloane's, Holt's—monitors flashing in unison. In the upper-right corner of each screen, a small red icon pulsed: Alert: Incident flagged.

Sloane leaned in and read the line that scrolled across. "Robbery in progress. Service doors sealed. Panic calls from inside. Matches our profile."

Tara grabbed her jacket. “We’re not letting the locals fumble this one. We’re going.”

The task force moved as one. For the first time, they weren’t just sorting the past. They were running straight into the present.

Chapter Eighteen – The Threads Tighten

The SCIF had no mornings. It just allowed people in.

Tara keyed the system awake and watched the wall glass populate: case numbers, cities, short lines under HOW and WHAT. She wrapped a hand around coffee that had already gone bitter and waited for the screen to finish building.

Sloane came in behind her, jacket on the back of a chair, coffee in a white paper cup. "Start basic," she said, sliding into place. "Location, date, time. Then build out."

They put down the bones: City, Venue, Date, Time. Under that, Loot, Entry, Crew Size. The board widened in neat rectangles.

"Crew of one here," Sloane said, tapping a line.

"Witnesses swear twenty in this one," Tara answered, flicking to the next.

The jobs refused to behave. Loud smash-and-grabs sat next to quiet surgical pulls. Some over in minutes, others stretched into hours. Coins and bullion shared space with antique pistols, medals, estate silver, a carved idol, a family Bible. And then there was the clutter.

"Binder of baseball cards," Tara read.

Sloane snorted. "Sure. Walk out with a fortune and grab Little League on your way."

Another file scrolled up: Assorted costume jewelry, logged beneath an estate inventory.

“Like stealing a Mercedes and taking the fuzzy dice,” Sloane said.

The short laugh that followed did what laughter does—let the pressure drop half an inch—before the silence folded over them again.

Rachael sat off to one side with a secure terminal, red pen parked in the crease of a legal pad out of habit. She drew a line through a word in the affidavit on her screen, initialed the margin, saved, and moved to the next. No commentary. The neat initials were the commentary.

Each time a note was written, each affidavit draft tightened, each margin marked, the system demanded the same ritual. Rachael scanned the pages into the slot at her station; the scanner hummed, codes assigned themselves in the corner of the glass, and the files slipped into their correct case folders. The war room didn’t just collect evidence; it archived in real time. Even Tara’s shorthand on witness notes, Holt’s corrections on autopsies, or Sloane’s preservation requests—every scrap became part of the digital vault. A mistake couldn’t vanish; a decision couldn’t hide.

A case with a fatal hovered at the edge of the board. Tara touched it and turned her head. “Doc?”

Holt leaned forward, eyes on the autopsy photos. “Report lists three rounds to the torso,” she said, voice even. “Photos confirm four. Correction filed.” She scanned her notes, watched the confirmation code appear, and returned the case to its folder. Then she went quiet again.

They kept filling the board. The rectangles multiplied. The contradictions didn’t lessen.

“We’ve been at this for days,” Sloane said finally. “Every time we think of a new angle, we redraw the whole thing.”

Tara nodded. "We need to add factors one at a time and let the system do the sweep. Trucks. Uniforms. Service doors. Vendor lists. Each time we add one, it runs across the whole cache."

"Baseline's easy," Sloane said. "All these cases came out of the same hidden folder. From there we keep layering."

Ty had been listening from the edge, pen on a pad. "So you don't want to redraw charts," he said. "You want the system to remember your questions, and each time you add one, it polls the lot and shows overlaps."

"That's it," Tara said. "We don't care how. We just need to keep asking."

Ty wrote quickly, then read it back. "Baseline: cases in cache. Criteria added one by one. System sweeps everything each time. Results show matches."

"Perfect," Sloane said.

"I'll walk it to Marcus," Ty said. "He'll get it to Daniel."

He left. The door sealed behind him. The room returned to what it was—stillness and glass.

Tara and Sloane went back to the grind. They added Injuries, Property Damage, Security Footage Available. Holt stirred when a second autopsy file surfaced. "Trajectory listed as upward," she said. "Photos confirm downward, right to left. Correction entered." She placed the file into the right folder and sat back with her arms folded.

They kept at it until even the silence felt heavy. On Sloane's terminal, a line of text made her frown.

Ty wasn't back yet, but she was used to asking out loud. "This field—does that mean content?"

"Timestamp," Rachael said without looking up. "Access, not content."

"Good enough," Sloane said, relieved. "We can use that."

They were still building when the day finally ended, and the SCIF released them one by one into the hallway that sounded too loud every time.

The SCIF dissolved for Ty the second he stepped through Rachael's door that night. She was barefoot in the kitchen, hair loose, a glass of wine in her hand and the smell of garlic warm in the air. They cooked because it gave their hands something to do—chopping, stirring, moving around each other the way two people who are learning a new rhythm do. Flour dusted his shirt again. She laughed and brushed it off with her wrist, then left her hand there like she meant to wipe more than flour.

By the time they reached the bedroom, a trail of clothes marked the path like breadcrumbs: his jacket, her blouse over a chair, his tie abandoned halfway down the hall. They fell into the sheets laughing, breathless and talkative until they weren't.

Later, when the room had settled and the only sound was their breathing, she found his hand under the sheet and laced her fingers through. "Good thing there aren't neighbors," she murmured into his shoulder.

"Even if there were," he said, "we'd tell them it was about freedom of expression."

She laughed again, quieter, and the laugh carried them until sleep did.

In the small hours, she stirred once and saw him watching her with the faintest smile, like he wasn't quite used to the idea of waking up next to someone again. Neither said anything. That silence, softer than the SCIF's, was its own fragile truth.

Before dawn he slipped out, jacket over his arm, soft steps on familiar floorboards. It had been the same all week: long days in the SCIF, longer nights in her rooms. He told himself they'd slow down. He didn't believe himself.

The next morning the SCIF acted like it had never met them. That was how it worked. Tara keyed the board back up and added Vehicles Noted and Uniform Mentions. Sloane pulled interviews into a panel and skimmed.

"Vendor swore he saw Reverend Drayton at Charlotte," she said, eyes on the screen. "Said he looked like he was soaking it in."

Tara glanced over. "His alibi?"

"Children's hospital that afternoon, cameras everywhere." Sloane layered a second file—Birmingham. "Another vendor: 'saw him, tall, smiling, walking slow.'"

"Locked down again?"

"Live sermon. Broadcast."

A third note out of Atlanta matched the first two. A fourth from a smaller show echoed the same. Handsome man. Big presence. Enjoying the room.

"People see what they expect," Tara said. "Note it, move on."

Sloane logged it under a small heading—WITNESS: RED HERRING (NOT ACTIONABLE)—and pushed the panel aside.

They went back to the chart. It was better now—more columns tugging at the chaos—but it still refused to be generous. The new criteria Ty had carried to Marcus hadn't arrived yet; they were still feeding the glass the old way.

Midday, the door sealed and Ty came in, setting his notes on the table. "Marcus has the request," he said. "I wrote it in plain English. You add a factor, the system remembers. Each time you add one, it polls everything and returns matches with case numbers and timestamps."

"How long?" Sloane asked.

"He didn't give a clock," Ty said. "Just said it would be handled."

Tara turned back to the board. "We don't wait," she said. "Add Service Doors (Off-Hours)."

Sloane logged the column. A handful of dots appeared—doors popped before public hours. "We've got something," she said. "Not a lot, but something."

"Add Vendor Roster vs. Payroll," Tara said. "Names in one list and not the other."

Two more dots lit up—"maintenance" entries with no paperwork to match.

"Add Truck Linger (Lot)," Tara said. "Anything that showed up too early and didn't move."

Three dots. None of it spectacular. All of it just enough to keep going.

They worked until their necks hurt. Holt corrected two more autopsies—a miscounted wound path here, an amended time-of-death estimate there—and returned to silence. Rachael finished a preservation letter and dropped it in the queue. Ty took notes for a second message to Marcus: "door cycles indexed," "truck linger time," "vendor roster cross-check," nothing more.

At the end of the day, the SCIF let them go again. And again the night was theirs.

A bath this time, steam curling the bathroom mirror. Ty sank back and Rachael rested between his legs, her hair damp against his chest. "This is the first time I've stopped moving all week," he said.

"That's because I'm smarter than you," she said, reaching up to trace a wet line down his forearm. "And because there isn't a neighbor for half a mile."

He laughed, kissed her shoulder, and let the idea of morning stay outside the door.

By the third day the request reached the glass like a whisper—no announcement, no fanfare, just a small button on the wall: ADD CRITERION.

Sloane didn't smile; it wasn't in her to thank software. "Start simple," she said, and typed truck linger with a pointer to logs and parking records. The board didn't hum or blink. It just came back with a thin line of dots.

"Two in state," Tara said. "One out."

“Next,” Sloane said. Coveralls / maintenance into interviews and notes. Five hits, none in the same city. “Service doors before hours.” Four more.

“Vendor names not on payroll,” Tara said. Two names. No paperwork. “Temp staff,” a manager had written. No one could produce the contract.

It wasn’t a miracle. It was work that felt like progress.

Rachael slid a cleaned-up preservation letter to Sloane’s terminal: widen video windows—morning-of, day-before, vendor build-in days—so the angles they had never asked for could be asked for now. Sloane sent it because the only other option was to wish for luck, and that had not worked yet.

Holt looked up when Tara pinned another fatality. “Autopsy lists two rounds,” she said. “Photos show three. Correction logged.” She filed it and went still again.

They added Door Cycles (Off-Hours) and got three more dots. Then Staff Re-interview Flag keyed to the words janitor, cart, bin, truck. The system marked a handful of interviews where people remembered ghosts on the floor—men in coveralls pushing empty bins in lazy circles, doors propped open for no reason, a panel truck parked early and still parked when the show ended.

“Not casing,” Sloane said. “Rehearsal.”

“Put ‘Dry Run Indicators’ on the board,” Tara said.

The room gave them what they asked for. It did not give them a face.

On the fourth day—the one where the coffee tasted like the inside of the pot and Ty had left his tie at Rachael's apartment without noticing—Sloane planted both hands on the table and let out a breath that had more bite than humor. "Maybe the only thing in common is that they don't have anything in common."

The silence let the sentence settle.

"That's it," Tara said slowly. "That's the pattern."

Sloane kept her eyes on the glass. "No two robberies look alike because someone made sure they didn't. Loud here, quiet there. One thief here, twenty there. Different loot, different methods. On purpose."

"And if you're hiding under noise," Tara said, tapping the board with her pen, "you don't improvise. You plan. You stage trucks hours ahead. You put men in coveralls and roll bins through service doors like you belong there. You run dry runs. You drill roles so no one freelances."

"Meticulous," Sloane said. "Trained."

They didn't congratulate themselves. They wrote a new list on the wall—REWIND VIDEO (morning-of, day-before), VENDOR ROSTERS vs. PAYROLL, TRUCK LINGER, COVERALLS / BINS, DOOR CYCLES, DRY RUN INDICATORS—and left it there, a recipe they could hand to anyone who walked in after them.

The day ended the way the others had. Ty left the SCIF with the rest, went the long way down the hall, and an hour later stood at Rachael's door with a bottle of wine he hadn't meant to buy. They cooked again because it was habit already, flour finding its way to places flour shouldn't go. Their clothes made a trail again, laughter turning into something hungrier again.

In the dark afterward, with her cheek on his shoulder and his arm hooked around her waist under the sheet, he thought about the word the wall had given them and how it applied to everything in the room: threads.

By morning he was gone before the first light had figured out the blinds. In the SCIF a few hours later, he passed behind her chair and their hands brushed for half a second. No one noticed. No one was supposed to.

The glass took their orders the way it always did. It gave them dots when they deserved them and nothing when they didn't. Holt corrected one last autopsy, trimming emotion from a county report with a single sentence. Rachael stripped adjectives from another affidavit that didn't need them. Marcus existed the way anchors do—out of sight, still holding. The televangelist remained a line in a log the system would remember and the investigators would not chase.

"Run the new door-cycle field across every case," Sloane said into the quiet.

Tara did, and the board added a few more thin lights to the work they'd pinned down. It wasn't enough to call anyone. It was enough to come back tomorrow.

They powered the glass down. The door unsealed with its soft mechanical hush. Outside, the building sounded like the world again. Inside, the word that named their work finally belonged to both halves of the day: the case, and the people solving it.

The threads were tighter. That was enough for now.

Chapter Nineteen – Auto Pilots

Glass broke in a low line, contained and careful, like someone opening a seam. The sound didn't travel far. Traffic a few blocks away carried louder stories.

The systems man went first. He didn't announce himself. He did the thing he'd been assigned to do—quiet the room—and gave a brief hand signal that meant other people could begin theirs.

Two lookouts held the edges of the lot the way ordinary workers hold late hours—backs to the fence, posture easy, shadows that could wave to a passing cruiser and look like they belonged there. They weren't there to be convincing. They were there to be unremarkable.

Inside, the loaders fanned across the pads under the white showroom lights. They didn't talk. They moved to the vehicles they'd rehearsed, eased them out of their display squares, rolled them in a slow glide to the bay. Doors shut without slams. A row of engines whispered alive and waited like animals that had been trained to heel.

At the rear, the drivers had already positioned the carriers. They breathed in time with the backup beeps—short, infrequent, the way experienced people turn noise into a kind of punctuation. Ramps came down. Straps found their buckles. Tarps fell clean. Each piece had a place and a second for it; no seconds were wasted.

Cameras along the side stayed blind, their lenses caught in a sprayed fog that made them stare at nothing. Where the fog didn't reach, a small light went steady instead of blinking. The systems man had walked that map days before and wrote time in his head. Tonight, he kept to it.

The rhythm held: pad to bay, bay to carrier, carrier easing off the line. No shouting, no hurry on the surface. It was hurry underneath, but the kind that was practiced—the kind that hides in a steady hand.

Before the hour had grown big enough to bother anyone awake, the showroom had lost enough steel to buy a building. What it gained was light; where cars had stood there was now a glare that made the floor look unfamiliar. A pedestal in the front office stood hollow. A frame on the wall hung skewed. Those were details for morning. Tonight, the work was the work.

The lookouts took a last pass with their eyes and became regular people again—a man crossing the street for a coffee, a woman checking her phone as if waiting for an Uber. The carriers made their simple turns at simple corners and were gone, one by one, into a city that was full of trucks doing ordinary jobs.

They left an absence behind them that was worth counting.

Morning did the counting. Staff walked in on light that threw the emptiness into relief. Where Ferraris had thrown red onto the glass there were polished squares. Where the Lamborghini nose had filled a frame there was just its outline in clean tile. The manager's first sound wasn't a word. He made it small, then made it loud, then looked for a pen and missed the page twice.

Twenty vehicles. Ten to twenty million dollars. Keys missing where keys used to be. Camera footage that stopped at a number someone could read aloud but couldn't explain. A velvet-lined stand sat bare at the end of an office shelf. A set of framed stamps that showed old exotics on tiny paper was only frames now. None of it was louder than the VIN lists—pages turning with lines circled and void where they had been concrete.

The first squad car rolled in and made blue shapes on the building. Tape went up because tape always does. Reports began because they have to. People said what they thought they remembered and handed over clipboards like excuses.

Local news framed the glass with their own rectangle and put a number under it that made good television. Organized crew steals fleet of exotics, loss up to $20 million. It was the kind of headline people click before a meeting.

The SCIF flagged it at noon.

ALERT — Miami, Florida. Prestige Imports. Organized theft. Estimated loss: $10–$20M in exotic vehicles.

The red header blinked small, then pulsed priority. It didn't offer a theory. It wasn't built for that. It shoved the event across a line and waited.

Tara read it once and the shape that came into her head was not a plan. It was just scale. She pressed her thumb against the console and let the map draw itself toward Miami.

Sloane skimmed the line and her mouth went a little flat. "That number doesn't happen by accident." She didn't add anything to it; there wasn't anything to add.

Ty leaned from his terminal. "Value flag only. No metadata yet. Locals are still counting." The light on his screen made his eyes look tired.

He straightened, jacket already on, and moved toward the door without touching the screen. He was carrying policy, not reaction—the standing rule Marcus had set before any of them ever sat at this table.

"You're the right kind of eyes," Ty said, almost conversational. "Same posture as always. Maybe you can offer help; don't take command. See it clearly and send it home."

Tara zipped her bag. "We go." She didn't say why; the number said it for her.

Miami pressed against them in a wet heat even after the sun had dipped. Cranes along the waterline looked like a row of patient animals. The rental car smelled like plastic and someone else's cologne. The hotel in Doral took them in without being interested. That was what they wanted.

Sloane tuned the police band on her handheld and waited for the chatter to pick up. It did: units at the tape, manager requesting additional inventory assistance, night security requesting to make a clarifying statement that would come out wrong the first time.

"Still active," she said.

Tara pulled the sedan into the stream and watched the neon make glass into mirrors. "We look," she said. "We mark. We don't touch."

"Free labor," Sloane said, the way someone repeats a rule for the sake of not breaking it.

Prestige Imports under floodlights looked like a showroom and a stage at the same time. The Xs on the glass were first-day-of-a-storm Xs. The light inside created absence the way a good photograph does—by showing you too much of what isn't there.

A Miami-Dade sergeant kept a clipboard between himself and everything else. He took in the badges in one look and didn't move them closer. "You two are…?"

"Part of a Government Multi-Agency Task force," Tara said, hands visible. "We were in the area, caught it on the band. If you need extra eyes, we can help outside your tape. If you don't, we're gone."

"We're not here to run your scene," Sloane added. "Just to do the boring parts if you want some free help."

The sergeant's jaw worked around the words he wanted to keep and the ones he wanted to send. He compromised. "Perimeter. Nothing inside unless I tell you. No pictures unless your phones are the kind that file things the way lawyers don't hate."

"Ours are those phones," Sloane said. "We push straight home."

He nodded once. It was the slow acceptance of a man who has fewer hands than he has jobs. "Then be boring in the places I can stand it."

They were. Tara marked cameras with her secure device—front domes intact, three on the side blinded with a paint that had dried into a chalky sunburst, a DVR cabinet at the rear eave hanging loose on one side. Each tag blinked, timestamped, and sent itself up the line where it would be paired against models and manuals without anyone having to carry a thing.

At the rear bay, the metal frame had a rub mark where paint had given up and a smear of oil that looked new. Tara didn't bend for a closer look. She didn't need to. She tapped her phone and typed two words—fresh oil—and let the SCIF decide if that mattered later.

Sloane talked quietly to the manager within earshot of a uniform. "Twenty cars?" she asked. The manager's mouth moved like someone learning to say something he would have to repeat many times. He handed over initial lists that were more blank than not, names of models and colors that felt like words for a language no one had time to speak.

“Alarms?” Sloane asked.

“Didn’t go,” he said. “Footage stops at… two forty-something. I can get you the numbers.”

“Log it,” Sloane said, tapping her device. She wrote: footage stale 02:43 (manager claims), bay open. She added: maintenance roster reviewed—two names unrecognized by payroll. She didn’t write what she thought of that. This wasn’t the room for thinking.

A uniform pointed to the office case that had been cleared. The velvet pad in the pedestal was the color of the sky before lightning; it had no burden now. Frames hung slightly askew where something had been pulled off hooks.

“Logged,” Tara said, and tapped her phone. She didn’t linger. The weight of the morning was not in velvet or paper. It was in the clean squares of floor and the lists of cars.

Across the street, a condo line looked down like bleachers. One balcony had a faded plastic chair and, tucked behind it, the neat black eye of a consumer camera facing the lot. Tara saw it because she trains herself to see that kind of thing. She tagged the GPS point and typed, possible alt cam. The SCIF would send a polite letter later.

They made a slow circle of the block, noting city traffic cameras at a corner pole and a gas station canopy cam half a block away. They didn’t ask for footage now. They logged what they could ask for later, when a chain of paperwork could be compelled and a system could stack it against other nights.

They didn’t talk about trucks. They didn’t talk about containers. They marked what was in front of them and passed it home.

The sergeant came back to them with an exhausted face and a question that wasn't hostility so much as fear that the paperwork would multiply. "You got enough?" he said.

"For tonight," Sloane said. "We'll send formal requests for DVR pulls first thing: day-of and a window before. We'll flag traffic cams in a radius. No promises. We know the rhythm."

"That makes two of us," he said. He looked grateful in the way people do when they finally allow themselves to.

They gave him their cards and the ways to say no to people who didn't have a right to ask. He nodded again in that slow lawman way that acknowledges the lie about control that everyone in a uniform has to live with.

They didn't celebrate in the hotel room. They didn't analyze either. They did the thing they were supposed to do: sync devices, verify tags, send up requests with simple language and no demand, only the quiet audacity of professional persistence.

Tara sat with her back against the headboard and scrolled through the list. CAMERA—FRONT; CAMERA—SIDE BLIND; DVR—REAR; BAY—FRAME RUB; OIL—FRESH; MANAGER CLAIM—FOOTAGE STOPS 02:43; ROSTER—TWO NAMES UNVERIFIED; ALT CAM—CONDO; TRAFFIC CAM—POLE (NE CORNER); GAS CAM—CANOPY.

Thirty-six entries pulsed in green as they reached the server. None of them said anything yet. That wasn't their job. Their job was to become part of a conversation the system could hold with the rest of the world when it was asked the right way.

Sloane built the preservation letters they'd need for the morning—DVR, city cameras, the condo's polite request, gas station canopy, any privately owned cams within a reasonable map. She wrote them in the same purposeful language she would want to be spoken to with. She left the fields for times blank until the manager could confirm numbers.

"We'll get the inventory lists tomorrow," she said. "VINs, models. Confirm the number, not what the news says."

Tara nodded and let her eyes close for exactly four breaths before she opened them to catch the last blink of a data packet going uplink in the corner of the screen.

"All we have is a hole," she said.

"For now," Sloane said. "We count the edges and see if they match another hole we've got."

Tara didn't smile. She threw the spare blanket over the end of the bed like a flag and watched it drape. "We go back at eight," she said. "I want the DVR cabinet photographed by their people. We ask for a copy when it's boxed."

"We keep asking," Sloane said, not like a question and not like a promise. "We keep asking."

Outside, the city's impatience made light skip on the hotel window. In the SCIF, the case number found its box in the grid and sat waiting for company—other entries that would give it shape, or not. They had been handed a number and a kind of emptiness. That was all they wanted. They had learned to be patient with emptiness.

They turned off the lights without leaving the room. That was the trick of the work: you make a dark that still contains you and then you wait until the next thing you can do is ready.

Morning would bring inventory, and calls, and someone's face that looked like they hadn't slept yet. They would walk the perimeter again and mark calmer, write more polite words that meant we're not going to stop. If there was a pattern hiding in the ordinary, it would declare itself in pieces the way real things do. If there wasn't, they would put this box next to the other boxes and watch it until it moved.

For now, $10–$20 million worth of cars had gone somewhere in the quiet, and the only honest thing to say in the face of it was the oldest thing the job knew: we'll see.

Chapter Twenty– Bread Crumbs

They started with what they already had: a binder.

The dealership's inventory manifest sat in the middle of the SCIF table like a ledger someone had dropped and dared them to balance. VINs, models, trim codes, colors, locations on the floor. A second stack—key vault logs—listed fob withdrawals by time and user. There were photocopies of insurance riders, a neat list of consignments, and the kind of notations managers leave for themselves in the margins when they think no one else will ever read them.

Tara turned a few pages with two fingers, not for the sake of discovery but to feel the weight of it. "Everything's here," she said. "They live on paper. This is their heartbeat."

Sloane stood at the end of the table with her laptop open and a soft beep coming off the secure line. Preservation letters had gone out the night before; the subpoenas were the next step. She walked through the checklist in the plain voice of someone asking a clerk for a form. "DVR serials, camera IDs, time window. Traffic cams within the half-mile grid. The causeway poles. Yard cameras at the port entrance. We keep it narrow."

Rachael sat beside her with a yellow legal pad and a cup of coffee she kept forgetting to drink. She crossed out adjectives and tightened verbs. "No 'likely,'" she said. "No 'appears.' You put that in front of a judge and they'll hand it back for wasting their time."

She penciled in the numbers and circled the identifiers: DVR: 11874; CAM: 12–17; TIME: 01:30–06:00; PORT ENTRY: Gate C, Lane 4. A second packet requested city traffic-camera pulls for the same window, plus a gas station canopy three blocks over. She trimmed a line that had grown into "all logs that may indicate operator action" down to "system logs indicating operator access or maintenance activity."

Tara leaned on the edge of the table. "We also want poles along the feeder road to the causeway. If anything rolled out after three a.m., it had to touch that artery. Give us those cameras for the same window."

"Add it," Rachael said. She didn't look up.

Sloane tapped the secure line and spoke into the headset. "Keene? Packet inbound. Prestige Imports theft, twenty vehicles. DVR cutoffs at approximately 02:43. We're requesting DVR exports, traffic cam pulls, and port-yard entrance feeds for 01:30–06:00. Also requesting preservation of yard manifests for the same window."

Keene's voice came back flat and even, the sound of paper turning. "Send me a one-pager and attachments. Facts only. I'll submit."

"Yes, sir."

Sloane listened to the last of the call, arms folded. When the line went dead, she stepped forward, nodding toward the list on the wall—CAMERA / DVR / PORT ENTRY / TRAFFIC POLES.

"If we need imagery," she said, "I can request archived satellite tiles from our federal partners. It won't be miracles. Just whatever's already been collected over that sector. Keep your expectations modest."

Her tone stayed practical, procedural. Every word stayed inside her lane.

"We'll ask if we have to," Sloane said. "Paper first."

The packet went north electronically; a courier took the paper for the clerk. The magistrate never left chambers when he signed, if he signed. He would look for precision and probable cause, the two things a room like theirs could provide when it remembered to be humble.

The answer came back in a thick envelope eight hours later. The clerk set it on the table without ceremony. APPROVED stamped the top sheet in the judge's neat square hand.

"Good," Rachael said, scanning the margin. The judge had added exactly one note: Scope reasonable. Custodians to comply within ten business days. She hit the corner of the packet with two firm taps and slid it aside. "Now we wait for the returns."

They didn't wait by staring at the wall. They waited by working the edges. Tara built a quiet grid on the glass: the dealership at the center, the causeway arcing east, the port entrance labeled with thin text, the gas station and condo windows that pointed toward the lot. She marked each camera as a dot—CAM 12, CAM 13, POLE NE-1, POLE E-2—and colored them when responses arrived.

The first DVR export said things they already knew: recording until 02:43, a system log noting "maintenance," then nothing until daylight. The office camera showed a security guard rubbing his eyes at 01:51. The bay camera's last useful frame—02:39:52—was an empty rectangle of concrete reflecting the inside light.

The traffic poles came in next—lower quality, higher utility. Night makes city light into noise. Trucks become smears if the exposure is wrong. They ran the feeds anyway. The system didn't make promises; it simply combed pixels for anything that fit the size and shape of what they might care about.

It was a smear that broke the monotony. A single frame at 03:12:41 from a pole three blocks west of the port entrance—rain dots on the lens, a heavy vehicle framed on a diagonal, the back half of a license plate half-obscured by a bracket and grime. Tara froze it and rolled back three seconds. Sloane muted the audio and watched the smear become a shape. Rachael squinted and found three digits and the twist of a county sticker. It wasn't enough to write down with confidence, but it was enough to ask for more.

At 03:14:09, another pole—north of their first—caught the same vehicle from the other side. The light swelled as the truck rolled under the lamp. The plate flashed cleaner. The system took the two frames, averaged what was true between them, and offered up a guess that didn't feel like a guess anymore. Numbers and letters made a partial complete.

"Run it," Sloane said.

Tara drafted the addendum, and Rachael stapled it behind the existing order. The request went back through Keene. He signed without commentary. In the evening, the response returned from the state registry: commercial account. Beneath the company name line, their grid filled in with the kind of simplicity you only get when you stop trying to be clever.

Registered owner: The Southern Sacred Order, Inc. (SSO).

No shell. No PO box. A street address.

It wasn't criminal to own land—what mattered was how often land like this appeared near places that bled quietly.

"Occam's razor," Tara murmured into the quiet, and tapped the address with a fingernail.

Property records put the address into a rural parcel in Georgia: a farm deeded outright to SSO. The deed wasn't fresh. It had been theirs for years.

They didn't talk for a long thirty seconds. The SCIF hummed the way rooms do when they're waiting for people to catch up to the obvious.

Sloane clicked open her browser and typed the name into a search box. The public site loaded with a glossy photo of men in shirtsleeves walking through green rows. Welcome to the Southern Sacred Order Farm — a place where the faithful may gather to be one with the Lord. Beneath it, the verse in a serif font: Hosea 10:12 — Sow for yourselves righteousness; reap steadfast love; break up your fallow ground, for it is the time to seek the Lord, that he may come and rain righteousness upon you.

"That's not rumor," she said. "That's theirs. Their name, their words."

Tara thought about the vendor statements from other robberies—the ones who had sworn they'd seen the televangelist strolling aisles, smiling at nothing in particular. "And witnesses put him in rooms we care about."

Rachael flipped the deed page to the signature block and set her pencil tip on the ink. "Names on land aren't proof of a crime," she said. "But they're proof of ownership. That's enough to watch."

They didn't push past that. The work didn't reward people for racing ahead of what the facts could carry.

"Now what?" Sloane asked, not because she didn't already know the answer, but because she wanted to hear them say it.

"Eyes," Tara said. "Quiet ones. We don't serve papers to prayer meetings. We watch from the trees."

“Then we’ll need imagery,” Sloane said. “And we’ll need to earn it.”

Keene took the call when she made it. The ask was clean: archival satellite tiles for the farm parcel for the last two weeks, if they existed; any civil flight imagery archived by federal partners for the same window; preservation of any gate logs tied to the driveway off County Route 17. Keene didn’t offer warmth. He didn’t offer resistance either. “Send the parcel number, lat/long, and date window,” he said. “I’ll route the request. Don’t ask for tasking. Ask for what exists.”

Sloane placed one quiet call after she hung up—no names, just a favor to make sure the request floated above the pile instead of under it. She didn’t tell anyone he did it. She didn’t have to.

The imagery came back as it does when you’re lucky: a series of tiles with timestamps burnt into the corners. Afternoon passes showed nothing but the geometry of a farm—silos, sheds, a long structure with a metal roof, a lane that bent into trees. Two night tiles—grainier, but readable—gave them more. On a Tuesday at 02:19, a flatbed sat in a clearing, tight under a tarp that made a clean rectangle in the infrared spectrum. On a Friday at 03:01, two vehicles with boxy outlines idled near a shed. The images didn’t scream crime. They whispered activity when the rest of the county slept.

They compared those timestamps against the dealership’s DVR cutoff and the traffic pole times. They didn’t match perfectly. They never do. But the windows overlapped in a way that tested as more than coincidence. They added the tiles to the file and climbed over the urge to name what they wanted the pictures to be.

The phone on the far side of the table lit up with a call from the Miami sergeant. He sounded more tired than yesterday. "We pulled your plate request through our DMV channel," he said. "It matches what you've got: your nonprofit owns the rig. Your time window at the port shows nothing recorded for that entry. That's a hole where a record should be." He made a noise that wasn't quite anger. "You get us a broader order, we'll pull two weeks of gate logs and see if that plate came through under another label."

"Send the request language to my email," Sloane said. "We'll route it through our channel."

She ended the call and turned to the wall map. The grid now had two anchors: Miami at the bottom edge and Farm Parcel—SSO in Georgia planted mid-state under a belt of green.

"We're not serving papers," Tara said again, more to remind herself than the room. "We're not taking anything. We're looking."

"How do you want to do it?" Sloan asked.

"Long lenses. Good cover. Two cars. No lights. Distant ridges if there are any. If that fails, we use the road and we keep moving."

Sloane wrote the word surveillance on the board and underlined it once. "We'll need a legal umbrella," she said, turning to Rachael. "We're not searching. We're observing from public land. Keep the memo clean."

Rachael nodded and drew up a short paragraph that said exactly what it had to say: observation from public vantage points requires no warrant; recording what is visible to the naked eye from those points is permissible; no expectation of privacy attaches to what can be seen from public roads. She attached case citations and tucked the memo into the folder under a tab marked Field Protocol.

Ty formatted the imagery packet and the plate returns into a bundle the other clothes-hangers in the federal closet would actually be able to hang on. He didn't interpret. He made sure the data could be read. He made life easier for people they depended on without exposing them.

Keene forwarded a short email that said everything it needed to and nothing extra: Imagery queued. Additional port logs pending. Continue.

It was enough.

They built a short list on the whiteboard that anyone could stand in front of and understand in the space of a breath:

- SCIF: ingest tiles, traffic-cam returns, port logs; match timestamps
- FIELD: recon drive (public road only); mark entry points, structures
- LEGAL: draft / file additional preservation requests (gate logs, yard cams); memo re: observation from public land
- LIAISON: imagery pull—archival only; no tasking
- NEXT: set eyes on site at first light, no contact

Tara took a road map from the slot by the door and traced the county. There were two feeder roads that didn't have names on the map, just numbers. One sat west of the parcel and ran a ridge line; the other dipped through low ground and would be a river when the sky decided it. She circled a turnout that looked like it had room for one car and a ridge of brush to tuck behind.

"Tomorrow," she said.

Sloane capped the marker and slid the lid back on the pen like she was sheathing a knife. "Tomorrow."

They closed the binder and left the SCIF with the room still humming—machines doing what machines do, lawyers' words fixed into requests that would either produce or not. The thing that mattered hadn't changed. The number that made Miami a problem had found its echo in a quiet dot on a rural map with a name the whole country would recognize if someone said it out loud. The simplest line between those two points wasn't proof. It was opportunity.

The room had a rule about opportunity: don't talk it to death; put eyes on it.

They turned the lights down and let the glass go back to a dim, neutral glow. Upstairs, the building felt like any other office after dark. Outside, the street was ordinary. Somewhere in Georgia, a patch of pine trees held a driveway with ruts in it and a sign on a post with a name that had never meant what it said.

They would go look at it in the morning—not to confront it, but to see what it did when it believed no one was watching.

Chapter Twenty One — Right Place, Wrong Time

The road shed its paint and shoulders as it left the last subdivision. Pines closed in until the sky narrowed to a strip of white, the asphalt breathing heat in small mirages. Tara drove with two fingers on the wheel and the other hand resting where a pen would go if she were taking notes. Sloane sat beside her, credentials in her inner pocket, eyes moving the way they always did when she was counting what a place could see and what it couldn't.

They had rehearsed the lines twice between exits. Now they let them settle.

"Blue Ridge is our bridge," Sloane said at last, voice low. "Female government agency employees in law enforcement, retreat finished an hour ago, we were carpooling back. I got the call and asked you to ride with me to talk to a possible witness. We keep it calm, we keep it brief."

Tara nodded. "We're not hunting a confession. We're looking for the driver."

They found the turnoff by a handmade sign half-swallowed by wax myrtle: The Southern Sacred Order Farm. The posts leaned a little, but the paint was fresh. Beneath the name, someone had stenciled a verse in patient, black letters:

Hosea 10:12 — Sow for yourselves righteousness; reap steadfast love; break up your fallow ground, for it is the time to seek the Lord.

"Not shy," Tara said.

Sloane didn't answer. She was already mapping the place: rows of pines hiding the first curve, a long gravel lane that would keep tires loud, a bend before the clearing that would block any straight view out to the county road.

The lane opened on fields and sheds picked out by the noon sun. A corrugated warehouse anchored the yard. Three white straight-trucks sat nosed under a lean-to, their sides painted with green lettering: SSO Produce Division. A fourth, smaller box truck idled with its hood up. The air carried diesel, cut grass, and something metallic from the shop.

Two men in work shirts stood at the loading dock, one with a rag in his hand, the other half-perched on a pallet jack. Both looked up when the sedan rolled in.

Tara pulled to a stop where the lane widened, killed the engine, and stepped out. Sloane joined her, credentials already in her hand.

"Afternoon," Sloane called, steady and clear enough to carry without sounding like a challenge. She held her wallet open. "Special Agent Sloane Carver, FBI — Atlanta Field Office. This is Tara Whitaker, on assignment with the National Security Agency.

We'd been carpooling back from a retreat in the Blue Ridge for female government agency employees in law enforcement when I got a call to interview a potential witness in a criminal matter down in Florida. A witness mentioned seeing one of your produce trucks making deliveries that morning, and we'd like to speak with the driver."

Tara added, conversational and unhurried, "Sometimes drivers notice things without realizing they matter — unusual cars, men loitering, someone following them. We just want to know if one of your drivers saw anything out of the ordinary that morning."

The man with the rag squinted, wiped his hands, and didn't move off the dock. "We haul produce," he said.

"Understood," Sloane said. The words were neutral. "We're not suggesting anything else. We're simply trying to pin down routes and times. If one of your drivers was out that morning, they may have seen something that helps."

The second man shifted off the pallet jack and came to stand beside the first. "Who said they saw us?" His tone wasn't hostile, just flat.

"Can't disclose that," Sloane replied, the line clean from use. "We're trying to be thorough while details are fresh."

The rag man looked toward the shed. "We've got four rigs. They go south regular. Which one do you think you saw?"

"Plate was partial," Sloane admitted. "Could have been yours, could have been another with similar paint. That's why we're here." She kept her chin angled so the sun glinted off her badge exactly once, then no more. "If someone could point us to the driver logs for that morning, we could save you time — we're only looking for a route and a name."

The second man shook his head. "Paperwork's in the office. Reverend runs that."

"Reverend?" Tara asked, using their word and not the one she'd heard in every statement she'd logged.

"Brother Zeke," the man said, like the name explained the place, the trucks, the verse on the sign. "He'll know if you want to poke around files."

"Is he here?" Sloane asked.

The answer was the only one it could be. "Travels," the rag man said. "Does sermons. Doesn't keep regular hours here."

There was a small pause — not confrontational, just waiting to see if the women would push.

Tara took a plain card from her pocket and set it on the dock rail, a gesture without demand. "If someone can call us when the logs are handy, we'd appreciate it. Driver doesn't need to go through anyone else." She tapped the card with a fingernail. "You can reach us direct."

Neither man reached for it. That was fine. They weren't here for a handover. They were here to look.

Sloane's eyes slid past them to the trucks under the lean-to. Two men stood near the front bumper of the center truck, heads tilted together in quiet talk. The nearer one turned at something the other said and looked across the yard.

For a heartbeat, distance misbehaved.

The face in the shadow was familiar enough to tug at memory like a fish line — the square jaw, the careful hair combed back from the forehead, the way the mouth held still when the eyes moved. Every witness line Tara had logged in the last months came up like subtitles:

Looked just like him.

Smiling. Taking it in.

I swear it was him.

Tara kept her body turned toward the dock and spoke without moving her lips. “Tell me you’re seeing that.”

Sloane didn’t tip her head. “I see him.” Her tone stayed where anyone watching would hear only small talk. “Don’t look again.”

“I’m not,” Tara said through her teeth. She had already looked again, but only in the mirror of the rag man’s sunglasses — a quick field trick that kept your eyes where they were while you stole an angle. The man by the trucks had already turned away, climbing into shadow. The second followed, all motion and no words.

Tara picked up the card and set it back down so it made a small sound on the rail. “We’ll wait for the call,” she said to the dock. “Thank you.”

Back in the car, they shut the doors like ordinary people and let the sound of them closing cover a small exhale neither had meant to make. Tara started the engine. Gravel popped under the tires.

“You think it’s him?” she asked under the engine’s idle.

“No,” Sloane said. “I think it’s close enough to make me believe the witnesses were looking at the right ghost.” She typed a note into her phone with one thumb, nothing eloquent: lookalike by trucks; jaw/hairline; cadence of glance; not approached.

Tara eased them down the lane. She didn’t hurry and she didn’t crawl. At the bend, the lane lifted them just high enough to see the side yard. A small security camera sat on the eave of the office porch, half the lens fogged by a spider’s web. Tara tapped a fingertip against her thigh once. Sloane marked it without looking: porch cam, south.

The county road felt wider than when they had turned in. They didn’t speak for three miles.

“Stonewall,” Tara said finally.

“Expected,” Sloane said. “But now we’ve got pins to pull.” She clicked the note closed. “Here’s what we need without being greedy: any county traffic cams on this stretch. Convenience store canopy down at the T, if they’ve got one. The feed on the porch. And archived satellite tiles for the last week, two-to-five in the morning.”

“Keene will want the one-pager first,” Tara said.

“He’ll get it with identifiers and nothing soft. Rachael can scrub it on the way.” Sloane scrolled. “I’ll ask for preservation on anything county-owned before I ask for production. That buys us time if someone decides to clean a drive.”

“Good,” Tara said. “And we drive the grid while we can.” She turned right at the next crossroads and let the road tell her where it would hold a car and where it would hide one. Long, straight stretches with no shoulder. Low spots where fog would settle before dawn. A cut where an old farm lane dog-legged into woods and then disappeared.

They didn’t stop. They never stopped their first time through any place, not for a mailbox photo or a friendly talk. They drove like two women coming back from a conference, which was, after all, part of the truth.

At a crossroads five miles out, the county had put up one of those new four-way poles with a camera the size of a fist on top. It wasn’t much. It only looked one way. But if a truck rolled through heading to the main highway before sunrise, the camera might have caught a plate or at least a profile. Sloane pinned it and typed the pole number off the placard for the preservation letter later.

“Fuel along here?” Tara asked.

“Two options within ten miles,” Sloane said. “A co-op pump with cards only and a Lucky Star with a clerk and coffee that tastes like burnt toast.” She dragged a finger on the map and left a note beside the star. “If any driver swiped a fuel card the morning after, it will live for a while on a ledger we can subpoena. If they paid cash, the clerk might still remember who paid with a roll of tens at five a.m.”

Tara glanced at the clock. “Not today.”

“Not today,” Sloane agreed. She wrote Lucky Star clerk — early shift and put a pin there, too.

They looped back toward the highway on a road that ran a ridge above the farm parcel. From the top, through a break in the pines, Tara could see a sliver of tin roof and one corner of the lean-to. She didn’t slow. But her eyes measured the pull-off with room for one car behind scrub, and the way a tripod could stand in the brush without anyone below noticing if you kept light off the glass. She said nothing. Sloane wrote ridge turnout, east of parcel—public shoulder.

By the time they reached the first town, the sun had shifted to that late angle that makes everything look like it has more weight than it can carry. They parked in a spot that faced the courthouse and left the windows down two inches to let the car breathe. Sloane called Rachael on the secure line and read her a list.

“Porch cam, south. County pole NE-17. Canopy cam at the Lucky Star if it exists. Preservation letters first. We’ll need production after the judge stamps the subpoenas, but let’s not spook anyone until we have to.”

“Understood,” Rachael said. You could hear her pencil clicking in the background, the metronome of someone who liked the line to be straight before she walked it. “Keep it tight. No adjectives. Times and identifiers only.”

“Always,” Sloane said. She paused. “We also need a memo for observation from public vantage points. Tara found a ridge shoulder that gives us eyes on the parcel without stepping off the county road.”

“Easy,” Rachael said. “I’ll cite the cases and drop it in your folder.” A beat. “Anything else?”

“Just one note for the file,” Sloane answered. “We were told the Reverend doesn’t keep regular hours on-site. There is a man on the trucks who looks enough like him to make me believe the witnesses we dismissed months ago weren’t as wrong as we thought.”

Rachael didn’t use adjectives either. “Logged,” she said. “And remember the difference between recognition and speculation in any report you sign.”

“Always,” Sloane said again, and hung up.

They walked into the courthouse not because they needed to that minute, but because it normalized their presence in town. They used the bathroom, bought two waters from a machine that had eaten its share of quarters, and walked back out like people who had nothing to hide.

On the drive back toward the interstate, they took one last pass down the county road that ran past the farm. This time there was a church van at the end of the lane, a woman in a denim skirt unloading paper plates and a bag of charcoal.

Kids kicked a half-flat ball in the grass and ran shrieking when it bounced into a ditch. Nothing about the scene looked like an operation that could empty a dealership of twenty cars and make them vanish before dawn. Everything about it looked like a place where people did ordinary things under a name that made them feel seen.

"Occam's razor," Tara said, almost to herself, again. "Their name is on the deed. Their trucks run south. Their own site says this is where the faithful gather."

"And a witness saw a truck on a morning we care about," Sloane said. "That's a line, not a circle."

"Then we draw the next line," Tara said.

It wasn't about belief—it was about logistics wearing faith like a uniform.

They reached the interstate as the light went the color of old brass. The sedan slotted into traffic and became one more ordinary thing going home.

They didn't talk about the man by the trucks again on the drive. They didn't need to. The image had already done what images do when they land right — it had made every prior witness statement feel less like noise and more like the beginning of a map.

At the SCIF that evening, they didn't change the map yet. They added dots. County pole NE-17. Porch cam south. Ridge turnout east. Lucky Star canopy. They wrote preserve first, produce later at the top of the whiteboard and underlined it once.

Keene replied to Sloane's one-pager with the thing she needed and nothing extra: Preservation approved. Route subpoenas when identifiers return.

Rachael slid the observation memo into the field folder with case citations that would read as dull and correct if anyone ever demanded them in court.

Tara printed the verse from the sign on a scrap of paper and pinned it to the corkboard beside the deeds and plates and the word SSO in black marker. She didn't write a note under it. She didn't have to.

"Tomorrow," Sloane said, and meant satellite tiles and ridge at dawn and Lucky Star clerk with the burnt-toast coffee.

"Tomorrow," Tara said back, meaning quiet, long lenses, patience.

They turned the lights down in the war room and left the glass humming, the way they always did. Outside, the city made the same small hushing sound pines do when wind slides through them. Somewhere to the south, a white truck slept under a lean-to with green letters on its side, and men who looked like other men they were not supposed to be sat and talked where no one could see them if they did not already know where to look.

The work would be slow. That was fine. They had learned to love the slow things because they were the ones that lasted.

Chapter Twenty Two – Americano with a Shot

Sloane Carver liked mornings best when they didn't ask anything of her. Neutral air, neutral coffee, a neutral half hour where the world existed without urgency. Atlanta was already warming, light hitting the glass in long, slanted strokes, but the streets still held that brief, forgiving hush that made a person believe the day might behave.

She locked her apartment, walked the three blocks to Brewline on Piedmont, and breathed the smell she wished she could bottle—espresso, scalded milk, a hint of cinnamon someone had spilled an hour earlier, and the faint paper smell of new pastry bags. People talked in low morning voices, half eyelids, half smiles, everyone still forming the edges of themselves.

She ordered her usual—a double Americano, no room—and didn't bother giving her name. The barista, maybe nineteen, already knew it, nodded, and wrote C-A-R-V-E-R on the cup with a smiley face she pretended not to notice. Sloane stepped to the end of the counter, checking her messages with the habitual speed of someone who had learned that emergencies had no respect for hours.

Her phone chimed once. Keene — 10:00 a.m. briefing moved to 9:30. Be early.

She exhaled. "Of course it is."

The barista slid her drink across. "Here you go, Agent Carver."

"Thanks," she said, taking the cup. It was warm enough to anchor her but not burn. She turned toward the door.

That was when she felt it first: a ripple in the air outside the glass. Not dramatic. Not obvious. Just wrong.

Sloane paused, instinct shifting her weight back onto her heels. The kind of shift that wasn't conscious but trained—the body moving into a state of readiness before the brain earned its say. Outside, traffic rolled normally. A bus hissed at a stoplight. A man walked his terrier, leash loose in hand. Nothing dramatic.

Except—

A silver sedan sat idle at the curb across the street, engine running, exhaust curling in soft white breaths even though the car hadn't moved for minutes. The driver's seat was occupied, but the window glare made the figure shapeless. Sloane's brow lifted. No parking signs lined that stretch. Engines running with no movement usually meant one of two things: a ride-share waiting for a passenger—or people who didn't want to commit to being parked.

A small instinct whispered in her ribs: Mark it. Don't fear it. Just mark it.

Sloane stepped outside. The air hit warmer, brushing her cheek with a faint humidity that promised a hotter afternoon. A group of college kids crossed her path laughing, a lattice of limbs and backpacks and caffeine. She stepped aside to let them by.

Her car—a government-issue gray sedan—was just twenty feet down. She clicked the key fob, heard the chirp, and walked toward it. Nothing unusual. Nothing alarming.

A man stepped out from behind the SUV parked beside her.

Hood up. Shoulders too tight. A moment of nothing—and then the shine of a weapon emerging from the pocket of his sweatshirt.

Sloane didn't think. She reacted.

"Gun!" she barked, loud enough that the group behind her froze and scattered.

The man lunged. His voice broke into a snarl, "Give me the keys!"

Sloane moved sideways, buying space, her coffee cup flying out of her hand and exploding into a brown arc across the pavement. Her right hand went to her holster by muscle memory.

He was fast.

Her fingers brushed the grip of her weapon but didn't close.

A gunshot cracked the space open.

The round hit the pavement near her foot, spraying shards of concrete. She jerked back, heart slamming.

"Drop it!" a man shouted—another voice, to her left.

Another attacker?

No. A bystander.

A truck driver who had been loading crates into his cab now stood behind the bed, a pistol braced in both hands, face white but steady.

The gunman spun toward him, weapon rising.

Sloane didn't hesitate. She threw herself sideways, boots scraping, a hollow shout ripping from her throat.

The second gunshot folded the gunman before he finished turning. He fell at an awkward angle, knees buckling, hands twitching once before stilling.

Silence cracked open the moment.

Somebody screamed. Someone else ducked behind a mailbox. A car swerved and braked hard.

Sloane stayed low, palm braced to asphalt. "Everyone back! Call 911!"

The truck driver stared at her over the bed of his truck, pistol still raised. His hands shook violently now that the danger was over.

“You okay?” he called, voice cracking.

Sloane nodded once. “Put the gun down. Slow. Set it on the truck bed. Step back.”

He obeyed immediately, breath hitching with adrenaline. “He—he was gonna shoot you.”

“I know.” Sloane rose carefully, weapon now in her hand, trained on the downed man as she approached at an angle. Her pulse thudded in her ears. “You did what you had to do.”

The attacker lay facedown, jacket riding up slightly at the waist. Blood spread in a dark bloom beneath him. No movement.

Sloane nudged the weapon from his slackened grip with her foot and kicked it farther away. She kept her pistol trained. “Sir, stay behind the truck. Do not approach.”

He nodded, swallowing hard.

Sirens wailed in the distance—multiple vehicles responding, growing louder, echoing down Piedmont like a warning.

A woman from the sidewalk approached cautiously. “Agent Carver? I—I think he tried to rob you!”

“Ma’am,” Sloane said, steady but firm, “please back up behind the tape line when officers arrive.”

Two APD cruisers skidded to a stop, doors opening in unison. Officers spilled out, weapons drawn, fanning into a perimeter.

“Drop your weapon!” one shouted at Sloane.

She kept hers pointed down and away, held in a safe ready-low. “FBI. I was the target. Attacker down. Weapon kicked clear.”

An officer approached, eyes wary. “You armed?”

“Yes. Holstered now.”

She re-holstered, slow and deliberate. Hands wide.

The officer swept the scene: the gunman down, the bystander behind the truck pale as wax, shaken college kids against a wall, spilled coffee bleeding into pavement.

“Medic!” the sergeant barked to the second cruiser. “We need EMS and a supervisor.”

Sloane stood still, letting the scene stabilize around her. Her pulse throbbed but her breathing had already begun to smooth—the trained reflex of someone whose job required returning to neutral after a spike in seconds.

An officer knelt by the attacker, checked for a pulse, shook his head once. “He’s gone.”

The sergeant turned to Sloane. “You injured?”

“No.”

“You firing officer?”

“No. Civilian bystander. He’ll need statements and counsel.”

The sergeant nodded. “We’ll secure the scene. You want an APD ride back to HQ?”

Sloane shook her head. “No. I’ll wait for FBI Evidence Response. And the Medical Examiner.”

“You’re staying?”

“Yes,” Sloane said. “Chain of custody starts now.”

The sergeant didn’t argue. FBI agents who knew the rules made his job easier.

He stepped away to coordinate the arriving units. EMTs crouched near the body but only long enough to confirm what everyone already knew. A white-sheet protocol bag waited nearby.

Sloane looked once at the gunman's body. His jacket had ridden up farther in death, exposing a strip of skin along his ribs. Pale. Unmarked. Nothing visible that meant anything. She turned away. There was no reason to fix anything in memory.

Not yet.

Thirty minutes later, the Medical Examiner's van pulled up. The CSU techs moved like they always did—measured, calm, indifferent to the emotions of a scene. They photographed the body, the angles, the weapons, the casings, the pattern of blood, the coffee splash, the arc of her skid marks.

Only when every image was sealed and logged did the ME investigator kneel and roll the man for bagging.

The jacket shifted.

His shirt lifted slightly.

A tech paused. "Huh."

Sloane, standing beside the sergeant, didn't notice the soft intake of breath until the ME investigator spoke.

"He's been branded," she murmured. "Left ribcage. Oblique. Unusual placement."

Sloane turned—but too late to see clearly. The body bag closed.

APD's sergeant asked, "Does it mean something?"

The ME shrugged. " Could be nothing. We'll document it at the lab. No field conclusions."

Sloane nodded. "Let the autopsy run its course."

Her voice was neutral, unassuming. No flicker of realization. She hadn't seen enough to interpret anything—and even if she had, field analysis wasn't protocol.

She gave her statement last, clean and clinical, then let APD wrap the scene.

When she finally returned to her car, her coffee long evaporated on the pavement, she sat behind the wheel and let her hands rest on the steering wheel.

A robbery attempt. Or a carjacking. Or someone desperate. That was all it needed to be.

She started the engine.

But she kept seeing the idle sedan across the street—the one she'd marked and dismissed.

When she looked now, it was gone.

Just a coincidence, she told herself.

But her pulse took longer than usual to settle.

GBI / Cobb County Medical Examiner's Office — Early Morning

Dr. Carolyn Holt pushed through the swinging door with a thermos under one arm and a file under the other. Autopsy Suite Two already hummed with the soft white-noise of vents. Stainless steel trays gleamed. A tech adjusted overhead lights until the body on Table Three lay under a clean cone of illumination—still clothed except for the cut-away panel of the shirt.

"Case 25-3476," the tech said. "Male, mid-twenties. GSW to chest. Taken from the attempted robbery on Peachtree. No ID on scene."

"Scene photos uploaded?" Holt asked, setting her file down.

"In your queue."

Holt snapped on gloves. The familiar latex sound was as close as she ever came to ritual.

“Let’s begin.”

She started the external exam—a slow, methodical choreography she could probably do in her sleep but refused to. Respect lived in precision.

“Single entry wound, anterior chest,” she dictated. “Close-range stippling minimal… ballistic trajectory straight through thoracic cavity. Exit wound posterior, slightly right of midline.”

She peeled back the remaining clothing, noting soot, faint powder transfer, the clean surgical line the bullet had carved through fabric.

“Any identifying marks on scene?” she asked.

“None visible,” the tech said. “He was fully clothed. Vest, jacket, gloves.”

“Alright. Full surface scan.”

As the tech repositioned an articulating lamp, Holt lifted the man’s left arm, scanning the underside, shoulder to elbow. Nothing unusual. She moved to the right.

Something dark caught the light.

“Pause.”

She rotated the arm gently until the mark came fully into view: high on the right ribcage, partially obscured by dried blood. A symbol. Stark. Deliberate.

Not gang.

Not prison.

Not any extremist brand she recognized.

A stylized emblem: a circle broken on one side with two radiating bars—almost a crude brand.

"Get me a macro lens," Holt said.

The tech handed her the camera.

Click.

Click.

Click.

Holt leaned closer, studying the pattern. "Database hit?" the tech asked.

She shook her head. "Nothing I know. I'll run it, but… feels new."

Meaning dangerous.

Meaning organized.

"Make sure Atlanta PD gets a clean copy of the report," she said. "Not the detectives—send it directly to their violent-crimes inbox and the duty sergeant. This belongs to them, not the task force."

"Understood."

She finished the exam, dictating findings with that same even tone she used for children, felons, and victims who would never be identified.

The brand photographs printed. Holt slid one into the case file, one into her personal notation binder, and set a small sticky tab on the page. She didn't like coincidences. Brands didn't appear from nowhere.

They belonged to groups. Groups had motives.

She removed her gloves and dropped them into the bin. "Prep for internal," she said quietly. "I'll be back in ten."

As she walked out, she carried the binder tight to her chest—not out of fear, but because something in her bones said this symbol wasn't going to stay small.

Not after yesterday's attack.

Not with a dead man wearing a mark no database could name.

Chapter Twenty Three – Practicing the Faith

The horn cut the night clean. It was a blunt sound — metal and breath and an authority that did not ask. Windows unlatched and doors opened along the barracks like the peel of a long, thin bell. Men moved first, then women shepherding children, and by the time the last slat of sleep fell away the compound had arranged itself into a shape it knew by rote.

Dawn here smelled of pine resin, engine oil, and the metallic tang of gun oil that never quite washed from leather slings. The yard was packed dirt, footprints layered like topography, the edges kept sharp by a line of low wire and watch posts. A banner, torch inside a ring of crude fire, snapped against the wind on the outer wall and drew every face up when the elder's voice hit its first cadence.

"The hands bear the fire," he called. The line answered — not politely, not hesitantly, but like a muscle remembering how to contract. The chant rolled across the field and through the rows of bunks, thicker than smoke.

The formations were military in habit. Two squads filed out to a measured cadence, rifles carried as if integral to the spine. Commands came down in short bursts and were obeyed without commentary. A teenager stumbled during a turn; an elder's hand corrected him with a touch that was more assumption than chastisement. The boy's shoulders straightened and he fell back into step, face set with the practiced neutrality of a man learning to lose himself to the group.

Women moved in separate, fluid patterns — water buckets, pots, bread stacked under oilcloth. They fed, washed, mended, and folded with the seamless choreography of people who spent their lives keeping other people ready to fight. The children, small and dusty, sat at the lean-to tables with eyes that watched more than they ate, learning which gestures would earn a nod and which would earn silence.

The Armory and the Shed

Between these choreographies stood the armory: low, cinderblock walls, a barred window that let in morning light in a thin, militant slice. The door bore a padlock and a tally of names etched into the frame. Inside, racks lined the inner wall like a shrine — rifles of differing ages, neat rows of magazines, boxes stacked with stenciled numbers. A workbench held oilcloths, spare bolts, and trays of parts that glinted in the fluorescent glare.

You could tell by how the boys treated the armory that it was a place of reverence. Under supervision, they laid out cleaning kits and ran barrels through cloths, fingers careful as if handling sacred relics. An elder moved among them, voice low and instructive. "Keep the hands sharp," he said, scanning the room. "The hands keep the fire." The refrain pressed like a rib against everything else that happened there.

Behind a locked steel cabinet sat heavier shapes: tubes and canisters shrouded in canvas. The elders never spoke of them, but every passing hand seemed to count them silently. Pipe bombs, small satchels, crude but lethal tools that reminded everyone here that fire meant more than ritual.

On the far side of the compound, the shed with the patched tin roof breathed steam in slow ribbons. No one called it by a tidy name. It was simply the shed. Its door was sealed with a hasp and a loop of wire; a small, constant fan thrummed against the humidity when the summer heat pressed in.

The air around it smelled sweet and chemical and faintly of ammonia. Women in aprons moved in and out of the yard carrying heavy buckets and sacks of fertilizer, their hands blackened at the nails from work that didn't show in the hush of prayer.

Inside that shed there were tables with glassware, not the neat, clinical arrangement of a classroom but the crowded, busy clutter of something lived in — beakers stained at the lip, tubing coiled like ropes, jars thick with residues. Men labored inside, their faces swaddled with makeshift masks and bandanas, moving with a purposeful economy that said they had done this many times.

Fans pushed one way; exhaust stacked to the eaves the other. No one talked about production and finance in the dining shed; talk here was practical and brief: loads, routes, money. The shed supplied that cash in ways people who lived outside the fence would never guess until smoke rose in a city street.

The Training Bay

The training bay sat like a clean secret, a long, low building set at the edge of the compound where the trees thinned and the ground flattened. From the road it might have looked like another storage barn, but inside the light was clinical and the smell was dry: rubber mats, cut plywood, and the faint metallic tang of gear that had been handled carefully and returned to place.

The floor was a grid of painted lines and removable panels. Against one wall, modular walls on casters could be rearranged in minutes to mimic an exhibition hall aisle, a service corridor, a loading dock — anything the men needed to run until muscle memory took over. Chalk lines tracked ingress and egress points, annotated in tight, neat handwriting. A bank of clocks on one end of the room counted off minutes and seconds.

Men moved through the house in small, precise teams. They were timed, critiqued, and sent back through the sequence until the motion looked automatic — a set of gestures that could be repeated without thought. Some practiced signaling with palms and glances; others ran silent communications into handsets that beeped with harmless tones. Role-players stood in as guards and confused bystanders, and the men rehearsed not just routes but restraint: how to move with speed that didn't turn into panic, how to cover each other's blind spots, how to stack and clear a space in a handful of measured breath.

The Active Farm

The cover that made it all credible was the farm itself. To anyone who might glance down from a passing plane or scan with a drone, the crops looked neat and tended, the animals moved with the ordinary rhythm of rural life. Corn rows lined the eastern field, beans sprouted in patches to the south, and chickens pecked in an open run near the hog pens. A smokehouse shed turned pork into hams, a side barn cured hides into leather.

Women rendered fat into soap, stirring vats in open yards until the lye-smell carried through the compound. Livestock pens supplied meat, feathers, and eggs. Goats were milked at dawn, soap made at noon, cheese pressed in small wooden molds that lined up like hymnals on a shelf. Grain was ground into flour, not just for their bread but to bag and send outward, proof that this was a farm with output, not just a fence with secrets.

Delivery trucks rolled out twice a week, loaded with produce crates stamped SSO Farm Products. They carried more than lettuce and soap, but the outer world saw only the carrots on invoices and the jars of honey that passed inspection. Paper trails looked like agriculture, not arsenal.

Camouflage

They hadn't left the place naked to the sky. Everything at the compound that mattered had been married to the land — tarps patterned like pine duff stretched over storage roofs, painted netting thrown high on poles to break the silhouette of barns and lean-tos, and irregular tree lines pruned so shadows fell where they needed to. The sheds wore weathered tarpaulins cut and sewn to mimic patches of sunlit undergrowth; even the corrugated roofs had been dulled with matte paint, the flash of metal removed with a careful hand.

At the edge of the yard the training bay's low profile was deliberate: earth berms banked against three sides, bermed entrances that would look like farm contouring from above, and a dust layer on the access road deliberately left rutted and unremarkable. The armory's intake vent faced downward and was masked with grating and a false planter so a lens would read only textured foliage. The shed's exhaust routed through a long run of buried piping and a scatter of scrub so heat signatures smeared and softened on thermal passes. Even the perimeter watch posts were half-buried behind brush, their radio antennas short and dull.

From the ridge the effect was subtle but unmistakable: the compound did not announce itself. It blurred. Where others would show as hard edges — roofs, straight lines, corrugated glints — this place dissolved into the pines, a geometry designed to confuse a passing eye or a quick drone sweep.

Ridge Notes and Carrier Plans

From their vantage point Tara wrote in her notebook: Armory, shed exhaust, trucks under tarp, porch cam. Sloane tapped her tablet, then frowned.

"If we want to put names to faces," Sloane said, "we start with towers. Closest coverage sectors to this road are Tower 14-South and Tower 22-East. If a device moves with a truck, it'll hand off between those. Not precise — but directional."

Back in the war room, Ty laid the tower coverage map beside the ridge notes. "So we ask carriers for preservation: tower attachments, IMSI/IMEI logs — device identifiers — along with call and SMS activity, windows tied to Miami theft and nights the trucks moved. We don't ask for the county. We ask for those towers, those hours."

Rachael underlined the language. "Magistrates sign narrow. No adjectives, no speculation. Tower IDs, dates, times. If it's a burner, subscriber info won't help. But repeat tower hits make a pattern. Patterns justify scope."

"And business lines," Tara added. "This is a farm. Farms have dispatch numbers, manager phones. If we can tie their listed number to tower sectors when the trucks roll, that's a visible line. Judges understand visible."

Sloane nodded. "We'll preserve those accounts. CDRs — call detail records — tower logs, subscriber metadata. If we see the same number attach near the farm and hand off toward Miami, that's a corridor we can prove."

Ty typed a draft into the affidavit: Preserve carrier records for Tower 14-South and Tower 22-East, dates X–Y, times A–B. Preserve CDRs for farm-listed numbers. Preserve telematics if registered to SSO fleet units. He slid the laptop toward Rachael.

She crossed out two phrases. "Lose 'possible suspicious movement.' Replace with 'observed truck activity logged by investigators.' Admissible, clean."

Keene's reply came by secure line: Queue preservation. Draft subpoenas narrow. File one-pager for magistrate review. Do not expand scope without PC language.

Tara closed her notebook. "So we start with preservation, run the logs, and see what holds. We're not proving identity in one pull. We're building a corridor of movement. If the same device shadows the same truck on multiple nights, we put a name to a pattern."

Nobody argued. It was slow, legal pressure, the kind that made secrets leak without a breach.

Trial by Fire

When dusk slid its long hand around the trees, the compound's center cleared for the trial by fire. The semicircle left an open patch of dirt, and a recruit stepped into the gap like a lamb into an arena. His arm was bare to the elbow, thin skin pulled tight over bone, eyes fixed on the banner. The torch was brought close, the flame low but deliberate, a touch of heat that made the air shimmer like something unreal.

The moment stretched. Voices held in a hush so thick a dropped coin would have sounded obscene. The torch kissed skin with a hiss like a small animal yelp, then the sound flattened into the ritual cadence: a cry stifled, a man pushed forward, a gesture of acceptance. A blistered mark bloomed, the flesh gone red and angry for an instant before the leader swept a cloth over it and lifted the boy's arm to show the scar. They nodded in slow approval, a tide moving through the semicircle, and the recruit's knees gave, not from the burn alone but from the weight of joining.

Behind the men, the women whispered prayers that were both supplication and accounting. Children were turned to face away, told to sing a different hymn. The doctrine was practical: ritual confirmed loyalty, scars confirmed belonging, belonging confirmed obedience. The chant moved them into the night like cattle led to water.

Night Sermon

Dark pulled the compound into the hall. A low building strung with bare bulbs, chairs scraped against concrete as men and women filed inside. Children shuffled to the back row, eyes wide, mouths pressed shut.

At the front, a projector hummed, throwing shaky light onto a hanging sheet. The image flickered but held: Ezekiel "Zeke" Drayton, arms spread wide above a crowd miles away. He was larger than life here, his voice rolling through tin speakers with the cadence of revival.

"Hold high the torch of Revelation! Bear the fire against a world that mocks His word!"

The hall vibrated with his rhythm. To outsiders, it might have sounded like metaphor — preacher's thunder, television faith. Inside the fence, the words landed as command.

Men shouted amen, fists tightening as though gripping torches not yet lit. Women bowed their heads, lips moving in sync with the chant. Even children, voices small and uncertain, echoed the refrain.

The insignia flashed in the corner of the screen — torch inside the ring of fire — as Zeke's voice rose higher.

"This world will call you strange! This world will call you fools! But you — you are the hands of Revelation! And the hands bear the fire!"

The chant came back in waves: The hands bear the fire! The sound rattled the thin walls, pushed into the rafters, rolled out across the pines.

The service ended not with dismissal but with direction. Men stood taller, eyes bright as if waiting for orders. Women moved in clusters, already planning the next morning's labors. Children clung to their mothers' skirts, still whispering the refrain under their breath.

The hall emptied into night. Smoke from the cook fires drifted low. A scarred recruit sat alone on a bench, arm wrapped in cloth, jaw set like stone.

From the ridge, two women sat in a car with the lights off, lenses balanced across the dash. The glow of the hall and the faint steam of the shed blurred against the trees, camouflaged but not invisible to those who knew where to look.

Sloane tapped her notes, her shorthand clinical: armory, training bay, shed — production, camouflage layered, dual-use farm as cover, towers preserved.

Tara closed her notebook and whispered, "They believe this is divine order. But what I see is an army, hiding in plain sight."

Sloane didn't disagree. "And funding itself one pallet at a time."

They let the quiet sit, the echo of chants carrying faint through the trees: The hands bear the fire. It was creed, commerce, and cover all bound into one.

Chapter Twenty Four – Full Disclosure

The war room wasn't loud. It never had to be. It worked in screens and timestamps, in maps that pulsed and logs that stacked themselves while the people in the room learned to breathe a little shallower.

Sloane glanced at the wall clock and lifted the secure handset. The blue banner across the console told her the line was clean.

"Keene."

"ASAC, Special Agent Sloane Carver. The task force is coming over. We'll need a secure room to meet with you."

A beat, then: "When?"

"Within the hour."

"I'll have a room cleared."

She logged the time, set the handset back in its cradle, and looked around the table. "He's expecting us."

Nobody packed a folder. There weren't any. Ty touched the small, tamper-tagged drive that sat on a foam pad by his keyboard and watched the console confirm the hash he'd just signed. Rachael saved a last line into the manifest and locked it. Tara scrolled a containment map one more time and committed the throat of every road to memory. Holt snapped her notepad shut; there were three words on it, nothing more.

Before they left, each of them gave the room one last look. It wasn't habit—it was reverence. The screens still pulsed, the bot still sat waiting, the logs still stacked in their quiet order. Nothing would stop here just because they walked out, and that was its own strange comfort. Ty slipped the drive into his jacket pocket and for the first time let himself feel the weight of it. Not metal, not plastic—responsibility.

Rachael's pen tapped once on her closed pad, her tell for nerves. Tara stood by the door, arms folded, already rehearsing the roads in her head. Holt lingered half a second longer, her hand brushing the glass as if touching a patient before leaving the room.

"On the way," Sloane said, and the room kept humming as they stepped out. Nothing here ever stopped.

They threaded into late traffic in a plain sedan. Atlanta did what cities do at five o'clock—widened into noise and narrowed back again. Ty drove with a steady, lawyerly caution. Rachael rode behind him with her hands flat on her knees and her eyes closed for half a minute at a time. Tara watched the skyline past Sloane's shoulder and let the shape of the day settle into place.

The first few minutes were silent. The kind of silence that came not from comfort but from calculation—each of them replaying what the next hour meant. Rachael finally opened her eyes and exhaled. "This is the first time my boss has seen any of this," she murmured. "If we've overreached—"

"We haven't," Sloane said, sharper than she meant. "And Benton's no fool. Once she sees it, she'll understand why you called her in."

Hayes, crammed into the back seat beside Holt—the state tactical liaison—leaned forward.

"You'll see soon enough," Sloane said. "Lobby will be flat and forgettable. No brass, no seals. Security will be tight: badges scanned, faces checked. Visitor log. No phones past the desks. They'll issue our temporary credentials and walk us straight to a room they've already killed from the network."

She shifted, glancing at Hayes in the mirror. "Keene himself? Measured. He doesn't flash. He won't pretend to be impressed. He'll want to see it work and he'll want to know it's auditable. If he believes what he sees, he'll widen the circle—legal, tactical—and ask them what they need to begin. He won't tell them how."

She let the thought hang a moment. "Don't expect handshakes or pep talks. He'll test us by silence. That's his tell—he doesn't fill space unless he's certain."

Benton's voice cut in, cool and lean. "What will he ask me for?"

"Discreet contact with the Governor," Rachael said before Sloane could. She didn't turn around. "State resources on quiet hold. Aviation, troopers, whatever they can earmark without a press release. He'll want your office for magistrate coordination, too. Narrow language only."

"Of course," Benton said, jotting something in a shorthand no one else could read.

Tara shifted in her seat and watched the city slide by. "He'll call it a posture, not a plan," she said. "And he'll want his people to see it themselves."

Holt didn't say anything. She didn't have to. The car knew what she'd need—contamination lanes, refrigeration, a quiet way to insert if the worst happened. The list moved through the car like a river under ice.

Ty kept his eyes on the lanes and spoke only once. "I'll drive the screen from the war room," he said. "Sloane will narrate. After, I'll hand the drive over. Manifest and hash match the copy I just signed. It's everything minus the front end."

Rachael exhaled softly, almost a laugh but not quite. "She's going to see it all in one sitting. My boss. Months of work, laid out like we meant it from the start." Nobody answered, but Sloane reached across the seat and gave her hand one quick press before letting go.

They took the turn for downtown and let the little inanities of the street—the brake lights, the green signs, the single bird on a wire—be normal for one minute more. Then they turned into the field office lot and normal went away.

They signed in like it was a vault. No one asked for a reason; no one gave one. The guard read their names off his screen and into the ledger and stamped the times down next to them.

CARVER, Sloane — 17:58

WHITAKER, TARA — 17:59

MATHIS, TYLER — 18:00

Garrison, Rachael — 18:00

HOLT, CAROLYN — 18:01

HAYES, LEONARD — 18:02

BENTON, CLAIRE — 18:03

Hayes muttered as he clipped the badge on, "Feels like walking into a jury box before you've been called." Benton's reply was dry: "At least in a courtroom you know what case you're about to hear."

The badges snapped onto lanyards with a sound that always registered as more final than it should have. They followed an escort down a corridor where the air was a little too cold and into a glass room whose glass had been turned to walls by the push of a button. A single console hummed on a credenza. Keene stood at the far end of the table. He said their names in order as if calling a roll he already knew.

"Carver. Whitaker. Mathis. Garrison. Doctor Holt. Captain Hayes. District Attorney Benton."

There were no handshakes. There was a table, a screen, and a question everyone in the room could feel, even if no one asked it out loud: show us.

Sloane nodded to Ty and he nodded to the intake tech. A wire jumped from Ty's laptop to the wall panel. The Bureau logo flickered, then yielded to a plain field that said READ-ONLY – AUTHENTICATED SESSION across the top.

"This is our environment," Sloane said. She didn't step toward the screen or reach for the keyboard; she let the bosses have the wall and kept her voice the thing that walked them through. "What you're about to see is how we pulled the threads together. It's not theory. It's aggregation."

Ty typed a short query. The map pane bloomed with pins as if someone had thrown a handful of salt across the country. He tabbed into a results list: time, date, location, field tags. He opened the first line and metadata stepped onto the wall like a second set of coordinates.

"Headers, timestamps," Sloane said. "Vendor receipts. CAD logs. Coroner indexes. Every file is wrapped with a hash when it's ingested so we can prove it hasn't been altered. Every query is logged. Every field is auditable."

Keene didn't speak. Hayes didn't either. Benton's pen stopped moving.

Hayes cleared his throat. "So it's not guessing. It's the system telling you when different reports rhyme."

"That's how isolated cases start to show the same mistakes," Sloane said. "Same habits. Same sloppiness. You don't need a mastermind for that—just crews copying what works."

"Sometimes thieves grab strange combinations," Sloane said. "Coins mixed with costume jewelry. A relic tossed in with silverware. It usually means panic or opportunity—maybe someone grabbed whatever was closest when they ran."

Benton raised an eyebrow. "Does that help us?"

"Sometimes," Sloane said. "Odd choices can point to who was on which aisle or who moved fastest. Nothing mystical. Just human behavior under stress."

Ty swept to another query, narrower: service door + off-site transport within four hours + odd item flag. The list shrank. The pins shifted. The same thread ran through the ones that stayed.

"The point isn't the keyword," Sloane said. "It's the cross-check. The engine flags when independent records repeat the same anomalies in different places—timing, routes, handling. That's how isolated cases start to look like the work of the same operator."

Benton tilted her head. "Odd items? What do you mean by that?"

"Things that don't fit the crime scene but appear anyway," Sloane said. "Again, like costume jewelry taken with rare coins, or a dinosaur egg alongside modern art. They don't matter in value, but they show the thieves were willing to take what interested them."

Benton scribbled a note fast enough to dig into the page.

Ty opened another file. The map recentered on Georgia. MARIETTA COIN SHOW bled into the top corner in small letters. The timestamp matched the one in Tara's head. Holt read the autopsy line without inflection. Rachael slid a short paragraph toward Benton—a magistrate-clean sentence built of verbs no judge throws back. Benton read it and nodded once.

"Now the piece that matters for why we're here," Sloane said. "We built a watch on top of this. A bot. Not to guess—just to alert when enough of the fields we defined line up. Service-door entry. Duration inside. Off-site transport. Odd items. Unusual vendor names. The moment the thresholds are met, it flags us."

It doesn't decide. It just notices when thresholds we defined are crossed.

She tapped the timeline. "When that first alert fired, we moved faster than the locals could have, because we already knew where to look. We asked for perimeter footage for the six hours before the alarm window, not the twenty minutes after. That's how we picked up a produce truck making a delivery where it didn't belong. The partial plate on that truck matched a shell company that kept showing up in manifests tied to the cache."

Benton's voice was almost toneless. "The farm."

"The farm," Sloane said. "The plate and routing data led us to Mobile Logistics LLC—paper company. Property records put a parcel in Georgia in their chain. The parcel belongs to a ministry. We subpoenaed tower data, requested preservation for manifests, and the farm showed up on our overlays."

She let them have one heartbeat to own that and then gave them the last line the system hadn't created but the case had needed.

“While the bot was doing that, witnesses in other cities started giving us the same description on first interviews: a familiar face walking the aisles in the days before the hit. They swore it looked like the televangelist—Zeke Drayton. In three cities. Different venues. We treated that as a separate thread. The engine flagged the movement; the witnesses pointed at the face. Property records linked the farm to the ministry. Those things lined up enough that we couldn’t call them coincidences anymore.”

Hayes let out a breath through his nose. “And not one of my people saw the link.”

Sloane answered without apology. “They weren’t supposed to. No single file gave it away. That’s why we built this.”

Benton’s voice followed, quieter but edged. “A grand jury will want every link spelled out. Keep your audit trail clean.”

Sloane gave a short nod. “It already is.”

She stopped. The only sound was the console’s fan.

Keene watched the screen for one more breath and then gave a nod you could miss if you weren’t a person who did this for a living. “All right,” he said. He didn’t turn toward Ty or reach for the keyboard; he looked at the intake tech. “Record the handoff.”

Ty set the small aluminum drive on the table. No flourish, no speech. The tech scanned the serial and read the hash Ty had printed. The console chimed when the numbers matched. On the wall, a line blinked into a box:

CHAIN ID: C-2025-117

SOURCE: NSA NODE (READ-ONLY)

RECEIVER: FBI ATLANTA INTAKE

PAYLOAD: AGGREGATED CASE FILES + AUDIT NOTES (NO FRONT END)

STATUS: VERIFIED (HASH MATCH)

No one cheered. No one ever did at a moment like this. They just breathed differently.

Keene let the quiet sit long enough for the logic to draw itself. He pressed a button by his elbow and didn't raise his voice. "Bring in Tac One and Tac Two. Legal as well."

Sloane glanced at Tara. Hayes's jaw flexed without the rest of his face moving. Benton set her pen down.

Two plain-clothed commanders came in with a woman in a dark suit who carried a slim binder. They signed their names into the log in the corner of the room and took their seats without introductions beyond the nod Keene gave them. Ty re-ran the queries without being asked. The pins reappeared. The list built itself. The wall did its work.

They sat through the same ten minutes everyone else had. The technical lead's attention sharpened. The ground commander's posture changed by the smallest angle. The legal liaison's pen hovered but didn't write yet.

Benton leaned back, pen now still, and said softly to herself, "Now the Governor will understand why I called." Hayes gave one stiff nod. Even Keene, unreadable as always, tapped his pen twice against his pad before folding his hands again.

Keene didn't posture or plan. He said the one thing a boss says when everyone who needs to see it has seen it.

"You've all seen the evidence," he said. "Tell me what you need to begin."

Keene didn't look back at the wall. He looked at the people.

"This is no longer an investigative posture," he said. "It's operational."

No one spoke. The distinction landed without explanation.

"What you've shown establishes intent and capability," Keene continued. "Explosives. Coordinated diversions. Targeting designed to influence Vice Presidential movement. That elevates this from organized criminal activity to a national leadership threat, regardless of outcome."

He let that sit for a beat.

"The group demonstrated willingness to kill, experience with bomb construction, and comfort operating across jurisdictions," he said. "They also demonstrated discipline. That matters."

He turned slightly toward the woman in the dark suit.

"Legal?"

She opened the binder but didn't read from it. "We're clear under domestic terrorism statutes. Conspiracy, explosives, homicide where applicable. Search and seizure will be warrant-backed. Detention authority will be federal with state coordination."

Benton nodded once. "My office will handle magistrates. Quietly."

Keene looked back to Sloane. "You're not requesting a raid," he said. "You're requesting activation."

"Yes," Sloane said.

Keene gave a single nod. "Approved."

Keene reached for the phone set flush into the table. He didn't dial from memory; he pressed a single labeled key.

"Activate joint operations," he said. "Glynn County."

No one reacted. No one needed the acronym spelled out.

Hayes shifted his weight. "FLETC," he said, not as a question.

Keene nodded once. "Federal Law Enforcement Training Centers. Glynco. We're not asking them to build a team—we're aligning one that already exists."

Rachael glanced at Hayes. “That’s not just training,” she said.

“No,” Keene said. “It’s where federal units cross-attach before deployment. Marshals, ATF, FBI, tactical medics, EOD. Same language. Same procedures. Same command discipline.”

He looked down the table, making sure the distinction landed.

“They’re not gearing up,” he continued. “They’re being pointed.”

The woman from Legal flipped a page in her binder. “We’ll route warrants and authorizations through the task force liaison there,” she said. “Search, seizure, detention authority will travel with the team.”

Benton nodded. “My office will coordinate state participation. Quietly.”

Keene tapped the table once, decisive. “They’ll receive the case package, not the analysis. Targets, known capabilities, prior use of explosives, demonstrated intent to influence Vice Presidential movement. Nothing speculative.”

Hayes exhaled through his nose. “So they’re told what this group has done. Not what we think they are.”

“Correct,” Keene said. “Intent and capability. That’s all an operational team needs.”

Sloane spoke again, steady. “Timeline?”

“Immediate,” Keene said. “Initial alignment tonight. Movement when they’re ready—not before.”

No one asked how long that would take. At Glynco, readiness wasn’t scheduled. It was assumed.

Keene rose, signaling the meeting’s true end. “From this point forward, this is a federal operation with state support,” he said. “You’ll stay available. You’ll answer questions. You will not brief outside this room.”

He paused at the door.

"And you will let the people whose job this is do it."

He didn't fill the space he'd just made. The room, full now—federal, local, state, medical, legal—understood the sequence. Tactical and legal would ask for what they required; the bosses would make the calls that cleared the path. The next chapter of the case would be built of those quiet calls and neat signatures.

In the war room across town, the map on the glass kept pulsing. The bot kept its watch. The screen in the field office went dark. The work had changed addresses.

Chapter Twenty Five - Tip of the Spear

The horns blew at dawn, flat and commanding across the pines. Doors banged open along the barracks row. Men filed into the yard with rifles already slung. Women pulled kettles from shelves, children herded into lines before their eyes were fully open. The sound was order.

The first business of the morning was the guard shift. Men climbed down from the night posts, faces stiff from cold, mud striped across their cheeks. Fresh sentries climbed the ladders and slid into hides built into the trees above the fence line, boots testing the platform boards by habit. Dogs passed from one handler to the next, harness buckles checked twice, muzzles pressed to the earth. Passwords changed hands in low voices. A line of men disappeared into the barracks while another rose to meet the light.

Scripture rolled from the long hall before the kettles hissed to boil. An elder lifted the book and read without theatrics, words made strong by use.

“Cursed be the man who eats food before evening, that I may be avenged on my enemies.”

He closed the verse and turned the page.

“But Jonathan tasted the honey, and his eyes brightened.”

He read from Samuel, shaping the words the way elders always did.

He shut the book. “We do not weaken the body in the name of false zeal. Eat, and be ready for what the Lord sets before us.”

The horns sounded again, sharper, shorter.

Smoke already lifted from the cookfires. Women crouched at long stone-lined pits, stirring kettles of porridge and beans. Older children built the flames with careful hands, faces streaked with soot. Younger children gathered eggs from the henhouse, palms cupped around warm shells. Goats bleated as milk pails filled, foam bright on the surface; tin buckets of cow's milk steamed in the cool. Inside the kitchen shed, bread loaves came out of blackened ovens with a crust crackle like quiet applause.

Breakfast moved down the lines in practiced rhythm. Bowls of porridge. Bread torn into hunks. Goat cheese crumbled by hand. Eggs boiled hard in their shells. Tin cups of warm milk passed hand to hand. A brace of fowl turned on spits over coals, fat hissing into fire and drawing a line of scent through the yard.

Men ate standing, one hand on their rifles. Children chewed and were hushed. A keeper tapped a small wrist when a crust fell to the dirt. "The Lord provided this. Waste nothing." An elder walked the row, the cadence of his voice steady as a pendulum. "Swine is filth. But the sheep and the goat, the cow and the fowl, are gifts from the Lord." The line repeated the words like a refrain. A boy licked a spoon of honey from a clay jar and the keeper smiled despite herself. "Jonathan ate the honey, and the Lord gave him sight. Eat. Be strong."

When the bowls were stacked and the last of the milk was wiped from chins, another horn split the mist. This one was for drill.

Men fell into staggered lines, boots thudding the packed earth. Morning mist clung to the clearing, softening the shapes of berms and bunkers until the first rifle cracked. The sound cut the fog. Instructors fell into their own rhythm: move, cover, reload, move.

"Cover fire! Advance! Reload on the move!"

Chaos turned to choreography under the repeated words. Plywood silhouettes stood against the berm, bodies punched with tight groupings. Brass spilled and skittered. A recruit fumbled a magazine and it clattered against his boot; the instructor slammed a hand into his shoulder, not cruel, not gentle, a calibrated blow that steadied hands and set the sequence right again. This was not theater. It was a habit carved into bone.

The horn across the yard blew two short notes and the formation broke into the next drill. Ropes hung greased between a pair of old pines; men clipped harnesses with gloved hands and learned again how to travel the fixed lines without shouting to the ground what they were doing. The quiet hum of pulleys, the soft grunt of landing, the slice of a boot through leaf litter—these sounds stitched themselves under the louder ones. Every motion taught speed without spectacle.

Beyond the range, the armory crouched against the treeline, padlock bright against concrete. The air inside tasted of oil and iron and the sour back-note of fertilizer that never really left the air. Crates rose in neat stacks. Oilcloth-wrapped rifles lay along a low shelf; shotguns leaned like tools in an orderly row. Cases of ammunition filled a pallet until the wood bowed. Coils of detonation cord spooled like scarlet rope; blasting caps sat in tidy rows under a glass-front cabinet like seeds in a nursery. Nails rattled in coffee cans. Ball bearings gleamed in the lamplight like a scatter of cold eyes. Every item had a place and a tally. A recruit read numbers aloud while another matched them with the cramped handwriting in the ledger.

Underfoot the earth hollowed into tunnels. Timber beams braced damp clay. Lanterns hung on nails driven into shoring posts. A false stump hid one exit; a chicken coop, another. A tunnel ended in a thicket where bramble grew old and heavy.

Water drums and sacks of grain lined the walls against collapse and hunger. The diesel tang of a buried generator laced the air like a stubborn memory. A pair of men walked the length with careful steps, counting braces and checking for drip. No one called the bunker a sanctuary. No one had to. Its shape said it.

Above ground, defenses dissolved into the land. Spotters crouched in trees with faces smeared in mud, binoculars tucked into elbows, rifles balanced across knees. Greased ropes ran from trunk to trunk to carry a man without crashing through brush. Snares lay buried under leaves. Pits were covered with brush that matched the understory so closely that even men who had built them stepped around the place by memory, not by sight. To borrowed eyes, the place read as a farm: corn rows, stacked wood, smoke from cookfires, livestock penned and loud. To those inside, it was a fortress.

The office bore the record of obedience. Tables sagged under binders and spiral notebooks. Rosters lay in cramped ink: names, dates, duties, initiations complete. Margins held shorthand that needed no key: watch, rotate, vet. Maps crowded a corkboard—cheap printouts and torn atlas pages; circles over malls, stadiums, convention halls; arrows scratched over with blunt pencils to make choke points and exits. On the far wall a calendar hung bristling with red marks coded into a rhythm only the faithful read: drills, sermons, gatherings. All leading toward something that was never written down.

Between horns, chores filled the hours. Men hauled water and split wood and patched fence. Women stirred kettles, kneaded dough, stitched clothes, rendered soap from fat and lye, blocking it in wooden molds for cutting. Children recited lines from psalms and proverbs under the eyes of keepers; when voices faltered, the words were started again without sharpness. They learned the chant-lilt by ear before they learned the meaning.

Bees worked the hives at the treeline, honey gilding the mouths of jars and the edge of wooden spoons. A pair of men wrestled a lamb onto a rough-hewn table and worked with quiet hands to take its skin for drying, meat for stew, bones for broth. No one hurried that work; the time it took was the time it took.

At midday the horns called four notes in quick succession. Men dropped drills, women pulled kettles from fire, children were called from recitations. The kitchen shed thundered with movement. Sheep were driven into pens for the butcher. Chickens were plucked by children whose small fingers moved quickly under sharp eyes. Cauldrons of stew bubbled, beef simmering with carrots and onions and potatoes pulled from the garden. Goat turned on a spit; a pan of greens hissed when a ladle of fat hit the iron. Wheels of cheese were cut and crumbled over bowls. Tin cups filled with milk still warm stirred a sweetness in the air.

Food went down the lines. A bowl, a hunk of bread, a ladle of stew, a cut of goat, a spoon of greens, a cup of milk. It was plain food, but plentiful and strong. Men bowed their heads long enough for a prayer; then hands moved and mouths did their work. A child tried to throw away a bone and was stopped by a light hand and a look. "The Lord provided this," a woman said. "Do not despise it." An elder passed and intoned again the litany of clean and unclean, the covenant of bread and meat. The people repeated, not as a chant so much as a way to make the meal part of the day's strength.

After the bowls were wiped with crusts and stacked, the horns called men back to the range. The afternoon drills wore a different shape: teams practiced silent movement through marked courses, one man with eyes closed and a hand on another's shoulder, counting steps between obstacles; another chambered rounds and learned to rely on touch as much as sight. The instructors used fewer words when men were tired; the body learned the lesson louder in quiet.

Inside the smokehouse, salted strips of beef hung next to racks of fish taken from a river miles east; a boy learned to turn the crank of a grinder while a woman taught another to split the sausage casing with a thumbnail. In a corner a pair of girls grated hard soap and laughed into the dust of it, making a storm in a sunbeam that came through a crack. The medic sat under the eaves and re-wrapped a man's hand, redressed a burn on a woman's forearm, pressed a palm to a child's forehead and declared him fit to recite again. His hands heard the stories skin doesn't speak in words.

When the light softened and the line of sunlight moved off the berm, the horns blew a long, low note that rolled into the trees. Families filed into the hall; chairs scraped concrete. A projector hummed and warmed, and a face larger than life bloomed on the hanging sheet. Ezekiel Drayton smiled with the ease of a man who never worried the camera would catch him from the wrong side. His voice rolled in a cadence that knew how a crowd breathes.

"As Jericho fell to God's trumpets, so shall every enemy who comes against us. Every blast is a covenant—your obedience to Him, your defense of His kingdom."

The horns answered him, punctuating his words in sharp measures. Men raised fists. Women bowed their heads. Children mouthed amens they did not yet understand. The word "fire" hung in the air more like inevitability than threat. The walls seemed closer, heavier, with each note. An elder in the second row whispered the response lines along with the recording because he had learned them by heart and because there was comfort in call-and-response.

Two elders stepped back from the front as the sermon swelled and spoke in the hush behind the curtain, faces turned toward the hallway where a little light still touched the floor. Clipboard corners ticked against paper. One put a palm on a calendar square as if testing for heat. They spoke in shorthand: the next drill, the next gathering, a phrase about deliveries. Their voices never rose; their fingers moved with the attention of men who had handled books for a long time and now held a ledger for a different kind of faith.

Outside the perimeter the spotters kept their watch. A man in a hide let his binoculars hang and rubbed a cramp out of his shoulder; the rope he would ride later hung slack and darkened with grease. The dogs along the fence paced without urgency; they had learned the scent of every goat and child and shirt in the place and now had only the air to argue with.

The day had moved through its shape from horn to horn, from bread to bone to prayer. It felt, for the width of a breath, like routine—weighty, rehearsed, real. The projector fan whined and the elder leaned toward his chair, eyes on the screen, the psalmist's words on his tongue, ready to feed the flock their last amen of the day.

The burner at his belt buzzed once.

The cracked little screen glowed through worn leather. Two digits shone pale: 23. The elder didn't look around. He looked only at the number, let it move through him, and slid the phone back into the pouch. He leaned toward the curtained wing where the trumpeters stood and spoke a single syllable that carried no farther than their ears.

The horns rose.

The first blast was wrong. Too long, too sharp. Then another, then another, tumbling into a pattern the compound had been taught to fear and to honor. It wasn't for meals. It wasn't for curfew.

Men surged to their feet. Women swept children into their arms and moved toward the hidden doors behind the smokehouse. Spotters shifted higher in the trees. Dogs lunged against chains and found the line they would run when released. The alarm became continuous, a scream of brass rolling over the compound until the earth itself seemed to vibrate.

An elder lifted his voice, scripture cutting clean through the sound. “He will never be defeated when he opposes his enemy at the city gates.”

Amen rose back like a tide. The horns did not stop.

Men: rifles up, lines along the berms, pairs ghosting into tree-hides, hands checking magazines by feel. Women: kettles pulled to quench the smoke, sacks of food and water carried down into tunnels, vents covered with rags soaked in thin vinegar. Children: herded in quick, steady lines, reciting the shepherd psalm as their feet found the ladder rungs. Elders: in the yard’s center, voices low and exact, turning fear into liturgy. Spotters: binoculars up, eyes on the road and the tree line, mouths quiet, bodies still. Dogs: loosed along the fence where the gate’s shadow falls, noses low, barking turning to a rhythm under the horns. The medic: kit in hand, walking the corridor to the bunkers, checking his own list the way a man checks the air before a storm.

No one asked who had sent the number, or from where. The message did not explain. It did one job. It told them to move.

They tightened. They waited. The horns kept speaking. The compound took its breath and held it. The night leaned closer. The next sound would decide what the day had been training them for.

Chapter Twenty Six – Storming the Castle

The alert came like anything else in that house of ritual: quiet, precise, and immediate. It was a short, scrubbed message pushed to the compound's emergency burner—the sort of text that could have been sent by a dozen hands and traced by none.

23. Stand ready. It was the kind of signal that read like a verse and tasted like war.

Protocol Twenty-Three—their emergency alert, drawn from the Twenty-Third Psalm.

"Thou preparest a table… in the presence of mine enemies."

Outside, the peacocks screamed first. Their shrill cries cut through the trees in uneven bursts, echoing down into the yard. Dogs followed, a chorus of chain-rattling and guttural barks, their bodies straining toward the fence line. The sound jolted men from cots, women from their low tables. A runner at the western berm froze, certain that the noise was no accident. The birds only called that way when something larger than foxes or stray dogs had crossed the line. The alarm spread not by radios, but by instinct. Everyone knew the peacocks were never wrong.

Inside the bunkhouse, the horn that marked meals and prayers took on a new, serrated cadence. Men snapped up from benches; women exchanged looks that were both practiced and raw. Commands rolled down the line in clipped syllables, twice-checked and sharpened by training: gather, arm, move to ingress points, secure non-combatants.

For a minute there was movement and not panic. That was part of the discipline—the difference between terror and purpose. Children were scooped up by taut-shouldered mothers. Older boys were sent to haul water and ration tins. The elders—men with scars and the slow certainty of those who had been given the responsibility of making choices for others—slid into leather coats and belts that carried small tools and the cross-slung tangle of a rifle. They did not shout; they methodically locked things that needed locking and handed instructions like lit matches.

Down behind the mess hall, the bunker door had been fitted with a steel ramp sunk into earth and camouflaged with pallets and soil. The hatch gave on a hinge that took two hands and a grunt. Men with flashlights and face masks moved first, single file, lanterns guttering as they descended. The air under the compound smelled of damp earth and old oil. It took a moment for eyes to adjust.

Inside the bunker, the dim was practical and stripped of worship. Bunks lined the side, stacked three deep. A low generator hummed. Maps were pinned to cinderblock walls. The elders split the group into escorts: women and children with food kits and water; senior fighters and a handful of "cover" teams that would hold the surface if they had to. The younger men—thick-limbed and fast—were sent to the tunnel mouths to check the charges. Old hands at the controls clicked booby traps back into place, a small, ugly art: concealed pits, tripwires wired to scrap-metal charges, a scatter of spring-loaded caltrops packed into burlap.

They called them booby traps in rough humor, then swallowed the laugh. There was no ceremony to this. It was logistics: hinder the following, protect the retreating.

Above ground, the compound reordered itself. Lookouts mounted into the trees, cloaked in branches and scent-muffled, rifles at the ready. Dogs snapped at the ends of their chains, nails clawing at dirt. Women lit diversion braziers in shallow pits that, if stoked at the wrong time, would throw up thick smoke and confuse the air. Elders walked the lanes, glancing up at the peacocks still screeching from rooftops, weighing whether the birds had given them minutes or only seconds.

They had time enough, minutes measured in ritual pace, and the discipline of practice. A watchman on the eastern berm checked binoculars and saw nothing unusual: tree-line, a strip of gravel road, the river like a black seam. He did not know the convoy of black SUVs had slipped through fields and laneways, hours earlier, until a runner arrived from the west with a face gone pale from too few hours' sleep and too much knowledge.

They moved into the tunnels in small groups. The elders took the lead with ritual calm; women and children followed under the escort of two men each, their hands steady, their faces blank with focus. They moved through narrow corridors whose ceiling was low enough to force bowed heads and whose walls had been hand-carved, soot black where torches had burned. The noise of it—the shuffle of feet, the whisper of fabric, the soft clink of baby teeth against a promise of bread—was intimate and human, and it cut differently across a compound built to be seen by no one.

Above them, the compound's defenders did everything an organized militia should: they camouflaged observation points, they checked red-light beacons, they rotated shift changes into triple speed, they set lookouts into the woods to track the horizon for mechanical glints. They reheated old lessons about defenses: block the roads, slow the advance, funnel the attackers into channels they had set with their own hands. They sealed gates, they stacked makeshift barricades, they wired doors with springs and thin, hungry noises.

At the staging area miles away, the convoy breathed low. Engines ticked in dark, unblinking rows. Lights were off, but men checked weapons under the quiet glow of map lamps—rounds slotted, optics zeroed, NVGs clipped into place. State troopers in black and blue straps, county sheriffs with soft voices and louder hands, municipal tactical units, and a roll of tactical medic teams had all been called; the call had been made and answered.

It was the kind of choreography that required many hands and the sort of planning that kept those hands busy: logistics officers with clipboards, line commanders counting men, comms techs bridging frequencies. Tactical commanders murmured into radios, checking lanes of fire, confirming timing, making sure every sector was aligned. Comms officers traced signals through the dark, tested the encrypted nets, and gave clipped affirmatives. Medics laid out their kits again and again, running hands over bags they already knew by heart. Deputies moved along the vehicles, noting numbers, jotting plates, rehearsing the language they'd use when they closed roads on startled locals.

Sloane and Tara sat in the command vehicle, sidelined by design. They watched feeds glow on darkened screens, silent observers in a room that neither required nor invited their words. Their presence was procedural, nothing more.

When the convoy rolled, it did so in a silence too exact to be idle. Vehicles eased out of the staging lot like shadowed beetles, moving in pre-ordained lanes to avoid observation. No headlights until the last possible mile. Routes wound along service roads, through fields, slipping past houses with shutters closed. Support teams fell in behind: a convoy of deputies closed secondary roads and checked plates, troopers manned choke points, specialized teams established an outer ring.

The plan was simple in its architecture: approach dark, surround wide, constrict narrow. They would cut a circle of containment every mile in every direction. The ring would be wide enough to eliminate escape routes by car and narrow enough to keep resources focused on the compound itself. Aviation units flew a grid overhead but far enough up to be unseen—satellite and drone feeds streamed to the command van.

As they closed, the groups split the countryside into sectors. Team One went north to close the county road and set the first checkpoint—squad cars, jersey barriers, the low, legal voice that says the road is closed for an emergency. Team Two slipped west to a farm lane, where they angled vehicles to block both directions with no room for a vehicle to find a turning radius. Team Three, a composite of state tactical and federal operators, formed the outer ring, raw boots on dirt and eyes in scopes. They moved with the tacit ease of people who had rehearsed their roles enough times to know them by muscle memory.

The outer ring called in the first of those small satisfactions: no one getting past. Plates were checked, IDs verified, the bones of the plan reading clean. Every mile was a stitch sewn to the next, and the compound at the center of the fabric had only the fences to bind it.

At the chosen point, the convoy went to stealth. Silent vehicle routines slid the stack to the edges of cover. Night vision sprang the world into green. The leaders counted on fingers. Ten. Nine. Eight.

Then the breach stack folded inward like a carefully controlled animal. Breachers, weighty with packs and charges, moved in tight. Shield teams unhooked ballistic plates. Sniper teams crept into ridges like ghosts. Medics checked IV kits and turned on the small red lights that would not show from above. The stack eased forward on foot.

Outside, the compound had reached the moment in which all small rehearsals hardened into a single axis of action. Lookouts screamed into radios that the sound of engines had shifted; binoculars found dark masses moving in the fields. Men who had drilled for this day did not panic; they slotted into posts and began the slow, deliberate process of fighting a defensive action: staggered firing positions, slipping out behind stacks of wood, shadowing the attackers' approach with clean, practiced bursts. Mothers checked children in the tunnels and pushed them deeper, as harried hands closed wooden doors and braced things in place.

At the gate the breachers dropped to their knees. There is a moment in every breach that is all breath: the placement of the charge, the last check of the tape, the eyes of the man holding the detonator finding the faces of the people around him and seeing nothing but work reflected back. They set shaped charges with calm hands. The safety pin clicked. Red lamps blinked faintly.

The charge went off with a roar that rattled teeth. The shockwave flattened the grass outward, snapped branches from the nearest pines, and sent dust sheeting over helmets and shields. For a split second the night was white with flash, then gray with smoke. The gate fell inward like folded paper.

Muzzle flashes answered from windows and from shadowed apertures; disciplined operators flowed through the breach with shields up and rifles forward. Hand signals sliced the air: left—clear; right—clear; center—move. The compound, drilled for this, returned fire with a voice as fierce as prayer. Men in the yard fired from behind crates and overturned farm tables. Guns cracked like a chorus; the night sharpened into fragments of light.

The first contact was a measured violence: quick, precise, the cadence of practice. Snipers on the perimeter fed clean shots that dropped silhouetted defenders who had exposed themselves beyond cover. Operators vaulted over splintered wood and into doorways; they cleared rooms with the blunt, careful choreography of trained teams. Explosions farther back—booby traps—detonated in the tunnels, a savage counter that shook support teams and sent up showers of earth from the escape hatches.

The sounds—metal, wood, the human breath—folded into one other. A Molotov struck a barricade and sent a sudden blaze licking across oilcloth, turning the yard into a ring of orange. Crewmen trained for that too: foam hissed, men pulled hoses, extinguishers were sprayed into the fire until the heat recoiled.

Inside the bunker, the elders had made the hard decisions: split into three groups and push through the older, deeper tunnel where the booby trap was a dead man's promise. They lit no torches; they listened. Mothers cradled infants, whispering scripture like lullabies. The tunnels had exits at different points on the property—an old root cellar, a shed under a tarp, a drainage culvert half-hidden in kudzu—and each egress spat them into tall grass in the dark.

The attackers were not blind to that strategy. A small team had been assigned to the tunnel mouths; they moved in with care, sensing the soil and the pattern of breath. A booby trap—set to collapse and to send scrap into the throat of anyone who slithered through—went off with a feral, metallic scream, and a man staggered back, hands full of blood and agony. The operators cursed and moved to treat him, their training pulling forward again even as the world edged into chaos. Another team sweeping the woods triggered a pitfall covered in brush; an operator dropped waist-deep before teammates yanked him out, shaken but breathing, his vest scored by sharpened stakes. The medic cursed as he wrapped the bleeding, and the sweep slowed, every man's eyes on the ground as well as the trees.

By the time the initial fury of the breach settled into the first order of clearing, the ring had held. Vehicles on choke points stopped traffic for a mile in every direction. The local sheriff's deputies had set humane cordons to shepherd away farmers who had woken and wandered from their fields; troopers held the perimeter and swept for anything crossing the road. One deputy stopped a pickup nosing toward the cordon, its driver wide-eyed at the glow on the horizon. "Road's closed," the deputy said, voice clipped. The man muttered, turned, and was guided back toward the county line, headlights swallowed by the dark. Medics established a triage site on a hill and called in for additional ambulances.

The compound was no longer their own world. It was a place under the law and the weight of tactic. The chant that had rung in the yard the week before was now a background noise beneath the sound of measured commands. The men who had thought themselves invincible had been forced into the one thing they feared most: exposure.

The fight would rage another hour, then two. The stack would surge and be pushed back and surge again. Men would be wounded; medals would not be given for the small courage of those who simply did what was needed. Children would be drawn from hiding, blinking at a sky full of dust and the way the world held itself when it was being rearranged.

Sloane sat silent in the command vehicle, watching feeds on a darkened screen. Tara beside her did the same. Neither spoke, neither moved to involve themselves. Theirs was the role of witness, sidelined, uninvolved.

This was the strike. It was a chapter of action that would be reduced later to reports and logs and statements that read plain on a page. Tonight it was men and noise and the small, stubborn courage that keeps people moving forward when all the world pushes back.

When the dust finally settled, someone would write "Operation: containment successful" and stack the file into a drawer. The medics would list their casualties. The magistrate would sign the preservation orders. The reports would flatten into prose.

For now, in the dark and the ricochet and the smell of burned cordite, they were doing what they had been built to do: move together, hold the ring, get through the chaos and find what had been hidden inside.

Chapter Twenty Seven – Armageddon

Dust hung over the yard like breath held too long. The torn gate leaned inward, a jaw cracked and set wrong. The first seconds after the blast went thin and empty—then the world came back hard.

Rifle fire snapped from windows and doorways in ragged bursts. Sparks crawled along twisted steel and died. Operators rose from their crouch, shields up, rifles shouldered, and pushed into the teeth of it.

"Left—clear. Right—hold."

They moved like water poured into the shape of a plan. One flowed to cover; another slid past—three strides, a pause, a shot. Brass skittered across dirt. Someone hissed "Up," and the next man answered with a short, precise volley that clipped a figure half out of a doorway. The body folded without ceremony.

From the yard came a hoarse chorus—scripture shouted as if sound could correct aim. Men behind barricades of crates and tables fired through gaps, muzzles stabbing the dark with light. Bullets chewed splinters and rang shields. A young voice cracked, "The fire proves the faithful," and vanished under the clean pop of a rifle that shattered glass and made his sentence into smoke.

The yard lit in pulses—green in NVGs, orange where flames licked oilcloth. Two operators stabbed a hiss of foam into the flare and stepped through as heat skated back across the floor.

"Barricade—suppress."

Three rifles answered and the barricade grew teeth in the wrong places. An arm extended too far; it dropped boneless before the hand fully let go of the weapon.

The stack split at a fork of buildings and went to work. The first barracks door blew inward under a boot. The room was bunks and smoke and plaster dust. A figure in the doorway raised a rifle—fell. Another sprinted for the far exit—caught by a shot that turned his run into a quiet heap in the frame. A third froze, dropped his weapon, hands up, eyes glassy. No one rushed him. The room was cleared twice—under bunks, behind lockers—before zip ties bit his wrists and a hand steered him down to the floor.

"Barracks one—clear."

Two operators came out bleeding—the thin line of a graze along one arm, a bruise blooming under a vest where a round had smacked and lost. Medics slid in, shoved gauze where it needed to go, taped, slapped a shoulder, and the wounded moved back into line with their teeth bared in something like a grin.

"Left, eyes." A shutter flapped, a muzzle peeked, and glass burst outward. The sound of the shot arrived a fraction late. The silhouette toppled forward, half into air, half into the room, then slid down like laundry off a line.

The yard howled in pieces—men shouting, dogs barking inside the fence, wood splintering, the hiss of foam, the thin whine of ricochet. Over it all the comm net held clipped and clean—the tight grammar of a fight measured in corners and distance.

A door on the right slammed back and light poured out of a low cinderblock building in a greasy, unnatural orange. Air spilled from it that stank—fertilizer's sour ghost, solvent, something sharp with a sugar edge. Tables sagged under jars and trays, lengths of tubing hung like loops of gut. Timers—crudely wired, some blinking, some dead—nested in plastic bins. Masks dangled by their straps, lenses pocked with dust.

"Hold," the team lead said, and they stacked on the jamb and breathed twice and went in together.

Glass flashed near the ceiling. A bottle arced and broke against concrete, fire sprinting across liquid like it had an order to obey. A table leg caught, a curtain coughed flame up its length.

They moved like they had rehearsed. One hosed flame with foam; two shouldered past and put the figure in shadow on the ground. In the doorway, someone coughed into a sleeve and blinked until tears cut clean tracks through dust.

"Possible chem prep," a voice said. "Tag and hold. No handling."

A marker went on the jamb. A camera flashed—wide, detail, tag. Someone kicked a can of solvent away from heat and its rattle sounded like bones in a cup. The team moved to the back—a short hall, a closet of nothing, a door that stuck and then gave. A tiny fan turned and turned and changed nothing.

They came back out into air they could swallow.

"Lab secured," the lead said.

The stack pivoted. The shack to the left coughed a man into the yard. He ran five paces, tripped on a plank, and physics did the rest. A shot landed after, and he went down as if asleep.

"Clear left. Push center."

The defenders had built a world out of discipline and a story out of fire. It still wasn't enough. They fired too long from the same places; overwatch wrote those mistakes in sharp glass and blood. Shoulders exposed to throw, to shout, to preach turned into lessons on dirt.

Inside the warehouse, men dragged crates across the floor, their boots slipping on powder. Some shouted verses, others barked orders that cracked at the edges. One man ripped a banner from the wall and tied it around his arm as if cloth could be armor. Another tried to brace a door with a desk while his hands shook. A boy held a torch high, voice breaking as he recited, "The faithful do not fall." His voice failed him before the torch did. In a back corner, two women pressed children deeper behind stacked hay bales, whispering prayers over their heads. Fear hung in the air, acrid as the smoke that already seeped under the rafters.

One defender climbed onto a crate, voice hoarse, and shouted for the men to hold the line. His face was lit by fire and pale with sweat. For a moment the chant caught, a surge of voices shaking the rafters. Then another blast outside sent dust raining down, and the shout thinned again. Someone muttered that God would not abandon them. Another answered that God demanded proof. Their argument lasted only seconds before the next volley from the yard struck the walls and drove them both to the floor.

On the ridge, a sniper pair watched a man crawl onto a roof and angle a long weapon across shingles. He had a lane for three seconds and did not use it. He had none at four because a single round folded him backward into shadow.

"Roofline—quiet."

A sweep team found a tripwire at a tunnel mouth a heartbeat late. A packed jar under brush coughed metal and dirt. An operator swore behind clenched teeth; the medic slid in, wrapped a forearm bright with blood, and shook the man's shoulder once, hard. The sweep slowed. Eyes went to ground as well as forward.

Farther downslope, a second pair followed a faint path to a drainage culvert hidden under kudzu. The grate was cut; the earth below tamped smooth by many feet. They marked it, covered it, and posted.

A long shed on the east edge gave up hardware—rifles wrapped in waxed paper, shotguns greased against rust, crates of ammunition, coils of wire, bags of nails. A camera popped and popped again—wide, detail, tag. Hands in gloves lifted, set down, repeated. The rhythm was the piece of the night that felt like sense.

The fight intruded into short halls and narrow rooms. A barracks on the south side had two rooms and a corridor that could be crossed in four strides. Four strides were enough to change a life. Two men pressed through and turned left. Two shots. A third dragged a boy—not yet twenty—into the hall, pushed him down, knee set in the small of his back, plastic biting wrists. The boy said something that might have been an apology and sounded like a curse. No one answered.

In the mess hall, a door stood crooked on one hinge. A chair lay at an angle that only made sense if you'd run through a room in a hurry. In the corner near a woodpile, someone had chalked a verse on cinderblock; a hand had smeared the last line into a gray blur.

A K-9 team slipped through the service corridor by the kitchens, the dog's tail stiff, nose dragging the floor where powder and sweat tangled. It pulled toward a stack of crates, stiffened, then looked up; the handler's palm flattened and the animal went down like a switch had been thrown. One crate was eased open—shotgun, wrapped in oilcloth; beneath it, a roll of fuse and a bundle of nails. Tag, photograph, bag. The leash went taut again and the team moved on.

Near the livestock barn, two operators cleared a row of empty pens by red light. Something scuffed in the straw—then a goat bawled, rearing against a rail. Hearts stumbled, rifles checked; a hand went up, palm out, and the breath everyone was holding came back in a rough laugh no one wanted. The doorway to the tack room stood ajar. A single rifle lay on a feed bin, still warm to the touch. Tag. Photograph. Tag again.

At the perimeter, deputies and troopers held the roads against the night. A farmer in a truck insisted he had to check his herd; a trooper told him the road was sealed and pointed to the fields behind his house. A teenager with a drone kit tried to lift off from a ditch; the jammer sang and the drone dropped back to dirt. Farther down the road, headlights clustered.

Deputies went car to car, telling locals and curious onlookers the same flat line: "Emergency operation, turn back." Every word was written down in the log by flashlight, every plate number captured against a clipboard. A man with a camera tried to argue he was press; a deputy pushed his lens aside and sent him back toward the highway. His protest was swallowed by the engines of waiting cars.

Detainee lines lengthened. Knees pressed into rock, wrists cinched, faces streaked with soot and sweat. Some spat words pulled from sermons; some said nothing and stared at the ground. A boy—scar raw and blistered on his forearm—cried openly. Tears cut tracks through ash. No one told him to stop. An older man muttered prayers that fell apart into sobs. One detainee smiled faintly, shoulders slumping as if relieved to be done running. Another whispered questions about his family—no one answered him. The line shifted as more knees hit the dirt.

"Gate two secure."

"South wall clear."

"Detainees—mark lane Bravo."

"Medic—east side—shrapnel chest. Tourniquet applied."

A tunnel under the old chicken coop exhaled dirt. The roof had been cut and braced with fence posts; the brace had failed. One operator dropped to a knee, coughed grit, and slid back as a section of earth slumped into the trench. "Collapse—coop tunnel. Mark and bypass." The paint stick scrawled an X and the team moved left instead of down.

Inside a storage room, a ledger lay open with columns neat and tight. A hand held it down for a camera. Coins had been used as paperweights; knives too. A pocket radio in the corner whispered static and a fragment of verse. A gloved finger clicked it off. In the corner of a footlocker: two passports, a stack of cash bound with a rubber band, three cheap cell phones with battery doors missing. Photograph, tag, collection slip slid into a sleeve.

Near the warehouse, the compound's last defenders pressed their shoulders into crates. One man recited verses between gasps, another tried to load a rifle with trembling hands. A woman clutched a Bible to her chest as if the cover might be armor. Children were herded to a corner where shadows were thickest, their eyes wide, mouths hidden under palms to keep them quiet. The warehouse was no longer a storehouse; it was a place for the last stand.

One defender knelt by the doorway and whispered a prayer into the floorboards. Another jammed nails into the seams of a crate, trying to turn it into cover. The air smelled of smoke, sweat, and fear. A voice near the rafters cried, "He will never forsake us," but the echo was thin. The sound of boots outside the wall came closer, steady, unbroken, and the defenders' voices faltered.

A woman came from a pen that stank of lanolin and hay, a child wrapped in a blanket clutched to her chest. An operator went to a knee, took the bundle with both hands, and rose. The woman nodded once and let herself be steered into the lane marked by cones. It was the first motion she had made that wasn't a reflex.

On the fence line, a trooper ran a light over tire tracks and said, "Not from tonight." A deputy wrote the note on a damp card and tucked it away. The card would becomc a photograph; the photograph would become a number; the number would become a sentence read under oath.

The defenders' chant thinned. Courage bled at the edges. A handful tried one last run—three silhouettes against smoke, rifles held too high—and the yard wrote them into stillness in three quiet bursts. The echo fell flat. Even the dogs in the pens had gone to a low, uncertain growl.

The team lead raised his hand and the stack halted, breathing together. He looked left, right, center, then lifted two fingers toward the big building at the yard's edge—the warehouse. Corrugated skin caught orange where light touched it. Through broken panes, shadows jerked. Inside: scripture and swearing, rage and prayer. A barricade scraped across concrete. Barrels rolled and stopped with a knock like knuckles on a table.

"Warehouse," he said into the mic. The word came back three times, three breaths.

They moved sideways through shadow, shields up, rifles low. A breacher team knelt at the corner of the big sliding door and went to work. Sparks skated over metal and went dark. The chemical hiss of persuasion drifted on the air like something that shouldn't be heard.

The yard's noise settled into a new pattern: shouts clipped into words that did work, small eruptions of flame with boundaries, men still moving forward because momentum had become muscle. In the warehouse, metal flexed. Crates clattered. Bolts rattled under a nervous hand.

"Stand by."

Men took breath. The warehouse took positions. The night bent toward something no longer controlled by the compound.

Chapter Twenty Eight – Fire and Brimstone

At the far end of the compound, militants crowded into the warehouse. Their voices clashed against corrugated walls—scripture shouted over curses, promises of fire rising above the metallic slam of rifles being chambered. A banner with the torch in a ring of flame hung skewed over the loading bay door. Someone tore it down and tied it around his arm like a tourniquet, as if cloth could stop what was coming.

Crates scraped over concrete as makeshift barricades were dragged into place. Barrels rolled and thudded to a stop. Nails rattled in coffee cans. Dust lifted and hung in lamplight, trembling with every impact. Sweat and smoke mixed with the raw smell of powder. Young men found gaps to fire through; older men took positions with torches and iron bars. In a shadowed corner, two women pushed children behind stacked hay bales and pressed palms over small mouths to still their breathing.

Outside, operators listened through closed throats.

"Lock it down," the squad Leader said.

Breachers dropped to a knee at the sliding door. Thermite strips unrolled with quiet finality. They pressed the charges into hinges and locks; tape hissed as it sealed tight. Sparks licked under gloved thumbs. The metal beneath began to glow, first a cherry rim, then white so bright the eyes watered.

Inside, voices rose like a bad choir. "The fire purges, the fire proves," someone shouted, and the men around him shouted it back, faster, as if speed could turn sound into a wall. A boy fumbled a striker on a lantern, singed his thumb, and bit his lip to keep from crying. The elder nearest him barked that the faithful did not need flesh to be whole. The boy nodded through tears and lifted the lamp higher.

The command net hummed with clipped reports.

"Contact left—"

"Suppressing—two down—"

"Thermite burning—door in thirty."

The yard flashed in staccato. Sparks stitched across the lip of the frame. Rifles barked in measured bursts. Shadows pitched against the warehouse skin in jittering silhouettes.

Heat crawled over the breachers' knuckles. The lock sagged, dull red, then drooled molten metal. Someone whispered "Set" and stood with hands open, palms outward, like a priest at an altar.

Shields rose. The stack shifted forward on practiced feet, shoulders low, rifles angled for the first deadly second. Boots rasped on gravel. Breathing came tight and even.

Then the world tore.

A thunderclap split the night. The roof peeled like tin, a sheet launched skyward on a column of pressure. For an impossible second it hung there, red at the edges against a black sky, like a coin refusing to fall. Then it folded on itself and crashed back in jagged arcs, scattering embers and shrapnel. Fire bloomed out of the door in a greedy wave.

The shockwave slammed operators to the dirt. Ears rang with a high, needling whine. Glass in the barracks and sheds exploded into sleet. Radios screamed static and then caught themselves as if nothing had happened. Boots slipped in ash. Men dragged one another upright, helmets gray with dust, shields angled toward flame without thinking.

Heat rolled over them in sheets. Smoke boiled, thick and black, clinging to lungs and eyelids. Flames licked rafter and banner and breath. Crates collapsed, spilling rounds and nails into fire, popping like brittle chestnuts. A ladder fell and clanged against concrete, then vanished into orange.

Inside the warehouse, scripture turned to screaming. The torch-and-ring banner tied to an arm flared and vanished in a wash of light. The barricade nearest the door went from wood to ghost in seconds. Someone tried to haul a barrel back into place and dropped it, hands blistering; the barrel rolled and thumped against a wall like a heartbeat.

"Push!" a voice barked from the yard, and the line surged. Rifles swept, shields locked. Men moved as if willed by a single muscle, not their own. Overwatch on the ridge picked off the figures who burst out of side doors, their silhouettes bright against the fire. Each body fell before it made three strides.

Medics slid under raised shields and pulled a man back, his vest stitched by shrapnel. Foam hissed where sparks found the slick on the floor. An operator nudged a canister away with a boot and marked it with a grease pencil, a quick skull and crossbones sketched in white.

A booby trap went off near a tunnel mouth with a metallic cough. Soil leapt. An operator reeled back clutching his hand, fingers cut and bright with blood. "Tourniquet," someone said, and a strap bit down above the wound. "Move him," another answered, and the man went to his feet because that was what men did here or they did not breathe again.

Inside, the last defenders pressed their shoulders into crates. The elder with the lamp climbed onto a pallet and shouted for the line to hold. His voice shook; the flame trembled with him. Another man jammed nails into crate seams like a ritual. Children curled around themselves behind hay bales, eyes wide, small hands pressed over smaller mouths.

A woman by the far wall clutched a book to her chest, the cover slick with sweat. She whispered words she had learned by heart but could not make the meanings stay. When a beam shrieked and sagged, she hauled a child by the arm and shoved him toward a gap in the stacks. The child went, because he had been taught to go when pushed.

On the ridge, a sniper pair watched a man crawl onto a roofline and angle a long weapon across shingles. He had a lane for three seconds and did not use it. He had none at four. "Roofline—quiet," one said, and the night held that sentence in its mouth because there was no need to answer.

At the perimeter, deputies turned back a coil of headlights with slow hands and patient words. "Emergency operation. Turn back, please." A man with a camera argued he was press; a trooper placed a palm in the space where the lens wanted to go and directed him toward the highway with two fingers. The glow above the pines pulsed and drew insects and people alike. The line held.

In the yard, operators flowed along the graveled edge of the warehouse. Each step sent soot into the air like breath. The stack hugged the wall, found the next door, felt heat through the glove and understood it in the bones. One man reached for a handle that had fused to the frame and stopped. Another tapped the metal with a boot and listened to the pitch. "No," he said, nothing else, and they moved, because the word was enough.

The door on the west side gave under a shoulder. Inside, heat roped up and curled a strip of skin off the cheek of the man who broke in. He blinked, blinked again, and fired into a shadow that lifted a rifle. The shadow dropped on its side like laundry.

The blaze chewed through barricade and sermon alike. It found the stack of timbers meant to prop a wall and ate through the center first and left the ends until last and then decided last was now. The world shifted. Metal groaned and bent with a sound like a voice made of steel.

"Back!" the squad Leader shouted, and the line slid away from the wall in one smooth pull, like being drawn by a string. A section of roof skin collapsed in sheets. Sparks fountained. Shards skipped across gravel and pinged off shields like hail.

A boy, maybe sixteen, flung his torch. It landed short and rolled and crawled flame toward the threshold. He tried to run for it and fell. He got up. He fell again. A hand reached out and caught the back of his shirt and pulled him into the crook between wall and crate and pushed his face into the shadow there. The hand shook. The fire came on anyway.

Down by the service yard, a deputy stopped a truck backing up to a gate. "I've got goats," the driver said, and his voice cracked and the deputy said "Not tonight," and they both understood that some sentences were for saying and some were for hearing and this one was both.

Back near the breach, an operator moved with the deliberate slowness of someone who knew everything after this would be different. He stepped over a body without looking at the face and marked the floor with a chalk line and a number that would turn into a bag and a tag and then into a chain that would hold in court if the men who carried it did their jobs.

A cinderblock side room coughed a ledger onto the floor. Pages fanned out and turned black one corner at a time. A gloved hand scooped the book back into itself and pressed the spine to make the edges square. A camera flashed: wide, detail, tag. The burned parts made their own grammar. Another page slid and showed neat columns—the kind that serve as proof when memory refuses to stand.

Somewhere behind the mess hall, another tunnel under the chicken coop exhaled dirt; the ceiling had caved in. A team who had meant to go down marked the lip with orange paint and a cross and moved left. There would be another way. There always had been. Men had hollowed this place the way a stream eats through limestone—quietly and over time.

The warehouse became a collapsing heart. Metal ribs bent and showed orange inside; beams peeled away like thin bark. From within, screaming thinned, then shredded into breath, then into the low animal sound fire makes when it eats alone.

In the yard, detainee lines lengthened. Knees pressed into rock. Plastic cut wrists. Faces streaked with soot and something older than soot. Some men spat words pulled from sermons; some found no language to stand on. A boy with a fresh scar across his forearm cried openly. Tears carved tracks through ash. An older man mouthed a prayer and was cuffed gently because the hand that cuffed him had learned that some things should not be broken when there is no need.

"South wall clear."

"Gate two secure."

"Detainees, lane Bravo."

"Medic, west—blast ear."

A K-9 team slid along the service corridor where kitchens fed the yard. The dog's tail grew rigid; the nose plowed dust; the handler's palm flattened and the animal folded to the floor without a sound. A crate eased open under the light: shotgun in oilcloth, roll of fuse beneath, bundle of nails below that. Tag. Photograph. Bag. The leash tugged again; the team moved on.

Near the livestock pens, straw shifted. A goat bawled and reared against a rail and scarred a beam with its horn. Rifles checked; a palm went up; everyone breathed again because even fear has to laugh sometimes or it cracks. In the tack room, a rifle lay on a feed bin. The metal was still warm. The camera said so.

On the ridge above the road, a small drone nosed toward the yard like a moth toward flame. A crack from a high point in the tree line wrote its ending. It fell into brush and sulked itself into silence. The jammer on a trooper's shoulder sang to itself and the quiet stayed quiet.

The blaze guttered in sections and flared in others. The warehouse's long wall all but lay down. The door that had been set to be a door was only a mouth now, breathing heat into the open. From the interior, one last knot of defenders tried to break out—three figures holding rifles too high, running at angles that made sense to zeal and none to survival. Three clean bursts folded them. The echo fell flat.

"Hold," the squad Leader called, and the word meant three different things at once: do not move; keep it together; keep it safe.

Medics fanned to triage. Colored tags pinned to sleeves. Names written on forearms in wax pencil. One man muttered his wife's name and a medic wrote that down too because all names might matter later.

"Containment holds," a voice said on the net, and somewhere at a roadblock a deputy turned another car back toward the county line. Hazard lights winked in a string and then went dark as the road returned to itself.

In the husk of the warehouse, heat still worked on metal. The light there was the color the mouth of a kiln makes when someone who knows the kiln looks into it and nods. Operators posted watch on the openings and waited for the temperature to fall enough that work could begin that was not fighting but something else: the slow, dull business of proving what had already been done.

A team walked the yard in pairs, heads down, counting. Markers went into the ground at regular intervals. Chalk lines stitched numbers across concrete. Every scrap that meant something and much that meant nothing went into bags that would become boxes that would become rooms with lights too bright for anyone who wanted to lie comfortably.

At the far edge of the compound, a lieutenant reached for a radio and said a quiet line into a channel reserved for things whose words had to be exact. The county coroner was notified. With the scale of casualties, a message went through to the GBI Medical Examiner's Office in Decatur. They would come when the heat fell and the scene was declared safe, and what had burned tonight would sign its name again under brighter lights.

The blaze burned itself from roar to hiss. Ash fell in lazy spirals, a gray snow on shoulders and hoods. Smoke lifted in a long column that wrote a kind of punctuation mark against the stars and then smeared itself away. The compound that had built itself into a fortress and practiced for siege had been pulled apart in a few hours by men who practiced the same thing differently. The result was not debate. It was wreckage and people and the first careful motions of law.

The ring held. The yard held. Operators moved slower now, as if the air had thickened. Someone laughed once, a sharp bark, and then didn't again. A goat nosed a bucket and sent it skittering; the sound made three men flinch and then raise eyebrows at one another in the sheepish way of men who know they are alive and have to get used to the shape of it again.

By the time the flames settled into beds of coals and the beams stopped speaking, the night had made its decision. The compound was no longer a story it told about itself. It was a place where the ground was black and the air still tasted of pennies and old promises. It had been broken open. What was inside would be counted.

Spotlights swung. The line re-formed in a wide arc around the ruin. In the distance, a rooster tried the courage of dawn and failed. The peacocks had gone silent.

"Hold," the squad Leader said again, softer now, so it sounded like a sentence a person says to someone they want to keep safe.

The work after this would be slower. It would have more writing in it and less shouting. It would be done with gloves and pens, not shields. But the shape of it would be the same shape as the night: a group of people who knew how to move in lanes and did not let go of each other when the world tried to tear them apart.

Chapter Twenty Nine – Revelation

The yard was a haze of smoke and dust, floodlights cutting sharp cones through the drifting cloud. Operators staggered upright, coughing, helmets powdered gray from the blast. Radios crackled with overlapping calls:

"Two down but mobile—"

"Medic to the east wall—"

"Check your partner, check your partner!"

The warehouse was gutted. Its roof peeled back like a sardine tin, walls bowed inward, flames licking the twisted frame. Inside, shadows writhed against orange light. Scripture in broken voices thinned to a kind of rasp, then to nothing the fire could hear.

"Re-form perimeter. Push casualties back. Secure the yard."

The order cut clean. No panic—just process.

Shields lifted, rifles swept arcs. Teams pressed through smoke, boots crunching across glass and charred debris. Militants burst from doorways firing wild; return fire was short, precise—three-round bursts that dropped a shout before it finished the word. One man let his rifle fall and raised his hands. Zip-ties bit his wrists and his knees found dirt.

Barracks were cleared methodically. Bunks overturned. Trunks kicked open. Weapons stripped and racked. No celebration; no speeches. Only the deliberate cadence of men moving lane to lane, room to room.

Gunfire thinned, then stuttered into silence. For every militant who pulled a trigger, another surrendered—choking on ash, hands high.

Rows of detainees grew along the yard. Plastic cut wrists. Knees pressed against gravel. Operators paced behind them, rifles low, nerves still sparking from the fight. Some prisoners spat curses through cracked lips; others stared hollow-eyed, zeal burned out by heat and shock. A boy with a fresh initiation scar cried without guarding the sound. Tears cut clear tracks through soot.

The compound hadn't fallen quiet yet. But the fight was gone. Below the yard, past the collapsed tunnels, by the treeline, a team hauled two older men into the floodlight. Robes charred, hand scars raised and shiny, faces ashen. The elders had tried to slip the line under cover of smoke and an old shaft; the ceiling slumped and trapped them to their waists until operators dug them free. They stood now with plastic biting old skin, the posture of command still in their spines, authority scorched away.

"Leaders—tunnel exit," someone reported, flat.

As they passed the detainee line, younger militants lowered their gazes—not reverence, not fear, but something quieter: shame, bewilderment. The old men said nothing. Their silence carried more weight than any verse.

A K-9 unit led its handler along the tunnel lip and sat, chin lifted. The handler flattened a palm; the dog lay down like a switch had been thrown. A paint stick scrawled an X across the collapsed mouth. Another team moved to a second shaft and snapped photographs of fresh tool marks inside. The ground told stories that breath could not.

Evidence technicians moved in behind the operators. Gloves shone pale in the floodlights. Every seized item went through the same ritual: photograph in place—wide, then detail—tag, bag, log, witness. The cadence sounded like drill commands spoken sotto voce.

At the feet of the first elder, a phone slid from his robe and blinked before the screen dimmed. A tech tapped it awake and saw one unread message.

Timestamp: thirty minutes before the first breach charge blew the gate.

"Device shows a pre-entry text," the tech said—no opinion in it, only the fact. The phone was sealed in a sleeve and the sleeve into a bag. The tag received a number and the number accepted a time. Two signatures followed, faces impassive, voices low. The chain began.

Operators exchanged brief looks that meant more than they said. A warning had gone out. Someone beyond the fence had sent it.

The shed beside the mess hall surrendered a ladder and two crates of wax-paper-wrapped rifles. The air smelled of oil and cordite. Bands of ammunition gleamed like dull jewelry. Smaller boxes cracked to reveal nails, powder, wire—kits waiting their turn. A tech stood in the doorway and read out the sequence while another clicked the camera:

"Marker twenty-seven: long guns, wax-wrap, ten units."

"Marker twenty-eight: ammunition—banded, five cases."

"Marker twenty-nine: improvised component kit—wire, cut nails, powder, timers."

Every line echoed back from a second voice with a pen; every call ended with a soft "Logged." The battlefield changed shape under that word.

Behind the shed, a shallow pit held a tarp and a crate with its lid stenciled FEED. Inside: a coil of fuse and a paper bundle of nails. The photograph turned the lie into evidence.

At the compound's center, the bunker doors sagged on scorched hinges. A flashbang thudded inside; the stack stormed through. Smoke drifted from corners. Desks bowed under the weight of maps whose corners were pinched by coins and knives. Ledgers scrawled with tight handwriting lay stacked in neat columns. Radios hissed and burped scripture.

On the back wall, banners hung—the torch encircled by flame, painted bold on rough cloth. In the far corner, a child's drawing—colors bled by heat—showed a circle and hands.

Two militants inside the bunker dropped their rifles and sank to their knees. They were cuffed without a word. The camera did its work:

"Command map—wide."

"Detail—Georgia region."

"Paperweight—knife—tag."

"Ledger—open page—columns—date range."

Knives went into sleeves the way photos went into envelopes. Coins that had held paper in place received tags of their own. Every object was given a number, and the number was given a voice on a log.

This wasn't barracks. It wasn't a storehouse. It was headquarters. The lines on the maps weren't decorations; the ledgers weren't diaries. The bunker held management, not myth.

Dawn found the detainee lines longer. Medics moved between them with colored tags and gentle hands. Burns were wrapped. Shrapnel wounds were cleansed and packed. Ears were checked, pupil responses marked with tiny circles on forearms. Operators stood behind the rows, rifles slung, eyes on roofs and doors and breaths. A firefighter team hosed the last orange out of a beam. Mist hung in the floodlights like gauze.

In the floodlight spill, a CSU officer raised his voice enough to carry to the next table. "Marker thirty-six—chain started—initials." Another answered, "Marker thirty-six—received—photo logged." A third spoke from the evidence table: "Marker thirty-six—sealed." The words passed like parts along a line until the bag sat in a crate whose lid would be screwed down and signed.

By the time the sun lifted past the ridge, the yard had become a grid. Numbers and flags, cones and tape. The jargon changed: less "clear," more "document." Less "push," more "preserve." The men in helmets still moved like a single muscle, but the flex had softened into the work of patience.

An operator paused beside a detainee with a torn sleeve and a bruised face. The boy's initiation scar had blistered and broken. The operator set a water bottle on the ground in reach of bound hands. The boy looked up once, eyes glassy, and bent his head.

Beyond the outer barricade, reporters collected like crows on a fence. Cameras peered over fields. A woman in a blazer tried to step past a trooper with a badge clipped to his belt. "Just one minute of video—" she said. "Ma'am, the road is closed," he replied, no heat in it. A teenager with a drone backpack opened a case beside a ditch and closed it again when the jammer sang. Hazard lights blinked in a snake at the mile marker.

Inside the perimeter, none of that mattered. Teams moved through the remaining structures with discipline that made quiet. The kitchen yielded canned goods and ruined sacks. The classroom—a long room with rough benches—held notebooks filled with scripture passages copied in stiff hands. A locker coughed a shoebox full of cash banded with rubber and a rolled-up banner that smelled of smoke and something older. Photograph. Tag. Bag.

A small chapel space sat at the end of a hallway—the kind made of chairs and a pulpit on a crate. A poster above the crate carried a verse, chalked by a hand that knew the letters and not the meaning. Below, a ledger page bore a list: dates, locations, odd items, all checked off with a neatness that made the stomach tighten. The page was turned into a picture and then into a number and then into a bag because that was how this night would be forced to tell the truth.

By midmorning, the elders had been separated for questioning. Their robes now looked like costumes stripped of roles. A tech sat across from the older of the two and read him his rights with a voice trained to be respectful without softness. The elder did not reply. He stared at the tag that had been pinned to the hem of his robe and the bag that held his phone.

He had seen the message. He had lifted the burner and read it aloud to a younger man with a scar on his palm, and the younger man had blown the horn. Now the message was a number in a bag with two signatures and a time. 23 was no longer a verse or a code only the faithful understood. It was a clock.

By noon, trucks rumbled through the outer checkpoint—refrigerated vans for bodies, box trucks for evidence crates. A county coroner's van stood in the shade at the edge of the lane; within the hour, their work—slow, exacting, necessary—would begin under the guidance of state pathologists called in from Decatur. A triage tent had become an intake tent. Names were now spelled carefully and repeated. Birthdates were requested and often refused and recorded anyway. The list lengthened with the indifferent generosity of bureaucracy.

The CSU lead raised a hand when a crate came to his table. "Stop," he said, and three sets of hands waited, bag above box. "Sequence." Each bag in that crate had to read as one chapter of the same story. No skipped numbers. No missing initials. The silence that followed that word made a different kind of authority than sermons had.

A pair of operators stood at the bunker doorway, looking down the short hall where the desk had been. One of them nudged the sandbag with a boot and turned away. “Headquarters,” he said to no one, and the word was both answer and indictment.

Sometime after dark that week, the televangelist walked a stage in a suit that shone under hot lights, voice amplified to the edge of song. The crowd swayed in long rows, hands lifted like a crop bending in wind. Cameras rode tracks on either side of the pulpit, red lights burning. He spoke of trial and fire as proof, of a fallen world and a ring of flame that could not be crossed by the unclean. The audience answered with amens that sounded practiced and sincere.

Men in jackets threaded down the aisles in pairs, moving with the rhythm of the crowd until they reached the stage steps. Then their shoulders squared in a way the camera did not confuse for worship. A shoulder brushed drape, a hand lifted the hem, a foot met riser. One agent leaned into the microphone’s shadow and said words that did not amplify. The televangelist’s mouth opened. His Bible slid. The page edges flashed white and then lay dark against the stage.

The cuffs flashed once under the lights and then were just metal again. The sound that rose from the room was not amen, not no. It was the incoherent sound of people who thought they were watching one thing and now could not say what it was. Phones rose like a second congregation. Security moved because that was the plan for nights like this.

The agents walked him off through curtains sewn to look like heavens. Someone ran down the aisle with a hand out as if to help. Someone else shouted that this was persecution. Most of them did what crowds do: watched, recorded, said words that made sense only to them, and tried to understand what a raised Bible meant when it was not between two hands anymore.

On a screen in a quiet room, a tech froze one frame and circled a small glint at the edge of the stage. The cuffs looked like jewelry at that distance. The caption the network later chose was a line someone else had written long before: Justice served. It was not the truth, not in full, but it was a sentence the public could hold.

Back at the compound, floodlights still hummed. Evidence crates sat stacked in rows with lids screwed down and numbers stenciled on wood. The yard that had been church and training ground and market for fear had become an inventory. A CSU tech wiped ash off a tag with the edge of a sleeve before pressing it flat. A deputy stood at the outer line with his thumbs hooked in his vest and watched the curve of headlights in the distance like a tide.

A small flock of peacocks—so loud the night before—walked the fence line with heads bobbing, their feathers dulled by ash into a flat tarnish. Even their voices had gone hoarse. A goat nosed a knocked-over bucket and sent it ticking across concrete. Three men flinched and then laughed softly at themselves without joy.

The elders stared at the ground. Their hands shook only a little. The boy with the blistered scar had fallen asleep with his cheek on his shoulder and a line of drool had drawn a clean stripe through soot. An operator tucked a blanket over his back because some motions did not belong to one side or the other. No one said anything about it. No one needed to.

The CSU lead walked past the bunker door and stopped. He looked once more at the map pinned to the cinderblock—coins and knives gone now, paper edges curling where they had been—and wrote a number on a card with his thumbnail as table. He set the card under a tape strip with a kind of care that looked like tenderness. It wasn't. It was work.

By evening, the yard was dim and orderly. The world beyond would make its stories now—the clean ones and the wrong ones and the ones that were half both. In the ring of floodlights, a different story began: of signatures and seals, of sealed bags and locked crates and the long slow path from smoke to sworn testimony.

The raid had ended the compound. The arrest had ended the illusion. What remained would burn longer than fire—in paper and ink and the sound of a clerk reading names in a room too bright for people to pretend they didn't see. The circle of flame had been drawn smaller than the circle of law. Ash lay in the seams of boots and the weave of cuffs and the folds of a banner tagged with a number that would outlive the name someone whispered over it.

Somewhere past the ridge, a rooster tried the edge of dawn and barely made a sound. The peacocks did not answer. The wind moved ash like slow rain across the evidence table, and a tech brushed it away with the edge of a gloved hand as if the movement could erase what it had fallen on. It could not. But the hand moved anyway. That, too, was part of the work.

Chapter Thirty – Securing the Evidence

By dawn, the compound had gone quiet.

Floodlights washed the yard in hard white, flattening shadows and bleaching the smoke that still clung to the air. Where hours before there had been gunfire, now there was only the metronome of procedure: the click of camera shutters, the whispered rasp of zipper bags sealing, the scratch of pens on clipboards, a distant generator's pulse.

Operators had pulled back to the perimeter. The hot zone belonged to crime-scene specialists now.

CSU teams moved in with steady steps, boots crunching over gravel, brass, and glass. They worked in pairs and threes, each team trailed by a scribe with a clipboard and a tablet. Nothing was touched until it was photographed; nothing was moved until it was logged and read back. The battlefield had been redrawn into a grid.

Yellow placards sprouted across the dirt like a field of bright weeds: BULLET DEFECT 031, SHELL SCATTER 017, FIBER LIFT 009. Laminated cards marked blast lips at the warehouse threshold, footprint clusters at the base of the berm, a scuffed semicircle where a body had turned and fallen.

Near the warehouse husk, a CSU photographer lay prone to frame the edge of a laminated map half fused to the floor. He called, "Marker twenty-six—map fragment—wide shot," and the scribe echoed it and tapped the entry into the tablet. A second shooter climbed a ladder to catch the high angle: rafters scored by rounds, splatter arcs, the angle of a beam warped by heat. He dropped a laser pointer through the bullet track and watched the red line kiss the corresponding defect below. "Trajectory rod to follow," he said, and the scribe logged it.

At the collapsed tunnel mouth, a tech ran a total station survey unit on a tripod, its green eye blinking as it captured reference points. He called coordinates in a patient procession—"Northing… easting… elevation"—and a colleague taped survey flags into the dirt so the digital model would later align with the ground that had held men upright and then let them fall.

A drone buzzed overhead and traced a grid pattern, camera gimbaling, each pass tagged with GPS. Downrange, its operator murmured time codes for the onboard recorder:

"Pass two, north sector—warehouse roof collapse, point of origin… Pass three, bunker entrance—note placards."

At the edge of the work, Tara Whitaker stood with her hands in her jacket pockets. Her eyes followed the rhythm of the scene, the way lines of people stitched themselves across the ground, the way evidence tents popped up like small white punctuation over things that could not be left in open air. She did not speak, did not interrupt. She was the witness to a thing she had chased long enough to know how to let it be itself.

A few yards away, Sloane Carver stood with the same kind of stillness, an FBI badge clipped visible, jacket zipped to the throat. She kept close enough that a supervisor could find her with a glance, far enough that no one mistook her for command. When a CSU sergeant met her eyes and lifted an eyebrow toward a stack of crates, she gave the smallest nod: present, not directing.

They watched; others worked.

In the intake tent, the rhythm was its own. Belts and shoes in one bin, wallets and cards in another, jewelry and pendants in a third. Phones were slipped into anti-static sleeves, screens photographed with time stamps, bags sealed and initialed. A CSU tech lifted a burner, saw a message still visible—23—and did the steps exactly: photo of the lock screen, photo of the message, time stamp captured, bag sealed, tag completed with three signatures in their small careful hands. The phone slid into a crate lined with foam, one number now with another, a quiet museum of things that would tell a story if the right questions were asked.

The elders' robes went into garment bags, each singed hem photographed, the burnt threads caught with tweezers and tucked into a coin envelope with its own number. A scribe read back the chain aloud—"Item E-41, elders' outer garment, brown; E-41-A, hem debris; logged at oh-seven-thirteen by CSU three-two; witnessed by CSU three-four"—and the repeating of it made the chaos feel honest.

At the bunker door, butcher paper went down like an altar cloth. Inside, the air still carried scorched dust and the mineral tang of heated concrete. On the paper, CSU techs staged each recovered item in order. Ledgers lay opened and flattened under small weights so pages could be photographed without distorting the lines. Coins that had been used as paperweights were slipped into evidence sleeves stamped with edge impressions.

A pocket radio with tape over its call button hummed a thread of static into the tent until a gloved finger turned the knob and the sound died. A serrated knife used as a paperweight went into a sleeve, the serrations pressed into soft wax to record their pattern—useless to a jury, maybe, but the habit of care had to be consistent.

"Map board—Southeast region," the photographer said, angle finder nested at the corner of the frame. "Wide. Detail—pins with date flags." He worked in a rhythm: wide, detail, tag, step.

In the lab shed, an explosives specialist crouched like a man at prayer and sifted ash with gloved hands, his face shield fogging at the edges. He coaxed out a sliver of timer casing, bagged it, and held it to the light until the etched serial woke. "Timer fragment, 127-alpha," he said. The scribe—eyes already pink from smoke and sleeplessness—repeated it and added the date, the time, the initials of the specialist, the GPS coordinate. An ATF tech labeled jars of residue—amines, nitrate traces—a stuttering chemistry set turned into evidence.

At the fence line, a county deputy said for the twentieth time, "Back up, please. Media staging is down the road." Lights on cameras winked like eyes. A man with a press lanyard tried to film over the deputy's shoulder and captured only the blur of the deputy's palm and the floodlit shoulder of a barn. "This is an active federal scene," the deputy said without heat, and guided the lens toward the mile marker where it would do no harm.

Behind the barricade of vehicles near the road, a refrigerated van idled with its doors closed and its future inevitable. A county coroner's white wagon sat in the shade, its logo catching light as someone walked in front of it. The call had gone out hours earlier to the GBI Medical Examiner's Office; their pathologists would take custody for autopsy, but nothing moved until the ME's chain of authority made a clean line over the scene. A CSU sergeant briefed an arriving coroner's investigator in low tones; the investigator took notes with the patient strokes of someone used to an alphabet of grief.

In the yard, a CSU photographer worked toward the collapsed tunnel, bracketing exposures to capture the subtle shift from dirt to the darker band where the ceiling had slumped. He slid a fiberglass trajectory rod through a bullet track in the berm wall and watched the red string line up through the air toward the rafter defect. He whispered, "High-angle fire," to the scribe, not to infer, only to connect the visible.

Tara let her eyes drift along the line the rod drew in nothing, imagined the way it had lived in the breath of a man above her hours earlier. She did not speak the image aloud. The work of the mouth belonged to others now.

Sloane stood in the same place long enough that dew settled in her hair. She watched a CSU lead read out each crate's seal number to a federal supervisor, watched the supervisor read each number back before the crate lid closed and screws bit down like teeth. The steps were slow, deliberate—designed to survive memory. She didn't call for speed, didn't ask for more hands. She watched and wrote nothing down; there would be time later to handle the language that traveled with the boxes.

Near the intake tent, a CSU photographer knelt to frame an image of a rosary half buried in ash. She brushed grit gently away with the tip of a brush until the beads showed a path. She took three shots—wide, detail, detail again from a different angle—and then a gloved hand eased the rosary into a small bag. The scribe wrote, religious article, found near bunker threshold, no more, no less. The adjectives stayed in the dust.

At the perimeter, the line of onlookers thickened. A deputy with a bullhorn repeated the same two sentences every twenty minutes, his voice thinner each time. A woman in a visor asked whether she could bring water to the "officers out there," and the deputy said yes and thank you and told her where to take it. A boy on a bicycle coasted up to the tape, pointed at the floodlights, and asked his father if the "bad guys" were still there. The father said no. His voice didn't carry.

By late afternoon, the compound looked less like a battlefield and more like a museum mid-installation. Evidence crates sat in neat stacks under shade tents. Plastic tubs labeled FIBERS, GLASS, METAL FRAGMENTS lined a folding table like drawers pulled from a tidy cabinet.

Photographs—printed by a portable unit in the command tent—hung from binder clips along a string, flapping gently as people brushed by. The image of the bunker map with its pins had been printed twice: one copy for the crate, one for the board that would travel to the war room.

In the bunker, the last ledger page was photographed, its edges rounded from handling and a smear of ash caught in the gutter. A tech placed a small weight on the page corner to keep it flat just long enough. He looked down at the writing—tight block letters, dates and locations in neat columns—and felt a shiver of something like anger, then pushed the feeling into the part of himself that wasn't allowed to touch anything and took the picture he was paid to take.

Outside, Tara watched a CSU lead lift an evidence tent, fold it with practiced hands, and carry it to the next marker. Sloane shifted her stance and rubbed a thumb along the seam of her glove. Neither woman moved to help, or to hurry, or to comment. They were witnesses whose job was to absorb and remember what everyone else was making into proof.

"Last sweep," a CSU sergeant called, and teams took a final walk-through of each sector, eyes low. A photographer caught an overlooked shell glinting near the base of a fence post and logged it as if it had announced itself at the first second. Another tech brushed a boot print cast and decided it had cured enough to move. He lifted it like a newborn tile and set it gently into a box.

A federal supervisor walked the rows of sealed crates with a clipboard and read each seal number aloud to the scribe who repeated, "Verified," and wrote them down. When they reached the end, the supervisor and the scribe signed the page, then the supervisor signed the page again for the copy, then the copy was clipped to the outside of the transport manifest. The repetition had a religious feel, not because it was sacred, but because it was a ritual believed in by all present.

At the outer lane, the refrigerated van's doors finally swung open and body bags were loaded under the coroner's eye, each tag read aloud twice—name if known, description if not, the place and time of recovery, the initials of the person who cut the scene tape and those of the person who tied the bag. A GBI pathologist checked the seals before the doors shut and signed a line that said custody transferred. Someone closed the van. The sound of the latch was softer than anyone expected.

In the war room, Rachael saved her last affidavit draft and slid the notebook to the side. Ty checked the final upload and sent a note to the CSU sergeant: Thanks. Perfect chain on the bunker crate. Holt clicked off her recorder and set her hand flat on the cool desk, knuckles whitening and then easing.

Back at the compound, the last placard came up. The last photograph was taken. The last screw bit down.

Tara let a breath out she hadn't admitted to holding. Sloane did the same, but only in the way a person who has taught herself to be a wall would allow it.

Floodlights still glared. Smoke still hung low. The wind moved ash along the ground in a line that looked like a sentence losing its subject.

The fire that had burned had gone out hours ago. What remained would burn long after—in paper and ink, in photographs and signatures, in sworn statements rehearsed and repeated until the words themselves felt like objects. The yard had become a grid. The grid had become a case. The case would become a story told under oath in a room with lights too bright for anyone to pretend they didn't see what the numbers said.

The line of vans pulled away in order: refrigerated, evidence, equipment. The drone case closed. The mast collapsed. The total station went into its box with a soft click as precise as any trigger. The perimeter thinned to patrol cars and tired men.

Tara and Sloane stood under the last floodlight as it hummed. They said nothing. They did nothing. They watched the last crate lift, the last latch close, and the compound settle into the quiet that follows when a place has said everything it had to say.

They turned toward the cars.

The yard was emptying of people and filling with history.

Chapter Thirty One – Compilation

The compound woke to a different kind of order.

Floodlights still burned even though the sun had climbed above the pines, humming faintly in the pale air. Their cones of white cut across ground churned by boots and bullets, revealing brass that winked like dull teeth, splinters from torn barricades, and ash lying in delicate drifts along the edges of the ruin. The racket of the night—rifles, shouted commands, men falling and being dragged—had drained away. What remained moved on a metronome.

A hundred small precisions replaced the violence.

CSU technicians in white coveralls walked the grid they had strung across the yard in the dark. Cord lines marked lanes between numbered placards. At each one, a photographer crouched, framed wide, medium, and detail, and stepped aside for a gloved partner to lift the item with tweezers into a bag whose mouth had been labeled in block letters before dawn. Everything was spoken twice, written once, then spoken again for the recorder that rode on a strap against the scribe's chest.

"Placard one-eight-seven—rifle casing, five-five-six, brass intact. Bag four-seven-nine," a voice called.

"Confirmed. Placard one-eight-seven logged, bag four-seven-nine," another answered, already moving his pen.

The cadence ran like a low prayer across the yard.

At the collapsed warehouse, the sift screens rattled on sawhorses as ash fell through mesh and timer fragments chimed into metal pans. A tech steadied his hands against the lip and coaxed out a warped crescent stamped with an unreadable number; he set it against a scale card, pressed the shutter, and slid it into a clear sleeve that fogged at the first breath of warm air. Another spooned a clump of fused ball bearings into a jar, twisted the lid until the seal squeaked, and printed a barcode number that the scribe read back twice before sticking it straight on the plastic.

Inside the bunker, a table salvaged from the corner wore butcher paper taped at the edges. Heat-puckered ledgers lay open on the paper, their pages curled like dry leaves, the writing inside still tight and legible in a practiced hand. A photographer worked the book as if it were an old patient—wide, medium, detail, detail again on the margin where a greasy thumb had smudged the month and year. A CSU supervisor spoke crate assignments as if he were reading a will.

"Ledger one, pages one through twenty—photographed and sealed—assigned crate two-two-four. Ledger one, pages twenty-one through forty—crate two-two-four-A."

He didn't look up as he spoke. His finger moved down a list, and a second voice echoed the words into the recorder before a third wrote them into a log that would outlive memory.

Even the small, human detritus did not go untouched. A child's sneaker burned at the heel but still showing the flecks of glitter that had once made it special. A hymnbook with its spine singed shut. A wristwatch melted into a lump, band fused to casing as if the wearer had put his palm flat against a stove and decided not to move. Each was framed, bagged, given a number, and made equal to all the other numbers.

The medical tent held another kind of ritual. Four stretchers remained under the canvas when GBI pathologists returned, coffee gone cold and faces reset to procedure

“Male, approximate fifty. Recovered bunker corridor. Tag one-five-three. Photograph series M-09 complete. Custody transferred to GBI at zero-seven-thirty-one hours.”

Another voice repeated the words; a hand signed the line. The zipper rasped closed. Two techs lifted the bag, and plastic wheels clicked across aluminum rails before the van swallowed the weight. The doors closed with a hollow boom that made people stop in place and breathe once, then moved them forward again, because the work didn’t bend for thoughts.

The last body left like the first—named without a name, numbered, zipped, recorded—and the white van rolled out from under the trees, shadow sliding up the tents as it passed. The sound of tires on gravel traveled to the fence where the press pool strained against tape and shoulders and hope.

“How many casualties?” someone asked. “Is there a terror link?” “Was the televangelist—”

“Scene’s closed,” a trooper said, voice polite and flat, as he had said at five-thirty and six-twenty and six-fifty-five. “Step back.”

Along the north road, deputies unwound the crime scene from the countryside: tape peeled from fenceposts and wrapped around gloved hands into bright rings; metal barricades folded and stacked into pickup beds; orange cones gathered in twelves and leaned into one another like skinny cattle seeking shade. A sergeant stood with a radio pressed to his jacket and called out rings to be lifted, one at a time, in the order the Bureau had specified.

"Outer ring, east—released. Outer ring, south—released. West gate remains until convoy clears."

It happened as slowly as it had been created, as if the yard were being rewound.

Under the last tent, a table filled with pieces that had smelled like war until the action of cataloging made them something else. Magazine springs laid out like metal snakes coiled to sleep. Three black rifles made empty and safe and tagged with numbers that made them the rifles of no one. A slab of concrete cut from the bunker threshold and transported to the table in a crate that had originally held fruit but now held ruin. A tech ran a gloved finger along a smear of soot and lifted it away like a print from a ghost.

The convoy lined up under the thinning hum of the floodlights. Dollies rattled as crates moved from tent to ramp to truck bay and were ratcheted tight with webbing that squeaked and creaked under hands used to this. A CSU lead leaned over a clipboard. A federal agent leaned in with him.

"Crate two-two-seven—ledgers A and B—seal intact—tape initialed alpha-bravo."

"Confirmed. Two-two-seven—ledgers A and B—seal intact," the agent said, his finger trailing a line on his own sheet. The CSU lead tore off a copy, kept one, handed one to a second agent, and a third went into a plastic sleeve that sealed with a dry sigh.

They repeated it for crate two-three-one (small arms, sealed), for two-three-two (improvised devices, sealed), for two-three-six (electronics, sealed). Each number pulled another bit of the night out of the yard into custody that wasn't the yard's to give but was the Bureau's to claim.

Engines rumbled to life in an order that had been briefed an hour before. SUVs moved first, idling into position at the head and tail of the line, lights dark. The lead truck rolled, and radios cracked in voices that were all brisk syllables and missing pronouns.

“Unit one clear.”

“Unit two moving.”

“Convoy established.”

The dust that rose behind them drifted east, then settled back as if breathing.

Near the fence line, Sloane Carver stood with her hands in her jacket pockets and her badge visible on her belt. She had been there since the first rumor of light and had not raised her voice once. She followed the last truck with her eyes until it slid from the frame the floodlights had held all night.

Tara Whitaker stood a few yards away with her arms crossed and her jaw set. Five years of stubbornness, five years of being mocked under breath in hallways, five years of looking at the same picture and making the same argument had brought her to a morning where she needed to do nothing. She marked an ending she had been told would never arrive.

They didn’t look at each other. They didn’t need to. There is a relief so sharp it feels like grief, and sometimes the only way to honor it is to let it sit between you without putting a name on it.

The war room was already dim when they arrived.

Screens that had once spilled color and panic were dark except for a clock face in the upper corner and a board that sat as green as a field. Files lay in squared stacks; a still-warm mug left a ring on a paper towel beside the sink; the hum that carried from the server room through the glass pressed its indifferent hand against the quiet.

Rachael Garrison sat at the table with her notebook closed and her pen laid across it. She had written as if writing alone could hold the case together: narrow scope, lean verbs, a language emptier of pride than law required. Now there was nothing left to write. The Bureau owned the paperwork the way their trucks owned the crates. She kept her hands folded on the dark tabletop and listened to the room forget how to breathe fast.

Ty Mathis leaned forward, forearms braced, elbows a little too far apart. The bones around his eyes showed the weeks. He stared at the board, at the green that had meant good news when it was rare and meant final when it was everywhere. He had argued them out of mistakes and back inside the lines so many times he could have done it in his sleep. There were no lines to argue anymore. It was both a mercy and an insult.

Sloane set her reports on the table and kept her words short, stripped of anything but facts.

"Chain of custody intact. All evidence sealed and transferred to Bureau. GBI has remains. Perimeter broken down. Convoy departed zero-seven-fifty."

She flipped a page; the paper made a sound like wings.

"One anomaly noted. Burner phone recovered from figures at the compound. Last message reads '23.' Time-stamped thirty minutes before breach. Evidence sealed. It's in Bureau custody."

Tara did not add a syllable. She nodded once, and it stood for everything she could have said and didn't.

Ty's jaw made a small motion that would have been a word if it had been allowed to be one. Rachael's fingers tightened where they lay on the notebook—barely a millimeter, but enough for skin to blanch around the joints. They did not ask who sent the warning. That question now belonged to people who used different doors.

There are ways to make a room end. Some are loud. This one preferred the gentler kind of punctuation.

Terminals logged out, screens fading through gray to black—one, two, three, four—down the line. Drives popped free from their ports with a small hollow sound and slid into envelopes whose tape was signed across in two neat hands. Keys on rings turned the steel covers locked over the empty ports. Envelopes dropped into bins with the soft thunk of paper obeying gravity.

Chairs pushed back into rows; their legs spoke briefly against tile and fell quiet. Coffee mugs got rinsed in the sink and left upside down on a folded towel. Someone gathered spent pens into a drawer; someone else pulled the shade two inches lower on the glass door to signal to a hallway that this was not a place to walk into right now. If a room can lay its hands flat by its sides, this one did.

Rachael slid her notebook into her bag and left the pen across it like a bar across a door. Ty gathered the loose sheets he had carried and sorted and scolded and saved and squared them on the table with a gentle smack that might have been affection if the object hadn't been paper. He bound them with a rubber band and moved his palm once over the top as if to smooth their hair.

Sloane removed a folded notepad from her jacket pocket, folded it again, and slipped it inside the inner pocket where she kept things she owed to other people. Tara unclipped her badge and set it face down on the table, not in defiance and not in surrender—a neutral act marking a point on a line.

Silence put its hand on their shoulders.

Rachael leaned back; her shoulder brushed Ty's arm, and her gaze lifted because she had taught her body to do that when she needed to withstand a thing. He turned his head a fraction because he had learned to notice. Under the table, her fingers slipped sideways and tapped his knuckles twice, then remained still. He let his hand turn palm up to meet hers and closed around it for a breath, not long enough to be an announcement, long enough to be an answer.

"You holding up?" he said, the words not much more than a movement of jaw and air.

Her mouth made a small shape that might have been a smile in a better room.

"I'm fine," she said, quietly, truth wrapped in what truth can get away with in places like this. "We made it through."

The contact broke because the world wants things to be separate even when they aren't.

Sloane glanced at the clock. Tara studied the board with a focus that didn't belong to any task and therefore could be indulged. The air from the server room turned a degree cooler and kept doing what it always did—the work of machines that do not need closure to continue.

No one said anything for a time that might have been three minutes or ten, everything in the world that mattered being without weight for once. Then Ty took in a breath that made the skin below his collarbone move and said the sentence a person says when all the verbs have been used up.

"Then it's finished."

The words landed somewhere between the table and the glass and made the quiet change shape.

No one contradicted him.

Outside this room, people with credentials would say other words in other rooms—pressers and podiums and seals on the wall behind. At precinct desks, someone would initial a paper and put it in a drawer. In vans on the highway, drivers would pass from shade into light and back again and not think about their cargo. Somewhere an evidence truck would stop for fuel, and a man would wipe diesel from his palm with a towel whose fibers would never see a lab. Somewhere a reporter would rehearse a question and rehearse her face and rehearse still not being let in.

None of that belonged here.

Here, there was a board the color of certainty and a table that had taught itself the shape of their forearms. There were chairs that had learned how far to roll and a lamp that had learned not to flicker. There was a hum that was both the sound of support and the sound of indifference. There were people who had come farther than they had believed they would be allowed to and had the sense not to ruin the moment by talking it to death.

The gate was shut.

If something moved on the other side of it, the sound did not carry.

Chapter Thirty Two – Wrapping Up

The story the public would carry home did not include grid lines and evidence placards, ash sifted from timers, or the way CSU folded a scene into crates. The story would be told against backdrops: flags, seals, marble steps, the American Sign Language interpreter's hands bright with movement beside a row of microphones. It would have a beginning and an end, and the middle would be whatever fit between quotes.

The first press conference was called before the coffee urns in the lobby had finished emptying. A pool camera rolled at the back of the room; local crews jockeyed just behind it, tripods nudging one another like animals in a pen. Producers in headsets whispered into phones, palms pressed over their free ears to hear better. Reporters stood shoulder to shoulder, badges swinging, notebooks lifted like small shields.

A long table sat on the riser beneath three flags—United States, Georgia, and the FBI's seal rendered in blue and gold. Two lecterns had been pushed together so that a single bank of microphones could catch every word. Staffers adjusted them in fussy, precise increments until someone from the Bureau lifted a hand: ready.

A Special Agent in Charge from the Atlanta field office walked on first. His suit held its creases. His face did not. He set a printed statement on the lectern, smoothed it with the side of his hand, and then looked up over the top of his glasses. The room stilled the way rooms do when they recognize a voice that will not be interrupted.

"As of last night," he said, each word clipped, "a militant compound in White County has been secured. Multiple arrests were effected. Weapons and explosives were seized.

Evidence relevant to the Marietta Coin Show robbery and related incidents has been transferred into federal custody. The individuals responsible for those crimes have been identified and neutralized. This case is closed."

The Director of the Georgia Bureau of Investigation stepped in and played his part with a different music—measured, almost academic. He did not make promises; he made statements of process.

"Our forensic teams worked through the night and into the morning to document and preserve evidence," he said. "Trajectory analysis has been completed on recovered scene defects. Ballistics comparison is underway for weapons found on site. Ledgers and electronic devices are in custody and will be examined under appropriate warrants." He closed his folder on the last sentence as if to close argument. "We are confident the evidence will support the charges as presented."

The Chief of Police from the jurisdiction where the raid had unfolded spoke last. He did not read. "Our officers, deputies, and first responders stood shoulder to shoulder with state and federal partners," he said, hands flat on the lectern. "They contained the perimeter, kept civilians safe, and brought this to a close without further loss of life. Their professionalism cannot be overstated. I am proud of them." His medals caught the camera lights and threw back a wink of gold.

The ASL interpreter's hands translated all of it as pure action—secure, seize, protect, neutralize, closed—verbs thrown into the air like cords meant to tie a thing to the ground.

Behind the cameras, they watched.

Tara Whitaker leaned against the rear wall, arms folded tight, jaw set. She said nothing. She did not want a microphone, had not been offered one even if she had. She watched the Governor's staff point to reporters they preferred, watched the SAC step exactly where a staffer's tape mark told him to stand, watched the Director of the GBI check his watch twice with his thumb just under the edge of the cuff and then smooth the edge of his folder again. She watched the word closed land and break over the room like a wave.

Sloane Carver stood a few feet away in the shadow of a column, hands clasped behind her back, chin level. She said nothing. Her presence with the federal contingent required nothing more than posture. She watched the Bureau own the room in the way rooms are owned without force: podium, flags, statements, refusal to speculate. She watched reporters get managed, watched questions get rewritten in the asking by whoever controlled the microphones.

She and Tara left by a side door when the applause began again. Their job here was to be seen by no one in particular and remember.

By noon the Governor had carried the show to the Capitol steps. Marble made a cleaner backdrop than flags. The sun glossed the edges of columns. Staffers fanned into a half circle behind him, faces composed to the thin smile of victory without gloating.

"Evil came to our doorstep," he said, one hand spread open to the press and the other planted at his sternum, "and Georgia shut the gate." The line was designed to travel. It did. He did not take questions. He had another event across town and another after that and a statement to tape for the evening shows.

Across the plaza, the Director of the GBI did his own smaller availability with charts and printouts clipped to foam boards. Lines on a diagram showed bullet paths slanted through air to defects labeled with neat numbers. A photo of a ledger page had notes circled in red grease pencil. He pointed to the lines and the circles and said words like confirm and consistent and match and preserve. He let the camera cutaways work for him: science, numbers, the appearance of certainty.

Outside the local headquarters, the Chief of Police stood flanked by patrol cars and plainclothes detectives, and spoke with the pragmatic grace of a man who had come up through midnight shifts and checks cashed at kitchen tables. "We held the roads," he said. "We kept people out who needed to be out and let in who needed to be in." He told the press where his officers had stood—"north road, west gate"—as if naming posts explained courage. He said thank you to three mutual aid departments by name, and his officers clapped in a roll that sounded like a flag being shaken out.

Between events, cameras had their own choreography. Producers begged for better angles and cleaner quotes. Photographers traded positions like chess pieces. One station's lighting kit went down and three competitors stepped around it like it had become part of the floor.

In newsrooms, writers tightened phrases so that they would fit into six-second soundbites and three-line supers. Web editors pushed "justice has been served" above the scroll. Assignment editors asked for live hits at noon, five, six, ten, and eleven.

By late afternoon, the courthouse steps belonged to a single voice. Microphones bristled on the risers. Camera lights washed the stone in a hot, even glow.

A crowd gathered at the bottom of the steps, some out of curiosity, some holding phones for the selfie that might have a day's worth of news at its back.

Rachael Garrison stood just beyond the riser, bandaged arm folded close to her body, jacket cut to read professional without invitation. She was close enough to be seen, far enough to remain unscripted.

The microphones belonged to others.

Cameras found her anyway—once, twice—before aides subtly redirected lenses back toward the podium. Her name rippled through the press line in murmurs rather than shouts, a different kind of attention, quieter and more durable.

She did not step forward. She did not speak.

When a reporter leaned sideways and called out, "Ms. Garrison—can you comment?" an FBI press officer slid smoothly into the space and answered without answering, voice practiced and firm. "All statements are being made from the podium. Any additional questions will be handled through official channels."

Rachael met no one's eye. She held her posture, allowed the moment to pass, and gave the cameras nothing but stillness.

That restraint would not stop the narrative.

By the time the feeds cut, a chyron was already forming in a producer's head—SURVIVOR TURNED PROSECUTOR SEEN AT COMPOUND RAID ANNOUNCEMENT—and it would travel just as far without a single quote attached.

When the lights dimmed and the microphones were lowered, the crowd surged forward with phones raised, hands outstretched. Rachael stepped back into the shadow of the building's columns, two agents in suits adjusting their positions without drawing notice. She did not smile. She did not frown.

She let the story belong to whoever needed it to end cleanly.

Tara watched from the plaza's shade and did not step into the sun. She did not clap. She did not frown. She folded her arms and watched the public receive the ending it wanted.

Sloane spoke to no one and texted a time and a place to the Bureau's press officer for a follow-up that would never truly be a follow-up, only the appearance of one.

Holt was not here. In a quiet office miles from the marble, she slid the final autopsy reports into envelopes, wrote names and numbers in exact script on each label, and stacked them into a drawer already packed with other endings. "Entry wounds catalogued," she said into the recorder for the last time, the microphone catching the rasp of the file cabinet as she closed it. "Trajectories logged. Findings consistent across multiple sites. Autopsy reports finalized." The cabinet's latch clicked. That was her applause.

The war room sat dark and ambient as evening cooled the glass. Screens were dead-faced. The evidence ports were locked with steel covers whose keys had been sealed and witnessed. The board, when someone brushed a knuckle and woke it by accident, glowed solid green and looked like the absence of weather.

Marcus did not appear in the lobby. There was no silhouette against glass, no shoulder-broad question. He had a business to run. He had been asked for nothing today and therefore did nothing. Cylentra's building worked on its timers and its badge readers and its maintenance schedule; the people who had needed it had taken what they needed and then left it to be a place again.

Ty passed through reception once in the late afternoon, jacket folded over his arm, tie slid loose and crooked, fatigue pulling at the corners of his mouth.

He did not stop at the board. He didn't need to see a color to know what it meant. He glanced toward the iron door down the back corridor, blinked once like a man clearing grit from his eye, and kept walking. The receptionist nodded to him and returned to her screen.

The Governor's office sent out a formal release at five. The GBI added a bullet-point list of "Key Forensic Takeaways" at five-fifteen: trajectories, casings matched, ledgers catalogued. The local Chief posted a photo at five-thirty of his officers in a line, sleeves rolled, faces open, captioned with three words—Proud. Grateful. Ready.—and a row of emojis someone in the media unit thought did no harm.

By six, the lead in most broadcasts was the podium speech cut clean: "This case is closed." The second package was Rachael's courthouse statement cross-dissolved with file footage from the pavilion and aerials of the compound. A lower-third read COMPOUND RAID over a still of floodlights bleaching the clearing. The Governor got thirty seconds. The GBI got twenty. The Chief got fifteen and a smile at the end.

Across the city, people watched from couches, from bars, from treadmills, from the backs of Uber cars, from deli counters where the sound was always off and the captions clean and fast. They nodded because endings make rooms cozier.

Tara sat at her desk in a building that had stopped expecting her to do anything heroic and pulled the battered legal pad she had carried since the robbery out from beneath a stack of new forms. The first page still bore three names written in the thick rush of that day:

Walter Garrison — DOA

Rachael Garrison — GSW, stable

Frank Harper — GSW, critical

She drew a neat line under them. She turned to a fresh page and wrote a single word in block letters that dug grooves deep and cut faintly into the sheet beneath:

CLOSED.

It was supposed to feel like victory. On paper it did. In her chest it felt like a room with a light left on for someone who hadn't come home yet.

Rachael arrived back at her office hours after the cameras had moved on and stood with both hands on the windowsill looking out at a city that had put its dinner on tables and its kids into baths and its worries into smaller boxes for the night. She touched the bandage at her arm and considered replacing it and decided to wait one more day. She set her phone face down on the desk and let it buzz twice without checking the screen.

In a newsroom downtown, a young producer clipped the last sentence of the SAC's remarks and slotted it over B-roll of the podium. She put Rachael's line next, then the Governor's gate metaphor, then the Chief's pride. The piece ended with a wide of the marble steps the moment after the microphones lowered, the crowd pressing in. She watched it once with headphones and once without. It worked both ways.

On a cleaning cart in a hallway outside the war room, two glasses clinked together when the cart hit a seam in the floor. The custodian steadied them without looking and kept walking. He had been told not to dust the room with the glass wall tonight. He would come back tomorrow and do it right.

News crawls rolled. Press releases landed in inboxes. Commentators filed takes about extremism and resilience and lessons. An hour later, another story took the top slot in two markets because a video had gone viral of a dog riding a skateboard. The world is generous with how quickly it forgets.

No one in public asked about a single number sent thirty minutes before a breach. The Bureau's property clerk had that phone in a sleeve in a bin in a cage in a room that didn't care about applause. That would be for later, if ever. For now, the day had been shaped until it was something that fit in a headline and could be held in one hand.

At the edges of the shape, where soft things live until they are named or left alone, there was the sense some doors were only latched. But the cameras had rolled, the microphones had been lowered, and the flags had been folded and wheeled back into closets where they would wait without complaint for the next time a story needed to end.

Chapter Thirty Three – Power Down

The war room was no longer a battlefield.

For weeks it had been alive with alarms, scribbled notes, hasty meals, and voices layered on top of each other until no one could tell who had said what first. Now it breathed in silence. The board glowed green from edge to edge, every circle resolved. The table, once buried under maps and evidence, had been reduced to order: three sealed envelopes stacked squarely in the middle, each one signed and countersigned.

They were all there.

Holt leaned against the wall of the evidence bay, her coat folded neatly, recorder tucked into her bag. Sloane sat at the end of the table, her phone face down, as if refusing to acknowledge the constant vibration still pushing through it. Tara sat half turned toward the door, jacket in her lap, the faintest of smiles tugging at her mouth. Rachael stood close to Ty, her bandaged arm across her stomach, her shoulders straight but softer than they had been in weeks.

No one spoke for a long moment.

The board glowed green from edge to edge. The room no longer asked anything of them. What had been carried was now held somewhere else.

Holt slipped her recorder into her bag and nodded once, already halfway back to procedure. Sloane checked her phone, silenced it, and slid it face down on the table. Tara stood and pulled on her jacket, pausing at the door as if expecting the room to argue.

Rachael remained standing beside Ty, her bandaged arm resting across her stomach, eyes fixed on the board. When she finally moved, it was with care, as if balance itself were something she had to relearn.

One by one, they left.

The door sealed behind the last of them with a sound that felt more final than any words.

For a few minutes the war room didn't feel like a war room. Holt told a dry story about a mislabeled case file that had sent her entire lab chasing the wrong set of samples for three weeks. Tara admitted she'd written a resignation letter when the coin show case went cold, kept it in her desk for nine months, and never thought she'd tear it up. Sloane muttered about the bureaucratic maze still waiting for her—"ten signatures for every warrant we already executed"—and shook her head.

Then Tara, uncharacteristically, added more. "Chief called me this morning. Said he's putting me up for a commendation." She gave a short laugh. "First time in my career the man's acknowledged I can tie my own shoes. Vindication doesn't usually come with a plaque, but I'll take it."

"Good," Sloane said, lifting her cup again. "You earned it."

Sloane hesitated, then added, "My ASAC says I'm being 'quietly considered' for a bump in rank. Which means they want me to smile at twice as many press conferences and fill out four times as many reports. Promotion disguised as punishment."

Tara grinned. "At least the paycheck's real."

Rachael looked around at them, then sighed. "The Governor cornered me after the press call. Said I should think about running for statewide office one day. Attorney General, maybe."

That landed heavy. Even Holt lifted her eyebrows.

"Governor doesn't waste words," Holt said.l

Rachael shrugged, uncomfortable but not dismissing it. "He said the state needs more people who won't look the other way. I told him I wasn't planning that far ahead. But…" She let it hang, the unspoken possibility filling the room.

Ty caught her eye. "You'd win."

Rachael gave a faint smile, but said nothing.

The moment softened again with laughter and quiet teasing. Ty poured second rounds, and even Holt joined in the banter.

When the bottle ran low, the rhythm faded. Holt pushed off the wall, slipped into her coat. "I've got a judge tomorrow who thinks autopsies are poetry. I'll remind him they're facts."

Sloane picked up her phone, sighed at the screen. "Chain of command. If anyone asks, I was here, smiling."

Tara swung her jacket on, pausing at the door. "If that board ever goes red again, I'm moving somewhere without power."

Before they left, Ty raised a hand. "Hold on. We've been sealed in here too long. Let's see how the world's spinning it."

He tapped the console. The wall screen shifted from green task circles to the bright red banner of CNN.

Breaking News: Federal Task Force Raids Militant Compound in North Georgia.

The anchor leaned toward the camera: "We are following major developments overnight. Federal officials say the raid dismantled a militant compound responsible for armed robberies across thirteen states, with losses totaling nearly one hundred million dollars in stolen property and assets."

The chyron scrolled: "$100M Robbery Spree – 13 States Hit by Network."

The screen cut to a correspondent standing before floodlit tape. "Behind me, you can see what remains of the compound after last night's assault. Officials tell CNN dozens of suspects were taken into custody. Weapons, explosives, and documents were recovered, pointing to a coordinated campaign of robberies across the Southeast."

Graphics filled the screen: arrows linking crime scenes on a map—Marietta Coin Show → Birmingham → Charlotte → Nashville → the compound raid. A second panel slid in: Key Facts — 13 States. $100 Million. 67 Arrests. 4 Dead. Explosives Recovered. The anchor repeated each line as though stamping it into memory.

Then came the press conference clip. The Governor stood at a podium, flanked by FBI Leadership and the county Sheriff. His voice carried the measured gravity of a man who knew every word would land in headlines: "These criminals thought they could terrorize our communities, but Georgia families are safer today because of the courage and skill of the men and women who stood in their way."

The FBI official leaned in: "This was a coordinated Bureau-led effort spanning multiple jurisdictions and multiple states. Across thirteen states, more than one hundred million dollars' worth of stolen property has been recovered or traced. Firearms, explosives, and evidence of further planned attacks were seized. This is one of the most significant domestic law enforcement operations in recent history."

Then the Sheriff, voice rougher, local pride shining: "Our deputies stood shoulder to shoulder with federal agents and never flinched. I couldn't be prouder of them, or of this community for standing strong."

Reporters' voices erupted:

"Was Drayton acting alone?"

"Are there more compounds like this?"

"What about the children removed from the property?"

The Governor took one: "This was the hub of their activity. The investigation continues, but authorities are confident this network has been dismantled."

The FBI dodged another: "We are not going to comment on intelligence regarding other potential sites at this time."

The Sheriff cut in on the last: "The kids are safe. They're with state services now. That's what matters."

The chyron changed: "Officials: Multi-State Militant Network Dismantled."

The anchor's voice cut back in: "Officials also confirmed televangelist Ezekiel Drayton as the Leader of this network. Investigators say Drayton used a doppelgänger to provide alibis, even appearing at televised revivals while robberies were carried out elsewhere."

Split screen: Drayton at a pulpit, arms wide, the crowd roaring; then grainy stills of his double near service entrances at crime scenes.

Then: "We're just getting new video into CNN."

Shaky phone footage filled the wall—agents hustling Drayton in handcuffs toward a black SUV, his suit wrinkled, face pale. He twisted, shouting about persecution before stumbling as hands shoved him forward.

"Let's bring in the man who shot this video." A college kid appeared by phone, voice nervous but thrilled: "I was driving by, saw the lights, pulled out my phone. At first I thought, no way, that's the preacher from TV. But it was him. You can see the cuffs."

The chyron blared: "Exclusive: Televangelist Arrested – Mobile Video Shows Ezekiel Drayton in Custody."

The correspondent pressed on. She walked the camera through the debris of the compound: a burned warehouse with smoke still curling, FBI evidence tents, crates displayed like trophies—rifles laid in neat rows, bundles of cash on folding tables, a bucket of crude pipe bombs sealed in evidence bags. Behind her, neighbors spoke to cameras:

A farmer: "We saw trucks in and out late at night. Figured it was farm work. Should've said something."

A shopkeeper: "They bought fertilizer in bulk. Said it was for fields. I didn't question it. I wish I had."

A woman from a nearby home: "I heard chanting some nights. Thought it was church singing. I had no idea."

The anchor closed the segment by recapping in bullet points over graphics: "Thirteen states. Nearly one hundred million dollars in stolen property. Explosives. Dozens of suspects in custody. And tonight, authorities say the case is closed."

Reactions rippled across the war room. Holt muttered, "Weeks of work, and it'll be this shaky clip people remember."

Sloane stiffened. "The Bureau will love the headline. FBI-led, always FBI-led."

Tara flinched as her name scrolled under: "Detective Tara Whitaker – From Pariah to Vindication." Her jaw tightened.

Rachael froze when Walter's name was mentioned—"beloved local coin dealer killed during robbery"—and then gone in less than a sentence.

One by one, the women gathered their coats. At the door, a secure drop tray waited.

Holt went first. She slid her NSA badge into the slot with the precision of a lab note, placed her temporary credential on top, and straightened it before walking out. Clinical to the last.

Sloane followed, flicking hers down with a muttered, "Bureaucracy never ends," but her pause at the tray betrayed pride. For once, she had carried something important to the end.

Tara laid hers down more slowly. Her fingers rested a heartbeat longer on the card. The badge had given her access, but also vindication. She turned away sharply before anyone could read her face.

Rachael lingered. She traced the badge with her thumb, thinking of Walter, then set it gently into the tray. When she looked back, her eyes found Ty's. "Don't stay too long." Then she left.

The heavy door sealed shut behind them.

Ty sat back at the table. The bottle sweated into a ring, the paper cups sagged inward. The board glowed clean, untroubled.

For a moment, he walked the room. Past the evidence bays now empty, past the chairs pushed back just enough to leave shadows on the floor. The war room smelled faintly of champagne and burned coffee. It looked like victory, but it felt like exhaustion. He touched the stack of paper cups with two fingers, then let them fall.

Marcus joined him briefly. He rubbed his jaw, scanning the clean board. "Strange, isn't it? Months of chasing ghosts, and it ends with champagne in paper cups."

Ty gave a dry laugh. "Closure always looks cleaner on TV than it feels in here."

Neither pressed it. Silence held.

Then the side door opened again.

Marcus rose. "Looks like that's it. We're closing it out."

Ty nodded.

The door opened again. Daniel entered. He didn't look at them. He went straight to the console, unplugging cables, coiling cords, sliding drives into sleeves.

Marcus watched him. "Daniel. We couldn't have done this without you. You closed this case."

Ty added, "He's right. You pulled it together."

"All requested Team parameters have been satisfied," Daniel said.

He paused.

"All parameters have not."

Ty looked up.

Marcus frowned. "What?"

Ty leaned forward. "The compound's down. Evidence sealed. The Bureau called it," he said carefully. "What do you mean it isn't closed?"

Daniel tapped a key.

The central screen flared awake. Circles filled it—most white, some red, thin lines stitching them together.

He turned from the console.

"Unresolved discrepancies remain."

Marcus's voice sharpened. "Discrepancies?"

"I've been closing loops," Daniel said.

Ty stood. "Show us."

Daniel walked to the iron door. His palm failed the reader. Marcus reached, but Daniel blocked him. "Not logged. Not authorized."

Ty pulled a slim card from his wallet. Daniel scanned it. A chime. Bolts withdrew.

Marcus stared at Ty. "You never told me."

Ty slipped the card away. "Wasn't supposed to."

The door swung open. Cold air spilled out. Silence heavier than sound.

They stepped inside.

Rows of towers blinked green and red, soundless, cables arched like ribs.

At the far wall, the display lit: white circles glowing, red ones pulsing.

Marcus whispered, “What is this?”

Daniel: “Encrypted forum. Years ago. Chatter about an attack at LAX. Detailed. Credible. I dropped the file into the FBI’s urgent queue.”

Marcus laughed. “Ridiculous. There was never an attack at LAX.”

“No,” Daniel said. “Because they stopped it.”

Ty froze. “Wait. I was asked to vet a file once. Anonymous. No origin. I told them ninety-five percent probable. They acted. That was you?”

“Yes,” Daniel said.

Ty slammed his hand on the table. “You can’t just query federal systems without a judge.”

“I didn’t,” Daniel said. “I used the channel they gave me. Authorized.”

Marcus shook his head. “So you’ve been running two systems. Ours. Theirs.”

Daniel: “Front end: intake. Back end: anomaly resolution. White means explained. Red means not.”

The silence broke with a printer’s sudden clatter. Paper slid out, warm and steady. Daniel lifted the stack and handed it to Ty.

On top lay the cipher of symbols.

Marcus recognized it. “That’s the one.”

Ty turned it.

Daniel said, calm: “This is where you understand.”

Chapter Thirty Four – Final Report

Ty lowered his eyes.

The page in front of him was warm from the printer, the paper faintly curled at the edges. Symbols filled it—circles, squares, triangles, crosses—arranged with the same impassive precision they had seen at the beginning of the case. No words. No annotations. Just structure.

He laid it face down on the black table.

"Show me," Ty said. "From the start. And don't skip."

Daniel didn't clear his throat. He didn't hedge. He turned the wall display to a time slice the system had already processed.

"At intake," he said evenly, "there were unresolved conflicts."

"They appeared as soon as the initial parameters were run," Daniel said.

"They were not surfaced because they were outside the requested scope."

The lattice widened. Borders vanished. A map without names filled the wall. White circles held steady. Four red circles pulsed. A thin band of timestamps ran along the bottom like a ruler.

Ty kept his hands flat on the table. "Unresolved how."

"Evidence that did not settle existing explanations."

Marcus leaned forward. "Meaning something didn't fit."

"Yes."

Ty nodded once. "What happened next."

"The system did not close the file," Daniel said. "It expanded its search."

The wall shifted. Intake logs scrolled—bag numbers, examiner initials, photo hashes. Dry. Procedural.

Marcus frowned. "Expanded how."

Daniel answered only that. "It tested whether the inconsistency appeared elsewhere."

Silence hung.

Ty translated. "So it didn't assume the heist explained anything. It treated it like a question."

Daniel inclined his head a fraction.

One red circle dimmed and turned white.

"Resolved here," Daniel said.

A line stepped off the Southeast and stretched across the Atlantic. Fields unfolded—manifest numbers, courier signatures, receiving stamps. Mundane shipping data. The kind people overlook because it looks like noise.

Ty squinted. "What am I looking at."

"Repeated attributes," Daniel said. "Packaging measurements. Stencil spacing. Pallet dimensions."

Marcus stared. "You're telling me it noticed how crates were built."

"Yes."

"And that mattered?"

"Individually, no."

Ty waited.

"When the same attributes appeared across multiple incidents," Daniel continued, "probability changed."

Another case appeared. Different year. Different country. Same measurements.

Marcus exhaled slowly. "So one odd detail didn't matter—until it kept showing up."

"It stopped being coincidence," Ty said.

Daniel did not respond.

Ty pointed at the wall. "What did that open."

"Additional linked records."

Marcus grimaced. "Plain English."

Ty didn't look away from the display. "It went looking for other things that might explain why those details repeated."

"Yes."

The lattice widened again. Corporate filings stacked along the margin—shell companies, nominee directors, trusts designed to exist without owners. A single mailing address threaded through them, stubborn and persistent.

Ty felt the shift before it was named.

"So the coin heist wasn't the objective," he said quietly.

Daniel answered only the question. "Correct. It was another equation."

"The system tested outcome dependence," Daniel said.

"Vice Presidential survival did not resolve or invalidate the model."

"The pavilion event was not treated as a failure state. Both actions were modeled as co-primary operations—each generating constraint and distraction value for the other."

"The system tested outcome dependence," Daniel said.

"VP survival did not resolve or invalidate the model."

"And the pavilion event was not treated as a failure state. Both actions were modeled as co-primary operations, each generating distraction value for the other."

"This led the system to add an additional parameter to look for additional similarities, like expanding the search to earlier time periods."

Daniel advanced the system.

Another red ring went white.

"This closure came from a museum incident," Daniel said. "Documents only. No objects of market value."

Marcus frowned. "That was written off as vandalism."

"The structure matched," Daniel said. "Selective removal. Custodial records targeted. Inventory ignored."

A side-by-side filled the wall: scorched ledger fragments from the archive on one side, the coin-show book on the other. Different handwriting. Identical internal logic.

Ty's jaw tightened.

"So whoever ordered this," Marcus said slowly, "knew exactly what they wanted."

"Yes."

"And knew it mattered."

Daniel didn't answer. He didn't need to.

Shipping records aligned. Free-trade zones surfaced. Receiving entries matched donor shells that resolved to trusts. Another red circle dimmed.

Closed.

Ty watched four become three.

"Keep going."

The system obeyed.

A pallet barcode in one case matched a receiving scan in another. A third red circle turned white.

"Repetition increased confidence," Daniel said. "Confidence resolves conflicts."

Ty leaned back. "So it doesn't search for answers."

"It tests explanations," Daniel said. "Anything that explains everything else survives."

Marcus rubbed his jaw. "How many of these inconsistencies were there."

"Approximately fifty," Daniel replied. "Cells. Names rotate. Structure does not."

Symbols again. Clean rows. Same grammar as the page that had started everything months ago.

"With the transatlantic nodes resolved," Daniel said, "the system inferred a substitution map."

Ty raised a hand. “Before we touch that—show me one more closure. I want to see how it kept pulling.”

Daniel returned the display to an earlier point, just after the first resolution.

“At this moment,” he said, “the system ranked external datasets.”

The wall updated—customs entries, AIS ship tracks, CDN cache logs.

Another red ring dimmed.

“Closed.”

Ty nodded once. “All right.”

He reached for the symbol page and turned it.

He did not read it aloud.

He folded it once and slid it into an evidence sleeve.

Marcus watched him. “So upstairs—”

“The case is closed,” Daniel said.

“And here,” Ty said.

“No.”

Ty sealed the sleeve into the secure box at his feet. The latch clicked.

“That’s enough.”

Daniel lifted his hands from the keys.

They stood in the cold air and the readable silence.

On the table lay the printed directive page. On the wall, two red circles pulsed without sympathy.

The door had sealed behind them at the beginning of the hour. The answer that would open the next one sat locked inside the box.

None of that belonged to the outside yet.

Daniel checked the screen.

The red rings hadn't moved.

"Upstairs," he said, "they'll say it's finished."

"And it won't be," Ty said.

Daniel advanced the display.

The wall went dark.

Then it filled with symbols.

No text.

No words.

Only structure.

Ty's eyes returned to the wall. Two red circles still pulsed.

"What's left."

"Two unresolved issues."

Daniel did not elaborate.

Ty waited him out. "Name them."

"The identity of the Investigator," Daniel said. "And the identity of the authorizing signature."

Marcus went very still. "That's the whole case."

Daniel reached for the printer.

A single page slid into the tray.

◇◆●■ ■✚◇□ ★◆◇● ☒■✶◇ ◇☑■◆

■●◇☑ ◆◇■✦ ●✚■◇ ★□◆◇ ✶■◆◇

✶■◆◇ ◇☒●■ ◆◇☑■ ●★◇✚ ■◇◆□

■◇◆□ ●✦■◇ ◇◆☑★ ■✚●◇ ◆◇■☒

◆■◇● ☒◇✚■ ●◆■◇ ★□◇✦ ■☑◇◆

■☑◇◆ ●✶■◇ ◇◆★■ ☒◇●✚ ◆◇■✶

★◇■◆ ✚●☑■ ◇◆■✶ ●□◇☒ ■◆◇★

◇■●◆ ■□✚■ ◆★●◇ ◆◇■☒ ●◇✖■

◆◇☒★ ✦◆◇● ◆□■◇ ●◆◇▲ ★◇◆✶

■●☑◆ ◆◇▲□ ●◆✚■ ☒■◆◇ ✶◇■★

◆◇■● ★●☒◇ ■◆✦□ ●◆◇■ ▲◇☑◆

★◆◇☒ ■◇◆● ●☒◆✚ ▲◇■◆ ■●◆□

◆☒■● ◆◇■□ ●☑■◆ ◆◇☒◇ ✶■●□

●◆◇■ ◆◇☑◆ ■☒◇✖ ●◆□■ ◇◆■★

◆◇☒■ ■◇◆□ ●◆◇■ ★◇☑◆ ■◆◇●

●☑◆◇ ◆◇■□ ◆◇☒■ ★■●□ ◆◇☒▲

■□◆◇ ●◆☑■ ◆◇✖□ ★◆◇■ ◇☒◆■

★◆◇☒ ■●□◆ ◆◇■★ ●☑✶◇ ◆■□★

◆◇■☒ ◇☑■◆ ●◆☒◇ ■□◆◇ ◆◇✖●

Daniel advanced to the next screen which presented the fully decrypted message:

Curator Garrison in violation.

Repeated failure to complete acquisition within approved temporal window.

Evidence indicates retention beyond custodial authority.

Risk to continuity assessed as unacceptable.

Review conducted.

Supporting materials compiled.

External interference anticipated.

Termination authorized.

Execution delegated.

Pavilion incident confirmed as corrective action.

Holies' Investigator: Rachael Garrison

Designation approved following post-event assessment.

Pattern recognition and closure capability confirmed.

Retention recommended.

— Holy T

Epilogue - The Halo Effect

Rome — Six Months Later

Evening stretched thin over the Piazza della Rotonda.

The air smelled of rain and espresso and old stone. Street musicians packed up their violins, the fountain murmured at the center, and the last light brushed the Pantheon's columns gold.

A woman crossed the square alone. Her hair was dark now, cut short enough that the wind could find her neck. Sunglasses hid her eyes even though the sun was nearly gone. She walked like someone accustomed to being followed but no longer afraid of it.

Rachael Garrison—or whatever name was on her passport—stopped at a café tucked under a crooked balcony.

Bar della Mano.

The sign was nothing special to tourists, but the logo—a palm encircled by a thin flame—made her pause. Old habits noticed things before her mind did.

She chose a table at the edge. The waiter didn't ask for an order; a small cup of espresso appeared, black as ink. She wrapped her hands around it, more for the warmth than the caffeine, and watched a priest cross the piazza with his cassock caught in the wind.

A man had been waiting across the street, reading a paper he hadn't turned in ten minutes. He folded it now, left coins under his cup, and came toward her with the slow precision of someone long practiced at being unremarkable.

When he reached her table, he smiled as if they were strangers meeting by chance.

"Signora," he said. His English carried the soft drag of old money and older schooling.

"Your Italian's better than mine," she answered, not smiling.

"I remember when your American accent was thicker," he said. "Atlanta, wasn't it?"

Rachael's fingers tightened around the cup. "You've come a long way to say that."

He eased into the chair opposite her. "And you've come farther to hear it."

The waiter drifted back, set down another cup, and vanished. The man slid a folded envelope across the table. The seal was wax, embossed with a symbol she had hoped never to see again: a ring of fire around a torch.

"You still use that crest," she said.

"Tradition is a form of continuity," he replied. "Even faith needs branding."

She didn't touch the envelope.

"What is this?"

"Instructions," he said simply. "There's always another ledger, another node, and more requests. You understand that now."

Her mouth twitched—a smile, a grimace, maybe both. "I understand how things end."

He leaned forward, eyes reflecting the thin candle flame between them. "No, Investigator. You understand how they begin."

The word made her flinch. "Don't call me that."

"But it's who you are," he said. "You found threats, just as the last Curator was meant to. You closed the circle of faith. That's why you're here."

She glanced toward the fountain where tourists laughed, unaware. "I closed it because people died."

He lifted his cup. "And because someone had to."

Rachael looked down at the envelope again. "What happens if I walk away?"

He sipped. "Then another will open it. But they won't be as thorough. The Holies prefer precision."

She exhaled through her nose, the sound half a sigh. "Is that what you call faith now—precision?"

He smiled, faint and real. "Faith is just discipline applied to the invisible."

She touched the envelope's edge with her fingertips. The wax was warm, as if it had been sealed moments ago.

She did not look at the envelope.

"Naming your Uncle would not have been easy," Holy T said. "But personal attachments cannot be permitted to interrupt continuity."

Rachael inclined her head once.

"Understood."

He regarded the cup between his hands, as if it were older than the table.

"The pavilion corrected the exposure," he said.

She took the envelope and slid it into her coat pocket.

"And then everything was contained," she said, "or so we thought until the laptop showed up".

For a long moment neither spoke. The sound of plates clinking drifted from inside. Rain began to fall lightly, dimpling the square.

Rachael took the envelope at last and slipped it into her coat pocket. "If I open this, I decide what comes next. Not them." She let the words stand, not as defiance, but as fact.

"Of course," he said. "Choice is the most elegant illusion we've ever built."

He regarded the cup between his hands as if it were older than the table, older than the room.

"People misunderstand what we do," he said. "They imagine urgency. Emotion. They imagine violence as an end."

The ledger had burned once before, long before computers learned how to remember—but it had never been lost.

He smiled faintly, the way men do when correcting a child without intending cruelty.

"But our work has always been custodial."

Rachael did not interrupt.

"Relics outlast nations," he continued. "Ideas outlast dynasties. Every age places guardians in positions of trust—and every age produces those who mistake stewardship for ownership."

He lifted his eyes to her then, calm and assessing.

"When that happens, correction becomes necessary."

The word sat between them, unadorned.

"Sometimes a man must be removed," he said, almost gently.

"Sometimes a movement must be redirected. Sometimes an entire structure must collapse so that something older may continue unbroken."

He inclined his head, a gesture that was neither approval nor apology.

"Distractions are not regrettable when they preserve what matters."

Outside, Rome moved on—tourists, priests, students—centuries brushing past one another without noticing.

"You understand this," he said at last.

Rachael did not nod. She didn't need to.

He stood, buttoned his jacket, and placed a coin beside her untouched espresso. "You were never terminated," he said quietly. "Only promoted."

Then he stepped into the rain and was gone, vanishing into the blur of umbrellas and neon reflections.

Rachael sat still until the candle guttered. Then she rose, left enough cash to pay for both cups, and walked toward the Pantheon. The envelope pressed a line against her ribs, steady and insistent.

A gust pushed through the piazza. Her reflection flickered in a puddle—brunette, pale coat, eyes unreadable—and for an instant the torch symbol gleamed in the water before the ripples took it.

She looked up at the dome. Through the oculus, the last of the daylight poured down like a single column of fire.

Rachael didn't look back.

When she disappeared into the narrow street beyond the square, the wind scattered the first dry leaf of summer across the table she had left behind, a thing moved without burning.

The envelope remained sealed.

As Rachael walked away, she thought of Ty once — not with regret, not with warmth.

He would notice the absence eventually. That was his strength. It was also his risk. He was intelligent. Persistent.

He might come looking. Or she might decide to surprise him.

About the Author

M.S. Canton is the pseudonym of Georgia native Glenn Weintraub, a storyteller who blends sharp investigative detail with page-turning suspense. Born in Albany and now based in Roswell, Glenn is an alumnus of both Georgia Tech and the Georgia State University College of Law.

A lifelong reader and keen observer of human nature, he draws on his professional background and deep interest in justice to craft thrillers that explore the intersection of belief, betrayal, and the human cost of secrets.

His debut mystery/suspense novel, The Holy Take, follows a detective and a federal agent as they unravel a conspiracy where stolen history funds extremist faith.

When he's not writing, Glenn enjoys spending time with his wife, Jodi, daughter, Frances, son-in-law, Dehn, and two grandchildren, Lucas and Elena.

Made in the USA
Columbia, SC
10 February 2026

79005185R00202